CONSTANCE HEAVEN

The Love Child

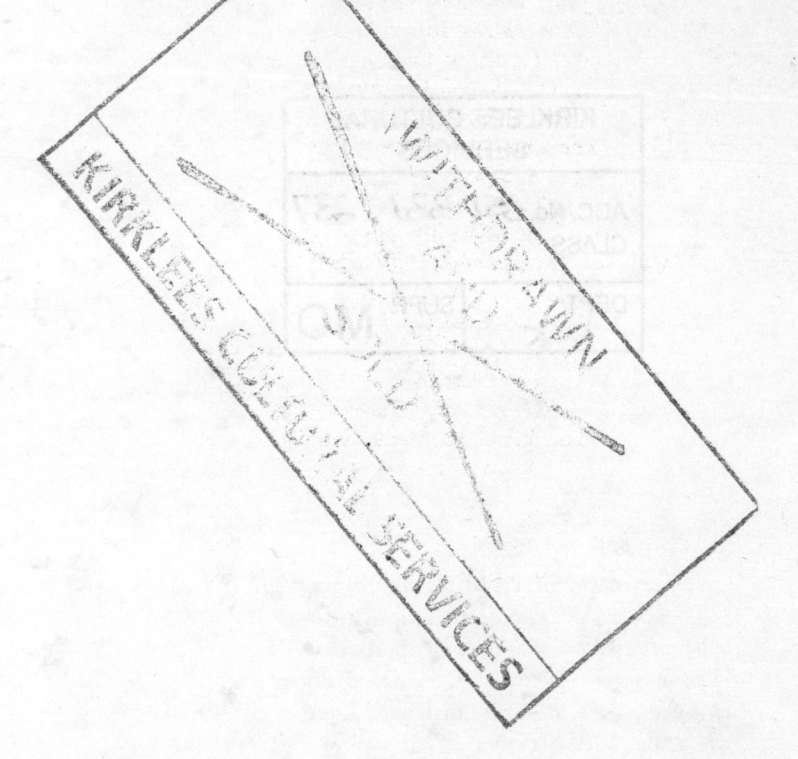

HEINEMANN: LONDON

First published in Great Britain 1997
by William Heinemann Ltd and
by Mandarin Paperbacks
imprints of Reed International Books Ltd
Michelin House, 81 Fulham Road, London SW3 6RB
and Auckland, Melbourne, Singapore and Toronto

Copyright © Constance Heaven 1997

A CIP catalogue record for this title
is available from the British Library
ISBN 0 434 00371 9

Typeset in Baskerville by Deltatype Ltd
Printed and bound in Great Britain by
Clays Ltd, St Ives plc

PART ONE

The Love Child

Chapter 1

It was one of those golden summer afternoons, rare in England, when it seems as if nothing could ever go wrong. David Fraser, stretched on a rug in the dappled sunshine under the ancient walnut tree, was drowsily content, a somewhat unusual state for him, since he was only just emerging from that adolescent certainty that he was always in the right while the rest of the world – especially his stepfather – were always in the wrong. He had his share of good looks: light-brown hair with an obstinate curl that sometimes fell engagingly across his forehead, thickly lashed grey eyes, a handsome face with a touch of weakness, of immaturity perhaps, something time would no doubt remedy.

Sounds drifted to him from the croquet lawn: the click of the mallets, little cries of triumph when a ball shot through a hoop, his sister's voice saying indignantly, 'That's not fair. You cheated!' and his grandfather's amused reply, 'Nonsense, child, you can't accuse a High Court judge of cheating, it's unethical.'

Garden parties at Bramber, Sussex home of the Warrinders for generations, always had this quality of timelessness. This afternoon they were celebrating Grandmother's birthday. He could see her, elegant as always in lilac taffeta and cream lace, yielding nothing to her sixty-five years, chatting with Aunt Margaret and smiling down at her favourite nephew lounging on the grass beside her chair. John Everard was twenty-four, on leave from the Guards, and much inclined to lord it over his younger cousins. There was the chink of cups and the sound of subdued voices as the servants prepared the tea trolleys, loaded with wafer-thin watercress sandwiches, chocolate cake and luscious strawberries from the kitchen garden with jugs of thick yellow cream.

David stretched lazily. It was true that he had only just managed to scrape through his law finals at Cambridge, but after a great deal of hard argument he had won his stepfather's grudging consent to three months' holiday before he must begin the next stage in his legal career, something he would never have achieved without his mother's strong support and the unexpected backing of his grandfather, who had said surprisingly, 'The boy's already twenty-one. Let him off the leading strings for a few months and he'll work all the harder afterwards.' He'd been promised a few weeks in Paris with his Uncle Harry, his mother's brother, who contrived to combine a very high lifestyle with a brilliant career at the Bar, and after that Germany, Italy . . . a dazzling prospect. He was smiling to himself and very nearly asleep when the sharp tip of a parasol prodded him painfully in the ribs.

'What are you dreaming about to look so pleased with yourself?' asked a voice with a distinct rasp in it.

He sat up abruptly. Cousin Clara was looking down at him and he felt his heart sink. It was a firm belief among the younger set that if Cousin Clara caught you in her spider's web, it was impossible to break away without being downright rude. If he had seen her coming, he would have taken good care to make himself scarce, but now it was too late.

'Don't get up,' she went on as he struggled to his knees. One of the servants had followed her and was placing a chair with exaggerated care. 'I shall just sit here beside you and you can talk to me.'

Even the Garden of Eden had its serpent and regrettably so had Bramber. Cousin Clara fitted the part exactly, even in the clothes she favoured. She had a passion for dark rich greens shot with purple, for silks and satins and velvets, always in the very height of fashion, with her hair swept up in two shining black wings, and she had the tongue of an adder. Everyone in the family called her 'poor Clara', and he could never understand why, since she was richer than they were, richer even than his grandfather, and had a wide circle of acquaintances who attended her dinner parties and soirées only because they feared her bitter tongue if they didn't. His mother once said that the worst thing about Clara was that she always hit on the unpleasant truth. She had a nose for the worst in people and never failed to make use of it. The only one who spared her a kind word was his grandfather. Clara was the daughter of his elder sister who had died in childbirth.

'There is someone inside Clara who longs for the happiness she has never known,' Grandfather had said once. 'She'll surprise us one of these days.'

So the obligatory invitation would go out and everyone devoutly prayed that she would be struck down at the last moment but she never was. Unhappily she enjoyed robust health.

She was just settling herself in her chair when a boy and girl came running hand in hand across the grass accompanied by an exceedingly muddy little spaniel.

'We haven't missed tea, have we?' they exclaimed breathlessly and then stopped aghast at the sight of Clara.

Celia's white muslin dress with its wide blue sash was plentifully smeared with long streaks of green slime while Robert's knickerbockers, socks and boots were soaked through and caked with mud.

'Good afternoon, Cousin Clara,' they chorused politely, gave David a frantic look of appeal and started to edge away.

'Keep that disgusting brute away from me,' snapped Clara, poking viciously with her parasol at the spaniel which had just given itself a good shake and then gone to inspect her elegantly shod feet. He yelped and backed off.

'Don't do that. You'll hurt him!' shrieked Celia, forgetting her good manners. She grabbed up the dog, causing a great deal more damage to her white dress.

David, who had a soft spot for his younger half-brother and -sister, said warningly, 'You'd better not let Mamma see you in that state. What happened?'

'Rowley fell in the lake and we had to fish him out. He got all caught up in that horrible waterweed. We were afraid he would drown,' explained Celia, obviously the leader of the two.

'I see. Well, you can't have tea looking like that. You'd better go in and change.'

'But then we'll miss the strawberries and cream!' wailed Celia.

'No you won't. I'll tell Mamma I sent you in to wash your hands. Now cut along, both of you, and hurry.'

They beamed their thanks and fled towards the house.

'I can't imagine what your mother is thinking of, letting those children run wild like that,' said Clara, trying to brush away the muddy splashes on her silk skirts. 'No more than street urchins, the pair of them. But then that's hardly surprising seeing whose children they are.'

'Actually Daniel is very strict with them,' said David who would have defended his worst enemy from Clara. 'Robert is doing very well at his prep school and Celia has already started at the girls' college.'

'A lot of stuff and nonsense, filling the girl up with so much book learning. No man will want to look at her later on.'

'Isn't that a little old-fashioned, Cousin Clara?' said David with a touch of malice. 'My friends like a girl who can talk intelligently.'

The croquet match was over by now and the players were strolling towards the tea tables. His grandfather, Lord Warrinder, nearing seventy but still handsome and erect, was arm in arm with David's mother, who looked remarkably slender and pretty in her light summer gown. *Mamma must be a year or so older than Cousin Clara*, he thought suddenly, *but no one would ever guess it.*

His stepfather had his arm around David's other sister's waist. They were obviously enjoying some joke, for Isabelle suddenly burst out laughing and then stood on tiptoe to give him a kiss before running towards her mother at the tea table. David's frown at this little show of affection was not lost on Clara.

'Are you still at daggers drawn with your stepfather?' she asked with a deceptive lightness.

'We rub along.' Whatever he felt he was not willing to give anything of it away to the enemy.

'It's easy enough to see who is his favourite. Not surprising, really.'

He looked at her sharply. 'What do you mean by that?'

'Haven't you guessed already? No, perhaps not. No doubt they've kept very quiet about it.'

'About what?'

'My dear boy, hasn't it ever occurred to you? Your mother was out in the Crimea with your father on a medical mission with those doctor colleagues of his, wasn't she? And Daniel Hunter was out there at the same time. He and your mother had been writing to one another long before that. He had been madly in love with her for years till your grandfather put a stop to it.'

'But that was twenty years ago. What are you trying to tell me?'

'Isn't it obvious? Your poor father was struck down out there, wasn't he, horribly crippled, scarcely able to move at all, and when they returned to England he remained a helpless invalid and yet nine months later Isabelle was born.'

David stared at her for a moment before he said slowly, 'Are you expecting me to believe that after my father was injured and was lying helpless, my mother was rioting in bed with my stepfather?'

'It doesn't require much rioting to produce a child, dear boy,' said Clara drily, 'and two months after Isabelle was born, your father took his life.'

'I don't believe you. He died as the result of his terrible injuries, all the doctors said so. I was very young but I can still remember him, his sickness and his agonizing pain. He used to talk to me.'

'Ask your mother if you don't believe me.'

'I wouldn't shame her by asking such a vile question. Why do you dislike her so much? You do, don't you?'

'Of course I don't dislike her. You don't know what you are talking about, boy.'

'I know quite enough to realize that,' David replied in irritation. 'Why, Cousin Clara?' He wanted to grab hold of her, shake the truth out of her, wipe the smug smile off her face. But before he could make a move his sister had come running across the grass towards them.

'Mamma says will you come and join us, Cousin Clara? We'll be cutting Grandmother's cake any time now.'

'I mustn't miss that, must I?'

'Have you seen the children, David?' Isabelle went on. 'They seem to have disappeared.'

He was staring down into his sister's face as if suddenly seeing a likeness he had never noticed before: the bright brown hair, the clear hazel eyes, even the way she spoke.

'Tell Mamma that I sent Robert and Celia in to wash their hands. They'd been playing with Rowley and were filthy,' he said with an effort. 'I don't want any tea. I think I'll go for a walk.'

Before she could say anything he'd swung away, taking a path at random, hardly looking where he was going, and Clara smiled to herself. She had always hated Christine, hated her since they were children together because she had loving parents, because she had had two men who desired her passionately and had enjoyed both of them, because she had four healthy and attractive children. Riches had never made up for the fact that Clara's mother had died at her birth, that her father, who even now pursued his diplomatic career in Paris, Vienna and St Petersburg, had provided for her but never liked her, and had never once suggested that his only daughter should take her place at his side, act as his hostess, welcome his guests, become part of his distinguished life. The bitterness had suddenly spilled over and she was glad. If it festered in the boy's mind so much the better. She stood up, shaking out her silken skirts and smiling sweetly at Isabelle.

'Shall we go and join the birthday party, my dear?'

The day passed pleasantly enough. The iced cake was cut

amidst laughter and congratulations, the grandchildren presented their little gifts. There was a great deal of hugging and kissing and while Christine went on pouring tea, making sure that everyone had what they wanted and preventing Robert and Celia from stuffing themselves with too many strawberries, she wondered what had upset her difficult, moody son, and noticed the frown on her husband's face when her mother asked plaintively what had happened to David.

The shadows began to lengthen and a cool breeze blew up. Clara left early, to everyone's relief, refusing to stay the night and driving back to Greystone Park, the handsome house she had inherited from her father-in-law.

No more was said about David till later, when Daniel came into the bedroom where his wife was washing her hands and tidying her hair for supper, always a simple affair of cold meats and salads on Sunday evenings, to spare the servants.

'What the devil does David think he's doing, storming off like that in the middle of the afternoon?' he said with considerable annoyance. 'It is the height of bad manners. Your mother was very upset. You know how much she thinks of these little attentions.'

'Isabelle told me she thought Clara had said something to upset him.'

'Oh, for heaven's sake! He is twenty-one and surely quite old enough to stand up to her by now.'

'I'm worried, Dan. Did he say where he was going?'

'I went down to the stables just now. Paddy said he had asked him to saddle Jenny and told him not to wait in for him as he had no idea when he would be back.'

'But that was hours ago. You don't think he could have met with an accident, do you? Should we send some of the men after him?'

'If he chooses to dash off like that he must take the consequences. He's quite old enough to look after himself. He'll be back soon enough when he's hungry. Are you ready, my dear? Shall we go down?'

Supper was rather subdued that evening, even though the

children were permitted to sit up for it and squabbled noisily over who should have the last of the sherry trifle till their father's stern eye fell on them. Then Nanny Renfrew appeared to take them off to bed. They had long outgrown her of course but she had stayed on, a valued part of the family. John Everard excused himself and went off on some expedition of his own and the ladies retired to the drawing-room, leaving Daniel alone with his father-in-law.

'Shall we take our coffee and brandy in my study?' said Everard Warrinder. 'We'll be more comfortable there and there is something I want to discuss with you.'

'What is it about?'

'Clara, actually. Don't shudder. She affects me like that too, always has done, but unfortunately she is family and her affairs concern me whether I like it or not.'

Comfortably installed in the book-lined room where generations of Warrinders had retreated with brandy and cigars and dozed over legal problems, Daniel looked at his father-in-law and thought how much he liked and respected him, which was extraordinary since for some twenty years of his life he had loathed and despised him as a man whose brilliant prosecution had sent his own father to the gallows for a crime he did not commit, who had indulged in a passionate love affair with his mother which had given him an illegitimate half-sister and had driven him and Christine apart so that she had married another man. But life has a way of sorting itself out. They had learned painfully to know each other's worth and to value their friendship.

He leaned back in the leather armchair, sipping the fine old brandy, and said comfortably, 'What's all this about Clara? Has she been making more mischief than usual?'

'Not exactly. It's not really Clara this time, it's her father. I think you met him once, didn't you?'

'Yes, a few years ago, when he came over to England and called on Christine. I rather liked him.'

'Yes, well, James Ducane is a likeable fellow and something of a character. He is about my age or perhaps a few years younger, and was at one time what we used to call a high flyer. When he married my sister we thought he would settle down but she died giving birth to Clara. He took an unreasoning dislike to the child who had killed his wife, put her in the care of nurses and servants and went abroad, taking up a career in the diplomatic service where he has continued ever since in Paris, Vienna and now St Petersburg. He is a clever chap, speaks half a dozen languages, has done very well wherever he has been stationed and is very well thought of by his colleagues. Now all this time we've always assumed that he has led a bachelor existence, foot-loose and fancy-free, if you take my meaning.'

'And hasn't he?'

'No, by God, he hasn't. It appears he has had a permanent liaison with a French opera singer for the past twenty years, setting up establishments for her in the different countries where he has been stationed. Not only that, it seems he has a daughter by her who must be about eighteen or nineteen by this time.'

'Good Lord! Does Clara know?'

'Apparently not, and it seems he is still anxious to keep it from her. Now the point is this. In case of something happening to him, he is anxious to make provision for them. Clara has her marriage settlement of course and last year inherited a considerable fortune when her father-in-law, Lord Dorrien, died, but James seems to think that she still might feel aggrieved if he arranges to leave a large part of what he still owns to his second family. For this reason he would prefer not to employ the family lawyer and asks me to go to Russia, discuss the situation with him and act as one of his executors. This is where you come in, Daniel. Would you consider going to St Petersburg in my place?'

'But I scarcely know the man,' he protested.

'I don't think that matters. You are now part of the family and you can also discuss the matter more objectively than I can. It's a devil of a journey to Russia and the plain truth is that I don't really feel up to it.'

Daniel sat up abruptly. 'You're not sick, are you? You're not hiding something serious from us?'

'No, no, just a few twinges now and again,' he said impatiently, 'and I've been advised to take things easy. I've no wish to retire from the law just yet and I have a very heavy workload coming up in the autumn. It would be a great weight off my mind if you could do this for me. It should not take up too much of your time.'

'It would have to wait a few weeks,' said Daniel thoughtfully. 'I have work in hand that I can't neglect and it's a longish journey. The whole affair could take two or three weeks at least, especially as I shall have to meet the ladies concerned.'

'I don't think there is any great hurry. I imagine that James, like me, has been feeling Time's wingèd chariot hurrying near, as Marvell puts it,' he said wryly. 'Then I suppose there's always an element of danger in these countries. I gather from his letter that the anarchists have been up to their old tricks. The trouble with these attacks is that a great number of innocent people suffer. What do you say, Daniel? Will you take it on for me?'

'I'll be glad to do it if it will help you — but are you sure you're not keeping something back from us?'

'No, no, no, and for heaven's sake don't breathe a word of it to Clarissa. She will have me wrapped up in cotton wool and confined to bed in five minutes. The last thing I want! I'll brief you with all the details before you go.'

'Very well. May I tell Christine, or must I invent some fairy tale about an assignment taking me to Russia?'

'If I know my daughter, she'll worm the truth out of you. But don't forget to ask her to keep very quiet about it till the whole matter is wrapped up.'

'Right. And mind you take good care of yourself.'

'I'll do my best. Well, now that's off my mind, shall we rejoin the ladies before they start wondering what we're planning behind their backs?'

But when they entered the drawing-room it was to find

Christine alone. 'They're all worn out so they've gone to bed. I'm the only one left standing,' she said cheerfully. 'You're looking exhausted too, Papa. What were you two talking about for so long?'

Everard shot a half-humorous glance at Daniel. 'Nothing important, my pet. Just something I want him to do for me. As a matter of fact I think I'll join your mother. These family parties are all very well but they do take it out of you. By the way, where has David got to? Has he come back?'

'Not as far as I know, and I'm trying hard not to worry,' said Christine, 'but it is half-past ten, Daniel, and he's been gone since before five.'

'He's probably slipped in and gone to bed without a word to us. It's like him if he is in one of his moods. I'll go down to the stables and find out if he has brought Jenny back.'

'Don't be too hard on him, will you?'

'I treat him a good deal more leniently than I do Robert and Celia,' said her husband shortly.

'You can never quite forgive him for being Gareth's son, can you?'

'Rubbish! He enjoys a great many privileges and doesn't appreciate any of them. I shan't be long.' He went out, shutting the door with a little more emphasis than was quite necessary.

'You shouldn't have said that, my dear,' said her father quietly.

'Oh, I know, and I don't really mean it, but I feel in despair about them sometimes. They're like oil and water, they're always at cross purposes and more often than not I end up being the buffer between them.'

'You fuss over David far too much, Christine. You're over-protective towards him, you always have been, because he's Gareth's son and you feel you owe him a debt for dying when he did and leaving the way clear for you and Daniel.'

'That's a horrible thing to say.'

'But true. I'm not being harsh, my dear, but I am outside the pair of you. I can see how things are more clearly. That's why I backed David in asking for this time off from his career. Let him get away from you both for a time, free of your care and Daniel's determination to be fair at all costs, which so often goes wrong. It will give David breathing space in which to grow up and that's what he needs.'

'I don't know if you've noticed but every day David seems to grow more and more like Gareth. People have remarked on it. It's a constant reminder.'

'My dear, Gareth has been in his grave for twenty years,' he said gently. 'Old grudges should be forgotten.'

'They are, but all the same they leave scars.'

'Then it's high time they grew a protective covering. You know I'm right, don't you?'

'You usually are,' she said ruefully.

He put an arm around her shoulders and gave her a little hug. 'Lecture over. And now I'm going to bed before I'm reproached by Clarissa for keeping her awake. Good-night, my pet.'

He gave her a kiss and went off, leaving her to turn out the lamps and make her way slowly up the stairs, realizing that her father had probably hit the nail on the head but still worrying about her beloved son. On the landing Isabelle put her head through the bedroom door.

'Are you all right, Mamma?'

'Yes, of course. Are the children asleep?'

'Snoring like pigs, both of them. You just ought to see their clothes. They must have fallen in the lake, and Betsy said Rowley was so filthy and smelled so awful she had to bathe him. David must have covered up for them. Has he come in?'

'Not yet. Your father has gone down to the stables to find out.'

'You don't think anything could have happened to him?'

'Of course not. He's not a child. Go to bed, love, or you'll be fit for nothing tomorrow.'

'Good-night, Mamma.'

She gave her mother a quick kiss and Christine patted her cheek. Isabelle was always such a tremendous comfort, quiet, steady, sensible, affectionate, and very fond of her brother. Christine went on to her own room to undress, put on her dressing-gown and then sat anxiously waiting for her husband to come back.

When he left the drawing-room Daniel went out by the back door and across the courtyard, aware that what his wife had said was at least partly true. He fell over backwards sometimes trying to be just towards David, and yet at the same time he was conscious of irritation because the boy had so much and made so little of it. David had been sent to Harrow and Cambridge like his father. He had a background of ease and plenty and took it all for granted.

God knows, he himself had always taken very good care never to point out the differences between them, but they were still there. He had grown up in dire poverty with the stigma of a father hanged for his revolutionary ideals, a mother who had died in an appalling mill accident. There had been years in an orphanage, years slaving in the cotton mill, starving on a few pence a week, but he had somehow kept himself afloat, had painfully educated himself, learned how to absorb the life around him and turn it into vivid, memorable prose so that now, at forty-three, he was a journalist of some distinction. His trenchant, witty and hard-hitting articles were published in leading newspapers, he had been sent on tricky foreign assignments and brought back the goods, he had written a novel that was a thinly disguised story of his own early life in the despair and poverty of the London slums. It might not have become a best-seller like Mr Dickens' books, but it had received considerable critical acclaim, not least from the great man himself. It had been widely read, gone into several editions and was a standby in Mudie's circulating library. This last year he had embarked on a second and his publishers were urging him to finish it.

He had learned to hold his own with men of a very different background, men who had known each other at school and university, men who rode to hounds, shot grouse in Scotland, took their families to Paris and Florence for long holidays. He and Christine had established a circle of their own chosen from the literary and artistic worlds, an aristocracy of merit and achievement rather than birth and riches, free of the inhibitions and social restrictions that haunted the rising middle class, and it was only now and then that he knew a prick of resentment because despite his success it was not he who kept the household afloat but Christine's inherited fortune, not only from her husband who had died so tragically young but from Gareth's uncle and guardian, whom she had cared for until he died at the great age of ninety-four.

Daniel was actually more worried about the boy than he cared to admit and was relieved when he arrived at the stables to find that David had returned already, soaking wet, his clothes thick with mud, leading a weary horse who was limping badly. His relief at once turned to annoyance that the boy should have gone off without a word, caused a great deal of anxiety and come back expecting servants to be waiting up for him.

'What the devil happened to you? Your mother has been worried to death,' he said before he could stop himself, and provoked an immediate reaction.

'She had no need to worry. I'm not a child, and I did tell Paddy not to hang about for me. If you must know Jenny put a foot down a rabbit hole and I went over her head into a ditch. The poor old girl was lamed. I had gone a good long way and had to walk her back. How bad is it?' he went on to the stableman who was already on his knees, feeling gently down the mare's injured foreleg.

'Don't ee worry, Master David. I'll have a hot poultice on that leg in a jiffy and she'll be right as rain in a few days.'

'It's past eleven, Paddy,' said Daniel. 'Your mother will be worrying. I'd better send someone to tell her you're detained.'

'That's all right, sir. I nipped home for me tea and I told her then I might be kept late. I'll rub the nag down and see to that leg for you, Master David. You get home to your bed. You look fair done up.'

Servants fell over their feet to do things for David. 'Paddy's right,' said Daniel through gritted teeth. 'You'd better come up to the house and get those wet clothes off.'

'Thanks, Paddy, you're a brick,' said the boy, putting a hand on the stableman's shoulder for a moment, and then followed his stepfather up the path. They walked back to the house in an unfriendly silence.

Now and again David stole a look at the tall lean figure of his stepfather striding beside him, good-looking in his own way, careless in his dress sometimes but giving the impression of a formidable whipcord strength, and he wondered if Cousin Clara could possibly be right. He'd fought some kind of a battle with himself as he galloped across the Downs and had ended up deciding her vile insinuation was a lie. She knew David adored his mother, and nothing would have given her greater pleasure than to destroy that love. He'd not give her the satisfaction. Much as he disliked his stepfather, he could surely never have played such a filthy trick on a sick and dying man.

There was no rational cause for his jeaousy and dislike, but the plain fact was that it had been there from the start. He had been a child of barely three when, the Crimean War over at last, Daniel had come into his life. He remembered that first time and how instinctively he had drawn away, aware of danger that threatened the close life he had led with his mother and his baby sister ever since his father's death. After that first day Daniel had become a constant visitor; and once his mother had taken David with her to his lodgings in a dark and ugly part of London. There was an old woman there who had clutched him to her beaded black bosom which had a queer musty smell, hugging and kissing him, and he had hated every minute of it, fighting to get down. Afterwards he had sat silent, glowering at his mother laughing and talking with the stranger, and had refused stubbornly to drink his milk or touch the sweet biscuit on his plate though it was his favourite.

Then after a short time the stranger had gone away to a country called India, where there were black people killing the

British, or so his nanny told him, and every night when he said his prayers, he added a little secret one that the black people would kill the stranger too. But God apparently hadn't been listening because after nearly a year he came back looking leaner than ever and everyone congratulated him on his lucky escape from a place called Lucknow. Six months later, he and Christine were married and the lovely intimacy David shared with his mother had gone for ever. He couldn't run into her bedroom in the early morning and snuggle down beside her in the big bed because that man was there, laughing and picking him up, carrying him back to Nanny and saying, 'You're not a baby any longer, Davey, you're a big boy now,' and he hated him with a fierce childish hate.

Isabelle was different. She took to Daniel at once. She had only been a tiny baby when their father died so she didn't remember him at all. Daniel was Papa to her at once and she would run to him to be picked up and made much of, while David sulked and refused to call him Papa or even Father. He was the unwelcome stranger who had wormed his way into his mother's bed and into her heart. David had never really outgrown that childish resentment. It still simmered, causing his mother intense anxiety that one day it would flare up in a real explosion and she'd be left to make a choice between them.

All this had gone through his mind as he galloped across the Downs and during the trudge home leading the lame mare and his heart had sunk when he saw his stepfather waiting for him at the stables. He had braced himself for a battle but the expected lecture did not come. Instead, as they went in by the back door to avoid rousing the servants, Daniel said unexpectedly, 'You must be hungry. The kitchen staff will have gone to bed by now but go and take off those wet clothes and I'll forage in the larder and see what I can find.'

When he came back in his shirtsleeves he found Daniel had produced a loaf of bread and some butter and was busily carving thick slices of ham. 'Make yourself a sandwich,' he said, 'while I rake up the fire and put the kettle on,' and David suddenly realized that he had eaten nothing since midday and was ravenous. He clapped thick slices of ham between two pieces of bread and bit into it hungrily. A great deal more resourceful than he would ever have been, his stepfather had coaxed the damped-down fire into life, put on the black kettle, found the teapot and caddy and gone back to the pantry.

'I'm afraid the children finished the last of the trifle so you'll have to make do with this,' he said, coming back with a platter of cheese. 'By the way, did you hurt yourself? Do you need some of your grandfather's brandy?'

'I'm all right, only a few bruises. Tea will be fine.'

'Cook will probably have my blood for this in the morning so for heaven's sake leave everything tidy when you come up to bed.' He poured the boiling water into the pot, stirred it vigorously and went to fetch a crock of milk and three cups. 'Have you any idea where you want to start this holiday of yours?' he asked, beginning to pour the tea. 'Sugar seems to have gone missing so you'll have to put up with this.'

'Well, I did think of joining Uncle Harry in Paris. He happened to mention it before he went off a few weeks ago.'

'Good idea.' Harry Warrinder led a somewhat rackety life but could be relied on to keep a watchful eye on his sister's son, and it would get the boy off to a good start. After that he would have to take his chance and make his own mistakes. He poured two more cups of tea and put them on a tray with a large sandwich.

'I'm going to take this up to your mother. When we go back to town, we'll talk about money. You can't expect your uncle to fund you. We'll work something out together.' He picked up the tray. 'Don't forget to turn out the lamps when you come up.'

When he came into the bedroom, balancing the tray in one hand and shutting the door with the other, Christine was on her feet at once.

'Wherever have you been? I nearly came in search of you. Is David all right?'

'Perfectly all right. Apparently he went a lot too far, Jenny put a foot down a rabbit hole and threw him into a ditch. He has ruined a perfectly good coat and lamed the mare. He had to trudge home as he couldn't ride her. Poor Paddy is going to be up half the night poulticing her leg. In the mean time he is tucking into ham sandwiches with tea and cheese and is highly pleased with himself and his escapade.'

'Is that true?'

'Absolutely true, *and* I didn't say a word to him. Instead I raided the larder and promised to make sure he has ample funds when he sets off on his travels in the next few days – with Harry as bear-leader, you will be pleased to know. I thought you could do with a cup of tea and half my sandwich.'

'Oh Daniel, you are a fool, but I'm so very thankful.' She took the half-sandwich he offered her. 'I don't know why it is but worry always makes me terribly hungry. It's like old times, isn't it, when we used to share our supper in Ma Taylor's attic?'

They drank their tea and he told her something of what her father had asked of him that evening.

'My God,' she said, half laughing and half serious. 'Whatever will Clara do when she finds out?'

'There's not much she can do if the whole affair is legally settled.'

'I suppose not. Will you go?'

'Certainly, if it will help your father. Of course it will have to wait a week or two until I've settled what I have immediately in hand, and for heaven's sake don't breathe a word to a soul. Your father was very insistent about that. I'll have to invent some plausible reason for going off to Russia.'

'I'll be silent as the grave, but I hope I'm there to see Clara's face when the news is broken to her.'

'Isn't that just like a woman! She has nothing to worry about, she's rich enough.' He yawned and stretched. 'Come on, my love, bed. I'm worn out. So-called holidays are a lot more exhausting than hard work.'

Theirs was a happy and stable relationship. The early years of stress and anxiety, of parting and months of desolation when everything worked against the marriage between a beggarly teacher in a ragged school and the daughter of a distinguished barrister, had cemented the love between them into an enduring friendship still spiced with passion and filled with trust. They quarrelled sometimes, argued often, for both held strong views on a great many subjects, but they never allowed the divisions to descend into bitterness.

Lying close together in the big bed, they talked for a while and then, when Christine fell asleep, settled comfortably in the old position beside him, Daniel lay awake for a while thinking of David, thankful in a way that the boy would be off soon and he needn't worry too much about their relationship. Then there was Russia, a country he had not yet visited. He would enjoy seeing St Petersburg, might even get in a trip to Moscow if time permitted and all this business was settled with James Ducane and his pretty mistress. He never dreamed for a single moment that he was venturing on something that was going to wreak havoc here in England and threaten everything he held most dear.

Chapter 2

At much the same time, more than a thousand miles away, in a small villa a few miles from St Petersburg, Louise heard the amazing news that her father at long last was to marry her mother. It came as a shock, and she didn't know whether to be delighted, or fearful lest it should mark some unpleasant change in their lives.

Her mother told her at breakfast that morning and Louise stared at her, scarcely able to believe her ears.

'But why now, Mamma? Why now after all this time?'

'I know, my dear, it seems almost ridiculous after nearly twenty years, doesn't it? But your father wishes it.'

'Are you pleased, Mamma? Is it what you have always wanted?'

'Oh, I did once, of course,' said her mother, 'but in those days there seemed an insurmountable gulf between an English gentleman and a girl from the streets of Paris with nothing to recommend her but the ability to sing.'

'But afterwards, when you had become famous?'

'It didn't matter then. A few words spoken by a priest could not have bound us any closer; besides, the British Embassy, to which Papa was attached at the time, might not have cared for it.'

'And yet you never ceased to love him.'

'With all my heart.' Her mother smiled. 'You'll discover one day, my dear, that love does not need to be fettered to be lasting.'

'I understand that, so why does he want this now?'

22

'There are reasons. After all Papa is sixty, you know. Perhaps he now feels a need to regularize his life.'

'He's not sick, is he?' she asked in sudden alarm. 'He is not going to die?'

'No, no, Louise. I would have known if it were anything like that.' Her mother got up from the table. 'And now I must go and finish dressing. He wants me to lunch with him in town today and talk things over. There is a good deal to be discussed. It seems there are legal matters, and the church must be consulted.'

'Where will it be, Mamma? In St Isaac's Cathedral?'

'No, no, of course not. In some things Papa is still very British, despite having lived so long abroad. It will be in the English church and very quiet.' She smiled. 'After all, I'm not exactly a blushing bride.'

'You'll still be a very beautiful one,' said her daughter loyally. 'Am I to come with you today?'

'Not this time. When it is all settled, then of course you will be part of it. I shall take the pony carriage and hope to be back early this evening. You'll not be lonely?'

'No, of course not. It's a lovely day. I shall walk the dogs and then spend a little time practising for my next lesson. Last time Monsieur Vincent told me I was playing Chopin with the delicacy of a herd of elephants.'

'Rubbish! He is an old fool and you play very nicely.'

'Very nicely isn't good enough. You forget, Mamma, he's a perfectionist. He never stops telling me of the days when he worked with Franz Liszt.'

They laughed together. Mother and daughter shared a passionate love of music and Louise had a considerable talent for the piano.

Later she saw her mother into the small pony carriage, dressed elegantly for the city in a tight-fitting jacket and full spreading skirt of dark blue watered silk, a tiny flowered hat on her rich auburn hair and a lace-edged parasol.

'Give my dearest love to Papa,' she said as she kissed her mother goodbye.

'He will probably come back with me, so make sure Katya prepares something really good for supper this evening.'

'I'll tell her to choose all his favourite dishes,' Louise promised, and watched the carriage disappear down the drive before she returned to the house.

It was an attractive villa, built almost entirely of wood carved and painted in the style of a Swiss chalet, and stood in a corner of the vast estates belonging to Count Davitsky, who held an important government post but preferred to live outside the city on account of his wife's delicate health. The count had been happy to lease it to the quiet Englishman attached to the embassy who, to his secret amusement, apparently sustained a discreet and long-standing liasion with a French opera singer. The villa had been built originally to house an ancient and very formidable great-aunt, and had several bedrooms, a dining-parlour and drawing-room, with extensive kitchen quarters and stables.

Early June in St Petersburg could be delightful: the snow all vanished, the garden bursting into flower but the sun not yet possessing the fierce heat of full summer. Louise ran upstairs to fetch a light shawl and a shady hat. Toby, a small white woolly dog of doubtful ancestry which she had rescued from drowning at the hands of a couple of savage-minded little boys, came bounding out of his basket joyously. Together they went downstairs and out by the garden door to be joined by Mishka, an aristocratic Borzoi who was a gift from Count Davitsky when they had first taken up residence.

There was a small flower garden which she and her mother lovingly tended between them but she had the freedom of the whole estate, so today she took the path that ran through the plantation of silver birch, the slender trunks gleaming white in the sun. It led to the banks of a small stream that wandered through the estate, finally ending up in the ornamental lake in front of the big house.

She sat on the wooden seat carved by the estate gardener from a fallen tree trunk and thought over the startling news of the impending marriage and what it could mean, not only to her mother and father but also to herself. The fact that she was illegitimate had never particularly worried her, partly because she had been shielded by so much loving care. She let her mind run back over the years. She had been born in Paris but since her father had moved to Vienna when she was five she could not remember very much about it. The very first time she heard the word 'bastard' had been at a children's party at the British Embassy in Vienna; it had been the daughter of the ambassador who had flung it at her in a rage of envy and spite.

In the morning the children had been privileged to attend a special concert in the Golden Hall of the Musikverein in the presence of the Emperor Franz Joseph and his wife. Since Louise's mother was to sing several songs by Franz Schubert, the ambassador had rashly decided that it would be a delightful gesture for the famous singer's eleven-year-old daughter to present the bouquet to the Empress, who so seldom attended public occasions. Looking like a small angel in pristine white muslin, her golden hair braided, Louise had performed a faultless curtsy and had received in return a few gracious words and a kiss on the cheek that sent her into seventh heaven.

Later the children had been shepherded back to the embassy for coffee and cake, but a silly dispute had arisen among them as to who should have the privilege of cutting the magnificent *Sachertorte* sent in by the chef of the Hotel Adler, laced, they hoped, with kirsch and rich with strawberries and cream.

Louise had been pushed forward by the younger children, who all disliked the ambassador's daughter Jane for her way of crowing over them because of her father's status. She was, unhappily, a plain child, with straight, mouse-coloured hair that no curling-tongs could ever do much with and a pasty complexion not improved in summer by a flush of freckles, whereas Louise was one of those fortunate people who, dressed in rags and dragged through a hedge backwards, would still have looked outstandingly beautiful – not that she was aware of it. She was far too young, for one thing, and had been taught by a stern governess that vanity about looks given to you by God was a mortal sin. However, all these facts combined to stoke the smouldering fire of Jane's jealousy. She pushed Louise violently aside and snatched the silver knife out of her hand.

'Not you,' she hissed. 'You've no right to anything. You're only a common bastard!'

Louise had no idea what the word meant but guessed by the shocked silence around her and the sly grin on the face of the young footman at the door that it was shameful. She retaliated with spirit.

'Don't you dare to call me that.'

'Why shouldn't I? It's true!' screamed Jane, letting bitter jealousy carry her away. 'It's what my papa calls you,' a deliberate lie: the ambassador would never have used such a word in his daughter's presence. She must have picked it up from servants' gossip and now, flushed with success, she let herself go.

'Bastard, bastard, bastard!' she yelled triumphantly, and plunged the knife into the luscious cake.

Louise was not going to let her get away with that. She drew a deep breath and launched herself at her enemy. The knife flew out of Jane's hand, scattering cream and strawberries all over them. They went down together, scratching, biting, clawing at each other like two enraged kittens, and by the time Jane's governess, assisted by the young footman, had dragged them apart they presented a very sorry spectacle indeed. Jane had lost the white satin bows in her hair, which hung in lank strands about her face, adorned with a long bleeding scratch on one cheek. Louise was in a similar plight, one eye half closed and a huge rip in the beautiful white dress which was also plentifully bestrewn with cream, strawberries and blood.

The real cause of the quarrel was never revealed by anyone. Louise would have died rather than repeat the horrible word hurled at her, while Jane was led away, sobbing far too hysterically to say anything coherent. Louise was sent home in disgrace, with the young footman as escort.

Mademoiselle Yvette, who had been with them since Louise was five years old, first as nanny and then as governess, was shocked at her appearance but apart from saying that she did not know what Louise's papa would say to such outrageous behaviour, and in the embassy drawing-room of all places, she did not scold too much. Instead she helped Louise to change out of the muslin dress, now irretrievably ruined, and dealt with what seemed likely to be a magnificent black eye.

It was not till early evening, when her mother returned from the reception following the concert, that the truth came out. Her mother looked up as Mademoiselle ushered Louise into the drawing-room.

'You may leave us, Yvette,' she said. 'I'll deal with my daughter.' The governess nodded and went out, closing the door.

By this time Marianne Dufour was thirty-five but still a handsome young woman. It was easy to see from whom Louise derived her looks. Her hair, a little darker than that of her daughter, had been elaborately dressed that morning and she was still wearing the creation in black and silver lace which she had worn for the concert. Relations between mother and daughter had always been very close and Louise was not in the least afraid of her. All the same she knew she had committed an unheard-of outrage, so she remained standing just inside the door, staring down at her toes in their black sandals and waiting for retribution to fall on her head.

'Well, Louise,' said her mother, 'what is all this I've been hearing about you?'

She raised her head, met her mother's eyes, read the faintest suggestion of a smile in them and took heart.

'Jane called me a common bastard.'

'Did she indeed? And do you know what the word means?'

'I didn't know then but I do now. I looked it up in the dictionary Papa gave me.'

'And what did it say?'

'It said "illegitimate, a child born out of wedlock".'

'I could think of a kinder definition,' said her mother drily. 'What about "child born of love"?'

Louise frowned. 'Does that mean that Papa is not my real papa?'

'No, it doesn't, quite the contrary.' Marianne sighed. The child was growing up. It was a wonder she had never asked questions before. Now she must be told the truth honestly, and not as something furtive that needed to be hidden away.

'Come here to me, Louise. I want to tell you a story.'

'About you and Papa?'

'Yes, about me and your father and the great joy we have had in you.'

Louise pulled up a footstool and sat close beside her mother, her eyes on her face.

Marianne was silent for a moment, bracing herself for the inevitable, searching for the right words to make her child understand how much pity and anguish, kindness and love, had made the two of them what they were.

In the end she told it well, with a touch of drama that had an instant appeal. She had been the daughter of two strolling players who, unable to cope with a young child in their wandering life, had left her in the care of her grandmother, who kept a small *pension* on the left bank of the Seine. One of her lodgers sang in the Paris Opéra. A kindly middle-aged man who was fond of children, he had been struck by Marianne's instinctive response to music and her unusually beautiful young voice. He had found teachers willing to show an interest, and did his best to have her trained so that by sixteen, and with his influence, she was already singing in the opera chorus. A year or so later she had foolishly fallen in love with a wildly handsome young man in the company. For a year they lived together in bliss, till the day he walked out on her, seduced by the attentions of a wealthy widow entranced by his looks and with a great deal more to offer than a penniless young girl. It was at this time of heartbreak, when there seemed nothing to live for and the only solution to fall one night into the black waters of the Seine, that James Ducane came into her life, struck by her beauty.

'What was he like then?' asked Louise breathlessly.

'Much as he is now,' said her mother, smiling. 'Tall, handsome, very quiet, a little shy perhaps.'

All the girls at the Opéra were accustomed to dealing with admirers, some kind, some demanding, a great many who thought only of getting you into their bed as soon as possible. You had to learn how to pick and choose. But from the first James Ducane had been different. He was English, to start with, attached to the British Embassy, a distinguished linguist. He was no callow boy but a man just turned forty, a widower it seemed, whose wife had died giving birth to a daughter who lived in England.

Marianne was wary at first, determined never to be hurt again, but James was not like the others. He treated her as an intelligent being with a mind of her own, invited her out to supper, hired a carriage on Sundays and took her for long excursions into the country, introducing her to books and poetry, to things she had never had time or money for, almost like the father she had never known, and asked nothing in return except her company. Eventually she learned things about him. He was a man essentially lonely who had suddenly found an absorbing interest. Her reputation began to build, she began to sing major roles, and at the end of their first year he found an apartment for her in a quiet corner of Paris and their friendship slowly deepened into love. When Louise was born it was as if he had discovered at last something he had always sought without realizing it.

Looking down at her daughter listening with rapt attention, drinking in every detail, Marianne said nothing about the problems of living an irregular life on the edge of society, the occasional insults, the spiteful whispers, the frequent snubs. Why should she care what the stiff, self-righteous embassy wives said about her, or the cold looks she received, when very rarely she met up with them at some concert or reception? She had James's devoted love and the circle of friends – the artists, actors, writers – they gathered around them.

Louise was entranced. To her it was like some of the romances in the books and poetry she devoured. She had always known there was something different about her family. For one thing her father did not live with them quite like other fathers did, it was her mother who controlled their household; but these were things she accepted without question as children do. She saw no shame in it. She had never been sent to school and so had not been exposed to other children's spiteful taunts. She adored her father, not because he came loaded with gifts but because he shared so much with her, told her wonderful stories about the many countries he had visited, bought her books, talked to her in English so that she grew up bilingual, shared her love of music and was proud of her skill at the piano.

'Does it distress you, my darling, to know that Jane was in fact speaking the truth?' her mother said gently.

'Oh no, Mamma, I wouldn't change Papa for anything in the whole world.'

'Neither would I, Louise, neither would I.'

Six months after that her father had been called back to London and, when he returned, they had packed up and moved from Vienna to St Petersburg, the fact that he had recently added Russian to his many languages being far too useful to be ignored.

Louise had never forgotten her first sight of the city. It was winter and bitterly cold. Despite thick fur rugs, foot muffs and the stone hot-water bottles on their laps, the carriage was piercingly cold. They had driven through a white landscape and as they entered the city and followed the course of the river, she could see the dying sun hanging like a huge fiery ball above them, flushing the frozen waters of the Neva to a deep rose, gilding the statue of Peter the Great on his leaping horse and turning the branches of the trees to pink coral. It was a city of magic, and though she had seen it many times since and in all kinds of moods, it had never quite lost its glamour.

She was roused from her thoughts by Mishka's sharp bark. Then two hands were clapped over her eyes and a familiar voice said, 'Guess who?'

'Leo, you idiot!' she exclaimed, laughing as she twisted

round to look up at a young man in breeches and boots and brown leather hunting-coat. 'What are you doing here? Shouldn't you be at your university lectures?'

'I've been sent home for the rest of the term.'

'Oh no! What is it for this time? Have you been plotting revolution again?'

'Don't *you* laugh at me. The others are bad enough,' he went on gloomily, picking up the sporting rifle he had dropped on the grass and sitting beside her. 'Papa is furious, Mamma cries and cries and Michael treats me as if I was some kind of village idiot.'

'I'm not surprised. Is that why you've come out this morning ready to kill something, just to prove what a big strong man you are?' she said teasingly.

'Oh shut up, Louise. The gun is only an excuse to take myself out of the house. I don't often hit anything.'

'A very good thing too. What have the poor birds and squirrels ever done to you?'

'I suppose you think that's funny.'

'Oh, Leo, don't be such a goose!'

Louise had been on friendly terms with Leo ever since they came to live at the villa. Leo, a shy boy of fourteen, had arrived one morning with Mishka in his arms. Both of them were a little lonely and a friendship had started up. They had played games together, gone on picnics, fought, argued and laughed together very much like brother and sister, till this last year when their relationship changed and he began to demand more from her than she was willing to give. She liked him but was not in the least in love with him, and it troubled her sometimes.

Leo was the younger son in a brilliant family, the duffer, the one who always lagged behind, and he nursed a perpetual grievance because of it. His father was highly thought of politically and on friendly terms with the Tsar; his brother Michael, five years older, was a lieutenant in a crack regiment of the Guards and a great favourite with the ladies; his sister had made a wealthy and successful marriage; while Leo, whom

31

no one knew what to do with, had been sent to Petersburg University to study law and so far had failed dismally, for which of course he blamed everyone but himself.

Petersburg University at this time was a hotbed of discontent. The students split up into little groups who met in secret and wasted their time plotting to destroy the government and turn society upside-down, whether by fair means or foul. Mostly they were hopelessly ineffective but now and then they did succeed. Tsar Alexander had narrowly escaped being assassinated only because his carriage had taken a different route from that planned, but several innocent people had died and the Okhrana, the secret police, had mercilessly hunted down everyone who might have had a hand in it. One was hanged, several were sent into exile in Siberia. Leo had regarded them as martyrs and had argued passionately with Louise over the rights and wrongs of it.

'What happened this time?' she asked him resignedly.

'We were just experimenting, that's all, in the physics laboratory. Then the authorities clamped down. They will never allow anything new. We've all got to toe the line and follow old-fashioned ideas that have been exploded for centuries. It's all so maddening.'

She only half listened. She had heard it all before, many times. He was a dear boy but he did talk such a lot of nonsense. Given the slightest chance he would go on and on about the peasants, how they must be given an opportunity for a better life, granted more privileges, freed from a life of wretched slavery. She doubted if he had ever set foot inside a peasant's hut in his life, or knew as much about them as she and her mother did when in a hard winter they took food and medicines and blankets to the women and children in the count's village.

She let him work off his indignation at being ignominiously sent down and then got resolutely to her feet.

'Poor old Leo,' she said. 'I know how maddening it is but I expect it will blow over soon. In the mean time we do have the summer to look forward to, don't we? I really mustn't stay talking any longer. I want to spend the afternoon practising. My music teacher comes soon and I haven't done half of what he told me to do.'

'Don't go, Louise, not yet. I want to ask you something.'

She picked up her hat and looked around for the dogs. 'What is it?' she said a little impatiently.

'Will you marry me?'

'What?' She was so taken by surprise that she could scarcely speak. 'Is this a joke?'

'No, of course it isn't. I mean it.'

But she still couldn't take it seriously. 'Oh Leo, don't be so silly. Of course I can't marry you. Whatever would your father have to say?'

'I think he would be pleased. He is longing to be rid of me,' he went on morosely. 'He could set us up in a place of our own somewhere – he's rich enough – and then forget about us. I'd like that. We've always got on so well together.'

He was obviously in earnest but it was so absurd. She had never once thought of such a thing and the prospect appalled her. How to make him understand how impossible it was without hurting him too much?

'It's not that I don't like you, Leo. We've always had fun together, but I don't want to marry anyone, not yet. There are so many other things that I want to do first.'

'I thought getting married was all girls ever dreamed about. I know my sister did, from when she was a child. She was seventeen when she was married.'

'I'm not like your sister. Oh Leo, why did you have to say it? You've spoiled everything.'

'Why have I? We're still friends, aren't we?'

But in a way she was right. Their easygoing friendship would never be the same again and now she only wanted to get away.

'It's sweet and kind of you but you must know how impossible it is,' she said despairingly, disturbed by the mulish look on his face. 'And now I really must go. I have so much to do at home and I have to see Katya about our evening meal.' She called Mishka a little distractedly and picked up Toby.

33

'I don't know why you're so fond of that little mongrel. Goodness knows where he sprang from,' said Leo moodily. 'My mother would give you one of her Dachshund puppies if I were to ask her and they have pedigrees as long as your arm.'

'I don't want a prize lapdog,' said Louise obstinately. 'I like Toby. He's a fighter and he's very brave. He's a bit like me, I suppose, a bastard with doubtful parentage.'

She didn't know why she said it and would have bitten the words back. It had just slipped out, perhaps because she had been thinking about it so much that morning.

Leo stopped dead, staring at her. 'There you are, Louise, isn't that a perfect example of all I've been saying? That's just another of the hundreds of things we would like to change one day. I know your father is English but that makes no difference. It's so typical, keeping a woman to serve his pleasure and too proud to give to her and her daughter the status and position in society that they should have. It disgusts me.'

'Does it? In that case I'm surprised you condescended ever to talk to me,' said Louise, touched to the quick by the contempt in his voice.

'Oh Lord, I didn't mean . . . you know how much I think of you, Louise.' He was stammering a little. 'Haven't I just proved it? Only you must have had times when you resented it.'

'Well, I haven't. You don't know what you're talking about. My father is good and kind and generous, everything a father should be. In fact, he will very soon – and then she stopped abruptly. She had only been told that morning. It was still something very private. She couldn't blurt it out, and certainly not to Leo. 'You're only a boy,' she said with a spurt of temper. 'How could you possibly understand? It's all talk with you, isn't it, talk, talk, talk, with those friends of yours, talk about all the wonderful things you are going to do and what happens? Absolutely nothing. You can't even pass a few exams.'

'So that's what you think of me, is it? I thought you were

different, I thought you understood, but you're just like all the others.' He grabbed hold of her by the shoulders, swinging her to face him, staring down at her, his face gone white, his fingers digging into her. 'Well, I'll prove you wrong. I'll show you and Father and Michael that I've got more guts, more determination, more courage than any of you. I swear I will. You can laugh at me, but very soon now I'll make you sorry, I'm going to make you take back every single word you ever said to me.'

She hadn't expected such a violent reaction and it disturbed her. 'Leo,' she said quickly, 'Leo, you mustn't think . . .' but he thrust her roughly away from him, turned on his heel and strode down the path, disappearing into the grove of trees.

She stared after him until she heard a single shot followed by a tremendous whir of wings as the birds flew up into the sky. She hoped to God he hadn't done something silly like tripping up and shooting his foot off. She waited for a few moments, a little anxious, but there was no further sound and at last she turned and followed the path back to the house.

It was early evening when she heard the carriage and ran out to greet it. As her mother had promised, Papa had returned with her. Perhaps because of what Leo had said, she seemed that night to see him with new eyes. James Ducane was turned sixty but looked a good deal younger: tall, lean and still handsome with his charming rather shy smile.

'Well, my darling,' he said, 'glad to see me?'

'Oh Papa!' In quick reaction she flung her arms round his neck and hugged him.

'Hey, hey, what have I done to deserve all that?' he said, putting his arm round her as they went into the house.

Supper was a joyful affair. Katya had outdone herself. There was leek soup with chopped mushrooms and cream, followed by sole in a delightful sauce of her own creation, and tender chicken cooked with truffles and capers in a thin pastry crust, and they laughed as the cork flew up and hit the ceiling when her father opened the champagne. They discussed the wedding which was to take place in mid-July, barely six weeks away.

'We can't make it sooner,' he said, 'there are certain matters still to be settled. I have to make a new will, for one thing, and I've written to England.'

Louise wondered if it was his daughter to whom he had written and what she would be thinking, this half-sister of hers whom he very rarely mentioned. How strange to think that she must be almost Mamma's age.

After supper Katya served their coffee on the patio outside the tall windows. It was very warm and the garden was filled with the scents of the evening.

While her mother poured the coffee, her father said casually, 'I ran into our neighbour yesterday, and the count said Leo is in trouble again, failed his exams and got sent home for some silly student prank.'

'He was here this afternoon,' said Louise, 'but he really didn't tell me very much about it. What exactly were they up to?'

'Trying to make a bomb, if you can believe it,' he said lightly.

'A bomb?' repeated her mother. 'Isn't that very dangerous?'

'It would seem so, since it blew up, but fortunately the only victim seems to have been the college cat. They protested it was a purely scientific experiment that went wrong but the authorities weren't very impressed with that excuse and came down pretty heavily on them.'

'Quite right too. Next time they could kill somebody,' said her mother severely. 'Louise, pour a little brandy for your father.'

'I rather think that is the ultimate aim,' he said drily. 'Fortunately they're none of them experts.' He took the glass from Louise and smiled. 'In my young days we were not quite so lethal. The worst I remember was scaling the tallest spire in Oxford and attaching a pair of pink silk drawers to the summit.'

'Did you do that, Papa?' asked Louise.

'I'm afraid I did,' he said ruefully. 'Everard Warrinder, who is now a highly respected judge, bet me fifty pounds that I couldn't do it, and I wasn't going to let him get away with that. There was a shocking row and my father was furious with me, to say nothing of the young woman whose drawers they were.'

So the evening passed pleasantly, with talk and laughter and all kinds of plans for the future, including a decision to invite a small party of close friends a week or two before the ceremony.

'We can have them here,' said her mother. 'The evenings are drawing out now and it is very warm. We can move out into the garden.'

They went on discussing it till it was time for Louise to kiss them good-night. As she undressed she wondered if she ought to have told them of Leo's proposal, and then was glad that she had said nothing. Surely by now he must have realized how impossible it was. She fell asleep with the happy certainty that nothing now could spoil their quiet happiness.

It was Uncle Harry who suggested that they might include a flying visit to Russia during what he laughingly referred to as their Grand Tour. David had joined him in France soon after the garden party at Bramber, but the season in Paris was already coming to an end and society was beginning to move out into the country for the summer. They had spent a day at the races where Harry, with his usual acumen, had backed a winner and was in consequence feeling expansive.

'We might call on my Uncle James Ducane,' he said when they were dining together in a little restaurant of his choosing where the food was, he declared, as good as any served at Maxim's and a great deal cheaper. 'You know him, of course. He's brother-in-law to your grandfather, and Cousin Clara's papa. Did you ever meet him?'

'Once or twice when I was a child, but the last time he came to London I was up at Cambridge.'

'Charming old boy. When I was your age and studying at the Sorbonne, he was extremely kind to me. I remember being vastly intrigued to find out that he – seemingly a model of propriety – was in fact involved in a very discreet liaison with a young singer whom he made sure I never met. I wonder what happened to her. We could look him up and find out.'

After a hectic few days in Berlin, where David was introduced to some startling German nightlife and met some fabulous girls, they arrived in St Petersburg in time to receive a hearty welcome and be invited to what to all intents and purposes appeared to be an engagement party.

'He is going to marry her, by God,' said Harry that night when they were undressing in the room they shared in the Hotel Europa. 'If that doesn't beat everything! There will be fireworks when Cousin Clara finds out.'

'I don't see why. After all she's been living her own life for years.'

'My dear boy, she has always resented the fact that her father can't stand the sight of her. Hell hath no fury like a woman scorned, as someone said.'

'It was William Congreve, actually,' murmured David, glad for once to be able to score off his knowledgeable uncle.

'Was it? Well, whoever it was he knew his onions. Anyway, to find out that for all these years her papa has had a beautiful mistress will, I'm pretty sure, bring our Clara to boiling point.'

'What can she do? They're thousands of miles apart.'

'I dare say that's what Uncle James believes, but life sometimes has a funny way of upsetting the best-laid plans.'

Owing to their cab driver losing his way, they arrived a little late, to find the party in full swing. They were greeted warmly by their host and immediately presented to Marianne.

'*Enchanté, madame*,' murmured Harry, gallantly kissing her hand so that David, a little awkwardly, was forced to follow suit.

'We had thought that perhaps you had changed your minds and decided not to come,' she said, eyeing doubtfully these two English visitors from her lover's other life.

'No such thing,' said Harry heartily, 'wouldn't have missed it for anything in the world.'

'You've come prepared to stay overnight with us, I hope,' said James. 'It's all settled, isn't it, my dear?'

'Yes, of course,' said Marianne, 'that is if you don't mind sharing a room. We are a little pressed for space at the villa. Now you are here, you must come and meet our friends.'

There were perhaps thirty or forty people, men and women, circulating in and out of the two rooms and overflowing into the garden, people, it seemed to David, of all types and nationalities. Conversations in French, German, Russian, flowed around him on all sides. It didn't trouble Harry in the least. Fluent in French and with a good smattering of other languages, he could always give the impression that he knew far more than he did, but David, following closely after him, was at first frankly bewildered and half afraid to open his mouth.

At first he felt completely lost but then gradually he grew bolder and began to enjoy himself. This was nothing like stiff English gatherings where no one spoke to you unless formally introduced. These people looked at him with frank interest, asked him where he came from, commiserated with him on the hardships of travel, urged him to eat, plied him with wine, all in a variety of languages that included fractured English. He found that after all his schoolboy French stood him in good stead. It must have been close to midnight when, overcome with the novelty of it and a little drunk with excitement and the wine he had taken, he went through the long windows into the garden.

It was wonderfully cool and fresh out here, the air filled with the evening scent of the flowers. Although it was so late it was still not entirely dark. Up here so far north, summer nights were long with only an hour or two of darkness. There were other people here and there, walking and whispering together, as he went down the patio steps and plunged into the garden. He ducked under an arch hung with climbing roses and came on to a wide grassy stretch with a gate at the far end. It was there, in the magic of the summer night with a sky like pearl, that he saw Louise for the first time. She was standing at the gate which seemed to lead into a stretch of meadow with a distant fringe of silvery trees. A gentle breeze stirred the wide folds of her white dress and blew tendrils of hair across her forehead. For a moment he stood quite still, afraid to move lest the vision should disappear as dreams inevitably do. Then he took a step forward, she turned to look at him and in that instant it seemed to him that never in his whole life had he seen anyone so beautiful. She came towards him, stretching out a hand, smiling, speaking in an English that was only slightly accented.

'You must be one of Papa's friends from London. He told me you were coming.'

'I am David Fraser. My uncle is Harry Warrinder.'

'And I am Louise.'

'You speak wonderful English,' he said, still holding her hand, still too bemused to realize what he was saying.

'I ought to,' she smiled. 'Papa has spoken English to me for as long as I can remember, just as I speak French with Mamma.' She gently withdrew her hand. 'When I was small, I used to get the two muddled and could never understand why they all laughed at me. We don't have many visitors from England. You must tell me all about it.'

'Doesn't your father talk to you about it?'

'Not really. He says very soon he is going to take me there and then I shall see for myself, but there is so much I would like to know. Are you a relative?'

'I suppose so, in a way, a sort of distant cousin.'

'Are you acquainted with Papa's real daughter?'

Her frankness startled him a little. He wondered if she had ever resented her illegitimacy. 'You must mean Cousin Clara.'

'Is that what you call her?'

'Well, she is really Lady Dorrien but she is my mother's first cousin and they grew up together.'

'Tell me about her. Do you like her?'

He was just wondering rather desperately how he was going to give an impression of Cousin Clara without disclosing the unpleasant truth when they were interrupted. Someone was calling for her and the next moment her father came hurrying down the path towards them.

'Our guests are asking your mother to sing, my dear, and she would like you to play for her.'

'Yes, of course. I will come at once.'

'I see you and David are getting to know one another,' he went on; 'excellent, but there will be plenty of time later. Come along, my dear, they're waiting. You too, David, if you enjoy music.'

He followed after them and took care to find a place where he could watch Louise at the piano, the light from the two candle sconces falling on the pure line of her cheek and finding gleams of dark gold in her hair.

Their sheer professionalism surprised him. He had often been dragged to musical parties by his mother and more often than not had endured hours of boredom, but this was quite different. Marianne Dufour's voice had a rich vibrant quality, tempered from the operatic stage to the drawing-room, while Louise's playing of the rippling accompaniment enchanted him. There was enthusiastic applause and calls for more until at last Marianne shook her head smiling.

'Enough is enough,' she said, but then with a little shrug glanced at Louise. Mother and daughter, hand in hand, sang a little Russian folksong in a rippling harmony that hushed the guests to silence and enchanted David.

He would have liked to take Louise away to some quiet corner and express his delight and admiration, but Harry had forestalled him, discussing with her and her mother the operas he had seen and the musicians he had heard on visits to Paris and Vienna with an expertise and fluency that David could not match, even though Louise held out her hand and drew him into their group.

It was long past midnight when the party broke up, the guests departed and the two Englishmen retired to the room prepared for them.

'Well, how did you enjoy your first venture into Russian society?' asked Harry with a huge yawn, beginning to peel off his evening coat. 'In at the deep end, I'm afraid.'

'I came up for air now and then. I wish I spoke as many languages as you do,' said David ruefully.

'My dear boy, I don't really speak them all. The art is knowing how to make the very best of the little you do know and looking intelligent about it. Quite a lot of people enjoy listening to themselves and an occasional nod will very well do for an answer. The girl's a beauty, isn't she? Takes after her mother. Uncle James is a lucky fellow. She'll cause a sensation when she takes her place in society.'

'She can't be more than eighteen.'

'Well,' went on Harry pulling his shirt over his head, 'this marriage is going to make all the difference to her, you know. Society here is not quite so hidebound by the conventions as it is in England, but prejudice does still exist among some of the old die-hards. However, one look at Louise and the young men will forget the marriage was celebrated somewhat late in the day. And James Ducane must have a tidy fortune tucked away. He can give her a substantial dowry no doubt. If she's not married off to some princeling within a year, I'll eat my boots.'

'You make it sound as if she were being put up for sale,' said David distastefully.

'Well, isn't that what the marriage market is? Everyone out for the best bargain. It's why I've always steered clear of it. We're not all so fortunate as your mother, who married the wrong man but was given a second chance with the right one.' He saw David frown and clapped him on the shoulder. 'It's true, you know, though you don't like to admit it, do you?'

'I've never thought much about it,' said David stiffly.

Harry smiled but did not pursue it. 'I saw you and the pretty Louise having a *tête-à-tête* in the garden. Have you fallen for her already? I don't think you stand much of a chance, you know.'

'We only spoke for a few minutes. She was asking me about Cousin Clara.'

'Was she, by Jove? What did you tell her?'

'I was just trying to think of the right thing to say when her father came looking for her to play the piano.'

'With any luck they'll never have to meet. For Louise's sake I devoutly hope they won't,' said Harry and climbed into the big bed.

Despite it being so late David lay awake for a long time, going over the events of the evening, dwelling on Louise and wishing they could stay longer so that he could get to know her better. He seemed to have scarcely closed his eyes when he was roused by the excited barking of dogs and a voice that was doing its best to quieten them. Harry was still sleeping so he crept out of the bed and moved over to the window, drawing back the curtains and looking out on the garden. A magnificent Borzoi and a small white terrier were chasing a ball, with Louise running after them looking as lovely as the morning in her flowered cotton gown, with the golden hair loosely tied back with a ribbon. As he watched he saw a young man come to meet her, a Russian, David guessed by his clothes. They stood talking together; David heard her laugh then she leaned forward and gave the boy a light kiss on the cheek, and for the first time in his life he felt a sharp spasm of jealousy. He swung the curtains across, then pulled off his nightshirt and began to dress.

Harry opened a sleepy eye and said drowsily, 'Do you have to get up at the crack of dawn?'

'It's not that early. I thought I'd take a look around outside. There was no time last night.'

'If you must,' sighed his uncle. 'Call me when breakfast is ready.'

Brass cans of hot water had been thoughtfully placed just outside their door but by the time David had washed, shaved and dressed and hurried down to the garden, Louise had disappeared. Only the Borzoi was stretched lazily in a patch of early sunshine and politely waved his plume of a tail in greeting. Disappointed, David explored the garden and leaned on the white gate for a moment; the land seemed to stretch flat and interminable to the horizon broken only by the copse of slender silver birch. When he returned to the house it was to find breakfast already in progress.

'You were up early,' said his hostess. 'I hope that doesn't mean that you slept badly. Louise saw you walking in the garden and we wondered what had become of you. Pour David some tea, my dear – or would you prefer coffee?'

'Tea, please.'

'I'm afraid that, after having lived so long abroad, I have rather grown away from the traditional English breakfast,' said his host apologetically, 'but we can provide something more substantial for you if you would prefer it.'

'No, please. All this looks wonderful.'

Louise had placed a tall glass of steaming tea beside him with lemon and sugar. The table was spread lavishly with freshly baked rolls, dishes of a creamy white cheese they called *pashka*, bowls of different fruit preserves and some magnificent peaches.

'Do you grow these yourself?' he asked.

'Good heavens, no. I'm no horticulturist and neither is Marianne, I'm afraid. They usually come from Count Davitsky's hothouses, don't they, Louise?'

'Leo brought them early this morning, Papa.'

'So that's who I saw you with in the garden,' exclaimed David.

'Were you spying on me?'

'No, of course not,' he said hastily. 'I heard the dogs barking and just happened to draw back the curtains and look out.'

'Did Leo say why he didn't turn up last night?' asked her mother.

'Actually he came to apologize, Mamma, and I think the peaches were a kind of peace offering.'

David would have liked to ask more about this young Russian who had seemed on such friendly terms with her, but at that moment Uncle Harry made his appearance, full of apologies for being so late, and the talk became general.

'Will you be staying long in St Petersburg?' asked Marianne.

'I'm afraid not, madame, though I'd like to. David and I worked out a fairly tight itinerary for the next few weeks. He wants to see as much of Europe as he can before he buckles down to hard work, and I have to be back in England by September when the holiday is over and the courts begin their sittings once again.'

'Are you a lawyer?' asked Louise. 'How do you say it – an *avocat*?'

'In English that's a barrister,' said Harry, smiling at her. 'Yes, I am, for my sins. Warrinders have been connected with the law ever since a certain Roger Warrinder indulged in some rather shady dealings for good Queen Elizabeth and was rewarded for them. He settled down at Bramber and founded a family. My grandfather was a judge, so is my father, and I suppose I'll end up on the bench one of these days, God help me. David is following in our footsteps.'

'And he's so young too, only twenty-one and passed all his examinations,' said Louise, her eyes wide in admiration.

'Only some of them,' said David modestly.

'It's more than Leo can do. He has failed miserably and tries to compensate for it by pretending to be a revolutionary.'

'Isn't that a little unkind?' said her mother.

'Perhaps, but it's true, Mamma. It's so silly to be sent down for trying to make a bomb and only succeeding in blowing up a poor cat.'

'The trouble with the young is that they are nearly always idealists,' said Harry easily. 'Even David here thinks me an old die-hard because I tell him you can't change a constitution that has lasted for a thousand years by shouting slogans in Hyde Park. You have to move step by step. Let's hope your Leo doesn't concoct something lethal next time and do some real damage.'

'It's all a lot of foolish nonsense,' said James Ducane impatiently. 'I know Count Davitsky thinks it's high time Leo grew out of it. I'm sorry you can't both stay to see us married,' he went on, turning to Harry. 'I wrote to your father some time ago asking if he would come. Everard and I haven't seen much of one another over the years but we've always been on friendly terms. However it seems he feels unable to make the long journey and his son-in-law will come in his place.'

'Daniel is a splendid fellow,' said Harry warmly. 'Have you met him?'

'Once, a few years ago when I was visiting Christine. He and I rather took to one another. I had thought of asking Everard to be one of my executors to look after these two if anything should happen to me.'

45

'Don't talk of such dreadful things, Papa,' said Louise quickly.

'One must be sensible, my dear. I've put things off too long already. In the circumstances do you think Daniel will be willing to undertake it for me?'

'He is an excellent choice, couldn't do better,' said Harry. 'Whatever Daniel agrees to do, he will carry out conscientiously. You can be certain of that.'

'Good. I was pretty sure that Everard wouldn't have suggested anyone who was not reliable. Apparently he has certain commitments to fulfil but he should be here in a week or so, in plenty of time for us to become acquainted with him.'

David had sat silent but he felt the old familiar prick of resentment. He knew it was unfair, he knew that his grandfather had a high opinion of Daniel, but all the same he felt irritated. It was so like Daniel to worm himself into something like this. He would come, he would be on familiar terms with them and with Louise, and he would charm them all, of course, while David himself was far away. It might be completely unreasonable, but it was just something else to notch up against his stepfather.

They spent the morning with Louise and her mother, walking together in the garden and venturing further into the wide estate of their neighbour till they arrived at the outskirts of the private gardens and caught a glimpse of the huge white house and the ornamental lake with its swans and its fountain sparkling into the air from a bevy of stone waternymphs. A bank of roses edged a stretch of lawn where peacocks strutted and screeched. If Leo was the son of a family as wealthy as this, perhaps James Ducane was already looking upon him as a possible son-in-law, thought David with a pang of envy, which was absurd seeing that he had only known the girl for a few hours.

On the way back, while Harry and Marianne engaged in a lively discussion of their likes and dislikes in the world of music, David walked with Louise and found her far more easy to talk to than Isabelle's friends or the sisters of his mates at college. She had none of their airs and graces, none of their silly coquetry, but chatted easily and frankly so that he found his usual shy reserve melting away as he told her about the dogs and horses at Bramber, about the trip he had planned with Uncle Harry, and how much he was looking forward to being free of college and exams and living his own life in London when he returned home.

'Mamma wanted me to be a doctor like my father, but I hated the very idea of it, so it had to be law because Warrinders have always been in law,' he confessed. 'What I would really like to do is to study fine art from its very beginnings. I love everything to do with it. I dragged my uncle round every gallery in Berlin and Paris, and we even managed to see some of the very newest work which the Salon has rejected and derided but we thought marvellously new and exciting.' He paused for a moment and then went on gloomily, 'However my stepfather wouldn't hear of it. He thinks studying art in all its aspects is far too much like fun, and my mother always agrees with him.'

She listened to him quietly and then said something so surprising that he stared at her. 'Don't you think you are making rather too much of it? Couldn't you have both, make the law your career and study art as a hobby? Many people do, you know.'

'Perhaps,' he said doubtfully. 'I hadn't thought of it quite like that.'

'I think you should. I do understand, you know. I used to dream about becoming a pianist, a real one in my own right, playing in concerts all over Europe like Clara Wieck, the wife of Robert Schumann. She came to St Petersburg for a series of recitals. Papa took me to all of them and I came home full of dreams. But I know it is impossible. I might work for years and still not be really good enough, so I'm happy with what I have. I play the piano as much as I can and it is my joy and my passion. And, if I still sometimes cherish a dream, well, I suppose everyone does about something.'

He had never heard any young girl speak like that and he was both enchanted and amazed. What a marvellous person she was, and how maddening that these few hours were all he would ever have with her.

'If you like painting and sculpture so much,' she went on, 'then you must go to the Hermitage. The Tsar has a wonderful collection and he does allow distinguished foreigners to look at it now and then. Speak to my father about it and I am sure he will arrange it.'

'That would be wonderful. I suppose you couldn't accompany us?'

'I've been there once and I don't really think I ought to desert Mamma after the party last night, but do go if you can. I'm sure you will enjoy it.'

They arrived back at the villa a great deal too soon for David, and then after luncheon it was time to leave. It was just his luck, he thought morosely, to meet a wonderful girl whom he really liked who lived more than a thousand miles away and whom he was very unlikely to meet again.

Louise's father was obliged to return to the city himself that day and invited Harry and David to drive with him. The groom could then bring the carriage back for the use of Louise and her mother.

They all gathered outside to say farewell. Marianne kissed David on both cheeks in the continental manner so that Louise, a little shyly, did the same. As her lips brushed his cheek she murmured, 'Perhaps we shall meet again next year, if Papa keeps his promise and brings us to England.'

Then they were in the carriage, the horse was whipped up and he could only look back at the two women, arm in arm, smiling and waving to him from the gate.

Chapter 3

Daniel could not leave for Russia till the beginning of July. Over the years he had built up a formidable reputation for deeply researched, often controversial articles on a variety of subjects – political, economic, social – so that he was often in great demand. Even the austere *Times* had been known to commission a series from him. He had to clear his desk of the immediate work he had in hand if he were to leave himself free for what could mean at least three or four weeks out of England.

A few days before he left he lunched at Simpson's in The Strand with Joe Sharpe, editor of the *Northern Clarion*, who was up in London for a few days.

The hard-swearing, forthright Yorkshireman, who had never feared taking risks, had sometimes been sued for libel and whose paper was occasionally forced to the point of closure, had nevertheless built up his northern newspaper into a force to be reckoned with a circulation extending far beyond its early boundaries. It was he who had given the young Daniel Hunter, living on starvation wages teaching in a ragged school, his first chance to show what he could do by sending him out to the Crimea as a medical orderly with a commission to report back, not only on the course of the war but also on the appalling conditions in which the Army were obliged to live and, more often, die. It was a start from which Daniel had never looked back, and over the years gratitude had deepened into a loyal and lively friendship.

'Russia is a bit out o' my road,' said Joe, tucking into roast beef and Yorkshire pudding with gusto, 'but you've always had a nose for the vital detail, Dan, so take a good look around you. There's something stirring over in that benighted country, the bear is waking out of hibernation, but it's damned difficult to get a smell of it in this island, so that's where you come in.'

'I shall be moving in rarefied embassy circles, I'm afraid,' said Daniel a little drily, 'more than likely out of touch with reality.'

'Don't you believe it. Things have a way of happening when you're on the prowl. I shall be bloody surprised if something doesn't break,' went on Joe, hesitating between treacle tart and apple pie and regretting that he could only tackle one of them. 'As a matter of fact I've something of a bone to pick with you,' he said: 'what about those articles you promised me on the growth of prostitution in London? Now I could build that up into something really spicy, lifting the lid on a sewer, so to speak, the grim reality beneath the gloss and glitter of respectable London society. It will cause an outcry of course but controversy is what makes people read newspapers.' He pushed away his plate with a sigh of satisfaction, took up his wineglass and grinned across the table at Daniel. 'Maybe you've thought better of it now you're well on your way to becoming a pillar of the establishment, with your father-in-law a law lord presiding over the bench, and that pretty wife of yours turning into a society hostess.'

'Christine would not thank you for calling her that, and I'm not exactly propping up the state. I'd still like to hit out at the complacency that closes its eyes to conditions it would prefer to believe don't exist and yet at the same time indulges itself in all the vices they have to offer.'

'Mind you, you could be stepping into a pit of snakes with that puritanical conscience of yours,' went on Joe thoughtfully. 'It'll be your undoing one of these days, especially if you've still set your sights on being elected to Parliament one day.'

'I've been considering it. Last time I had a go, I only lost by a whisker, and I have had another opportunity offered to me down in my old stamping ground, the Whitechapel constituency. Ezra Brown, who gave me my first job teaching in his

Methodist school, has built up something of a grocery empire and is willing to put me up for it. His support could carry a good deal of weight.'

'You take care, my boy: there's nobody so hidebound or so rigorously respectable as your wealthy tradesman aspiring to be a gentleman.'

'That's something we shall have to find out. It's early days yet,' said Daniel. 'About those articles you want ... I have amassed a deal of information one way and another. Give me time and I'll go ahead with them, even if I do have to watch my step.'

'Good man. That's the spirit I like. Someone who plunges in head-first and only remembers about drowning afterwards.'

They parted with mutual good will and Daniel set about his preparations for the long journey in front of him. Over the years, with assignments as far away as India and America as well as all over Europe, he had brought his packing to a fine art, but this time he had to take formal clothes if he were to attend the wedding, a good supply of clean shirts and underwear and what it amused him to call his 'fashionable faldirals'.

The two children sat on the floor watching him. Celia, whose view of Russia was derived from pictures of daredevil Cossacks riding shaggy horses and waving swords above their heads, was worried about his safety. 'Will there be wolves, Papa, and bears like that big brown one we saw at the circus Mamma took us to and which growled when I tried to stroke it?'

'I doubt if wolves and bears roam the streets of St Petersburg,' said Daniel cheerfully, and wondered what he would do if invited to join a hunting party. Riding spirited and unfamiliar horses was not one of his accomplishments – he had come to it too late in life. However he had once been obliged to join a tiger hunt, mounted on an elephant, and been forced to watch Redskins chasing and slaughtering buffalo. It was not likely to be very much worse than that.

Christine came in, sending the children to their tea and

helping him to shut and lock the bulging valise. He had always preferred to do his own packing, saying he then knew where everything was and did not have to turn the whole thing upside-down to find a pocket handkerchief.

She watched him put into a small bag the necessities for the five or six days he would spend in the train: plenty of reading matter for the long boring hours, books he had not had time to read in his busy life – Mr Dickens' *Our Mutual Friend* and the latest edition of Henry Mayhew's monumental work *London Labour and the London Poor*, which contained some interesting information about the prostitutes who thronged not only the slums but the Haymarket, Leicester Square and the fashionable streets around Piccadilly. With them he included a quantity of notebooks and a supply of pencils.

'Don't you ever stop working, Dan?' said Christine, shaking her head at him. 'Why not look on this as a holiday?'

'Life's far too short for all the things I want to do.'

She had bought Anthony Trollope's latest best-seller for him, knowing how much he admired the author's studies of men in politics, and he smiled as he took it from her. 'Remember how you used to steal books from your father's library and bring them to me at the school?'

'It takes us back, doesn't it? Over twenty years ago, Dan. Do you still love me?'

'I can't stop,' he said, kissing the tip of her nose before he packed the book into his bag.

'Don't forget this.' She handed him the silver flask filled with brandy for emergencies.

'Lord, no. I don't know how many times a nip of that has saved my life,' he said, packing it in with the rest. 'That's the lot, I think,' and he shut the bag with a snap and straightened up. 'I hope I've not forgotten anything vital.'

'I wish you weren't going on this trip, Dan,' said Christine suddenly. 'I wish you had refused when Papa asked you.'

'Good heavens, why? You've seen me go away often enough before. I always come back safe and sound, and this does seem more like a holiday than anything else. I'm looking forward to seeing a little of Russia.'

'It's silly, I know. No reason. I just feel this is different somehow.'

'What with Celia worried because she thinks I might be eaten by a bear and you with your megrims, I look to be in a very poor way,' he said jokingly.

'I know, I know, but all the same I'm coming with you to Dover tomorrow.'

'To make sure you see the last of me, is that it? What would I do without you?' and he put an arm around her waist and pulled her against him. 'Now all this is done, what about letting the children sit up for dinner for once, and we'll open a bottle of your father's champagne and drink the health of Clara's new stepmother and her half-sister.'

Christine giggled. 'If she only knew! Did I tell you the latest? She has gone off on a pleasure cruise in the Mediterranean with her latest beau. He is by all accounts extremely rich, devastatingly handsome, half French and owns a yacht.'

'How do you know all this? Gossip at one of your tea parties?'

'Far more than gossip.'

'You don't mean that it's serious this time?'

'I doubt it, but you know Clara. She does like to have a man in tow so long as he is rich and handsome and adores her.'

This was true, but whether she took any of them as a lover was a moot point. If she did, it was so discreet that no one was ever able to point a finger. Clara's husband had been a handsome wastrel who had been murdered in particularly sordid circumstances after a year of marriage, so it was little wonder that she had been wary of committing herself and preferred to remain a widow, tantalizingly wealthy but not yielding an inch to anyone.

'You know,' went on Christine thoughtfully, 'I think a really strong man, who would meet her on equal ground and stand no nonsense, would be the making of Clara.'

'She's not met one yet,' said Daniel drily.

'That's because they're thin on the ground. They say this one is half Greek too.'

'Do they? A Greek pirate, eh? Maybe he'll toss her into his felucca and sail away with her into the Aegean.'

'Wouldn't it be marvellous if he did?' said Christine, giggling.

Dinner that evening proved a riotous occasion. Discipline was relaxed. The children were allowed half a glass of champagne and made the most of it. Even Isabelle, who tended to be serious, joined in the fun. Daniel told some startling stories of things he had seen and done in the past and promised to bring them all back something typically Russian, only refusing point-blank to buy Celia a live bear cub.

Afterwards when they were preparing for bed he came up behind Christine as she brushed her hair in front of the mirror, slipping his arms round her shoulders in the thin silk dressing-gown and pulling her back against him.

'Do you ever wish that I had been able to come up with something like a yacht in the Mediterranean?'

'God forbid!' she said and meant it.

She turned, reaching up to kiss him, and he took the brush out of her hand, pulled her to her feet and carried her to the bed, despite the years and four babies still not much heavier than the girl with whom he had first fallen in love. They came together that night with a passion that surprised them both and proved that old fires could still burn as fiercely as they had ever done.

The next day she travelled down to Dover with him and saw him on to the packet, watching till it slowly moved out of the harbour, leaving her with the strongest feeling that in some way, when he came back, everything would be different, a feeling that with her usual good sense she put out of her mind as firmly as possible.

The train journey was every bit as long, hot, uncomfortable and boring as Daniel had anticipated. He travelled first-class, but all the same there were no sleeping compartments, no refreshment cars and no lavatories, which meant a fearful rush of passengers at station stops to use these conveniences and a hasty gulping of any food that was available before the warning bell sounded and the train steamed out again. At the border between Poland and Russia he had to change trains, since the Russian gauge was wider than the European one, and here his passport and special Russian travelling visa were closely examined. He was asked where he came from, where he was going and why; his luggage was turned out, his books closely studied and his notebooks, which he had half filled, examined with the gravest suspicion. All communication had to take place in limited French, with the Russian guards infuriatingly treating him as some kind of international spy. It held everyone up and he was regarded with hatred by the other passengers resenting the delay.

At last however, somewhat reluctantly, everything was returned to him and they were once more on their way. The railway line between Poland and St Petersburg had not long been built and was still suffering from teething trouble. There were numerous inexplicable delays and the journey took some thirty hours in the stifling heat of early July. He arrived at last in the late afternoon, tired, sweating and thirsty, his eyes gritty from lack of sleep, and longing for a cup of good English tea, a long cool bath and a decent meal, which he did not seem likely to enjoy, for a time at any rate. He had telegraphed James Ducane from Warsaw Station but the journey had taken far longer than he had expected so he took a cab to the Hotel Europa, booked in, dipped his face in cold water, put on a clean shirt and made his way to the British Embassy where he gave his name and asked for James Ducane.

The man at the desk stared at him for a long moment and then said in a stifled voice, 'I will enquire for you, sir,' and bolted. Daniel was left to cool his heels in the spacious hall, where a recent painting of Queen Victoria, in deepest mourning for Prince Albert, frowned down on him and he wondered what the devil could have happened to make the man so jumpy. After what seemed an age, he returned.

'Sir Henry will see you now, sir,' he said. 'Would you come this way?' and led him up the wide staircase, ushering him into a handsome furnished room on the first floor. A middle-aged man rose from behind a massive desk and came to greet him with outstretched hand.

'Daniel Hunter, I understand. I am Henry Russell. James told me that you would be coming in the place of his brother-in-law, Lord Warrinder. I am afraid that you must have had a long and very exhausting journey. Do please take a seat. Tea will be along in a second.' He went back behind his desk, leaving Daniel even more uneasily aware that something must be very wrong.

He said, 'I was expecting to see James here. I came at once to apologize for the delay. We had one or two lengthy hold-ups which I rather think are not infrequent.'

'Very true. The line from Poland has only recently come into operation.' Henry Russell looked up and seemed to brace himself for the inevitable. 'I am afraid, Mr Hunter,' he said heavily, 'that I have some very tragic news for you.'

His first thought was that something appalling must have happened to Christine or to the children. 'Tragic?' he repeated. 'In what way?'

'It grieves me to have to tell you that a bomb was thrown at the carriage in which James and his fiancée were driving through the city early this morning. James was killed outright, Madame Dufour died an hour later in the hospital.'

'Oh my God!' For a moment relief and horror combined to render him speechless. Then he said, 'But why, why? For what reason?'

Russell dropped into the chair behind his desk. 'That is of course what we all asked ourselves and it is only now, some hours later, that, with the help of the police, we can make a guess at what must have happened. The bomb was thrown by a student from one of the revolutionary groups at the university who have been giving trouble from time to time.'

'But this is appalling. Has the assassin been arrested?'

'Not yet. There was considerable confusion, as you can imagine. The driver of the carriage also died and several other people were seriously injured. Before the police arrived on the scene, he had made his escape.'

'But it's outrageous that innocent people should be murdered in this way!'

'I can't agree more, and you may be sure that the ambassador will be demanding a full inquiry into the matter, but in the mean time we do have certain information which leads us to believe that the bomb was not intended for James and his . . . his bride-to-be, but was a disastrous accident.'

'How do you mean?'

But at that moment there was a knock at the door and a young man came in with a tray. 'Ah, tea!' exclaimed Russell with obvious relief. 'Put it on the small table, William. I will deal with it.'

'Very good, sir.' The young man went out and Sir Henry moved to the table.

'Let me pour it for you. No doubt it will be very welcome.' He took the cup to Daniel and went back to pour one for himself. 'It would seem,' he went on carefully, 'that the Okhrana, that is the secret police, have been keeping an eye on some of these terrorists, and they rounded one of them up. They have their own methods of extracting information and it appears that the bomb was intended for General Trepov, the St Petersburg police chief, a man who has the regrettable reputation of being a sadistic bully in his treatment of prisoners and is in consequence heartily detested. Apparently, in order to deceive his enemies he is in the habit of travelling in an unmarked carriage, with a lady companion at times and takes very good care to change his routes at the last moment in order to confuse any would-be assassin. The plan must have been worked out by the conspirators, but gone wrong at the last moment, and it is easy enough to imagine the assassin clutching his dangerous home-made bomb, receiving the signal from his colleague and throwing it without looking too closely.'

'And you believe that is what happened?'

'It seems to me very possible, not that it makes the result any less appalling.'

In the course of his work Daniel had seen violence in many

parts of the world, but this had the quality of a nightmare, of an almost childish stupidity and negligence, and yet it had destroyed the whole future of the two people whose marriage he was there to attend. Then he remembered something else.

'There is a daughter, isn't there? What about her? Was she not with them?'

'No, fortunately. It would appear that Louise and her mother had come up to stay in town for a week making final preparations, seeing dressmakers and so on, and that morning James and Madame Dufour had to settle some details at the English church. They were all three staying at the Europa and I must confess I shirked telling the child the ghastly news – Louise is barely eighteen – and I sent my wife in my place. Lady Russell knows both mother and daughter well. She is with her now.'

'I booked in at the Europa,' said Daniel slowly, 'but I hesitate to intrude upon her now. She must be devastated at this terrible blow.'

'Wait till tomorrow, my dear fellow. I'll be along there this evening to fetch my wife. She will be able to tell us how Louise is taking it.' He shook his head sadly. 'I don't know what the future holds for that poor girl. As you already know, we were to have settled James's new will with the lawyers this week. We are old friends and he had asked me to be one of his executors along with your good self, but now ... I don't like to think what the outcome is likely to be.'

There was little more that could be done that evening so Daniel returned to the hotel, considerably disturbed by the shocking news and a little uncertain as to what he should immediately do for the best. The embassy would almost certainly look after its own. They would inform Clara of her father's death and no doubt arrange a suitable funeral, but the younger daughter was another matter. Daniel had sensed Sir Henry's distance even though he had been sympathetic. She was James Ducane's love child and, now, no one's responsibility. If only the tragedy had come after the marriage. He had no idea of the contents of the new will or whether any provision had been made for her future. Eighteen was a tender age at which to face alone a friendless, possibly hostile, world. While he bathed, changed his clothes and sat down without much appetite to the dinner provided, he wondered about his own position in the circumstances and what was likely to be expected from him.

Afterwards he was joined by Sir Henry and his wife. Lady Russell proved to be the type of woman he found particularly trying, good-hearted enough but obviously out of her depth, tearful, agitated and disconcerted because instead of a distressed, weeping child she had found a young woman of apparently strong and resolute character.

'I can't understand her,' she complained over and over again. 'She seems so hard, so unfeeling, and she is quite determined to stay on at the hotel, though I offered her our support and said she could come to us at least until the funeral is over.'

Daniel guessed rather cynically that she was mortally offended at the rejection of her generous suggestion when most of the embassy wives would have expressed their sympathy but taken good care to draw back from any further contact.

'I think I can understand that,' he said. 'I would feel like that myself' – the animal desire to hide, to face death and grief alone till it had become part of you and you could endure the well-meant kindness and ill-judged comments of others. His sympathy grew for this unknown girl.

Lady Russell eyed him with distrust and he knew what she was thinking: *Not quite the gentleman, not one of us*, but he was there in the place of Lord Warrinder, and so he must be accepted. In the first years of his marriage he had met this prejudice constantly and it had worried him at one time, on Christine's account, but not any longer. He knew his own worth and could rise above it.

'I would rather not ask to see her tonight,' he went on, 'but perhaps before you leave, Lady Russell, you would be good enough to tell her that I am here, staying in the same hotel, and very willing to undertake anything she should require of me.'

In one way, he thought, the Russells were grateful to shift the responsibility on to other shoulders. They parted, with Sir Henry promising to keep him informed of any developments. He spent a restless night and occupied part of it in writing to his wife. He wished that Christine was with him now. Her calm good sense would have known just how to deal with a young girl no doubt inwardly distraught with grief.

He was breakfasting when one of the waiters approached him with a folded note. 'Mademoiselle Dufour would be grateful if you could spare her a few minutes of your time this morning,' he read, and was touched by the attempt at formality.

'Tell her I will be with her in an hour,' he said to the waiter, and, when eventually he went up the stairs and knocked at the door indicated, he hoped to God she spoke reasonable English otherwise he would be at a considerable disadvantage.

He was not sure what he had expected when he went in but it was not this. For one thing he was struck by the girl's beauty, just as David had been in the moonlit garden a few weeks before. Louise was standing by the window, outwardly calm, inwardly trembling, her hands tightly clasped in front of her to stop their shaking. The simple black dress, long-sleeved, high to the throat, made her look very slim and emphasized the creamy pallor of her face. A ray of sun caught the dark gold of her hair, brushed severely back and tied with a black ribbon. She looked so young, so lonely, so utterly defenceless, that his heart went out to her. This surely was a child so hurt, so numbed with grief, that she dared not lose control, dared not give way to the easy relief of tears lest it sweep her away.

And what did Louise see in that fraught moment? A tall, lean man, informally dressed, quite unlike the stiff embassy types whose disapproval showed beneath their courtesy. She sensed his kindness and warmth.

A small white dog at her feet gave a throaty growl at the stranger. She quietened him with a whisper and impulsively held out both her hands.

'You must be Daniel Hunter.'

He took the small cold fingers in his own firm grasp. 'I wish I could tell you how it grieves me that we should have to meet at a time like this.'

He felt her tremble and then deliberately relax a little into the formal hostess. 'Will you sit down, Mr Hunter? I have ordered some coffee; it should be here in a moment, or would you prefer something stronger?'

He smiled, and it lit the ruggedly handsome face to an unexpected charm. 'Good heavens, no. Not at this hour in the morning.'

She let herself drop into the chair on the other side of the small table. 'Harry Warrinder told us a great deal about you.'

That surprised him. '*Harry* did? What on earth was he doing in St Petersburg?'

'He was on his travels with his nephew. Is the young man your son?'

'David is my stepson,' he said shortly. 'I understood they were making their way to Italy.'

'Oh, they were going on there afterwards. They could only spare us two days. Papa invited them to our garden party. It was only two weeks ago and now it seems to have happened in some other life . . .' Her voice trembled into silence.

He could think of no adequate answer and into that moment came the hotel waiter with the tray. He placed it on the small table, asked something in Russian and, when she shook her head, went out closing the door.

She took up the silver coffeepot. 'How do you like it?'

'A little milk and no sugar.'

She poured the coffee and pushed the cup towards him. Her eyes with their dark lashes, enormous in her pale face, were fixed on him. 'Harry Warrinder told us that you were utterly reliable and that anything you undertook you would carry through, whatever the difficulties.'

What on earth could Harry have been thinking of? Daniel stirred uneasily. 'I do my best.'

'It is very important, you see, because I do need a friend so very desperately.'

'My dear child, you must be surrounded by friends, all those who were close to your father.'

'No,' she shook her head. 'You're wrong. You don't understand. The British tolerated me because of Papa, but now he has gone, I have become an embarrassment. They can't wait to be rid of me as quickly as possible.'

'Are you being quite fair?' he said gently. 'Maybe it only seems so in the shock of what has happened. Hasn't Lady Russell been kind to you? Hasn't she done her best to help?'

'Oh yes, she was very good, she spent the day with me, but she made me feel that I should go down on my knees in gratitude because she had come, because she offered to let me stay with her and Sir Henry until the funeral is over.'

'Surely you are mistaken.'

'Oh no I'm not. It was quite obvious. She doesn't want me at all. She only thinks it is her duty, like giving money to a beggar or feeding a starving dog. She has daughters, you see. I might corrupt them.'

He was disturbed at her bitterness. She was learning too much far too quickly. He said, 'If there is anything I can do for you, you have only to ask.'

'There is one thing. I asked Lady Russell but she said it was impossible. I would like to go to the hospital. I want to see them.'

'There could be a reason for that,' he said gently.

'You mean that the bomb could have disfigured them. But you see, I love them, they meant everything to me. We were so happy yesterday morning . . . when they came and told me, I couldn't believe it, our whole life gone in a few seconds. I cannot bear the thought that I shall never see them again, never kiss them farewell. Would you help me? Would you find out if it is possible?'

'I will if you wish but I strongly advise against it.'

'Why should you say that?'

'Louise,' he said earnestly, 'I may call you that, mayn't I? I take it you are meeting death for the first time, and in a particularly tragic shape. Maybe you don't realize that when the spirit goes it leaves behind only an empty shell. Believe me I know what I'm saying. Don't let those haunting memories be the last you have of them. Remember them as you saw them yesterday morning, loving, warm, close to you. Don't ask me to do this for you, not because it may be difficult to arrange but for your own sake, and for theirs and for your future memories of them.'

'You really mean that, don't you?' she said, looking at him curiously.

'Yes, I do. It has happened to me and is full of a pain that I would spare you. It is not as if you sat by their bed in sickness. Violence such as this leaves its mark. Don't go, I beg of you.'

'Perhaps. I didn't think of it like that. But there is one other thing. Lady Russell told me that the embassy would arrange for my father to be taken to England to be buried with the rest of his family, but not my mother – oh no, she is of no account, she was only his mistress, but she loved him so much, she gave her whole life to him. They were so happy, and now, to be thousands of miles apart in death, it is cruel, unfeeling . . . Can you make them understand that? I know they will not listen to me.'

This could be more difficult. He thought he knew how Clara would react, a fierce refusal to acknowledge this other life of her father with the woman and child he had cherished for twenty years.

'It will depend on Lady Dorrien,' he said at last.

'My half-sister.' There was a note of resentment in her voice. 'Why should she want his body now he is gone? She never cared for him, never came to visit him, never laughed with him when he was happy and nursed him when he was sick like my mother did.'

'Maybe he never gave her the opportunity.'

'I don't believe that. Whenever he returned from a visit to England he was unhappy, not like himself.'

This was a situation about which Everard Warrinder would have known far more than he did, but he was on the spot and must deal with it as best he could. He said, 'I will speak to Sir

Henry. Perhaps some more suitable arrangement can be made.'

'I would be very grateful.'

He smiled at her. 'Well, now that we're over the first hurdle, and since we are going to see quite a lot of one another in the next few days, suppose you pour me another cup of coffee and tell me something about yourself.'

Her taut control relaxed a little. 'Do you really mean that?'

'Indeed I do. Tell me about your little dog. What is his name? Where did he come from? I have a young daughter who has a small spaniel which she calls Rowley and which sometimes plagues the life out of me.'

'Toby is not like that. He was a stray that I rescued from drowning. Now he is my friend.'

She responded to his easy, friendly manner, losing a little of her shyness so that by the time he left her half an hour later he knew a little more about her and could make a shrewd guess at much of the rest. During the next few days, in between necessary consultations at the embassy, he even persuaded her to walk with him.

'You mustn't shut yourself up away from everyone. It will make you ill,' he said to her. 'I am a stranger here. Show me a little of the city, the places you love most.'

At first she shook her head, but he could be very persuasive and so one afternoon she took him to St Isaac's Cathedral, with its enormous dome higher than St Paul's, with its magnificent paintings and walls of gold, marble, malachite and porphyry and told him of the magical moment at the Easter Mass when the cathedral was plunged from darkness into light with everyone holding candles and embracing one another as the great cry went up: 'Christ is risen!' Another time they walked in the Summer Gardens among the children and dogs. Walking beside the Neva she pointed out the slender spire of St Peter and St Paul on the opposite bank, and the dark fortress, the most dreaded prison in Russia.

'When the river floods, some of the underground cells are three feet deep water and there are rats bigger than cats.'

'In the Middle Ages, perhaps,' he said smiling.

'No, now. The Empress Catherine once imprisoned one of her ladies-in-waiting for daring to smile at her latest lover, and the poor creature was driven insane.'

He even coaxed her to smile once or twice, forgetting the numbing grief, if only for a few minutes, but all the time he was aware that she was perilously on edge, taut as a violin string which at any moment could snap, and he dreaded the inevitable breakdown.

The question of the funeral more or less settled itself. No reply had been received to the message telegraphed to Clara and he was able to inform the embassy that he knew her to be cruising in the Mediterranean with friends, so that the news of her father's death would in all probability not have reached her yet. In the circumstances therefore James Ducane was buried beside his mistress until such time as his daughter's wishes could be known.

The embassy attended the funeral in strength, together with certain members of the government and a large contingent of the artistic and musical world. Daniel, as the sole representative of James Ducane's family, stood beside Louise, submerged beneath her heavy black veil. Later, at the moment when the coffins were lowered into the ground, he saw her waver, and took firm hold of the small hand in its black glove.

The St Petersburg press, as eager as their British counterparts for a spicy story, were there in force, and Daniel did his best to ignore them, putting a protective arm around Louise. Walking towards the waiting carriage he caught a glimpse of a face he knew, a roving photographer from the *Daily News* who had mounted his camera on the flat surface of a tomb and gave Daniel a knowing grin. He would willingly have smashed the plate the wretched man had triumphantly slipped into his camera, except that the furore it would have caused might be worse than the effect of the photograph itself.

Back in the hotel, he was worried about Louise. She seemed to have grown thinner in the last few days, probably eating nothing of course, and there was still an ordeal to be faced.

The embassy were anxious to be rid of the whole wretched affair as soon as possible, and a meeting had been arranged for that very afternoon when all the details of the unsigned will would be thrashed out. He knew something of its contents already, and dreaded the effect on the friendless young girl.

Louise took off her hat with its shrouding veil and pushed back the waves of dark-gold hair with a sigh of relief.

'Are you sure you feel up to this meeting this afternoon?' Daniel asked. 'I can easily arrange for it to be postponed till later in the week.'

'No,' she said quickly. 'No, let us get it over with. I must know the worst before I can begin to live again.'

'Very well, if you are sure. I will order luncheon to be sent up to you and then come back to fetch you at three o'clock.'

'Don't go yet. I want to show you something.' Her only ornament was a locket on a thin gold chain. She unfastened it and took it off. 'You knew my father but you never met my mother, did you? Papa gave me this. Now it is all I have of them.'

She opened the locket and held it out to him. On one side was a portrait of James Ducane and on the other that of Marianne Dufour. The artist must have been highly skilled. The execution, though so small, was very fine, the face had a charm that was as much of expression as of flawless features.

'It is exquisite,' he said.

'It doesn't flatter. She was if anything lovelier than that.'

'It is easy to see that you are her daughter.'

'I'm not beautiful like she was.'

Perhaps not feature by feature, but the fine bones were there, with a rare quality of strength and dignity that seemed to have grown in the few days he had known her.

'Thank you for showing it to me,' he said. 'Now you must rest. And do make sure you eat a little before I come to fetch you.'

'I will try,' she said. 'Why are you so kind to me?'

He could not explain even to himself why her plight moved him so deeply, so he fell back on the easy explanation. 'My daughter Isabelle is about your age, and I know how she would have felt.'

He went downstairs to eat a light luncheon with a strong certainty that the afternoon with the lawyer was likely to be uncomfortable for everyone.

They met in Henry Russell's spacious office with its antique furniture. There were one or two fine pictures on the walls – Daniel thought he recognized a Canaletto – and he wondered if they represented Russell's expensive tastes or were simply part of the furniture of the room. Russell himself sat behind his desk with the lawyer. Nugent Webbe was a small man with the pointed features of an intelligent ferret. He was an Englishman who had made his home in St Petersburg for some thirty years, dealt with any legal quibbles that arose in the embassy and was kept busy looking after the affairs of British residents who preferred to deal with a compatriot.

Both gentlemen rose with a murmur of sympathy as Daniel came in with Louise. Russell indicated the place beside him at the desk but she shook her head, taking instead a chair that stood close to the window, open against the stuffy warmth of the July afternoon.

'I can listen just as well from here,' she said as she threw back the black veil, sitting very upright, very composed, with her hands tightly clasped in her lap.

'As you wish,' said Sir Henry, a little put out. 'Shall we begin, gentlemen? Mr Webbe, would you be good enough to explain the situation?'

The lawyer opened the portfolio in front of him, adjusted his glasses and cleared his throat.

'Some weeks ago,' he began in his colourless voice, 'Mr Ducane consulted me about making a new will. He told me that since his daughter Clara, Lady Dorrien, was already provided for in her own right, having married into wealth, he had decided to leave her only a small house he owned in London with all its contents. I understand an elderly family dependant lives there. All the rest of his estate, which is considerable, except for a few minor bequests would go to his . . .' he paused for a moment, then went on smoothly, 'to Madame Dufour, his companion for many years and whom, as you know, he was to have married in less than a week's time. I urged him very strongly indeed to have the will witnessed and signed immediately, but he felt that he should wait till Everard Warrinder, the brother of his late wife, could be consulted. Since Lord Warrinder felt unable to make the journey, and you, Mr Hunter, would be taking his place, it was decided the whole matter should be completed immediately on your arrival. However, as you know, Mr Ducane and his fiancée died tragically a few days ago, leaving the will incomplete, and I am afraid therefore legally null and void.'

Oh God, thought Daniel to himself, *if only I had not delayed so long in London, if it had not been for those damnable hold-ups on the train, I would have been here, the will would have been completed and Louise's inheritance secured, while now . . .* He glanced at her. She was sitting absolutely still, looking out of the window as if her whole future did not hang trembling in the balance; only the lift of her head, the slight stiffening of her straight back, gave any indication that she had even heard the lawyer's dry, unemotional voice.

'Now,' went on Mr Webbe, 'we come to the existing will, which was drawn up in Paris some twenty years ago.' He looked up, his eyes kindling behind his spectacles. 'I cannot tell you, gentlemen, how often I urge a client to reconsider his will at least every five years, but alas, few of them listen to me. They let it run on, and the amount of litigation, regret, hard feelings, bitterness and even heartbreak that can be caused by this neglect beggars belief.' Mr Webbe took off his glasses, rubbed them vigorously with his handkerchief, then replaced them and continued in his usual dry voice. 'Mr Ducane, I regret to say, was no exception. He went on cheerfully in the belief that he would live for ever with the result that his daughter, Lady Dorrien, whom it would seem he scarcely ever saw, inherits everything while Louise Dufour, whom he apparently greatly cherished, is left completely penniless.'

There was a momentary silence while all eyes turned to Louise.

'Surely, Mr Webbe,' said Sir Henry at last, 'when you forward these documents to Lady Dorrien, which of course will be done in due course, she will respect her late father's wishes and make provision for her ... for this unfortunate young girl.'

'That remains to be seen,' said the lawyer dourly. 'If you dealt with as many people as I do at these distressing times, you would know that reactions can be very different, and most heirs under a will are extremely reluctant to give away so much as a penny. What is your opinion, Mr Hunter? You must know Lady Dorrien well, since she is your wife's first cousin.'

Daniel could see Clara tearing up any documents in a fit of jealous rage and tossing them into the fire, but he only said cautiously, 'I think she will be very distressed by her father's death and I would not like to make any guess as to what her feelings will be in these unusual circumstances.'

'I see,' said Henry Russell. 'What then, I wonder, can be done for the best?'

'May I say something, gentlemen?' Quite suddenly Louise was on her feet, startling them all. 'When you have quite done discussing my future as if I were a tiresome and unwanted parcel,' she went on in a blaze of anger, 'perhaps you will allow me to tell you that I have no intention of living on my half-sister's charity. Perhaps, Mr Webbe, you would be good enough to let me know exactly what is still mine – my clothes, perhaps, and those of my mother, our few personal possessions, or am I to be stripped of those too? Am I to be left naked as well as penniless?'

'My dear Louise, you must not think that we would allow any such thing,' exclaimed Sir Henry in a fine burst of indignation, and was immediately interrupted by Mr Webbe.

'Allow me, Sir Henry, to explain more fully. Mr Ducane was in the habit, I understand, of placing a considerable sum every quarter in your mother's bank account, for household expenses and so on. This quarter's allowance is still there and, although the account has been automatically frozen at her death, I could possibly give you the equivalent out of the estate.'

'Thank you,' she said drily. 'How very kind of you. I shall at least be able to pay my hotel bill.'

'You must not concern yourself about that,' said Russell, taken aback by her sudden show of spirit. 'We shall be happy to settle any such expenses on your behalf.'

'I am grateful, Sir Henry, but I am afraid I must learn to be independent now, mustn't I? I would like to take the opportunity of thanking you and Mr Webbe for making my position so very clear to me. There's really no more to be said, is there? Mr Hunter, would you be good enough to call a cab for me?'

'At once,' he said. 'I will take you back to the hotel myself. Perhaps, Sir Henry, you would let me know if you require me for anything else?'

He went ahead of Louise, and by the time she came down the stairs the man on the door had already secured a passing cab. Daniel handed her in and as he took the seat beside her she lay back against the cushions with a long sigh of relief. 'Thank goodness that's over. I suppose you more or less knew about it already?'

'Some of it. I'm very sorry, Louise. I feel guilty. If only I had arrived a couple of days earlier, this would never have happened.'

'That's like saying everything would be wonderful if pigs had wings. I had a governess who used to be fond of that silly expression. At least I know what Papa intended for Mamma and me, even if it has all gone wrong.' She pulled herself upright. 'I'm not giving in. I'm young, I'm strong, I shall have to learn to earn my own living, shan't I? Fight my own battles. Mamma did when she was my age.'

'Till she met your father.'

'Yes, she was fortunate. Perhaps I will meet someone, a fairy prince perhaps, a knight in shining armour . . .' Her voice choked and she turned away her face.

'Don't be disheartened, Louise. Be brave. We'll work something out.'

She was looking at him through a mist of tears. 'What would I have done without you?'

'Managed very well, I expect.'

At the hotel he helped her from the carriage and went with her to her room. 'Now,' he said as she took off her hat, 'I have a suggestion to make. I'm going to order a tray of tea to be sent up. You will rest for an hour. Then I'll take you out to eat where it is cheerful and lively and for a little while you can forget your grief and your worries about the future and simply relax and enjoy yourself. What do you say? Will you come?'

She was looking up at him, her eyes shining, then slowly she shook her head. 'I wish I could,' she said wistfully. 'It would be wonderful to escape, even for an hour, but I can't, I mustn't. Lady Russell has already told me that I should not have taken walks alone with you. If I were to accompany you to a public restaurant, everyone would be outraged.' Daniel made an impatient gesture but she went on. 'They would, you know, and it would be you they would blame, not me.'

'Let them,' he said sturdily. 'I've never cared very much about what people say of me.'

'But I would care for you, and I would not be much of a companion. But you must go. You mustn't worry so much about me. Why don't you visit one of the gypsy restaurants? Papa took me once with Mamma and some of her friends from the opera to the Samarkand, on Apothecary's Island. It was wonderful. You must see it, and then you could write one of your stories about it.'

He smiled. 'It doesn't always work out like that. Are you sure about this, Louise? Why not defy convention and come with me?'

'No,' she said, 'it wouldn't be right. It's too soon. I should feel guilty somehow.' She smiled faintly. 'And I dread to think what Lady Russell would say about me and about you. But you must go, and tell me about it tomorrow.'

He gave in reluctantly. Maybe she was right. Convention

demanded heavy mourning, gloom, hushed voices, no break in the outward show of grief no matter how lonely and rebellious the spirit.

He said good-night and went downstairs to eat dinner at the hotel and then, feeling restless and remembering Joe Sharpe, decided to take Louise's advice and look for some local colour on Apothecary's Island. He took a boat across the Neva and landed at the Samarkand. It was a great smoky cavern of a place opening on to a splendid garden. Lanterns hung from the raftered ceiling and the trees while candles flickered on the many tables, glinting on the scarlet and gold of uniforms, on gowns of silk and satin, on jewelled necklaces and diamond bracelets. This was where the young and the rich indulged themselves. He sat at a table a little withdrawn from the rest, ordered wine (not yet having developed a taste for vodka), and was fascinated by the kaleidoscope of colour, by the throbbing vibrant life around him.

The gypsy orchestra were playing their balalaikas with a rhythm that stirred the blood and presently the dancers came threading their way through the tables in their whirling, many-coloured skirts, the flash of gold coins knotted into the shining black hair, weaving in and out of the customers, snatching a glass from some young man, drinking it off and holding it out for more, evading clutching fingers, sensuous, enticing, elusive.

He wished Christine had been with him. At heart she was still the unconventional girl who had stepped out of her gilded life to love a penniless schoolteacher, and she would have enjoyed it all, the brilliance, the music, the feeling of release and freedom. She would have laughed at his puritanical rejection of the girl who leaned over his shoulder, took the glass out of his hand, sipped the wine and then held it to his lips with invitation in the curving red mouth, the low-cut dress revealing a swell of honey-coloured flesh. He shook his head and the girl shrugged shapely shoulders and said something in Russian that was probably uncomplimentary. He had grown up in the strictest Methodist tradition and, though he had long moved away from its beliefs, it lived still inside him, bred in the bone and not easily tossed aside.

It was very late when he returned to the Europa. He sat for a while writing up his impressions of the evening that could prove the basis for a colourful short article; and then, when the candle was blown out at last, he lay wakeful, trying to find an answer to the problem of Louise. There seemed to be only two alternatives: to turn his back on her and leave her to find her own destiny, or to take her with him to England, into the shelter of his own home and the problematical meeting with her half-sister. He was not a man to abandon even a lost kitten, let alone a young woman of extraordinary beauty who was a relative, if only a very distant one. He sighed. Sooner rather than later the question must be decided. He could not afford to abandon his work for too long a stay in Russia.

Chapter 4

Louise too lay awake that night. It would have been a relief to go with Daniel, to forget for a few hours, to recapture if only fleetingly the joy and happiness of that last morning when she had thoughtlessly kissed her parents goodbye and lost them for ever.

The numbed grief had begun to recede a little. The afternoon at the embassy had forced her to face the stark reality: she was utterly alone. There was no one to whom she could turn for help. She had no status, no place in society, not even a name which she could properly call her own. She had been loved and cherished with a future full of promise, and in the few seconds it took for a bomb to explode all that had been swept away, the only resource grudgingly suggested being an appeal to a half-sister she did not know, something from which she shrank with every fibre of her being. It was a bleak prospect and she shivered despite the stuffy summer heat, the walls of the hotel bedroom seeming to press in on her till she could scarcely breathe. It was then that she made up her mind. She would escape, go back to the villa. There perhaps, amidst all that was familiar and beloved, she could come to terms with what had happened, discover her own identity in this new and frightening world.

The pony carriage that had brought them to the city was still housed in the hotel stables. She would settle the bill, have the pony harnessed and drive it herself. The thought of freedom, away from all the false sympathy, the barely concealed impatience, Lady Russell's unbearable condescension, gave her new purpose and strength. She was up and dressed very early and had packed her valise before the maid brought her a tray of tea. They had not brought a great deal with them, expecting only a short stay, and the luggage belonging to her father and mother could be left at the hotel for the time being.

It was not till she was drinking her tea that she thought of Daniel. He had been so kind to her, had tried to give her strength and comfort, she liked and trusted him – it would be churlish to go and leave him no word. She wrote a brief note: 'I cannot stay here any longer. I need time alone to think. I am going home.' She gave it to the hotel porter when she went downstairs. The stableman had brought the carriage to the door. He helped her up and handed her the reins. The air was fresh and cool, the sun only just beginning to break through the clouds. Louise felt the oppression lift a little as she took the familiar road out of the city.

It was a busy morning at the Europa, with guests leaving and new ones arriving, so it was near midday before the note was delivered to Daniel. He was immediately anxious and a trifle annoyed. So she had bolted, had she? And where the devil was home? Of one thing he was certain: in her present state of mind he could not leave her to spend days there alone. Who knows what she might do in a fit of despair?

Fortunately James Ducane had been a frequent visitor to the Europa and the hotel manager was willing to give Daniel information.

'Mademoiselle left soon after seven o'clock,' he told him. 'The villa is an hour's run out of the city on the road to Pavlovsk. One of the cabs will take you there, monsieur – at a price of course.'

'Good. Perhaps the porter will call me one.' While he waited he wrote a brief note to Russell and when the man came back with the cab told him to deliver it to the embassy as soon as possible. Then he was in the carriage and urging the driver to make haste. He was not sure what he was going to do when he arrived; it would depend on Louise. He could scarcely spend the night alone with her there. That would set the scandalmongers' tongues wagging with a vengeance!

*

When Louise reached the villa, everything was so quiet and peaceful, it was difficult to believe that the happy life she had spent there lay in ruins. She unlocked the tall gate and drove into the small courtyard. She unharnessed the pony and led him into the stall, leaving the carriage in the yard, as she had done often before when she and her mother had taken short country drives. The boy who looked after the stables for them would be coming up later and would see to the carriage.

Everything in the house was in order. Katya had been sent to stay with her sister in the village while they were away but she came up each evening bringing food for the icebox in the cellar and making sure everything was ready for them in case they returned unexpectedly. Louise realized that it was possible the terrible news had not yet reached her.

In the kitchen there was a used cup with a knife and plate on the table; this surprised her, as Katya was almost obsessively neat and tidy. She put them in the sink and went into the drawing-room, pushing open the long windows into the garden. Toby, delighted to be free of the close confinement of the hotel bedroom, careered joyously down the path, barking shrilly. Everywhere she walked was full of memories, painful and yet in a curious way healing. There was the climbing rose that she and her mother had trained over the wooden arch. A shower of golden petals fell into her hand as she looked up at it and she smelled the honeyed sweetness as she crushed them. There was a row of plants they had planned to put in that autumn and a bed which had been dug ready for a new shrub.

Back in the house she found herself wandering everywhere reliving more memories, stirred by the piano where she and her mother had sometimes played together; the faint fragrance of Marianne's perfume in the bedroom; her father's leather country coat on the chair where he had dropped it, the scent of his favourite cigars as she picked it up and buried her face in the silk lining. Was it a mistake to have come? She didn't know; she only know that she could not stop herself touching the familiar objects, remembering, as if she must somehow store them away against the bleak future.

At midday she went out to the stables with the intention of feeding the horse. She was just about to climb up the ladder to where the sacks were stored when someone seized her waist and swung her round. A hoarse voice said, 'What have you come back for? You should still be in Petersburg,' and she was staring up at Leo, but a Leo who looked quite unlike his usually neat self. His hair was wild, he hadn't shaved for days and his clothes looked as if he had slept in them.

'Why shouldn't I come back?' she said, frowning. 'What are you doing in the stable, Leo? Have you been sleeping here?'

'Did you come alone?' he whispered with a quick, furtive look around him.

'Yes, of course I did. What is all this? Oh for heaven's sake, come out of here. I can't see you properly in this half-light.' He followed her reluctantly into the sunshine of the courtyard and she turned on him, patience beginning to wear very thin. 'Is this one of those stupid games of yours? Was it you who left a used cup and plate in the kitchen? How did you get in?'

'A window was unlocked and I had to eat something, didn't I?' he muttered sullenly. 'I couldn't starve. I only took some of the bread and a little cheese.'

'Starve? What on earth are you talking about? Why are you hiding here? Have you quarrelled with your family again?'

He mumbled something and quite suddenly she knew. The realization shocked her so much that for a moment she could not speak.

'Oh God, it can't be true,' she whispered at last. 'Were you one of the group who plotted to throw that bomb?'

'I did more than that.' Dirty, dishevelled, hay and straw still in his hair and sticking to his clothes, he drew himself up with an odd dignity. 'I said I'd do it and I did. I told you I would show Father and Michael and the others that I had more courage than any of them. They made fun of me, told me I hadn't the nerve, but I proved them wrong, didn't I? And it wasn't easy standing there holding that bomb, but I held on and I waited till Petrov gave me the signal and then I threw it.' His voice rose on a note of pure exaltation. 'And I knew I had succeeded. It was I who killed General Trepov and his latest whore and I'm proud of it.'

For a moment she could only stare at him. A huge lump seemed to rise up in her, tightening her throat. It was so impossible, so hideously unbelievable that it should have been Leo, ineffective, bungling Leo who could never do anything right and now stood there boasting of it, believing he had rid Russia of a monster and instead . . . surely he must have known, he must have realized . . . She swallowed down the icy lump in her throat. 'You did not kill General Trepov,' she whispered.

'But I saw it, I tell you. I saw the explosion. It was magnificent. We got it right at last and it worked.'

'Oh yes, it worked all right,' she said in a dull voice. 'It worked very well indeed, only the victims were wrong. General Trepov was too clever for you. His carriage had taken a different route.'

'That can't be true. Petrov was watching. He gave me the signal.'

'Perhaps he did, but he was mistaken. It was James Ducane, it was my father and my mother who died. All that fiery talk of revolution, all those high ideals of yours achieved was the murder of two innocent people on their way to church to arrange their marriage, and I hope you and all the others burn in hell for it!'

He was staring at her, all the pride, all the feeling of justification, slowly draining out of him. 'I don't believe you. I saw it, I tell you, I saw it before I ran.'

'You saw two people blown to pieces, but you never attempted to find out who those people were.'

'Oh God, I didn't know. I've not seen anyone. I've not talked to anyone, I daren't. I've been in hiding here ever since.' He was shaking, sweat beginning to run down his face. 'What are you going to do?' he whispered.

She shook her head helplessly. 'I don't know. I can't think.'

A sudden loud knocking at the door of the villa jerked him into life. 'Who is that?'

'I don't know.'

'You must know. You wouldn't have come down here alone.' He grabbed her by the arm. 'You lied to me. You've known all along, haven't you, and now you've set the police on me!'

'How could I,' she said wearily, 'when I had no idea that you were hiding here?' The knocking went on, growing louder every minute.

'Oh my God, it's the Okhrana! You know what they will do to me, don't you?' He was gripping her by the arm viciously in a frenzy of terror. 'You must have known all the time, but I won't let you betray me, I'll kill you first.' His hands slid up her body and seized her by the throat. He was shaking her in a crazy panic. She struggled with him but his hands pressed closer and closer round her neck, strangling her voice as she tried to cry out.

Then in a sudden spurt of rage and terror he flung her away from him so violently that she stumbled backwards and fell, her head striking the stone steps. She lay stunned. The knocking had risen to a crescendo and Leo took a terrified look around him. Toby, disturbed by the noise, had come running from the garden into the courtyard and leaped up at him. He kicked him aside, then raced through the stable, climbed into the loft, smashed open the dusty window at the back and leaped through it, landing on the other side on his knees, bruised, bleeding and breathless. Then he picked himself up, raced through the garden and out into the park, sheer blind terror giving wings to his feet.

The knocking went on, someone was calling, 'Louise,' and she sat up groggily. Blood from the cut on her forehead was running down her cheek. She tried to wipe it away as she got unsteadily to her feet and groped her way through to the front door of the villa.

Daniel was just about to try and find some other way of breaking into the house when the door opened. With blood all over her face Louise gasped out his name and more or less collapsed into his arms. He picked her up and carried her through the first door he came to, finding himself in the drawing-room. He put her on the sofa and looked around him. There was brandy on a side table with a used glass. He poured a little of the cognac and took it to her.

'Take it slowly,' he said. 'You're all right now. I'm here with you. Don't be afraid.'

She swallowed a mouthful, choked and then tried to sit up. 'I feel so silly,' she gasped. 'I've never fainted before.'

'Don't move,' he said. 'Just lie there for a moment.' He went quickly out of the room, found what looked like a kitchen, soaked his handkerchief in cold water and came back with it. He gently wiped the blood from her face and then laid the soaked pad against her bruised forehead.

'I don't think it's very serious. What happened to you? Did you fall? I thought I heard shouting. Was someone here?'

She shivered. 'He was hiding in the stable.'

'Who was? Someone you knew?'

'It was Leo.' She was staring in front of her, still dazed and distressed. 'He was the one who threw the bomb. He thought that I . . . that you were the police. He was terribly frightened. He must have run away.'

It sounded crazy and yet it was obviously true, and he had to do something about it.

'As soon as you're feeling better, I'll take you back to Petersburg. We must inform the authorities at once. This is the man they are looking for.'

'No.' She clutched at his hand and held on to it. 'No, I don't want to go back, not now, not today.'

'But we must –'

'No!' She was trembling but resolute. 'Let him go. You see, I've known Leo for a long time. He is the son of Count Davitsky, who loans the villa to us. He didn't realize what he had done. He believed he'd struck some grand blow for the cause, and if they hang him for it, as they will, what good will it do? It won't bring them back and I shall feel like a murderer.'

She was still holding on to his hand, pleading with him in an agonized whisper, and he wondered perhaps if there had been a childish love affair with this wretched youngster.

'I don't like it,' he said. 'If the police find out you let him go free like that, they could blame you.'

'They won't know. Why should they? Please, Daniel, please.'

'Very well,' he said reluctantly. 'In any case, by the time we give the information he will have had some hours to make his escape. I'd better make absolutely sure he's not still here, hiding somewhere.'

He got up to go and she pulled him back. 'You won't go away, will you? You won't leave me here alone? Katya will be here soon. She comes every day to look after the house.'

'Don't be afraid. I won't leave you.'

'Thank you.' She let go of his hand and lay back amongst the cushions with a long sigh.

She looked so young and so frail, he touched her cheek gently. 'Lie quietly for a little and I'll take a good look around.'

He made a tour of the house and then went out into the garden. The white gate at the end of the main path had been flung open and told its own story. He came back to the stable. The door had swung shut and when he opened it Toby leaped up at him, whining and barking frantically. He soothed the little dog, took a cautious look around and then climbed up to the loft, saw the smashed window and guessed at the frantic flight. He carried down one of the sacks of oats, filled the pony's manger, checked its water and then went back to the drawing-room. He put the little dog beside Louise on the sofa. Toby scrambled up to lick her face and and her arms went around him, hugging him to her.

'I had forgotten Toby.'

'He was shut in the stable. The fugitive must have slammed the door as he left.'

'Poor Leo. I wonder what will become of him.'

'I wouldn't waste too much sympathy on him if I were you,' he said drily, and stood looking down at her. 'It's long past midday. I think I'd better explore the kitchen and try to find you something to eat. Does your maid bring any food?'

'She will have put it in the icebox in the cellar. I don't know what she will have brought with her. I'd better get up.'

He pushed her gently back. 'You stay here while I have a look.' He picked up the sodden handkerchief and examined her forehead. 'The cut isn't much but there is a very nasty bruise. Best to lie quietly if you don't want a bad headache.'

And so, while Daniel foraged in the kitchen, Louise lay back against the cushions he had piled behind her, still terribly shaken, a fierce anger at Leo's crazy irresponsibility, which had caused such tragedy, fighting with the years of childish friendship and the half-pitying affection she had always felt for him.

She guessed where he might have taken temporary refuge. It was a secret place of their own that they had discovered on one of their long rambles in a distant corner of the vast estate. It had once been a tiny hunting-lodge, a place where the sportsmen could shelter from the rain or heat a hasty meal during a shooting party, now crumbling into ruin and vastly overgrown with creepers and flowering plants, but with part of it still habitable. Louise had found it romantically attractive. She called it Bluebeard's Castle and they had made it their own, taken the dogs there, spread picnics on the dusty floors, acted out dramatic games of capture and rescue up and down crazy staircases, sharing the secret with no one. In the last year or two they had largely grown out of it, but it was still a treasured meeting-place. She wondered if she ought to tell Daniel, but then could not bring herself to betray what she knew. Let the wretched boy take his chance.

Daniel was nothing if not resourceful. He found fresh bread with eggs, cheese, butter, tomatoes and cucumber in the icebox, discovered how the stove worked, whipped up a very creditable omelette with sliced tomatoes and cucumber, then boiled a kettle for tea, serving it *à la russe* in tall glasses with slices of lemon and plenty of sugar, and when it was ready piled it all on a tray and carried it into the drawing-room.

'*Voilà, mademoiselle,*' he said with a flourish, 'luncheon is served.'

She stared at the tray and then at him. 'I never knew a man could do anything so useful. I don't think Papa could have even boiled an egg.'

'I had to look after myself for a great many years. You never forget the old skills.' He placed a chair for her. 'Now you must eat a little, if only to prove my efforts have not been wasted.'

She did her best to pick at the omelette and drank the tea thirstily but he was obliged to eat most of it himself. When they had finished he put everything tidily together in the kitchen and then carried chairs through on to the patio where they could sit in the cool shade and look out on the sun-scorched garden.

There was a good deal that needed to be decided but he put it on one side for the time being. Let her recover from what must have been a very unpleasant shock. It was quiet and peaceful here. Even Toby had given in and was stretched at Louise's feet. In this homely place it was difficult to believe in the trauma of the past week, the violence, the distress, the shattering effect of the will that left her to face her life alone and unprotected.

He thought she was sleeping but she surprised him by suddenly sitting up. 'Do you think I could keep myself by teaching?'

'As a governess, do you mean?'

'Yes, or in a school. I do speak four languages,' she went on, not boasting but simply stating a fact. 'English and French, of course, but German too and Russian, and some Italian. Papa insisted and I enjoyed it. We had always found it so worthwhile to read books together in the language in which they had been written.'

'Most people in England ask little more from their children's teachers than a smattering of French,' he said. The thought of this delicately nurtured girl struggling with some of the spoiled children of his acquaintances appalled him. 'There is translation work,' he went on thoughtfully. 'I have experience of that in the publishing world.' It was of course mostly done by men, but why not by a woman as intelligent and well-educated as this one?

'The only other thing I can do is play the piano,' she went on ruefully. 'It's terrible to feel so useless.'

'Louise,' he said gently, leaning forward and putting a hand on hers for a moment. 'You don't need to worry about things like that, not yet. There is still a great deal to be discussed and settled.'

She sighed. 'I suppose so.'

So the afternoon wore on, the sun disappeared and dark clouds rolled up across the sky, the heat becoming so oppressive that Daniel sweated just sitting still. He was just thinking of making some fresh tea, which with lemon and no milk he had found to his surprise to be very refreshing, when Katya arrived. She came bustling through the garden, plump and middle-aged, bursting into a flood of Russian, taking Louise into her arms with sympathy and concern and, believing Daniel to be some sort of relative, giving him too a kiss on both cheeks with little pats of consolation, much to his embarrassment. Mishka had come with her, adding to the excitement by forgetting his dignity and romping down the garden with his old friend Toby.

Greetings over at last, Katya wiped her streaming eyes and retired to the kitchen while Daniel said helplessly, 'What was all that about?'

'She has only just heard about the bomb, and she was always very attached to Mamma. She is very upset and says she will stay here with me for as long as I want her. So I shall not be alone any longer and you can go back to St Petersburg if you wish.'

'I shall do no such thing,' he said decidedly. 'God knows what might happen to you both here, alone and unprotected. Tomorrow perhaps, or the next day, we can go together. Besides, if I'm not very much mistaken we're going to have the very devil of a storm.'

It was only too true. Ominous streaks of saffron had appeared in the dark sky and the air was filled with that tingle, that tense expectancy that so often presages thunder. Even the dogs felt it and came in from the garden looking for somewhere dark and cool to hide till it was all over.

Katya did wonders with what was left in the icebox and produced a very appetizing evening meal. She brewed coffee for them and then busied herself with putting out fresh sheets and towels in the guest bedroom. Not expecting to make a stay, Daniel had brought nothing with him, and Louise offered him the choice of her father's wardrobe: 'Papa always kept clothes here. There is a clean nightshirt and his dressing-gown too,' but he could not bring himself to wear the clothes of a man whose presence still seemed so alive in this house. When they retired at last he simply stripped off jacket, shoes and socks and lay on the bed in shirt and trousers with no more than a sheet over him in the oppressive heat.

He had taken a book at random from one of the shelves downstairs but found he could not concentrate. The day had been too disturbing. More and more it had become obvious that he had no alternative. As the only relative, even if it was a very tenuous link, he felt responsible for Louise. He could not just turn his back and leave her to fend for herself. On the other hand Christine might not welcome a stranger with so doubtful a future into their close family circle. It was a taxing problem and there was no question of leaving immediately; too much remained to be settled. When they returned to St Petersburg he would cable Lord Warrinder and ask for advice. He had great trust in his father-in-law's judgement. The decision made, he turned out the lamp and resolutely settled himself to sleep.

He was roused from an uneasy doze by the sound of music. Someone was playing the piano, very quietly, but it seemed to pervade the whole house. For a moment, still half asleep, he lay and listened. It must be Louise, of course. What on earth was she doing playing the piano at this hour? A sudden flash of lightning lit up the room followed by a distant roll of thunder. He sat up. Perhaps he had better investigate. He was still worried by her disturbed state of mind.

He had left the door ajar because of the heat. Now he crept through very quietly; he listened for a moment at Katya's door, but there was no sound, so he went on barefoot down the stairs and into the drawing-room.

Louise had lit the candles in the sconces on the piano so that the light played over her, accentuating the pallor of her face, the gleam of dark-gold hair falling loose on her shoulders. The dressing-gown of some filmy white material flowed around her. He had no wide knowledge of music but he guessed that this was Chopin at his most dreamy, his most melancholy, filled with a sweetness that was unbearably poignant. He stood quite still, watching her, unable to stir, enchanted by the picture she made.

He was not sure how long it was, probably no more than a few minutes, but then there came a blinding flash of lightning followed by an ear-splitting crack of thunder that shook the whole house. It seemed to wake Louise out of a dream. Her hands fell on to the piano keys with a discordant crash and she began to weep, huge heart-rending sobs shaking her slender body. She slid from the piano stool to the floor, hugging herself together, weeping desperately. He did not stop to think but fell on his knees beside her, taking her in his arms, not saying anything, simply holding her close against him, realizing that the breaking point he had feared had come at last, and there was nothing he could do or say except try to make her feel that she was not entirely alone. The storm continued to crash around them while very slowly the paroxysm eased. She began to gulp and sniff, still trembling. He put a handkerchief into her hands and after a little she tried to sit up, still in the shelter of his arms.

'Did I wake you? I am sorry,' she whispered shakily.

'I wasn't asleep.'

'I couldn't rest. The whole day down here seemed to crowd in on me, filled with so many memories. They were all around me like ghosts. I couldn't bear it. I thought if I played something, the music we had all three of us loved so much, it would help. It would be like a farewell to Mamma and Papa ...' She choked and drew a deep, shaking breath. 'Does it sound very silly?'

'No, of course it doesn't. Music has a potent magic.'

'Do you feel that too?'

'Sometimes.'

The storm seemed to have partly blown itself out and was being followed by rain. They could hear it bouncing on the stone flags outside and beating against the windows. She shivered in a sudden draught of cool air and he pulled himself together.

'I'm putting you to bed, my girl. You need your sleep. There's a good deal to be got through in the next few days.'

'I know.'

He stood up, lifting her with him. She swayed a little from sheer emotional exhaustion and unceremoniously he picked her up. She felt as light and fragile as a child.

'I can walk,' she protested.

'Don't argue. I'm going to make sure you don't go wandering around the house again.'

He carried her upstairs and into a bedroom, all white and rose-pink in the mellow light of the lamp, obviously designed for a beloved daughter. It might have been better if she had never come back to the villa which reminded her too vividly of what had gone for ever. He put her on the bed and, when he would have straightened up, her arms locked around his neck.

'I've never thanked you, Daniel,' she whispered, 'but you've given me so much courage. Without you I don't think I would have wanted to go on living.' She pulled him down to her and kissed him full on the mouth. For a few seconds his arms tightened around the slender body in the flimsy nightwear, and a stirring of the blood, an almost irresistible physical urge swept through him. For a moment it held him in its grip, then he pulled himself away almost roughly.

'Nonsense, my dear.' He drew the disordered coverlet over her. 'I've done no more than any man would have done. Now try to rest. It's past three. It will be morning soon,' and he went quickly out of the room, disturbed, not trusting himself.

Until this moment he had never felt the slightest physical desire for any woman other than Christine. Even during the two years when they had been driven apart, when it seemed her life must remain with her crippled husband with no hope of them ever coming together again, his attempts to satisfy himself with other women had been a dismal failure; and yet he knew overpoweringly that for a few seconds he had wanted nothing so much as to go on kissing, had known a tremendous urge to make love to Louise.

'Christ!' He sat on the edge of the bed and loathed himself. All this time, all his concern for her, is that what it had been? She was younger than Isabelle, for God's sake! He must put it out of his mind, forget it. He loved Christine, didn't he? For him there had never been any other woman. It was ridiculous. He had allowed himself to be charmed by a beautiful child, it was a purely physical urge, and the sooner he put a distance between them the better. With that thought he lay down and tried to concentrate on the book he had picked up, but with very little success. It must have been six o'clock when he heard Katya stirring and he got up, washed, shaved with James Ducane's razor and prepared to face his responsibilities.

As for Louise, the fierceness of her grief purged for the time being by the emotional outburst of the night, she lay utterly exhausted and thought about Daniel. She had so little experience of men, only the ineffectual Leo; the few young men she had met in her mother's artistic circle, who paid her pretty compliments and stole an occasional kiss; her father's friends, so much older, who patronized her and treated her as a child. She had worshipped her father and in a way Daniel had stepped into his place, but he was younger and had the added charm of unfamiliarity. She had never met anyone remotely like him and wished to know a great deal more, never realizing the danger in their enforced intimacy at such an emotional time, the powerful attraction that drew her to him. She was only aware that the immediate future seemed a great deal less bleak knowing he would be there at her side.

Chapter 5

It was well into August before the legal problems were finally settled and Daniel could begin to make arrangements for leaving Russia. He had cabled Lord Warrinder and received a terse reply: 'Bring the child with you. She must not be left unprovided for.'

When he told Louise the decision, she felt a great leap of gratitude that he would still be with her and she would no longer be entirely alone – until doubts gradually began to creep in and she wondered how he really felt about the responsibility forced on him. There was still a great deal to be done. She must choose what personal possessions she wanted to take with her, books and clothes and those special items that had some particular meaning for her. Daniel stood out firmly against taking Mishka, foreseeing endless difficulties on the long train journey, but gave in to Louise's anguished pleading and agreed with some misgiving that Toby should accompany them. Nugent Webbe proved a model of efficiency, despite his dry unaccommodating manner, promising to undertake the disposal of certain articles of furniture and settling matters with Count Davitsky who, his wife prostrated with grief, was both angry and deeply distressed at the disgrace his irresponsible son had brought upon his family.

Only a couple of days after they returned to St Petersburg Leo had been arrested. He had been tracked down to that secret hunting-lodge, Bluebeard's Castle, where he and Louise had spent so many happy hours. How the police had discovered it she didn't know, only that Leo, filthy, starving, one hand badly infected from the smashing of the stable window, had been brought back to the city and imprisoned in the Peter and Paul prison, that dreaded fortress on the banks of the Neva, to await trial.

Britain, through her ambassador, was demanding the death penalty. They had no particular objection to Russians killing Russians – that was their own affair – but he had murdered an Englishman, a distinguished member of their staff, and must suffer for it. France too was causing trouble: Marinne Dufour had never renounced her nationality. Arguments went back and forth while Count Davitsky, citing his years of faithful service, was pleading with the Tsar for mercy.

Somehow Leo had found the courage to maintain a stony silence, refusing to implicate any of his former comrades even though General Trepov was not squeamish about the methods used to extract confession. In his secret heart the boy nursed an unreasoning and bitter certainty that it was Louise who had deliberately set the police on him after that meeting at the villa. They had been so close, she had been his dear friend, only she had known of Bluebeard's Castle – and she had heartlessly betrayed him.

Shut up in the dank cell where the walls streamed with water in the summer heat, his back bloody and painful from the inhuman flogging his stubborn silence had provoked, it gave him a sort of sour comfort to let anger and a desire for revenge seethe and fester in him.

Louise was greatly distressed. Though it was Leo's hand that had destroyed so much that was dear to her, she still shuddered to think he could hang for it.

'With his father so influential with the Tsar, he is more likely to be exiled,' said Daniel in an effort to comfort her.

'You don't understand. How could you, you're not Russian. To be sent to a labour camp thousands of miles away in Siberia can be worse than death.'

With Britain and France so persistent in their demands, the trial was hurried through and Daniel was proved right. The death sentence was commuted at the last possible moment to fifteen years' hard labour in the mines of Siberia. Sir Henry Russell, who had been keeping them informed of all the developments, told them that Leo would be hurried out of the city with a convoy of prisoners already condemned to exile.

Louise listened in silence but afterwards she said slowly, 'I would like to go to the station and see them leave.'

'No,' said Daniel, appalled at the very idea. 'No, Louise, there's nothing you can do and it will only distress you.'

'I was the only person who knew about that hunting-lodge. He will think that it was I who betrayed him.'

'What does it matter what he thinks?' argued Daniel. 'Listen, Louise, he destroyed the two people you love by an act of criminal folly. He must accept the consequences, however hard.'

'I know,' she said wretchedly. 'I know. But I'd still like to be there. His father, his brother, all his family have abandoned him. He will be so alone.'

'It's against my better judgement,' sighed Daniel, 'but if you must go, I will go with you.'

She gave him a tremulous smile. 'I was hoping you would say that.'

A large cattle-truck had been attached to the train to carry the prisoners to Irkutsk; it would be shunted from time to time, taking weeks to complete the journey. The file of prisoners shuffled forward and with deliberate cruelty Leo had been shackled between two hulking miners who had been convicted of a particularly brutal robbery. He looked helpless, young and frail. He had lost weight in the prison, the coarse convict clothes hung loosely upon him, his head was shaved to a reddish stubble. *A crazy fool he might be*, thought Daniel, stirred in spite of himself, *but by God what a pitiful one.*

The crowd, some of them weeping relatives but a good many who had come merely to stare and jeer, were being held back by police.

The line of convicts came to a temporary halt and Louise leaned forward. 'Leo,' she whispered, 'Leo,' and then added something in Russian which Daniel thought might be 'God go with you.'

Leo raised his head and stared at her across the barrier. The eyes, sunken in the pale face, burned with an uncontrollable fury and bitterness.

'Traitor!' he hissed, 'traitor!' and, leaning forward as far as the chains allowed, he deliberately spat at her.

Then the line moved on and he stumbled as the shackles on his ankles jerked him after the others.

Tears were running down Louise's face as Daniel put his arm around her. 'We've seen enough. We're getting out of this,' he said and forced his way through the crowd.

Back in the hotel room, with Daniel persuading her to take some hot coffee laced with a teaspoonful of brandy, Louise said wretchedly, 'He believes that I deliberately gave away our secret place.'

'Don't let it distress you,' he said firmly. 'It is over and done with. You must put it out of your mind. It's the future that is important now.'

'I know,' she said. 'You must think me very foolish – but Leo was part of my growing-up. I can't get away from that. He was part of the old life at the villa . . .' She choked and then went on quietly, 'Thank you for coming with me. I don't know how I would have survived without you.'

'Part of my job,' he said briefly.

'I'm sorry to be such a burden to you.'

'I've known worse,' he said and smiled. 'Now, if you will forgive me, I must leave you. I have a dozen matters to be attended to if we are to leave Petersburg in the next couple of weeks, but don't hesitate to let me know if there is anything I can do for you.'

Although this affair of Leo had drawn them close together, Daniel, aware now of the disturbing effect she had on him, had been careful to maintain a distance between them, a coolness that had not been there before and which troubled Louise greatly. The embassy, and Henry Russell in particular, were only too willing to shift the awkward responsibility on to someone else's shoulders. Daniel, whether he wished it or not, was obliged to take charge of her, travel with her to England, help plan her future.

There were nights when she lay awake trying to think of a way out and could not find one. The lawyer had advanced her a sum of money that would not do much more than pay her fare to England and perhaps provide a few weeks' lodging. She found the thought more and more unbearable and it came to a head one afternoon when she was lunching with Daniel at the hotel and he happened to mention that he really must do something about buying a few gifts to take back to his family.

'They wanted me to bring them something typically Russian,' he said, 'and to be quite frank I don't know where to begin.'

'Why don't you go to the Gostinny Dvor, that's the Inn of the Merchants? Everything there is typically Russian, not at all like what you could buy in the fashionable streets.' When he looked doubtful, she went on quickly, 'I will come with you if you wish and then I can interpret for you. There are stalls there with every imaginable kind of gift. You tell me what you would like and then we can bargain for it. We could go this afternoon.'

'Are you sure it won't be too much for you? I dare say I can manage it myself.'

She smiled. 'You are a foreigner, they would cheat you right and left. Besides, the market is really one of the sights of Petersburg. You shouldn't miss it.'

'Very well, if you say so.' He gave her a half-ashamed grin. 'To tell the truth I should be glad of your assistance.'

'Good. Then let's go.'

The Gostinny Dvor had been built a hundred years before under Catherine the Great to house the merchants bringing their goods to the city from all over Russia. It was an enormous yellow building covering a whole block, one side facing on to the Nevsky Prospekt and the other on to Sadoya Street.

He realized very quickly that he would have been hopelessly lost without Louise to guide him among the myriad stalls with the merchants in their blue kaftans and wolfskin caps, each of them doing his utmost to entice customers to examine and buy his goods. At the back of every stall a small red lamp burned before an icon, and the air was filled with the trilling of countless birds from the cages of nightingales, linnets and other songbirds that hung everywhere. *Here*, he thought, *you can see and taste and smell the real Russia.*

Together they chose a shawl of Persian silk in deep rich colours for Christine. The shopkeeper threw it around Louise's shoulders and then stood back, holding up his hands in admiration.

'What does he say?' whispered Daniel, but she only laughed and blushed, gathering the shawl around her, the brilliant colours over the sombre black lighting up her eyes and making her look so startlingly lovely that he caught his breath.

The same stall provided them with a blouse for Isabelle, in exquisitely embroidered fine white muslin, and it amused him to see how she bargained with the shopkeeper as he totted it up on his abacus, refusing to pay the sum asked, shaking her head, pretending to walk away until the price pleased her.

'They expect it,' she said when he protested. 'They would think you a very poor kind of a fool if you paid the price first asked.'

'You never cease to surprise me,' he said.

'I do? Why?'

'Most young English girls would pay up, and grumble afterwards.'

'But that's stupid. I know the value and so does he, it's only sensible to get it right. What is the next thing we must look for?'

'Robert wanted a knife with which to kill bears,' he said, laughing. She led him towards the stalls loaded with fine leatherwork; sorting through the dozens of items he found a curved knife in an embroidered leather sheath.

'It's an imitation *yataghan* which was traditionally used in bear hunts. This is made for use as a paper knife and is quite safe, see.' She ran a finger along the blade. 'He won't cut himself. Now, what about your little girl?'

'Celia is nearly eleven and asked for a bear cub, but I

thought a doll would be more suitable. She has quite a collection already.'

'Then she must have a *matrioshka*,' said Louise decidedly. 'It's a wooden doll which contains a whole series of other dolls decreasing in size, each one inside the other. Papa bought me one when we first came to Russia. You can have all kinds of shapes; the best ones tell a story. Papa told me they have been carved for children for hundreds of years and no one knows why. Some scholars say they began in pagan times and represent a kind of earth mother.'

'Sounds just the thing to me. Celia can confound her schoolfriends with her learning. She will enjoy doing that.'

They spent some time choosing among the hundreds on sale, from a foot or more high down to tiny ones of only a few inches; at last they settled on a doll painted to represent a peasant bride. Within her lay the bridegroom and the wedding guests, a baker, a carpenter, a dairymaid and so on, down to the tiniest of all, no more than two inches high.

Their purchases carefully stacked in a large bag of embroidered linen, they began to explore the bookstalls with their enormous volumes, many of them religious, superbly illustrated. Daniel was poring over a Greek Bible when Louise said suddenly, 'You've forgotten someone. You haven't bought anything for your stepson.'

He looked up. 'David is not a child. He is a little beyond the age when you demand presents.'

'Oh, but he will be disappointed. You can't just leave him out. It wouldn't be fair. I think I know exactly what he would like. I'll show you. Come and see.'

She took him by the hand and led him to a stall where icons of every type and size were spread out for customers to admire. Some of them were smoky and very dark; others vivid with brilliant colours picked out in gold; and still others pale, ethereal and quite incredibly lovely with a static, unearthly beauty.

'What makes you think David would like one of these?'

'Because he has a passion for art and paintings. He told me

about the galleries he had seen already in Paris and those he hoped to explore, especially in Italy. Has he never talked to you about it?'

'No, never.' Daniel felt guilty. All these years and they had remained so far apart, almost strangers, while this girl he'd met for a few hours already knew more of what moved and excited him than he did. Was it his fault, or was it the boy's dislike that had brought about the estrangement?

She turned the icons over till she found the one she liked, some martyred saint he had never heard of. The Orthodox Church possessed its own family of holy men and women. The face was infinitely haunting with an aureole of golden hair not unlike Louise's.

'This is the one. He will love this, but I'm afraid it is very expensive.'

'Never mind. If it's your choice, then it is mine.'

He paid for it and thought wryly that David would know well enough who had inspired such a gift.

It was late afternoon before they came out of the building and on to the Nevsky Prospekt. 'I couldn't have managed any of that without your help,' he said, taking her arm. 'You must be exhausted, so now I'm going to buy you some tea. Where shall we go?'

'We could try one of the Chinese shops.'

'Splendid idea. You lead the way.'

There were several of these distinctive teashops along the Nevsky, and stepping into one was rather like stepping into China. There were silken carpets underfoot, exquisitely painted satin panels on walls softly lit by lanterns hung from the ceiling, and over all was the pervading scent of the tea which was being wrapped in soft paper, encased in lead to preserve the rare fragrance and then packed into lacquered boxes for the wealthy customers who liked to come personally to choose their favourite brew. Passing through the beaded curtains, it was possible to sit at one of the bamboo tables and be served with the tea of your choice.

'What shall I order?' asked Louise.

'I'm no connoisseur, I'm afraid. I tend to drink whatever is put in front of me. You choose,' said Daniel, leaning back in his chair and thinking that he would like to strip off the grim shrouding black of mourning and dress her in the pale lilac silks of the girl who came soft-footed to serve them.

'Then I shall order lapsang souchong,' said Louise. 'It was one of Mamma's favourites.'

The tea came and she poured it in the long glasses, pale amber with slices of lemon, deliciously refreshing and unusual. He sipped it appreciatively.

'I think I must buy some of this in one of those elegant boxes,' he said, 'and take it back for Clarissa. She is my mother-in-law, a lovely lady with fastidious tastes.'

Every time he spoke of his family, his wife, his children, of Lord Warrinder who had been close to her own father, she felt her heart sink. The time was growing nearer and nearer and she dreaded it. What would they think of her, the stranger coming into their midst, making demands upon them? She shrank from the inevitable meeting with her half-sister who was so close to them, whom they had known all their lives. How much Daniel must have been regretting the promises he had made, the kindness and generosity that had been so freely given at first and were now wearing thin as the time came closer. Ever since they had come back from that brief stay at the villa she had felt the change, and now suddenly she could bear it no longer. She refilled his glass with the delicately scented tea and pushed the lemon and sugar towards him.

'Daniel,' she said hesitantly, 'have I done something to offend you?'

He looked startled. 'Offend me? Good heavens, no. Why should you think that?'

'All these weeks ... we were such good friends at first ... and now I'm beginning to realize how much is being asked of you, and it distresses me because I can see no way around it.' The words were muddled, not expressing what she really felt, and to her horror she found she was very close to tears.

He knew his withdrawal had been deliberate, for his own

sake as much as hers, and now he couldn't bear to see her distress.

'My dear child, you mustn't feel –'

'I'm not a child,' she said with sudden fierceness, 'and don't treat me like one!'

'I'm sorry,' he said helplessly, 'but you mustn't think it is anything you have done. If I have seemed preoccupied, it has been because there has been so much to be discussed, so many problems to be sorted out . . .'

'And you've been wishing every hour of every day that you could walk out and wash your hands of me and my troublesome affairs.'

'Never,' he said fervently, 'never for a single moment. I hope that very soon now you can put all this wretchedness behind you and begin to look forward to a new life.'

'Perhaps. Sometimes I feel strong and confident, and at other times I seem to face a mountain I don't know how to climb.'

'You'll not be climbing it alone.'

'Are you sure of that?'

'I'm very sure.'

He put his hand on hers and gripped it. A strong hand, she thought, a hand that had never drawn back from what had to be done, however painful. The pressure of his fingers tightened and she smiled tremulously at him, her mind flying back to that night when for a few seconds she had been in his arms and known such great comfort. Then two people came through the beaded curtain, talking loudly, and the spell was broken.

They set out for England at the end of August, accompanied by a huge leather-bound trunk that held all Louise's worldly possessions; two large suitcases; some small hand luggage with necessities for the journey; a picnic basket packed with useful additions to whatever meagre fare could be obtained on the way; and a small, excited dog who served one useful purpose by barking hysterically if any hapless passenger so much as poked his nose into their first-class compartment. On the whole, to Daniel's infinite relief, the journey turned out to be far less arduous than he had anticipated, becoming at times almost enjoyable.

To start with Louise was an excellent traveller, interested in everything and proving unexpectedly strong and resilient despite her fragile appearance. She did not grumble endlessly at the many discomforts and minor embarrassments; she cheerfully ate what food was available, which varied between palatable and downright abominable; and when they changed trains at the border and difficulties immediately arose, she quietly took charge, astonishing the guards by her fluent Russian and German and so confounding them that they never questioned anything, and scarcely even glanced at Daniel's bulging notebooks.

'How did you manage it?' he asked afterwards. 'I was nearly arrested as a spy when I came through in July.'

'I told them that you were an extremely influential member of the British government, a personal friend of the Prime Minister, and engaged on a secret mission.'

'And they believed you?'

'Every word. Papa always used to say that if you must lie then do it with panache, with an absolute certainty and confidence, and you will be believed. By the way, who is the British Prime Minister?'

'A gentleman called Benjamin Disraeli,' said Daniel, much amused, 'and he did just once nod to me at an official dinner I attended with Lord Warrinder. Did they ask you?'

'No, but it wouldn't have mattered what name I had said, they wouldn't have known in any case.'

Six days in the intimacy of a railway journey, forced to be in one another's company for twenty-four hours a day, made it almost inevitable that they would end up closer than lovers or as bitter enemies. Except for the stops at stations it was impossible to escape, no genius having yet designed a railway coach with a corridor, but they had brought a good supply of books, and they read, they dozed, and inevitably they talked.

Daniel, who was the least conceited of men, rarely bored other people with his own experiences, never quite believing that anyone with the exception of Christine would be interested, but Louise was different. She asked questions, one thing would lead to another and to his own surprise he found himself telling of his adventures in India at the time of the Mutiny, when the only way to get a good story was to take risks; the sorry tale of how he had narrowly escaped being shot as a traitor by both sides when reporting on the American Civil War; the months he had spent shut up in Paris besieged by the Prussians till he escaped in a balloon, which wandered off course and landed him in Spain; and at her urgent request telling her something of the gruelling conditions during the Crimean War.

'How very brave of your wife to go with you and share such a dreadful experience,' she said admiringly.

'Christine was not my wife then. Her husband was a doctor with a medical team. I was only an orderly in a different unit.'

For the first time she sensed reticence, an unwillingness to speak about that time, and she did not ask any further questions.

On the whole the journey was uneventful, except for one unpleasant incident. They had been obliged to change trains again at Berlin and it was very late by the time they boarded the express that would carry them on through Germany. They had begun to settle down for the night, Louise lying on the seat opposite Daniel, the travelling rug tucked around her. The dim light made it impossible to read at night and they were dozing when the train suddenly pulled up with a violent jerk that threw Louise across the carriage and into Daniel's arms. He gripped her firmly while the train juddered to a halt with a terrible grinding of brakes.

'Are you all right?' he asked, setting her back on her feet and rescuing Toby, who had been shot out of his basket and was buried under books, papers, a biscuit tin and other paraphernalia and was complaining loudly. He gave him to Louise. 'You stay here, my dear, while I try to find out what has happened.'

Outside there was pandemonium. Passengers were hanging out of windows demanding to know why the train had stopped so suddenly, railway staff were running along the bank, flares had been lit and someone gave a piercing scream.

Daniel opened the door and jumped down on to a grassy bank beside the track. 'We seem to be stopped outside a station,' he called back. 'Stay there and I'll walk down the line.'

'Do be careful.'

He disappeared into the darkness and she shivered, suddenly afraid. She put Toby in his basket, telling him to be a good boy and stay there, and then jumped out, landing on all fours on a kind of bank. She picked herself up, pushed the door shut and began to move towards the front of the train where a crowd had already started to gather. Someone told her to go back to the carriage and wait there but she took no notice. She reached the engine which towered above her like some huge ferocious monster, snorting and puffing out steam in the smoky light of the flares. The vapour eddied around her in great clouds but she thought she could see Daniel and forced her way towards him at the edge of the track. It was then that she saw what had caused the sudden stop. The body of a woman lay directly in front of the train, clothes disordered, long hair spread out, as if she had been flung there like some discarded puppet.

Daniel was staring down at her. A man in uniform carrying a lantern said agitatedly in German, 'Is there a doctor anywhere?' People looked uneasily at one another and Daniel said, 'I'm not qualified but I have had a good deal of experience.'

He climbed down to the still figure and the man with the lantern went with him. Louise held her breath, horrified and yet unable to move. The two men had knelt down beside the body, and she saw Daniel shake his head. Two more men climbed down and with great care they lifted the woman between them and carried her to the grassy bank. By then more station staff had arrived with a stretcher. For a moment, as they placed her on it, Louise saw the face of the dead woman. It was untouched, but deathly pale and very young. A blanket was thrown across her and Louise closed her eyes, feeling suddenly faint and sick.

Daniel's voice, rough with concern, was saying, 'What are you doing here? You shouldn't have come.'

'I wanted to be with you. Is she dead?'

'Yes. The driver had slowed down for the station and he stopped, but not before the train had hit her.' His arm had gone round her and she buried her face against his coat for a moment.

'Did she fall?' she asked in a muffled voice.

'I doubt it. This is not a station platform. She must have intended to kill herself. Now come away. We'll be moving on presently.'

Passengers were already climbing back into their compartments. She took his arm as they walked along the track.

'When I saw her lying there, I had the dreadful thought that it could have been me.'

'You? What are you talking about?'

'When I first heard the news on that awful day, after Lady Russell had left me I didn't want to go on living. I thought how useless I was, how unwanted.' She was staring in front of her, almost reliving it. 'I thought how easy it would be to go out into the night, climb down the stone steps and slip into the Neva, walking till the water closed over my head.'

'You would never have done such a thing. You have far too much courage.'

'I didn't, then. All that night I thought and thought about it and it gave me a wonderful feeling of release, because if I died, it would no longer matter to anyone. Then the next day you came and after that the despair began to recede. I wonder what agony that poor woman went through before she flung herself in front of a train.'

He was appalled to hear that the idea of taking her own life had ever occurred to her. They were back in the compartment by now and he took her by the shoulders, looking down into her face, so pale in the shadowy light.

'You are young, you are beautiful, you have everything to live for. Don't ever think of such a thing again. Promise me.'

She was looking up at him, her body pressed against him, her face only a few inches from his own. He thought he had conquered the crazy desire, had put it firmly behind him during the last weeks, and now suddenly, like a ferocious beast, it leaped into life again.

'I promise,' she whispered and reached up to seal it with a kiss.

For a moment he yielded. The kiss was hard, almost savage, then with an effort he pushed her down on to the seat and turned to the bag in which he carried the silver flask.

'I'm going to give you a taste of this. It'll steady us both after a very unpleasant experience.' He poured a little brandy into the silver cup and gave it to her.

She sipped it and then handed it back to him. 'I think you deserve it more than I do.'

He replaced the flask and shut the bag. 'I'll try to find out when we are likely to be moving on,' he said hurriedly, but before he could step down from the compartment the train had begun to jolt forward into Hannover Station, and there it stayed for several hours while police came and went; the train driver, considerably shaken up, was given restoratives; and station staff appeared with wagons dispensing watery coffee to disgruntled passengers.

'At least it's hot,' said Daniel, returning with two thick white china mugs and giving one to Louise. 'I'm afraid this delay is going to play the devil with our travel arrangements.'

He was perfectly right. They missed their connection at Calais and had to wait half a day for a ferry to carry them across the Channel, with another long wait at Dover due to the mysterious disappearance of Louise's trunk, so that by the time it was located the London train had already left. They had to spend several tiresome hours at a hotel and eventually arrived at their destination at least two days later than expected.

It had been raining hard ever since they boarded the train

at Dover and the London streets had never looked more dismal and uninviting. Louise shivered and looked apprehensively at the tall black and white house in Wimpole Street. Lamps had already been lit each side of the handsome front door, but blinds had been drawn at all the front windows and the house had a deserted look. Daniel was frowning as he helped her out of the cab and up the steps. The door was opened by a manservant before he had even taken out his key.

'Welcome home, sir,' said the servant warmly. 'Madam has been expecting you for the last two days.'

'We were delayed. Come in, my dear.' Daniel took Louise's arm. 'Mark, you had better send someone to help bring in the luggage. And why are all the blinds drawn? Has someone died? Where the devil is everyone?'

'Madam has taken the children to the seaside, sir. She said as how it was the last opportunity before they went back to school.'

'I see. Has everyone gone with her?'

'Oh no, sir, only Cook and Betsy. Nanny Renfrew is still here and the rest of the staff. It is only for a fortnight, sir, and she hoped you would follow them down there. She'll be very sorry to have missed you.'

'Yes, well, we must make the best of it, I suppose. Ask Nanny to come down, will you?' He opened a door to the right of the hall and ushered Louise into a large room which at one time had been Doctor Fraser's consulting-room and had now been transformed into Daniel's study, with a large desk, comfortable leather armchairs, a daybed, a tall cabinet and overflowing bookshelves from floor to ceiling.

Louise looked around her with a certain relief. During the last couple of days she had been nerving herself to face the ordeal before her. The intimacy of the long journey was over, and she would be meeting his wife, his children, all of them looking at her critically, judging her. Now it seemed it was to be put off after all. She felt grateful for the respite.

Through a fog of fatigue she heard Daniel saying, 'I'm sorry that my wife is not here, but Nanny will look after you. She has been with Christine since David was born. We'll soon have everything opened up.'

'It doesn't matter,' she murmured. 'Almost anything will be heaven after the train.'

Then Nanny Renfrew herself came bustling in and Louise was immediately reminded of Katya, because she was so comfortably plump and wearing a neat black dress with a white lace cap on her greying hair.

'Thank goodness you're here, Nanny,' said Daniel. 'I began to think I had been deserted.'

'We've been expecting you for days, Mr Hunter,' said Nanny with the familiarity of an old and valued servant. 'Madam will be most upset.'

'There was an unpleasant accident in Germany. It didn't affect us but it caused a hopeless delay. Nanny, this is Miss Louise Dufour, and she will be staying with us for a while. Will you see to a room for her and make sure she has everything she wants?'

'Yes, of course; the guest room is always kept ready and I will have a fire lit. The rain has made it chilly this evening. You come with me, Miss Dufour,' she said to Louise, 'I'll take you up at once. I expect you'll be glad to take off your things and have a nice wash. I will ask the kitchen to send up a tray of tea for you.'

'Thank you,' murmured Louise. 'That will be wonderful.'

'Ask Nanny for anything you want,' said Daniel. 'Mark will have your luggage sent up to you. By the way, Nanny, if Cook has gone with my wife, what are you all doing for food? I'd prefer not to have to go out to a restaurant tonight.'

'I should think not, indeed,' said Nanny, shocked at the very idea. 'As it happens, that Hannah who came to us when Cook had that bad turn some months ago has been cooking for us and has been doing very well.'

'Could she provide us with a light meal, do you think? Something you're having yourselves will do, and serve it in here. It will be cosier than the dining-room for just the two of us.'

'I'll look after it, Mr Hunter, don't you fret. I'll have a fire lit in here too. There's a pile of letters and messages waiting for you – Madam put them on your desk – and I expect you'll be wanting to take a look through them. You come with me, Miss Dufour, and the little dog too,' went on Nanny, patting Toby warily on the head. 'He'll be hungry and thirsty I'll be bound. Miss Celia will be pleased to see him. She's very fond of dogs. This way, my dear.'

Daniel had already turned to the papers on his desk as Louise followed the old servant out of the room and up the stairs.

It was a wonderful relief for Louise to strip off her travelling costume, to wash away the dust and stains of the journey in gloriously hot water, to put on fresh underwear, to shake out a clean silk blouse and skirt, still black, of course, which she had grown to hate. Must she continue to wear it now she was in England? Grief was in the heart and not in the clothes on your back. In a fit of rebellion she took out a little white lace collar and tucked it into the neck of her blouse. She brushed and brushed her hair till it shone dark gold in the firelight. Tomorrow, Nanny had promised, the house would be back to normal and there would be baths, so she could wash it. Now she swept it up very simply with two large combs. This evening, she thought, was the last one she would spend alone with Daniel and she wanted to look her best. She was quite ready when there came a timid knock at the door.

There had been a great deal of talk already in the kitchen about the young woman travelling alone with the master. Louise's coming had not been mentioned to the staff, since Lord Warrinder had impressed upon his daughter that he did not want a lot of gossip spread around, especially among the servants, before Louise could be introduced to her half-sister and the whole rather fraught situation straightened out. Speculation was rife as to who she was and why he treated her with such care and consideration.

The newest maidservant, temporarily raised to the position of parlourmaid, put her head around the door and bobbed a curtsy.

'The master says supper will soon be served and he would be happy if you would join him in the study as soon as you are ready,' she gabbled all on one long breath.

'Thank you.' Louise smiled. The girl was so very young and was gazing at her wide-eyed. 'What is your name?' she asked.

'Hetty, miss,' the child gulped, and fled, reporting to the kitchen that the young lady everyone was saying came from Russia actually spoke English just like they did.

'Well, she would to you, wouldn't she, silly?' said Hannah, proud of her temporary status as cook but a little flustered at the responsibility. 'Don't stand there gawping like a ninny. We've got to get a move on. Bring me the tureen for the soup.'

The study looked very welcoming when Louise went in. A small table had been placed near the fire, laid with glass and silver and lit by candles. Daniel was buried in an armchair, papers in his hands, a lamp at his elbow. He got up at once when she came in and tossed the letters on to his desk. He too had changed from his travelling tweeds. He was wearing black trousers with a velvet smoking jacket in a deep maroon colour. He was freshly shaved and his thick brown hair was still damp from washing and curled round his neck. He was no longer her fellow-traveller, with whom she had shared so many incidents, laughable as well as embarrassing, but the formal host dispensing hospitality in his own home. For a dizzying moment she regretted it. She had known him – how long? – scarcely more than six or seven weeks, but in that time they had shared so much she felt he had become part of her life. She didn't want this stranger but the man who had held her in his arms on that night at the villa, who had comforted her during that horrible moment on the train: protector, friend, lover ... she shied away from that last disturbing thought.

He was saying, 'I hope Nanny has looked after you properly. May I offer you a glass of sherry, or would you prefer Madeira?'

She pulled herself together. 'Madeira, please,' she said and came to the fire, taking the glass from him and sipping the rich sweet wine.

The food was simple but nectar after those hurriedly snatched and mostly unappetizing meals, making do with cheese and biscuits when there was nothing else, or dry cakes from the station wagons washed down by watery tea or bitter coffee.

She found she was starving and tucked into the thick vegetable soup, grilled lamb cutlets with fresh green peas and crisp roast potatoes, fruit salad with thick cream, enjoying it with the healthy appetite of a schoolgirl, sipping the cool French wine he poured for her and shaking her head regretfully at the array of cheeses placed before her.

While they ate, he told her about where he would be taking her the next day.

'The children call it Hunter's Lair, because most of the time it seems to belong entirely to us. It's on the south coast, rather wild and hemmed in by cliffs so that at high tide, unless you are a rock climber, the cove is shut off from the rest of the seashore. It was my wife who found it and fell in love with it. She does not care for seaside resorts like Brighton and Weymouth. She says they are too much like London by the sea. It was a ramshackle house built high up on the cliff so Lord Warrinder bought it for her and had it refurbished, and we've been going there ever since. Did your father ever take you and your mother to the sea?'

'Yes, once or twice. We went up to the Gulf of Finland, but the wind can be very cold and it is not very good for sea bathing. Mamma did not care for it. What is the sea like in England?'

'It can be cold here too, but the children don't seem to mind. They bathe and hunt for sea creatures in the rock pools and ride their ponies along the beach when the tide is out. We go down there sometimes in the winter. To walk along the seashore in the teeth of a howling gale and come back to hot tea and toasted muffins can be very exhilarating.'

It was a glimpse of a happy family life of which she had no experience, but this was his real life, not these last few weeks in St Petersburg when he had seemed to belong to her alone.

When the servants had cleared the table and brought coffee, they moved nearer to the fire. As she filled his cup, she asked him if he would be staying down there with them.

'Only for a day or so, I'm afraid,' he said, waving a hand to the piled papers on his desk. 'I have a backlog of work I need to catch up with: I had not expected to be away from England for so long. It will do you good to have a few days of peace and quiet by the sea before we begin to discuss your future.'

'Yes.' She wondered if he had guessed how much she was dreading it.

He offered her brandy with the coffee but she shook her head and, though he leaned back comfortably enough in the armchair, sipping the coffee, she guessed that he was itching to get back to the pile of letters demanding his attention, to the affairs he had neglected for her sake. Resolutely she put down her cup and stood up.

'I really am very tired. Would you forgive me if I went to bed?'

'Yes, of course. I've been very thoughtless. You've had a gruelling few weeks and the devil of a journey. You can have a good lie-in tomorrow. We won't be setting out for the country till the afternoon and I am sure Nanny will be only too pleased to coddle you like one of her babies and bring you breakfast in bed.'

'She has been very kind already.'

He got up to open the door for her and she stopped as she passed him, standing on tiptoe to kiss his cheek in her endearing foreign way.

'Good-night, and thank you for everything,' she whispered huskily.

It would have been only too easy for Daniel to pull her into his arms, to kiss the mouth, so temptingly close. *I wonder if she guesses what she does to me?* was his desperate thought as he did none of these things, simply touching her cheek gently for a moment.

'Good-night, my dear, sleep well,' he said, and closed the door after her.

He came back to his chair, poured a little more brandy into his glass and then stood looking down at it. He had shut the door once and for all on the disturbing effect she had on him. Tomorrow he would be delivering her to Christine and reporting on his mission to his father-in-law and the whole episode would be over. His responsibility would be at an end and he swallowed the brandy, turning his mind to the hundred and one matters requiring his immediate attention. He did not realize how very wrong he was.

They arrived at Hunter's Lair by early evening. The cove was tucked away in a stretch of coast between the fishing village of Hastings and the little medieval port of Rye. The cab from the station deposited them at some distance from the cliff-edge.

'Can't go no further, guv,' said the driver cheerfully. 'Afraid it's Shanks's pony from now on. Bit of nowhere this is and no mistake.'

Daniel smiled as he paid the fare. 'You'd be surprised at how many find their way here.'

'You don't say! Well, there's plenty of folks with funny ideas, ain't there? Thank ee kindly, sir.' He pocketed the tip and whipped up his horse.

'Come along. It's not far,' said Daniel, picking up the two cases and leading the way.

They followed a short, well-defined path from the clifftop which opened on to a kind of shelf, and there was the house, whose irregular outline was rather like the jumble of bricks a child might put together, with its red-tiled roof and sturdy walls that backed against the cliff. The main door appeared to be at the side but Daniel went on past it.

'The windows look out over the sea,' he said. 'We'll go round and surprise them.'

As they turned the corner she saw that the shelf had either been deliberately cut out or was a natural fissure in the chalky rock. There was even room for a small garden, where late roses bloomed and a welter of garden flowers struggling with native wild plants in a mass of tangled colour. A wide, well-built path wound in a zigzag down the cliff to the shore, and in the evening sunlight she caught a glimpse of a stretch of shingle, weed-covered rocks and the distant sea like rippling blue-green silk lapping lazily at the sandy edge.

Doors and windows opened from a room which seemed to run almost the entire width of the house. For a moment she saw the whole scene like a painted conversation piece in a picture gallery: two children lying on the floor, some kind of a gamesboard between them; a girl about her own age in a flowered cotton gown on a sofa with a small spaniel asleep on her lap, a young man leaning over the back of it, one hand almost possessively on her shoulder; a woman who must be Daniel's wife leaning back in an armchair, with dark hair which curled a little untidily on her forehead; a golden labrador who sprawled lazily at her feet; and all of them looking towards an older man with finely chiselled features and hair that time had silvered, who was reading to them. His voice had a practised cadence and for a few moments she stood there beside Daniel, entranced into listening.

> 'What if we still ride on, we two,
> With life for ever old but new,
> Changed not in kind but in degree,
> The instant made eternity,
> And heaven just prove that I and she
> Ride, ride together, for ever ride!'

He came to an end and shut the book. A kind of sigh ran around the room. The girl on the sofa was saying, 'Thank you, Grandfather, that was lovely,' the big dog stood up and shook himself and the small girl on the floor gave a sudden squeal, scrambled to her feet, screamed, 'Papa!' and launched herself through the door at Daniel.

He put down the cases and swung her up in his arms. 'Hello, my poppet!'

Rowley woke up to an intruder and began to growl, setting Toby off to bark shrilly, and with that the whole quiet picture broke up into a deluge of questions. 'We've been expecting you for two days. What on earth happened to you? Was there an accident? Is that what caused the delay?' and so on till at last Daniel raised his voice above the clamour.

'Stop it all of you, for heaven's sake. I'm here, that's what is important, and we have a guest. Listen everybody. This is Louise, who is going to stay with us for a while.'

In the sudden hush Christine came forward to take both her hands, saying, 'Oh, my dear, what must you be thinking of us, behaving like a pack of hooligans? I'm so glad you have been able to come to us, and after such a frightful journey. Now come and let me introduce you to everyone. These are my two scapegraces, Celia and Robert.'

The two children straightened up murmuring polite nothings till Celia said timidly, 'May I look after your little dog for you? What is his name?'

'It's Toby, and I think he would be glad of some water.'

'Of course he would, poor darling. I'll take him, shall I?'

Louise gave up the lead a little apprehensively and Christine said, 'Don't worry, he'll be quite all right. Celia has a way with animals. Now come and meet my daughter Isabelle and her friend Dr Alec Rawly, and this is my father, Lord Warrinder.'

'Call me Uncle Everard, my dear,' said the silver-haired man, taking her hand, drawing her towards him and kissing her cheek. 'You must think of me as an old friend of your father. Has Daniel been looking after you properly?'

'Oh yes, he has been wonderful.'

'Good. My only regret is that I couldn't have been there myself. I'm sorry my wife is not here but she has not been so well lately and the helter-skelter life Christine lives here does not always agree with her.'

'Oh Papa, really!' protested Christine. 'What will Louise think of us?'

'She'll soon realize what a wonderful gift you have of making everyone feel happy, my dear.' He turned back to Louise. 'As soon as you are rested and feel you can speak of it, you must tell us about yourself and your mother. We felt the tragedy of your loss very deeply and the suffering it must have caused you,' he went on kindly, wondering to himself if James Ducane had ever thought what a dilemma he had created. What were they going to do with this extraordinarily beautiful girl and what on earth would Clara say when she saw her? If he knew anything about her, she would go up like a rocket.

Celia, having produced a bowl of water for Toby, said in a loud stage whisper, 'Papa, did you remember to bring us you-know-what?'

'Celia!' exclaimed her mother. 'Is that all you can say to your father the moment he comes through the door? Asking him for presents?'

'Well, he did promise ...' she began, looking a little crestfallen.

'Yes, I did,' said Daniel, 'and I hadn't forgotten. Not a bear cub, I'm afraid, but something I think you will like just as well. But not till after supper.'

Food tended to be rather picnic-style at Hunter's Lair but Cook was with them so that, although most of it was cold that night, it was very good. There was poached salmon with shrimp sauce and tender roast beef with potato salad and her famous chocolate trifle with a jug of cream. Afterwards, as Daniel had promised, he brought out the big bag and distributed the gifts to the enormous satisfaction of all concerned.

Robert dashed about the room killing bears with his *yataghan* till his father threatened instant bed if he didn't stop at once. Isabelle was entranced with her muslin blouse; Christine threw the Persian shawl around her shoulders with the practised grace of a queen; and Celia knelt on the floor sorting out the team of characters from the body of her *matrioshka* while Louise knelt beside her and explained how each character was dressed in the traditional peasant costume for whatever trade he represented.

'Nobody at school has ever had anything like this,' exulted the little girl, 'just wait till I show it to them!'

The lacquered box of tea was handed over to Lord

Warrinder, who smiled. 'Good of you to remember her, Dan,' he said. 'She will be the envy of her friends at their afternoon tea parties.'

Celia, still rummaging in the opened bag, came up with another carefully wrapped parcel.

'You've forgotten one, Papa. Who is this for?'

'Leave it. It's for David.'

'David's too grown-up for presents and he's not here. Can we see what it is?'

'No, you can't.'

'Oh, why? David won't mind, will he, Mamma?'

'Your Papa says no and that's the end of it. Give it to me, Celia. I'll keep it till David comes home. And that's enough excitement for one evening. It's past nine and high time you were in bed, young lady. Now, no argument. Off you go.'

'It's not fair. You let Robert stay up.'

'When you're thirteen, you will be allowed to stay up too. Now say good-night to everyone.'

Reluctantly she went from one to the other, glaring at Robert, who looked smug, and coming last to Louise, who bent down and gave her a little hug.

'I'll tell you all about the rest of your *matrioshka* tomorrow, shall I?'

'Oh, yes please,' and she went on up the stairs, hugging the big wooden doll to her.

Later that night Louise stood at the window of her little room, listening to the sound of the sea that had come up to high tide, and thought that in the winter it must be like standing on the deck of a ship. She had weathered the first meeting and it had not proved nearly as difficult as she had feared. Though she knew it was only a brief respite before stepping into the unknown, it was a great relief.

She opened the casement wide and looked out over the sleeping garden, wondering whether Alex Rawly was in love with Isabelle. Shy, gawky, it seemed he had met her when they were both attending a course in pharmacy, and they had been awarded their diplomas on the same day. Now he was in his first year of walking the hospital wards. They were both so clever, she thought enviously. If only she had studied something worthwhile. All she had done was to learn foreign languages for fun and play the piano for pleasure.

She looked along the line of windows. Behind one of them Daniel would be with his wife, telling her about the young woman who had given him so much trouble, laughing about it perhaps as he took his wife to bed. Twice he had kissed her, twice it had thrilled through her and left her shaken, but that meant nothing. It was crazy to think of it but she couldn't help herself. Here in his own home she was seeing him in a new light, but she was still enthralled by him. Ridiculous, when he was twice her age and married and had his own busy and fulfilling life.

The breeze, laden with salt from the sea, blew in coldly, making her shiver. She pulled the window shut. Toby grunted and she looked down at his basket. The little dog opened one sleepy eye, turned himself round twice, then settled down again, which was what she must do. She pulled off her dressing-gown, climbed into bed and turned out the lamp.

In their room at the other end of the house Christine, already in her nightgown, was trying out the Persian shawl in a variety of dramatic poses in front of the long mirror.

'Did Louise choose this?' she asked suddenly.

'Yes, she did actually. Why? Don't you like it?'

'I think it's gorgeous. I shall flaunt it in the faces of all my acquaintances when we return to London. I just thought that you would have chosen something more sober, more matronly. It takes another woman to understand what a woman of my age might secretly covet.'

'That's too deep for me,' said Daniel, pulling his nightshirt over his head. 'She helped me choose all the presents. We bought them in the Gostinny Dvor, which is the Russian market, and she was very practical, haggling over the prices with the shopkeepers like some old fishwife.'

'Daniel,' went on Christine, folding the shawl carefully

before getting into the big bed, 'what are we going to do with Louise – not immediately of course, but in the future?'

'God knows. Tomorrow I must discuss it with your father. Is Clara back from her cruise yet?'

'I gather that she is not returning to England till early in October.'

'With the new lover?'

'I presume so.'

'I imagine it will then be decided for us. If Clara refuses to do anything for her, I don't think Louise will accept any kind of help, either from your father or from us. She has a strong independent streak and feels her position very keenly.'

'You seem to know her very well,' said Christine, looking at him curiously.

'Well, I should. I've been in her company more or less every day for the last six or seven weeks.'

'I suppose in those circumstances it had to be either love or hate. Which was it, Daniel?'

'Oh, for God's sake! A bit of both, I suppose.' He came to sit on the edge of the bed. 'Must we go on talking about Louise?'

'Why not? She is so young and lovely, isn't she? Much more exciting than your commonplace, everyday wife. It's a wonder you didn't fall in love with her on the spot.'

'Well, the plain fact is that I didn't,' he said with a little too much emphasis. 'As a matter of fact you very nearly lost me to a gypsy dancer.'

'Did I?' She sat up. 'Tell me about it.'

'On Louise's advice I visited one of the *tzigane* restaurants.'

'Did you take her with you?'

'I asked her but she said it wouldn't be proper.'

'Go on,' said Christine. 'Tell me the worst.'

'It's all very dramatic, very colourful: throbbing balalaika music, flashing eyes, coal-black hair, a lot too much to drink and a great display of beautiful flesh.'

'Heavens, it sounds wonderful. Did you fall for one of them?'

'So much so,' he went on, 'that I wished you had been there to enjoy it all with me.'

'Is that true?'

'True as I'm sitting here, and now shut up about it. There are more important things to be attended to.'

'Such as?'

'Such as this.'

He pulled her into his arms, kissing her so roughly that she gasped and struggled and then capitulated. He took her so fiercely that night that it surprised her. For a long time now their love-making had been affectionate and tender, filled with talk and laughter and ending in a coming together that was infinitely pleasurable and fulfilling. But this night it had a fierceness, almost as if he were trying to prove something to himself. It made her wonder a little before she yielded herself to it.

Chapter 6

The September sun still shone but the woods and hedgerows had already the golden glow of autumn. There were scarlet hips on the tangle of wild roses, and blackberries were ripening, fat and juicy, on many slopes of the Downs. A sharp little wind blew the sea into white crests as it crept up the beach and began to lap into the rocky pools where Robert and Celia were hunting for sea creatures trapped there before the tide swept them out again. Rowley was with them, watching intently as a small crab made its laborious way across a rock, prodded by Robert's finger.

Louise was walking at the water's edge, her feet bare, her white dress kilted up high above her ankles. It was Christine who had suggested that she might discard the dismal black down here in this remote place, and lent her one of Isabelle's muslin gowns, which fitted well enough if a little too big in the waist.

'You're so slim,' Isabelle had sighed. 'How I wish I could stop myself indulging in Cook's chocolate cream trifle!'

Toby was bounding along with her, barking fiercely when a wave broke too near to him, and then racing after the ball she threw for him as it receded. Since her parents' death, Louise had never dreamed that she could feel so happy. Of course there were still black moments when the whole hideous tragedy washed over her again, but the last fortnight had acted like a strong tonic, bringing her back to life. She had never been part of a family before and did not realize how very unusual this one was and how much the relaxed atmosphere, so warm and comforting, owed to Christine who, without seeming to be so, was the mainspring of the whole household.

When Daniel went back to London on the Monday after her arrival, she thought she would feel utterly bereft, but the others simply accepted her, absorbing her into their lives and taking it for granted that she would join in their simple pleasures, taking a picnic to the woods, spending a morning hunting for mushrooms, making a trip to Hastings to watch the fishing fleet sail in, buying a basket of fish straight out of the sea and taking it back for Cook to fry for supper, having tea in the Mermaid Inn in Rye and hearing about the smugglers who only forty or fifty years before had swaggered around the town, drinking and boasting of their exploits. She listened to the children talking about their father and looked forward as they did to his weekend visit.

Daniel was here now, lying on a rug beside his wife's chair, looking at Louise through half-closed eyes and thinking that in that white dress, with her hair escaping from its ribbon and blowing about her face, she looked like one of those sea nymphs – what did they call them? Nereids, wasn't it? Sometimes he regretted his lack of a classical education.

David was thinking much the same, only, his imagination stirred by the pictures he had seen in the great Italian galleries, he thought of fourteenth-century angels with their enigmatic smiles, and of Aphrodite, Goddess of Love, rising from the foam of the sea. He had arrived at Hunter's Lair half an hour before, called at the house and found Betsy setting out tea in the sitting-room. He caught her round her plump waist and she gave a little squeal of surprise and pleasure.

'Where on earth did you spring from, Master David? You gave me quite a turn! And us all thinking you were far away in foreign parts enjoying yourself.'

'So I was, but now I've come back. Where are they all?'

'Down on the beach, but they'll be up any minute now for their tea. It's too blowy to carry it down there this afternoon. You go on down. Your mother will be that pleased to see you, and looking so brown and well too.'

He left his small valise, tossed his hat on a chair and went down the path to the shore, pausing at the bottom and taking in the picture: his mother, reading; his stepfather stretched at her side, barefoot with trousers rolled up from playing ball with the children; Celia and Robert intent on their rock pool; Isabelle and her latest lame duck, the serious, awkward Alec Rawly, clambering over the seaweed-covered rocks soon to be engulfed by the advancing tide; and the astonishing sight of Louise, the very last person he had expected to see. For a few moments he stood quite still, savouring the moment.

He didn't quite know what had brought him back a good month before he was expected. It wasn't that he hadn't enjoyed his trip. He'd had a marvellous time with Uncle Harry, who was the best of company, both guide and boon companion, good-humouredly sharing sightseeing expeditions with him but also introducing him to a social round where he seemed to eat wonderful meals and meet splendid girls who were a far cry from the prim society he met at home, taking him to card parties (where he won a little and lost far more, and learned painfully how not to drink too much) and altogether giving him a wonderful feeling of being a man of the world.

Then at the end of August, Harry, feeling he had done enough for his sister's boy, had left him for the Mozart Festival at Salzburg so that, despite his new-found expertise and worldliness, David suddenly felt very alone. Basically shy and reserved, somehow the magic had vanished from the holiday without Harry to give it an extra sparkle. Florence was blisteringly hot and his new friends scattered to join families by the sea. He went on to Rome, and one night was invited to a literary gathering where Robert Browning would be reading his own work. Browning's elopement with the fragile poetess Elizabeth Barrett had been the talk of society before David was born, but she had been dead these ten years. He was not much given to poetry but Browning was his sister's favourite so he bought a copy of his poems and asked the great man to inscribe it particularly for her. Then, because everyone told him he should, he went on to Naples and wished he hadn't. Despite the fascinating history, the picturesque bay with its marvellous views of the sea, nothing could disguise the poverty, the squalor and the unpleasant reek of crowded streets grilling in the summer heat. He picked up a prevalent fever, spent three days sick and sweating and feeling sorry for himself while the thought of the cool sea breezes and quiet pleasures of Hunter's Lair seemed like heaven. Suddenly he made up his mind to return home.

The news of the bombing disaster had reached them shortly before Harry left him. He found it hard to believe that all the quiet happiness he had sensed in that villa had been swept away in a few seconds by some crazy terrorist. 'What will happen to Louise?' he had said to Harry, concerned for the girl with whom he had shared a few special minutes that he had never forgotten.

'No doubt her father will have left her well provided for – but what a tragedy for the poor girl, and what a pretty kettle of fish for Daniel to have to sort out. He must have arrived in the thick of it, poor devil. I've no doubt he will cope but I must say I don't envy him.'

The very last thing he had expected was to find her here, paddling unconcernedly along the seashore, enjoying Hunter's Lair as his family had always done.

No one had noticed him yet and he stood for a while longer, leaning on the gate and thinking that the months away had made quite a difference. He felt more detached now, able to view them all more objectively, even his stepfather. It was as if the cord holding him so close to his mother had slackened at last; not that he didn't love her just as dearly, but he had a new feeling of freedom. It was time to make his own life, and although he had no idea what the future held for Louise, the very fact that the lovely girl who had impressed him so deeply was here in his own home was an unexpected delight. He had apparently come back at just the right time, and he felt filled with self-confidence. At that moment of complacency it happened.

The wind had freshened and become much stronger, as often happened when the tide came up in this narrow cove. The waves had become rougher and far more boisterous, crashing in instead of lapping gently at the flat sandy shore. Louise, who had no experience of the sea's power, threw the ball too far. Racing after it, Toby was swept up into the receding wave and carried back out. Without stopping to think and with no knowledge of the dangerous currents that lurked amongst these seaweed-covered rocks, Louise went after him. A huge wave knocked her off her feet. David saw her head disappear and then come up again. She was struggling against strong waves and obviously could not keep her footing on the slippery rocks. She could easily be carried further out and drown before anyone could reach her. He tore off his coat and began to run but Daniel had been quicker. He had seen the danger at once and was on his feet already, racing down to the sea. An incoming wave flooded the children's rock pool and tossed a shocked Toby almost at Celia's feet. She snatched him up and watched terrified as her father plunged in after Louise.

They had all realized what was happening by now. Christine had come hurrying after Daniel and was watching anxiously at the water's edge. Isabelle and Alec came running from the rocky caves. No one had noticed David, who stood ready poised to dive in if necessary, though he was only too well aware of his lack of skill whereas he knew Daniel was a powerful swimmer. Louise had been carried further out, bounced from wave to wave. Twice they saw her head disappear and come up again, and they held their breath till with a gasp of relief they saw that Daniel had reached her and taken firm hold. He was supporting her with some difficulty but at last he turned to swim back, bringing her with him, the long hair streaming out behind her. He had a hard struggle against the strength of the waves, preparing for their final assault on the shore, then thankfully it was over and he was staggering through the surf carrying Louise. Willing hands stretched out to help him up the shingle to safety.

Daniel put her down gently and stood for a moment, struggling for breath before falling on his knees beside her.

'Is she all right?' Christine was kneeling on the other side and bending over Louise anxiously.

'I think so. Thank God she is still breathing.'

For a heart-stopping moment David looked down at her, lying so still, her hair spread out around her, her face sheet-white. Then Daniel raised her; she choked and vomited a little seawater.

'Toby,' she whispered, 'is Toby . . .?'

'He's quite safe. I've got him,' whispered Celia.

'I thought . . .' Louise shuddered and turned to Daniel, clinging convulsively to her rescuer, still shaken by the terror of the engulfing sea that had so nearly drowned her.

'You must go back to the house, both of you, as quickly as you can,' said Christine. 'You'll catch your death in this cold wind.'

'Take my coat,' exclaimed Alec, peeling it off and bending down to wrap it around Louise. 'Shall I carry her?'

'I think I can manage.' Daniel stood up and lifted Louise to her feet, holding her close against him.

'I'm all right now,' she murmured. 'I can walk.'

'Don't argue, girl.'

He lifted her easily and David, still standing outside the concerned little circle, saw how confidingly she slid her arm round his neck, saw, or thought he saw, intimacy in the look that passed between them, and was shaken by a sudden stab of sheer jealousy.

'Take care of her,' said Christine. 'Tell Betsy to get the fire lit and to give her a good rub-down. I'll be following you up to the house as soon as I can. It's much too cold to stay down here any longer.' She watched Daniel make his way a little unsteadily across the shingle and then turned to the others. 'Come along, all of you, pick up your things and bring the dogs. Be quick about it, now,' and it was only then, as she bustled the children along, that she saw her son and stopped in surprise.

'David!' she exclaimed. 'David! I can't believe it. What are you doing here? When did you come? Why didn't you let us know?'

'Didn't know I was coming till the last minute –' and then they were all round him, exclaiming, asking questions.

'Did you see what happened?'

'Yes, I did. I was just getting ready to dive in if Daniel had needed any help.'

'For a terrible moment I thought I might lose both of them,' exclaimed his mother with a shudder.

'Poor Mamma! What a horrible shock for you,' and he gave her a big hug and a warm kiss, shook hands with Alec, patted the children on the head and was heartily embraced by his sister.

Then they were all trooping back to the house, loaded with beach paraphernalia and all talking at once as they climbed up the steep path.

When they reached the house they stacked chairs, rugs, buckets and spades in the garden shed, together with two glass jars of revolting slimy sea creatures that Christine refused to allow Robert to keep in his bedroom, much to his indignation. In the sitting-room they found Daniel who had already changed into the ancient garments he kept for when his wife bullied him into helping her in the garden, and was kneeling by the hearth doing his best to coax the fire into a blaze.

'This confounded wood is too damp,' he said without turning round, 'it's never going to burn. Find me the old bellows somebody.'

'Your hair is still soaking wet,' scolded Christine, coming up behind him and putting her hand on it, 'and what have you done with your hands? They're bleeding.'

'I must have grazed them on the rocks. They'll be all right. The salt water will have cleaned them. Ah, that's my boy,' he went on, taking the bellows from Robert and setting to work on the fire again. 'Louise is upstairs. Betsy is with her.'

'I'd better go up and see how she's feeling. Isabelle, run out to the kitchen and find out about tea. We could all do with a good hot cup.'

'Ought I to go and take a look at Louise?' asked Alec a little nervously.

'She hates being fussed over. I'll take her up a tray of tea. Come on.' Isabelle grabbed his hand. 'We'd better go and find out about your coat. It's probably drying in front of the kitchen stove.'

The two children furtively eyed the table already spread with plates of sandwiches, sultana scones, cakes, biscuits and a particularly luscious trifle. It looked very tempting.

Daniel, still working patiently at the reluctant fire, said warningly, 'Hadn't you two better dry the dogs, or Mamma will be cross.'

'Oh goodness, I forgot.' Celia looked stricken. 'We left them in the shed. Come and help me, Rob.'

They dashed out together and Daniel sat back on his heels with a sigh of relief. 'That's done it. It's beginning to burn up at last. I swear there's a contrary devil lurking somewhere inside this grate who does his best to spite me.' He got to his feet, brushing the dirt off his hands, and saw David for the first time. 'Good God, where did you spring from? What happened to bring you home? Did you run out of cash?'

'Nothing like that. I just decided to come back, that's all.'

'Did you, now? And did Harry come with you?'

'No, he's gone to the Salzburg Festival.'

'Well, your mother will be pleased at any rate. She's missed you down here with the children. When did you arrive?'

'About an hour or so ago. In time to witness the drama.'

'Yes, well, it could have been worse.'

'And wasn't, thanks to you. I didn't expect to see Louise here.'

'I don't suppose you did. You heard what happened, I presume.'

'Yes, when we were in Florence. It was a frightful shock. We did meet them all, you know, in St Petersburg.'

'So I understand. Well, there was no help for it. Louise has been left more or less penniless. Your grandfather suggested I bring her back to England. He is coming over to take her back to Bramber till Clara comes home from her cruise. What are you thinking of doing? You can hardly start your pupillage in

Harry's chambers till he comes back, and we shall be shutting this place up for a few months since the children will be going back to school.'

'I should like to go to Bramber for a short while if it's all right with you and Mamma.'

'Good enough. You can ask your grandfather about it when he comes over this weekend.'

'Yes, I will. What is going to happen to Louise?'

'We shall have to hear what Clara has to say.'

'I suppose Clara inherits the lot?'

'More or less. Unfortunately her father's new will was never completed.'

'That's damned unfair.'

'I couldn't agree more, but there it is. There's nothing we can do about it.'

Despite an attempt at good will on both sides, they were still inclined to be edgy with one another and were relieved when Christine came down the stairs, saying that Louise had borne up very well considering she had nearly drowned and would be coming down to join them presently. Then the servants brought in the tea with freshly toasted muffins, the children came in with the dogs and they all gathered round the table.

It was a strange evening full of hidden tension.

They had been noisy over tea, laughing and talking together, but now it was cleared away they were quiet, Daniel reading, Christine frowning at imaginary pictures in the red-hot heart of the fire, Isabelle whispering with Alec over the book of Browning's verses which David had given her, Robert lying on the floor absorbed in a complex chess problem, his latest craze.

Daniel looked up as Louise came in, back in the sombre black with a little white lace at neck and wrists.

'How do you feel?' he asked.

'Fine now.'

'Good. Come to the fire.' He got up to give her his chair but she shook her head and dropped down close to him on a low stool beside the hearth.

'No ill effects?'

'None, only tremendously grateful to be still here.'

'That's something we all share.'

'Louise, my dear,' interrupted Christine. 'I think you know David, don't you? You met before.'

'Yes indeed. He came to our party at the villa.'

She was looking across at him, smiling, and David was gripped again by sheer magic, just as he had been that first time in the moonlit garden which seemed now as if it belonged to another world.

'It was a wonderful evening,' he said, 'and I can't tell you how grieved we were when we heard what happened. It must have been a fearful shock.'

'It was.' She turned her face away and he could have kicked himself for being insensitive enough to mention it now, of all times. He was saved from further blunders by Celia, who had been showing him the intricacies of her *matrioshka* doll.

'I've just remembered,' she said. 'Papa brought a present for you, David. He wouldn't tell us what it was. Has he given it to you?'

'Not yet.'

'Where is it? Shall I fetch it, Papa?'

'Your mother took charge of it.'

'It's in the bottom of my wardrobe, Celia. Run up and bring it down for David.'

The little girl pounded up the stairs and was back in no time with the carefully wrapped parcel.

'Shall I open it for you, David?'

'We'll do it together, shall we?'

He lifted the icon out of its protective wrappings and held it up. The mellow light fell on the pale, exquisite face, on the golden aureole of hair and the carved and gilded wood of the frame.

He drew a sharp breath of surprise and appreciation. 'It's the most beautiful thing I've ever seen. I don't know what to say . . .'

'Don't thank me,' said Daniel brusquely. 'It's Louise you must thank. It was her choice.'

He looked across at her, lost in wonder. 'How did you know?'

'I thought about what you told me – do you remember? About art and the paintings you hoped to see and what you felt about them.'

'I saw a few icons when your father took me and Uncle Harry to the Hermitage, but none of them more exquisite than this. It must have cost a fortune.'

'Not quite that,' said Daniel drily, 'but enough. I'm glad you like it.'

They all wanted to look now and it passed from hand to hand with exclamations of wonder and pleasure.

'It's a bit like Louise, isn't it, Mamma?' said Celia, leaning over her mother's shoulder to peer at it again.

'Oh heavens,' smiled Louise, 'I hope not. I'm not a saint or a martyr. I believe that poor girl was thrown into a vat of boiling oil because she refused to give up her Christian faith.'

'I think I'd rather have my head cut off,' said Robert seriously. 'It would be quicker and wouldn't hurt so much.' He proceeded to describe in vivid detail some of the more bloody deaths endured for religion that came from a book of martyrs which someone had unwisely given him, till his father put a stop to it. 'But they're all true stories,' he said indignantly.

'Maybe, but there are enough horrors in the present without delving into the past for them.' Robert went back to his chess problem in disgust at grown-ups, who never wanted to discuss anything really interesting.

There was a battered old piano at Hunter's Lair that had belonged to the original house and Christine had kept it so that Celia could bang out her exercises and they could all have a sing-song on the rare occasions when Harry spent the weekend.

David, remembering the party at the villa, said impulsively, 'Won't you play us something, Louise?'

'Oh no, I couldn't,' she said quickly. 'I'm hopelessly out of practice.'

'Oh, please. I know it's a frightful old piano but your magic touch will work wonders with it.'

Daniel, who knew better than anyone how closely her playing was still bound up with the loss of her parents, said quickly, 'Don't press her, David. She may not feel up to it.'

'I'm all right,' she said quietly and moved towards the piano stool.

'Can you play without music?' asked Celia with considerable awe.

'A few pieces, not many of course. It's quite easy, you know,' she smiled at the little girl, 'no more difficult than learning poetry by heart.'

She began a little hesitantly, with one or two simple melodies, and for some reason the old piano, with notes that occasionally stuck, responded wonderfully to the touch of skilful fingers. Presently, confidence returning and perhaps unconsciously influenced by the experience of the afternoon, she moved into the Chopin she had played that night at the villa, losing herself in memories.

Her audience listened in silence, taken by surprise at her expertise. *Daniel told me she played the piano but not like this*, thought Christine: *why hasn't he?* And she was shaken by a sudden passionate wish that Louise had never come to stay with them, never entered their lives. She had felt instinctively, almost from that very first evening when Daniel had brought her to Hunter's Lair, that Louise was fascinated by her husband: the way she looked at him, hung upon his words, longed to talk about him, had even found the copy of his novel in the bookshelves and cherished it beside her bed, that first book of his which contained so much of the young Daniel's passionate struggles. And what did *he* feel about *her*? What had happened during those weeks he had spent with her at such an emotional time? He had never said much about it except to show a deep concern, which he would have felt for anyone in similar tragic circumstances, but she guessed that there had been something more – and Louise was so young, so helpless and so achingly beautiful, she would tempt any man. She glanced across at him now. He was lying back in his chair, his eyes on Louise, his face unguarded as the music flowed around them, and it seemed to her that something passed between them, a shared memory that bound them together; Christine was flooded with a wild unreasonable jealousy before she firmly shut her mind against it, telling herself she was being ridiculous in looking for something that was not there.

David too had been watching them. He had been entranced by the music, and this thought was like a shower of cold water. Louise couldn't care about Daniel, it wasn't possible, he was twice her age for God's sake! And yet already impressions had been piling up: the trusting way she had clung to him when he carried her from the sea, the way she had gone to him as if no one else mattered, sitting close beside him as if by right. He had always known that his stepfather was attractive to women. When Daniel spoke at one or other of his wife's charitable activities, the women all swarmed around him afterwards . . . and Louise was so very young and vulnerable. Surely he had never . . . would never . . . David shut his mind against it. When his grandfather took her back with him to Bramber, he would make sure he went with them. For the first time in his self-absorbed life David was lifted out of himself, stirred by feelings he had never felt for any girl; if there was going to be a fight with his stepfather, then he was prepared for it.

Later that night, when everyone had gone up to bed and Daniel was dealing with the dying fire, Christine gathered up Robert's books, which as usual he had left scattered over the floor, put them tidily on the table and turned to look at him.

'I must say I'm very thankful that Louise is going to Bramber tomorrow.'

'Why? It seemed to me that she fitted in extremely well, seeing that she's not used to our kind of life.'

'That's just it. For the last fortnight everything has seemed to depend on Louise. The children have hung on her every word. Alec, who is so shy he blushes if a stranger speaks to him, has been her slave ever since she began to translate some German medical book he has been working on, and hardly gives a thought to Isabelle. Even Cook, who can be a tyrant, said, "Oh but Miss Louise doesn't care for curried lamb, madam, and she never touched that creamed rice"! There have been times when I wanted to scream.'

He set up the fireguard, carefully locking it into position before he turned to her. 'What is all this? You've never grumbled before, and heaven knows we've had some difficult guests from time to time.'

'Yes, I know . . .' but Christine, having once started, could not stop herself. 'And there's another thing. She is crazily in love with you!'

'Have you taken leave of your senses?' He came to her then, taking her by the shoulders and giving her a little shake. 'Now listen to me. If Louise has seemed to turn to me, it is simply because I was the only person who showed any understanding at a time of extreme wretchedness for her, the only one she could rely on and I suppose that in a way that feeling still remains in what must be a very different and alien world.'

'And what do you feel for her?'

'Oh for heaven's sake! What do you think? Concern, pity . . . Christine, what has happened? This is not like you.'

'No, it isn't, is it? I'm sorry.' She leaned against him for a moment. 'She is going away tomorrow and Clara will be coming home very soon now.' She raised her face to his. 'I don't dislike Louise, you know, I wish her well, I'd do anything for her. I just don't want her to live with us, that's all.'

He tightened his arms around her. 'It's not likely to happen so stop worrying. I'm dead tired and so are you. I've mountains of work waiting for me when we go back to London and I think I've got a cold coming on.'

She was all anxiety at once. 'I knew it. You never will take proper care of yourself. You've taken a chill. I'll make you a hot drink and bring it up to you in bed.' She suddenly buried her face against the rough tweed of his coat. 'I'm sorry, Dan,' she whispered. 'I'm sorry.'

He held her close, looking across her head towards the dark and distant sea, and knew that there was more truth in what she had said than he wanted to acknowledge. 'You go up to bed, my love. I'll forage in the kitchen and bring us both a hot drink. Would you like that?'

'Yes please.'

He kissed the top of her head, saw her go up the stairs, then went out to the kitchen, stirred up the fire, heated milk, poured a dollop of brandy in each cup and then took them up to their bedroom, shutting his mind resolutely against that agonizing moment when he thought he had lost Louise, and without giving a thought to wife and children had risked everything to save her.

PART TWO

The Half-Sister

Chapter 7

All who knew Clara had expected the worst and speculated with considerable misgivings as to what the outcome would be when she at last confronted Louise, the love child of her father's liaison with an opera singer, the daughter on whom he had lavished the affection and tender care that should rightfully have been hers.

When Lord Warrinder brought Louise back to London and invited Clara to meet her at his house in Berkeley Square, he asked Daniel to be present, since the latter had been in St Petersburg, had met the lawyer who drew up that last unsigned will and could answer any questions Clara might see fit to ask.

'To tell you the truth I'm not looking forward to it,' he said gloomily to his son-in-law. 'Clara has been a thorn in our flesh ever since she was a child. Heaven knows, Clarissa did her best for her, but she was always what Nanny used to call an aggravating child, as full of prickles as a porcupine.'

'How does Louise feel about it?'

'She is very quiet but that doesn't mean she is feeling happy about it. She has a good deal of self-control for one so young, you must have realized that. I've been impressed by her during these last weeks at Bramber. I did suggest that Clarissa and I would be very willing to let her stay with us if she wished but she is quite resolute about not accepting any more from me or from you, it would seem, and after all Clara *is* her half-sister and she should think of her father's wishes for this daughter of his. Matters ought to be settled suitably between them but I must confess I do have doubts about it.'

They did not have long to wait. Sharp to time the butler announced Lady Dorrien and Monsieur de Chaminard and was ushering in Clara, dressed magnificently in black from head to foot and accompanied by the man who was popularly believed to be her lover, and all their expectations proved to be completely wrong. No one could have been more charming, more friendly or more forthcoming than Clara was that morning.

'Dear Uncle Everard,' she said, throwing back her veil, taking his hand and kissing him on the cheek. 'How good it is to see you looking so well.' She extended a gracious hand to Daniel. 'I believe I owe you a debt of gratitude for all you have done for this unhappy child of my late father. May I introduce Jean-Louis de Chaminard, my very dear friend, who was with me when I received the tragic news of Papa's death and gave me comfort and strength when I needed it so badly.'

Courteous greetings having been exchanged, Daniel looked with curiosity at the man none of them had met and about whom they had entertained the liveliest curiosity. He was nudging fifty, Daniel thought, tall, good-looking, impeccably dressed and giving an unmistakable impression of controlled power. A man, he guessed, who knew where he was going, understood exactly what he wanted and would be ruthless about acquiring it. What neither he nor Lord Warrinder knew was that it was he who had brought about this unexpected change in Clara.

He had been with her in late August when his yacht had put into port to pick up mail and the French and English newspapers. His summer guests took their leave and, alone with him, Clara had given way to a savage fury which surpassed anything he had known (and he was not inexperienced in the ways of women). It took him the whole day and the utmost patience to calm her down, to sympathize with her outrage at the long deception, till at last, utterly exhausted and reduced to helpless tears, she was made to understand that the best way to counter the backlash of society, the tormenting certainty that everyone would be laughing at her for being deceived for so long, was to show magnanimity, express deep sympathy, hint that she had known all along and now felt only kindness towards the forlorn girl, an innocent in a distressing situation. She had wept in his arms but at last he knew he had won, helped by the astounding fact that for the first time in her forty-two years Clara had fallen hopelessly in love. Always before in her encounters with men, it was she who had led and they who had tamely followed, but Jean-Louis was different. He wanted neither her money nor anything she could do for him. He was a man who knew his own worth, his own strengths, and it was in fact that same steely quality in her which had first attracted him.

He was not yet her lover, not for any moral reason but simply because he had learned very early in life never to rush at anything. Confident of his power, he knew he could always have what he wanted if he waited for it, and it amused him to keep her trembling on the brink. He could capture his tigress whenever he wished. It was something he had inherited from his Greek mother, together with her raven-dark hair and olive skin. From his father, a high-born but impoverished French aristocrat, had come the grey eyes, the elegance and the devastating charm. *Certainly not a man to trifle with*, thought Daniel shrewdly at that first meeting.

Louise, when she came in, surprised them both. Clara had seen Marianne Dufour as an intriguing French harpy who had trapped her doting father into some impossible affair from which he could not free himself, and her daughter as a cunning little vixen determined to grab what she could. She was utterly confounded by this quiet girl in her simple black dress who was neither timid nor brazen, and composedly held out her hand.

'I understand, Lady Dorrien, that you are my half-sister,' she said. 'How do you do? Papa told me a good deal about you.'

Taken aback, Clara took the outstretched hand. 'It is my wish, as I hope it is yours, that we should be friends,' she said with an effort, drawing Louise towards her and kissing her cheek before turning a little helplessly to Jean-Louis. 'My sister, Louise.'

'*Enchanté, mademoiselle.*' He brushed his lips across her outstretched hand and thought, *She is quite* formidable *this little one, not quite what I had expected, a tiger cub and not a ewe lamb. I think we shall see the sparks flying before long*, and he was aware of a prick of sympathy for the girl who stood, so pale and yet so composed, giving no hint of the turmoil within her.

He too had suffered humiliating rejection. His father's aristocratic family had loathed and resented his mother, whose grandfather had been a horny-handed Greek fisherman with one boat, the forerunner of the fleet that had brought wealth to his son. The fifteenth-century château of Chaminard, buried in the apple orchards of Normandy, might be crumbling into ruin but to its owners the very word 'trade' was anathema. Jean-Louis was twelve when his father was killed in a hunting accident; the day after the funeral he and his mother were firmly shown the door. They were not poor, as his mother's father had made sure of her marriage settlements. Jean-Louis had studied at the Sorbonne and afterwards at Leipzig. He was trained in the law, and spoke several languages, and after his grandfather's death he successfully ran his shipping empire – but that rejection still rankled, and he sometimes took pleasure in playing on the anxieties of the blue-blooded aristocrats who now sought his favours so eagerly.

The preliminaries over, and a tray of coffee and biscuits having been provided, Clara – never one to waste time – got down to business.

'I am of course arranging with those concerned to have Papa's body brought back and buried in the family vault beside my mother,' she said briskly.

'Is that really necessary?' asked Lord Warrinder mildly. 'After all, James spent most of his life out of England.'

'He should be here where he belongs, and not in some foreign cemetery lying beside –' 'his whore', she would have said, but she bit the words back just in time, '– lying beside strangers.' Daniel saw Louise's quick intake of breath and remembered her passionate outburst, but now she said nothing and Clara went on. 'I am afraid that the settlement of the will is going to take a very long time, since communication with St Petersburg is necessarily so slow. Why Papa chose to employ this Nugent Webbe instead of the family lawyer I simply cannot understand. It makes the whole affair so excessively complicated.'

'Your father could scarcely have been expected to foresee such a sudden and tragic death,' said Daniel mildly.

Pulled up short, she gave him a glare before she went on. 'Monsieur de Chaminard has very kindly offered to look after my legal interests for me, but he thinks it will take at least a year, if not longer, and there is nothing I can do until it is finally settled.' She paused and gave Jean-Louis a hunted look. He smiled encouragingly and she went on with an effort. 'In these circumstances I would like to suggest that Louise comes to live with me until it is finally arranged. The house is large enough, heaven knows, and since my dear Miss Motford retired last year I've often felt the need of a young companion.' She turned to Louise. 'What do you say, my dear? It will give you a home while you decide what it is you wish to do, and I've no doubt there are many little things you can do for me just as you did for your own mother.'

Daniel remembered Christine saying that Miss Motford must have been a saint to put up with Clara for so long, and he wondered how Louise would survive such a life. 'I will certainly do my best,' she was saying calmly, 'if that is what you wish,' but he saw how pale she was and how tightly she clenched her hands in her lap. He had a crazy desire to say, 'Don't do it, Louise. You'll be shutting yourself into a prison from which you may never escape.'

Daniel gave Clara a brief account of all that had happened in Russia and it was decided that her carriage should call for Louise and at the same time pick up the large trunk that was still at Wimpole Street. Then it was time to make their farewells, Clara kissing her uncle and sending good wishes to

Aunt Clarissa, who was still down at Bramber. They saw her into her carriage, followed by Jean-Louis, who had seemed to Daniel to have watched the whole proceedings with an air of ironic detachment.

'Well, that's that,' said Lord Warrinder with a sigh of relief, as they returned to the house. 'I only wish I felt happier about it. Stay and lunch with us, Daniel.'

'I'd like to but I mustn't. I have to see my editor and my publisher, and I'm already late for both appointments. Christine is making sure that Robert is fitted out for his first term at Rugby and I have to take him down there myself tomorrow. He will be living away from home for the first time and I want to see him comfortably installed.'

'You're a conscientious father, Daniel. I remember my first term at Harrow: it was sink or swim, and I felt as if I had been abandoned. But boys of that age shake down after a while, you know.'

'Robert is a quiet child, but he feels things deeply.'

'Why are you sending him to Rugby?' said Lord Warrinder, pouring a glass of sherry and handing it to Daniel. 'Why not Harrow, like David?'

'I did consider it. It's what Christine wanted, but I met this Dr Arnold and talked with him. I liked his ideas. They're more progressive. Robert has a foot in two worlds after all, yours and mine, and he has to learn to find a balance between the two.'

'You may be right. He's a clever lad in his quiet way. I've never beaten him at chess yet.'

Daniel laughed. 'It's his latest craze. My God, look at the time. I must go.' He swallowed the sherry and put down his glass. 'Say goodbye to Louise for me.'

He was already half-way along the square when she caught him up, carrying a bulky parcel.

'Lord Warrinder said you left it behind you and it was certain to be important,' she said breathlessly. 'What is it? It's very heavy.'

'It's two-thirds of my new book. My publisher will murder

me if I turn up without it. He tells me it takes his copyist hours to read my handwriting as it is, but he is pressing me so hard, I simply haven't time to recopy it neatly.'

'Why don't you let me do it for you? Papa always used to say I wrote a very good hand. I once had a governess who bullied me so much and made me copy out so many exercises that now I couldn't write badly if I tried.'

'Copying out some hundred and fifty thousand words is a killing occupation. I couldn't possibly burden you with it. You don't know what you would be taking on.'

'I would love to do it for you.'

He knew he should go, but still lingered, looking down at her. 'How do you feel about living with Clara?'

'I don't know,' she said, 'but what is the alternative? I can't go on taking and taking from you and Lord Warrinder. It's not right. I've got to face up to it, stand on my own feet, and she *is* my half-sister. We are tied together in a way, and she does owe me something. Papa did wish it, didn't he? Only . . .'

'Only what, Louise?'

'It's just that I feel so alone, and somehow it frightens me.' She caught her breath in a tiny sob and he dropped the heavy parcel and put his arm around her, drawing her close against him.

'You mustn't feel like that. You're not really alone. We're all still here.'

For a moment she clung to him, her face pressed against his coat, warmed and comforted, but then she pulled herself away. 'Yes, of course, I'm being stupid, aren't I? It's just that I don't know her yet, but I will very soon. I've so much to be thankful for. You won't forget what I said about copying your book, will you?'

'I won't forget.' He desperately wanted to help her, but didn't know how. Suddenly she stood on tiptoe.

'Dear, dear Daniel,' she breathed, and kissed his cheek before she slipped away from him, running back to the house and leaving him shaken. He stood for a moment looking after her, then picked up his parcel, made his way to the main road and took a cab to Fleet Street.

'About time too,' grumbled the editor of the *Daily News*. 'Where the devil have you been for the last couple of hours?'

'What's the hurry?' The pace of life at the lively newspaper offices was always about three times faster than anywhere else, but by this time Daniel had learned to take it in his stride.

'Something has come up in Manchester that's right up your street. A chap on a building-site fell from the roof to the basement and broke his back.'

'Poor devil. Is he dead?'

'Not yet, but it looks pretty bad. He'll never work again, that's for sure, and he has a wife and four kids, all under six. There were no proper safeguards but as usual there will be no compensation, and it's brought up the whole question of a responsible trade union for building workers – and you know what that means. There's a fine old row brewing up there and they'll all be at each other's throats. Take a good look round and write me one of your flaming articles about the injustice.'

'It so happens I'm taking my boy to his first term at Rugby tomorrow, but I can go on from there.'

The editor stared. 'Too much mollycoddling is not good for growing boys, you ought to know about that. All right, all right, I'm not arguing with you, but get up there, Dan, as soon as you can, and do your stuff. You can telegraph it through and we'll keep a space for you.'

He turned to the next item on his agenda and Daniel went on to his publisher in Maiden Lane, thinking that he had begun to grow out of such journalistic assignments and it was now time to look for something more stable and satisfying. If only he could succeed in winning a parliamentary seat at the next election, he would be able to raise important issues with some hope of seeing them brought to a conclusion.

'I've got some good news for you,' said Mr Todd across his crowded desk: 'a damned good offer from the United States for your first book. There's a market for poor-boy-makes-good over there. It should do well.' He pulled out a bundle of script from the parcel Daniel had dumped in front of him. 'My God, your handwriting gets worse and worse. Spare a thought for your copy editor's eyesight!'

'I know. I'm sorry, but I do have other commitments and you've been pushing me so hard there hasn't been time to make a clean copy.'

'Get yourself a decent copyist, there's a good chap. You can afford it by now.'

'Maybe I will.'

They parted on amicable terms, with Mr Todd urging him to get on with the final section and not let the grass grow under his feet.

When he reached Wimpole Street at last, tired and hungry, Christine pounced on him, wanting to know every word of what had happened with Clara that morning. He gave her a brief summary.

'What's this new man of Clara's like?' she asked him, frowning.

'I should say two-thirds Greek pirate and one-third French aristocrat.'

'He sounds stunning.'

'I think in future it will be he who calls the tune and not Clara,' he said drily.

'It'll be for the first time. How is Louise taking it?'

'Putting a good face on it but with a certain dread I think.'

'I'll call on her as soon as she is settled in,' said Christine. 'Make her feel we are still here in case of a crisis.'

'It would be kind of you if you did.'

It was David who took greatest exception to Louise's future, and said so very fiercely that same everning. He came in very late, when dinner had been served and cleared away. The children were in bed, and Isabelle was spending a few days with a friend who had been accepted as a student at Newnham College in Cambridge. The university had at last opened its doors to women, though numbers were very limited. They would not be granted a degree, of course, and were strictly segregated and chaperoned. Isabelle had been badgering her father to allow her to join the selected few in the new year, but he was still very reluctant to send his beloved daughter to a city swarming with hundreds of male undergraduates. For the last few weeks he had been working every evening, sometimes till one or two in the morning, trying to make up for the time lost in Russia. But on this particular evening he was tired after a stressful day and was in the drawing-room with Christine, rereading Thackeray's *Vanity Fair,* which he greatly admired for its unsparing picture of fashionable society, when David burst into the room.

'What's all this I hear about Louise being forced to go and live with Cousin Clara?' he said explosively. 'I never heard of anything so infamous. You know, we all know, what Clara is like. She will make life absolute hell for Louise.'

'Who told you?' asked his mother. 'It was only settled this morning.'

'It was Uncle Harry. He heard it from Grandfather when he called in to see him this afternoon.'

'Did he also tell you that Louise made the decision herself? No one forced her to do anything,' said Daniel drily, looking up from his book. 'In fact your grandfather had already told Louise that she could stay with him and your grandmother indefinitely if she wished, but she would not agree to do so. Clara behaved very kindly and Louise will stay with her at Arlington Street till the matter of her father's will is finally settled.'

'But she doesn't know what Clara is like. You could have stopped her,' insisted David, facing up to Daniel. 'She looks up to you, listens to every word you say. You know what will happen. She'll make Louise pay for every hour that her father rejected her. Cousin Clara can be a cruel, vicious bitch when she feels like it.'

'Don't use language like that in front of your mother,' said Daniel sharply. 'The matter is settled and that's the end of it. There's no more to be said.'

'Sorry, Mamma,' muttered David, 'but when Uncle Harry told me, it made me furious.'

'Aren't you being a little foolish about this, David?' said his mother gently. 'Louise is not a child, you know, she is a very sensible young woman, and she has made up her mind that she wants to be independent and make her own decisions. She is not going to be shut up in prison, you know. She will be visiting us. You can call and see her if you wish. Why not take her to see some of the sights of London, with Clara's permission of course? Louise would enjoy that.'

'Yes, I suppose I could,' muttered David, unconvinced.

'It's very late, dear. Have you had anything to eat this evening?'

'I'm all right. Uncle Harry took me to dine at his club. He says I can settle in at his chambers next week. I've been thinking, Mamma. I'd like to move out of here and share rooms with a couple of the other chaps if it's all right with you.' He was speaking to Christine but shot a quick look at his stepfather.

'If your mother agrees, then go ahead,' said Daniel. 'I have no objection. It's time you were independent. I have to go up north tomorrow for a few days. When I come back, I'll call in and discuss it with Harry. Will that suit you?'

'Yes . . . thanks,' muttered David, expecting opposition and rather at a loss when there wasn't any. 'You do understand, don't you, Mamma?'

'I suppose I must,' said Christine ruefully. 'So long as you don't entirely desert us.'

'Of course I won't. I think if you don't mind I'll go to bed. It's been rather a day,' he went on. 'Good-night, Mamma.'

He gave her a kiss and she watched him go, frowning. 'Daniel, you don't think David is falling in love with Louise, do you?'

'He probably imagines he is, a knight charging to his lady's rescue,' said Daniel ironically. 'You worry about him too much, my dear. He's a man now, not Gareth's baby son.'

Up in his own room, David undressed gloomily, certain that all he had done that evening was to make a fool of himself – and yet he was sure that he had been right. The week he had spent at Bramber with Louise had been idyllic and at the same time frustrating. Alone except for his grandparents, they had spent a good deal of time together, walking, talking, going for long drives around Sussex in the dog-cart. To his great disappointment Louise did not ride and had declined his offer to teach her on one of his grandfather's gentle old hacks.

'I shall never master it in a week, and when shall I ever be able to afford a horse of my own?' she said sadly.

She treated him, he thought, very much as she treated the dogs: friendly and kind, yet the least mention of Daniel and her eyes would light up. *Why?* he asked himself angrily, and yet the more he saw of her, the more she made all other girls seem flat and uninteresting. It was all quite damnably frustrating, and now, if he wanted to see her – which he did, badly – he would have to face up to the abominable Cousin Clara. It was enough to make any man spit!

The cause of all this anxiety was not nearly so composed and resolute as she appeared. She was in fact quite sick with apprehension, and a kind of hopeless longing that something catastrophic – an earthquake perhaps – would effectively stop the carriage arriving to carry her to her half-sister's great house. Louise knew she was being childish but she could not stop shivering whenever she thought of Clara. It was of course completely irrational, but . . . When she was a child of four or five, her father had taken her to the Zoological Gardens in Paris. The elephants, though so enormous, she had loved at once, fearlessly feeding them buns; lions, tigers, even a rhinoceros might have walked out of her nursery Noah's Ark; but the snakes! Walking round their special house with its fetid heat and curious smell, she had seen a cobra raise its hooded head and strike it angrily against the thick glass, and watched a python uncoil itself until with a sick fascination she seemed to feel it wind itself around her own small body and in sheer terror had begun to scream and scream until they carried her out into the fresh cold air. This morning, when she had seen the rich black silk glittering with jet, when she had taken Clara's hand and felt her sister's lips on her cheek, she had been filled with that same unreasoning terror, and it had taken all her self-control not to jerk away.

What a fool she had been to refuse Lord Warrinder's offer to stay with him and Lady Clarissa. At first she had felt a little overawed at the sheer splendour of Bramber and Berkeley Square, so different from the homely atmosphere at Hunter's Lair, but beneath the grandeur there had been a real warmth and kindness and Lady Clarissa, who at first had seemed too much like the embassy wives, with their half-veiled contempt for her, proved to be unusually understanding. She had an endearing habit of losing everything: her book, her spectacles, her vinaigrette, so that Louise had run little errands for her, much as she had done for her own mother. Yet despite all that feeling of welcome, a proud independence had forced her to turn her back on the kindly meant invitation – and for what? She shivered involuntarily as she slipped her nightgown over her head and climbed into the big bed, making a little nest for Toby to lie on his own blanket close beside her, and, as an antidote to fears and grim anticipations for the future, gave herself up to thinking about Daniel.

She was still young enough to escape from gloomy thoughts into fantasies. He would suffer some unspecified calamity and she would be the only one to rescue him, take care of his hurts, watch over his sickness, bring him back to life: all absurd of course and bearing no relation to the real Daniel whose strength had supported her, who had a wife and children and friends to care for him. But somehow, when the future was so dark, it helped to let her imagination run riot, stopped her from dwelling too long on the loss of Mamma and Papa and that dear and happy life that had vanished for ever.

But no catastrophe occurred. Daniel left Robert at Rugby, shivering a little amongst a bunch of unfamiliar faces but bravely waving his father goodbye. Up in Manchester the unlucky labourer had died and his distraught widow, unable to go out to work since the youngest child was only three months old, was forced to sell up their little home with its few treasures and face the horrors of the dreaded workhouse and the grim certainty of the family being torn apart. Daniel wrote a scorching article for the *Daily News* and followed it up with one for his old friend Joe Sharpe at the *Clarion*, had his hand shaken gratefully at the funeral and was marked down by the bosses of the building company as one of those damned rabble-rousers.

He returned to London on the very day when Clara's handsome carriage collected Louise and her luggage and took her to Arlington Street, where she was greeted by Mrs Bolton, the housekeeper, an imposing figure in black bombazine who conducted her to a room on the second floor, just below the servants' attics, and told her that Lady Dorrien was at present visiting friends but would expect Louise to dine with her that evening.

The housekeeper frowned down at Toby. 'I'm sure I don't know what Madam will have to say about a dog. She has never allowed pets of any kind in the house.'

'Toby is very good. I will take care of him myself.'

'Well, we shall have to see, won't we? When you have settled in, perhaps you would care to come to the housekeeper's room, where there will be a cup of tea for you. The men will be bringing up your luggage directly.'

What was she supposed to be? thought Louise. Lady's-maid? Parlourmaid? Companion? It was hardly the welcome extended to a relative, a sister who had the same father as the lady of the house. She felt frozen, within and without. She dropped on the bed, suddenly as wretched and lonely as she had felt on that dreadful day in St Petersburg, before Daniel came and brought her comfort and hope.

The men came sweating up the stairs with her heavy trunk and asked where she wanted it put. When they had gone she pulled herself together and began to look around her. If this was where she was going to live, perhaps for a year or more, then she must accustom herself to it. The room was plainly furnished but not uncomfortable, and probably intended for the personal attendant of some honoured guest. The window looked out on a small town garden where a few late flowers still bloomed. It was a cold day for October and a sharp wind was whipping the branches of the tall lime tree. No fire had been lit and the room was bleak. She had a sudden memory of her arrival at Wimpole Street, the warmth of her welcome, Nanny fussing over her, sharing a meal with Daniel in the room that was so particularly his, and quickly she shut her mind against it. Toby, who had been exploring on his own account, came jumping up at her and she picked him up.

'I don't think you are going to enjoy being here any more than I am,' she murmured ruefully. 'We must comfort one another.'

He was wearing a new red collar. Celia and Robert had put their pocket money together and, with a little help from their father, had bought it for him as a farewell present, together with a medallion engraved with his name and address. 'You've made a mistake,' she had said examining it. 'You've put Wimpole Street.'

'Well,' said Robert seriously. 'It was Papa's idea really. You see, when we ordered it to be done we didn't know where you would be living so we thought if Toby did get lost, and a policeman or some kind person found him, they would bring him to us and we would be sure to know where you were.' And she had laughed and hugged them both.

That first night she dined with Clara, just the two of them at a massive mahogany table that might have seated twenty or more. She felt oppressed by the dark panelled walls, the enormous sideboard loaded with silver and crystal, the deep-red velvet curtains edged with gold braid, fold after fold swathed beneath the handsome gilded pelmet. While they ate, Clara told her what she expected from her.

'Just a few small tasks that dear Miss Motford was always so willing to do for me. I will discuss them with you every morning, one or two necessary business letters, sending out invitations from time to time, and of course replying to them. It will only take a few hours of your time and help to keep you occupied. You write a good hand, I hope.'

'Papa used to say so.'

'Good. I'm not asking too much from you, am I?'

'Of course not. I am very willing to do anything.'

Clara sat back in her chair, frowning a little. 'Mrs Bolton tells me that you have brought a dog with you. I don't care for animals in the house. They are unhealthy. They bring in dirt and fleas.'

'Toby has never had a flea in his life,' said Louise indignantly.

'Maybe not, but I should be grateful if you would keep him in your own room and out of my sight.'

'Yes, of course. I'll make sure he doesn't worry you.'

Afterwards in the drawing-room she poured the coffee when it was brought, placed the cup on a table at Clara's elbow, obediently fetched her a book and some of the latest Parisian magazines and placed an embroidered footstool at her feet, overawed and weighed down by the almost vulgar display of wealth. Small china-cabinets were filled with costly examples of Meissen and Limoges, and many expensive trifles – miniatures, elaborate snuffboxes, valuable *bibelots* of all kinds – were displayed on elegant occasional tables of alabaster and onyx. There were gilded chairs and sofas upholstered in the richest of tapestries. It was all too much, too overwhelming, a display of riches for the sake of it, and she had a longing for the simplicity of Hunter's Lair where everything was of use, where the few beautiful objects were treasured and where the piled-up books were loved and read.

The only object which she looked at with respect and longing was the grand piano, a magnificent instrument, now firmly closed and draped with an elegant embroidered shawl, obviously only for use at Clara's musical soirées. Louise wondered if she dared to ask if she might practise on it.

She was turning over the pages of an elaborately bound volume of German songs and wondering how soon she could decently escape to her own room when Jean-Louis was announced and Clara instantly sprang into life.

'You're late,' she said, rising at once to greet him.

'I know.' He took her hand and kissed her cheek. 'My apologies, *chérie*, I was detained. Your note said you wanted to see me urgently.'

'Yes, I do.' She glanced towards Louise and he turned, seeing her for the first time.

'Ah,' he said with that attractive smile of his. 'So you have arrived at last.'

'This afternoon, Monsieur de Chaminard,' she said and got up, closing the leather-bound book.

'I see you are interested in German *Lieder*. Do you sing and play yourself?'

'A little. Mamma loved many of these songs and sometimes I accompanied her.'

'Then you must give us the benefit of your skill one evening when you have tried out the piano.'

'I cannot think of anything more tedious than spending an evening listening to schoolgirl fingers mishandling my piano,' said Clara, lightly but with an acid undercurrent. 'My dear,' she went on, 'you've had a very tiring day so I am quite sure Jean-Louis will understand if you would like to finish your unpacking.'

'Yes, of course.' She was aware of Jean-Louis watching her with a faint smile, as if the obvious dislike between them amused him. 'Good-night, Clara, good-night, monsieur,' she said and went quickly, Clara's sharp voice following her out of the room as she called Jean-Louis back to her side.

Life in Arlington Street was not going to be easy, thought Louise as she undressed and slipped between the icy sheets. Already she was aware of the dislike, the bitter resentment, and this was only the first evening. Yet there was so much they might have shared, so many memories of their father, so much she would have liked to know about his early days! But she was not going to let herself be disheartened. She was determined to go through with it whatever it cost.

During the months since that dreadful day of grief and loss, her resolution had gradually crystallized. It was not so much the provision for the future which her father had intended to give her but the acknowledgement that she was his daughter, the right to a name she could call her own, that she wanted passionately, as much for her mother's sake as for her own.

Lord Warrinder, Daniel, Christine, had all accepted her generously, but it was only Clara who could set the seal upon that acceptance. To live with her as her acknowledged sister was only the first step. She shivered, pulled the blankets closer around her and tried to face up to what the future months might bring.

Chapter 8

On a bitingly cold mid-December day, Louise pulled a thick woollen shawl around her shoulders as she delved into the huge trunk that had come with her from St Petersburg, part of which was still not yet unpacked. One by one she lifted out her mother's gowns, which she had carefully laid between sheets of tissue paper during that last week and which she had not been able to bring herself to touch till now.

At last she came upon the one she was looking for, an evening dress in black corded silk trimmed with lilac velvet which her mother had worn only once because her father hadn't cared for it. She held it up against her. She and her mother had been much the same height, but it was too big in the waist. She would have to alter it to fit herself. Like many Frenchwomen Marianne Dufour had been clever with her needle and during her early years had often made her own dresses. Although later James Ducane's generosity had enabled her to buy from the most expensive and stylish of dressmakers, she had still insisted on her daughter learning something of her skills.

If only her hands were not so stiff with cold, thought Louise ruefully. An icy bedroom was one of those small acts of spite indulged in by Clara, who knew very well that to escape to her own room was Louise's only refuge from her barbed tongue. Servants tend to follow the whims of their employers and the staff, from Mrs Bolton downwards, treated her with scant courtesy and little respect as a poor relation living on Lady Dorrien's bounty. All the staff, except one.

Ada was a recent recruit, only fifteen years old. Tongue-tied with shyness, she was one degree above the ordinary maids because she had been taught fine needlework and how to care for delicate lace and embroidery, and could therefore act as assistant to the haughty Miss Pye, who was Lady Dorrien's personal maid. Louise had come across her one day, crouched on the stairs to the attics, in helpless tears because she had accidentally scorched a fine lace collar she was ironing. Louise had earned her eternal gratitude by showing her how to remove the scorch mark. After that Ada would sneak up the back stairs during the coldest winter days and put a hot brick wrapped in flannel into Louise's bed, or bring her a cup of boiling cocoa last thing at night before she herself was sent to bed.

Louise slipped off her dress and dived into the rich folds of silk and velvet. She pinned the places where it would need to be taken in and then looked at herself critically in the mirror. The stylish cut, the skirt skilfully draped into the fashionable bustle, the off-the-shoulder neckline softened by folds of lilac velvet made her look older, gave her added dignity and poise.

Louise was only very occasionally invited to join Clara's dinner parties, usually taking the place of some guest who had failed to turn up at the last moment. More often than not she dined off a tray and then was expected to appear in the drawing-room to serve the ladies with tea or coffee, or hand around the refreshments when it was one of Clara's musical parties. She was usually introduced with a deprecating smile as 'Poor dear Papa's little *protégée*, a legacy which, I fear, I must try to honour for his sake.' It never failed to make Louise seethe with hopeless rage. A good many of the guests knew exactly what that meant and would whisper to one another about it, but Russia was a long way off and only a few knew the actual details. Some of those whispers reached Louise's ears and once, when a lady muttered in French something about '*La pauvre petite bâtarde*,' she stopped in front of her and said coolly, 'Perhaps I should tell you, madam, that my first language was French.'

The lady turned bright pink, someone nearby tittered into a lace handkerchief and Clara was furious with Louise, just as she was furious when Jean-Louis spoke to her in French, as he did occasionally for his own amusement. She would willingly have flayed Louise alive when one day he happened to mention a work by Friedrich Schiller which he had not read since a boy and Louise said thoughtlessly, 'I have a copy. Papa and I read it together in German. Would you care to borrow it?'

Jean-Louis troubled her sometimes. She did not know what to make of him. Clara, usually so self-contained, so sure of herself, obviously doted on him and Louise thought that sometimes he purposely showed attention to her simply to make Clara angry and then prove his power over her. Was he her lover or wasn't he? Louise could not be sure, though often enough he would still be there when all the guests had left and she herself had been dismissed to bed. The one thing she did know was that the dinner party to be held in a few days' time was in his honour; she had been commanded for once to be there and she did wonder if it was at his suggestion.

'And for heaven's sake dress yourself suitably,' said Clara irritably. 'Isn't it about time you gave up appearing so ostentatiously in black? It provokes questions I do not care to answer.'

'I loved Mamma and Papa and it's not six months since I lost them,' she said stubbornly. 'It is right that I should mourn for them still.' But the sharp exchange did send her searching through the big trunk.

Along with the black dress she had taken out the casket that held her mother's jewellery. There was not a great deal – Marianne had never been greedy – but there were one or two fine pieces. She took them out one by one, remembering when she had seen her mother wear them. Then slowly she put them back. They were not for her, they belonged to the dead. One day she might have to sell them but not yet. She would wear the diamond earrings her father had given her for her eighteenth birthday, and the gold locket which had come to mean more to her than anything.

During the next few days, while she unpicked and restitched in the few minutes of leisure she had from Clara's constant demands upon her, she thought about the last two months and wondered if after all she had been wise. Perhaps it would have been more sensible to ask Lord Warrinder or Daniel to help her find some work she could do, and a modest lodging where she could live and forget about her father's will and her fight for acknowledgement. Clara seemed to take pleasure in making her life as difficult and unhappy as she could, and all with a feigned concern for her welfare.

There had been Christine's invitation to a little party for Celia's birthday, when Clara had suddenly found it absolutely necessary for Louise to accompany her to a charity concert. 'Write a little note expressing our regrets,' she said blandly.

'Do I have to go with you?' objected Louise. 'I'm not important.'

'My dear, of course you must. Lady Ancaster has asked most particularly for your assistance. It's such a splendid cause and you did so well last time. Send the child a little present and add something from me.' So reluctantly she went and knew that Clara had meant deliberately to slight Christine.

Then David called one day in very good spirits and was shown into the morning room, where she was attending to correspondence with Clara. She was so delighted to see a familiar face that she showed her pleasure only too openly.

'Uncle Harry has given me a day off,' he said gaily, 'and I thought I might take Louise out and show her some of the sights of London. Where would you like to go first, the Tower of London or Westminster Abbey?'

'Oh, the Tower, please. That would be wonderful. I remember Papa telling me how much he had enjoyed being shown all over it when he was a boy.'

'Good. We'll go there first and then, while we're lunching together, we'll decide where you would like to go in the afternoon. Go and put on your bonnet.'

To be free of the house, even only for a day, was so delightful she sprang to her feet. 'It won't take me a minute to get ready,' she said and was brought up short by Clara. 'Just a moment, my dear. David, don't you think you should have asked my permission first? Louise is only eighteen, you know, and she is under my protection. I really don't think it would be quite the thing for so young a girl to spend the whole day with a young man, including lunching in some public restaurant. Of course if you insist I could ask my housekeeper to accompany you. Mrs Bolton would be only too pleased to act as chaperon.'

'Oh no!' exclaimed Louise. 'Oh no! That would spoil everything.'

'Is all that necessary?' said David, facing up boldly to Clara's bland smile. 'I'm not a stranger, you know. We are in fact cousins in a distant sort of way. Mamma doesn't see any reason why Louise and I shouldn't spend the day together. In fact it was she who suggested it.'

'Oh, your mother!' said Clara. 'I'm greatly afraid Christine has learned very free and easy manners from your stepfather that are really not acceptable in good society. I am surprised at the freedom she allows Isabelle working down at that East End clinic and going around everywhere as she does with that penniless young doctor. It must greatly disturb your grandmother. Dear Aunt Clarissa has always acted with so much discretion and good taste.'

'Are you criticizing my mother?' said David dangerously, 'because if you are, I must tell you now I don't like it.'

'I wouldn't dream of it, dear boy. She has her ways and I have mine; but Louise is very young and a foreigner, so she must be guided to the right way of behaviour in English society.'

'Anyone would think I was planning to seduce her,' exclaimed David, his temper flaring up so that Louise quickly intervened.

'Don't let us quarrel about it. It's not that important,' she said. 'Perhaps some other time . . .' She checked his impatient movement. 'Please, David.'

'Oh very well, if you say so,' he muttered, disappointed at the collapse of his high hopes of spending the day with Louise.

'Can we offer you some refreshment, coffee perhaps?' suggested Clara.

'Thank you, no. I had better go.'

'I'll see you out,' said Louise quickly. 'I want to know how everyone is at Wimpole Street.'

'Why do you put up with her?' he said as they went together down the stairs to the front door. 'Why are you letting her make your life miserable? She is, isn't she?'

'Yes, sometimes, but I think I'm proving something to myself,' she said slowly. 'I intend to make her acknowledge that I am her half-sister and just as good as she is, even if Mamma died before she and Papa could be married.'

'Is that so important to you?'

'Yes, it is. I hadn't realized how important until now.'

'I don't like it. Cousin Clara is dangerous. I've always thought so. Mamma told me once that years ago she did her best to ruin Grandfather's career at the Bar. If she'd have lived in the Middle Ages, she would have gone around poisoning her enemies like Lucrezia Borgia.'

She laughed at him then. 'Oh David, don't be so absurd. It sounds more like a melodrama than genteel English society.'

'I'm not joking,' he said earnestly. 'I mean it. Clara would stop at nothing.' He turned to take his hat and coat from the stand where the butler had hung them, then suddenly gripped her shoulders and swung her round to face him. 'I wish you would let *me* take care of you.'

'And how do you propose to do that?' she said teasingly.

'By marrying me of course,' and though he knew it was foolish, he could not stop himself blurting it out like a schoolboy. 'I love you, Louise. I've thought of nothing else since the summer. You do like me, just a little, don't you?'

'Yes, of course, I like you very much, but you're much too young to think of marriage. Whatever would your family say? And what about your career?'

'Sometime soon I'll be called to the Bar and that means a good deal.' He hesitated, then suddenly pulled her close against him and kissed her hard on the mouth.

He had taken her by surprise. She did not struggle but after a moment put her hands against his chest and pushed him firmly away.

'Don't do that.'

'I suppose you'd rather it was Daniel,' he said angrily. 'He matters more to you than anyone.'

'Now you're just being stupid. Of course I like Daniel, why shouldn't I? He was very kind when I needed it most and I shall always be grateful to him.'

'Grateful! Is that what you call it?' he said wildly.

'I don't think you know what you are talking about,' she said coldly. 'I think you had better go. Remember me to your mother and sister,' she went on and turned her back on him, leaving him staring after her as she went up the stairs, knowing he'd behaved like a fool and filled with a mixture of longing, regret and anger. Then he jammed on his hat, slung his coat around his shoulders and slammed the door after him as he ran down the steps and along the street.

In the morning room Clara looked up as Louise came in. 'That young idiot believes he is in love with you.'

'What makes you say that?'

'It is obvious, isn't it? You'd better not encourage him, Louise. His mother may be careless in some respects but she'll look a great deal higher for her beloved son than the penniless bastard of a French singer.'

That stung, as it was meant to do. 'The bastard is also the daughter of an English gentleman, don't forget that, Clara,' she said steadily, 'and in any case the question does not arise. David is far too young to think of such things. Shall we finish the letters?'

If anything the little incident had hardened her resolution. If warfare was what Clara wanted, then she could have it. She had tried to be self-effacing, to accept everything and not argue, but from now on Clara would find she had an opponent who fought back. In the end one of them would have to lose.

Chance played a great part in what happened to Louise on the night of the dinner party. To start with she was late in coming down. Usually on such occasions she had slid into the drawing-room before the guests arrived and, moving quietly among them or keeping unobtrusively in the background, she had always avoided conversation. But since on one occasion Toby had escaped from her bedroom and been found cheerfully trotting from guest to guest, much to Clara's fury, Louise had always taken good care to arrange for Ada to keep an eye on him. That evening, however, the girl was distracted by the turmoil in the kitchen and came panting up the stairs at the last minute to where Louise was impatiently waiting for her. Toby settled, Louise went hurrying down to the hall at exactly the same time as a latecomer was being divested of his hat and coat and, taking this well-dressed young woman to be a fellow-guest, he stood back courteously to let her precede him.

'You're late,' hissed the butler. 'Madam has already been asking for you. In you go.' He opened the door and gave her a push so that, without in the least intending it, she made rather an impressive entrance.

She stood still for a moment, dazzled by the light from the great chandeliers. There was no doubt about it, she looked ravishingly beautiful. Her hair shone like burnished gold while the stark simplicity of the black silk softened by the richness of the lilac velvet seemed to make every other woman look overdressed. In a moment she would have moved away and it would all have been forgotten if it had not been for Jean-Louis. Like everyone else he had been startled and then amused. *The tiger cub is beginning to show her claws*, he thought to himself and walked across to take her hand.

'Ah, there you are, Louise, we wondered what had become of you,' and he led her much against her will to the little group gathered around Clara, whose first shocked reaction had hardened into a strong determination to make the girl pay for her cheek. This was intended to be *her* evening, and now it seemed as if that damned illegitimate brat, spawned by her father on a slut from the theatre, was doing her best to spoil it for her! All this went through her sharp as a needle even while she smiled and made light conversation and wished she had the power to strike Louise dead.

The guests for dinner that evening were very varied, some from the world of finance in which Jean-Louis moved so easily, others from the arts and the theatre. Louise, seated far down the great table, found herself beside the stocky gentleman whom she had seen arriving and who turned out to be Johann von Standen, a German singer of considerable reputation who had very little English indeed. After listening to his stumbling efforts to maintain polite dinner-table conversation, Louise took pity on him.

'Would it help,' she said courteously, 'if we were to speak in German?'

He smiled at her in astonished relief. 'You speak my language?'

'Yes. I lived in Vienna as a child. Papa was attached to the embassy.'

'Ach, so! For a time I studied there. You are also a musician?'

'Not really, I only play the piano a little, but my mother was a singer. She was Madame Dufour.'

'Madame Dufour!' he exclaimed. 'But I heard her sing many times. She was ravishing. But I was told that she died – some terrible tragedy in Russia. Isn't that so?'

'Yes. It was a bomb. My mother and father died together.'

'What a loss for you and for the world of opera!'

A man sitting on the other side of Louise turned to her with lively interest. Despite his impeccable evening dress he had a slightly rakish air, not quite the gentleman perhaps.

'We heard the sad news here in England, of course, but I had not realized that you were the daughter of the late James Ducane.'

'Yes, they were in the carriage together when the bomb was thrown. In another two days they were to have been married in the English church in St Petersburg.'

'What a cruel accident to lose both your parents at one stroke. I take it that you are at present staying with Lady Dorrien.'

'Yes, she is my half-sister.'

'Yes, of course,' he said thoughtfully, and Tom Harper, editor of the *Daily News*, smiled to himself. He had of course already received a guarded account of what had happened from Daniel, who had been careful not to say too much, knowing only too well how the paper might embroider it. But the editor nursed something of a grudge against Clara. She had inherited her father-in-law's share in the newspaper and, though she seldom interfered, she had been known on occasion to criticize his running of the editorial and his encouragement of radical and inflammatory political views. He had been invited this evening for the express purpose of writing up the occasion, and he would of course do so; but he would also take very good care to put in a few interesting comments about the striking young woman whom Lady Dorrien was obviously doing her best to hide away. *Stony-hearted bitch*, he thought to himself, *she's as rich as Croesus and looks to inherit a good deal more when her father's will is proved leaving this girl penniless*. A hint or two, judiciously dropped, would knock her off her high horse.

If Louise had realized to whom she was speaking, she might have been more careful, but she was tired of Clara's attempts to hush up her birth as if it were something shameful. For the first time since she had come to live at Arlington Street, she found it a relief to speak the truth and let people judge her as they would.

There was no doubt at all that the evening had been a great success, she thought later, looking down the candlelit table with the tall épergne loaded with flowers, the glitter of silver and glass. The food had been excellent, the wines even better, and the champagne that had come with the dishes of hothouse grapes and the bowls of nuts was of the choicest vintage. Clara would undoubtedly prove a splendid hostess for the man who sat at her right hand, handsome, elegant, giving an impression of power even in repose and who was now rising to his feet to propose a toast.

'I would ask you, ladies and gentlemen, our very dear

friends, to raise your glasses to our hostess, Clara, Lady Dorrien, who has honoured me with this wonderful farewell evening before I leave England – not for long, I assure you, but I do have commitments elsewhere. Clara, my dear.'

They were all rising then, lifting their glasses, as he took Clara's hand and drew her to her feet beside him. She smiled, she responded to their warmth, she looked radiantly happy, and no one would have guessed at the devastating disappointment in her heart. She had been so sure that this evening he would announce their engagement. He had hinted at it without actually promising anything. She had known him now for just over six months, and had known from the very first that this was the man she wanted as a husband, the man she had waited long years for, but Jean-Louis had been elusive, so close and yet yielding little, and soon he would be gone, promising to return soon, but there was no certainty. The evening she had thought would be the happiest in her life was proving one of the hardest to get through.

Louise, standing like the others, glass in hand, with no knowledge of what was in Clara's heart, saw Jean-Louis slip an arm around her waist and kiss her cheek lightly. She wondered what her father would have thought of this daughter of his and whether he would have come to England as he had promised, bringing her and her mother with him. For a moment the fantasy was too much for her and her eyes filled with tears. To hide them she took a quick gulp of the champagne and choked. The gentlemen either side of her offered their handkerchiefs but she shook her head, excusing herself, trying to laugh.

Then the ladies, led by Clara, left the table and retreated to the drawing-room, congratulating her on the wonderful evening. Louise took the opportunity to race upstairs, make sure Toby was safely tucked into his basket, bathe her eyes in cold water, put a dab of rice powder on her hot cheeks, tidy her hair and then run down again to the drawing-room just as the servants were carrying in the coffee and sweetmeats and they were joined by the gentlemen.

Card tables had already been set up and little groups formed around them, settling down to an evening of whist. Coffee was handed round, liqueurs offered and accepted, and Louise moved among the guests as usual, as unobtrusively as she could. Only this time, instead of passing unnoticed, she felt their eyes upon her, questioning and wondering.

The evening passed very slowly as usual. Louise was asked if she cared to join one whist table, but shook her head, and later she retired to a chair on the other side of the grand piano and took up one of the large leather-bound books of engravings that lay on one of the many tables, thinking regretfully of evenings at the villa, full of music and talk and laughter, of the cosy pleasure of Hunter's Lair, of the quiet dignity and intelligent conversation at Bramber, and longed to escape upstairs to the quiet of her own room and Toby's undemanding company.

Presently one of the nearby tables finished a rubber and broke up. Jean-Louis, strolling to the sideboard for a drink, noticed her sitting alone and examining with every appearance of concentration a fine study of Canterbury Cathedral. He indicated the glass in his hand and said: 'May I pour something for you?'

She shook her head. 'No thank you.'

He came to stand beside her. 'I have been very remiss this evening. I have not told you how very charming you look. Is it in my honour?'

'I am afraid it is nothing very particular. It is an old gown of my mother's which I altered to fit me.'

'Very successfully, if I may say so. It could have been made for you.' He looked over her shoulder. 'I never thought cathedrals were so fascinating.'

'Oh, they are. I have learned a great deal from them.'

He smiled at her gravity. 'So young and so earnest. It seems a pity. Why don't you play us something, Louise? Something beautiful and gentle to soothe the savage heart.'

'Oh, I couldn't. I'm shockingly out of practice.'

'Surely not, with an instrument such as this in the house.'

'I – I don't play it. Clara does not approve.'

He frowned. 'What nonsense. I'll speak to her about it.'

'No, please, don't. It's not important.' She hesitated and then went on. 'Actually I do manage an hour or so occasionally, but only when Clara is out of the house.'

The almost childish confession touched him and he surprised himself by saying impulsively, 'The apartment where I am living in Half Moon Street once belonged to a musician and there is a reasonably good small piano. Would you care to use that?'

She stared at him wide-eyed, wondering if he were a little drunk, trying to understand what could be behind such an outrageous suggestion.

'I would love to but I couldn't possibly do that. It would be most improper.'

'Would it? I don't know why. It stands there completely unused. I am out for most of the day and I could instruct my manservant to let you in whenever you chose to come.'

'You are joking, of course,' she said earnestly. 'I've not been very long in England but I am quite sure that to visit a gentleman's apartment, whether he is there or not, would be quite out of the question.'

'As you wish, of course. I thought only to help you.'

'It's very kind of you, but it is quite impossible.'

Clara's sharp voice broke in on them. 'Jean, we're waiting for you.'

'Coming, my dear.'

Louise hesitated and then put a hand on his arm. 'You won't tell Clara about my practising when she is out?' she whispered.

'Never,' he smiled. 'It shall be our secret.'

To him she still seemed hardly more than a child, a very lovely child in a damnably awkward position. He had made the offer with no ulterior motive but, English society being what it was, maybe she was right and in no time at all someone would find out and they would be calling her his mistress. He shrugged his shoulders and went to join Clara, unaware that she had watched the whole of the little episode with the utmost suspicion and anger, directed not so much against him as against that abominable girl who, not content with doing her best to spoil her evening, was now trying her wiles on Jean-Louis. A scorching pang of jealousy burned through her, making her breathless.

'Are you feeling all right?' he asked with concern. 'The evening is not becoming too much for you?'

'No, of course not.' She forced a smile. 'I'm just a little tired, that's all. What were you saying to Louise?'

'Nothing of importance. I thought the child looked a little lonely.' He smiled. 'You're not jealous, are you?'

'Do I need to be?'

Alone together for a moment, he slipped an arm around her waist and drew her towards him, his lips lightly brushing across her bare shoulder. She trembled at his touch. She had never felt like this about any other man. It was ridiculous. She might have been twenty-two instead of forty-two. She was so deadly afraid of losing him that even to see him glance at another woman was torture.

The party was beginning to break up now. Little debts were being settled at the whist tables; ladies were rising from sofas, shaking out their skirts, looking for vanity bags, yawning a little. 'They will all be going soon,' he said, 'and I must go along with them.'

'You could come back,' she whispered.

'No, *chérie*, it would not be proper.' He smiled. 'Maman would not like it.'

She knew all about his mother, the matriarch, nearing eighty now, who lived in a magnificent house on one of the Greek islands, the only woman in the world whose opinions he respected and valued. She had never interfered with his life, admired the acumen with which he controlled his inheritance and hers, was indulgent towards his pleasures; but when it came to taking a wife, then it would be different. She must be above reproach. He had been married before, many years ago when he was still only learning to control their financial interests. His wife had been very young, much the same age as Louise was now, and had died with her child in a boating accident within two years of their marriage. He had spoken of it once and then never again. Clara had learned very soon that it was a closed book and not to be reopened.

All these thoughts were chasing one another through her mind as her guests came to make their farewells, Tom Harper first, bowing over her hand, thanking her for a wonderful evening, anxious to get away and write his article so that it could be slotted into place as the paper's first edition went to the presses. Then all the others were thanking her until Jean-Louis took her in his arms, kissing her good-night before he went down to the waiting carriage and she could look down at the diamond he had given her, blazing on her hand but not on that all-important finger. He still remained tantalizingly out of her reach and she lay awake most of the night, tormented by a sense of failure.

Louise had expected a few sharp words from Clara since for once she had dared to assert herself, to prove she was not a nonentity living on her half-sister's charity but a person in her own right, but she was totally unprepared for the storm that broke over her head.

Everyone, including the servants, seemed to oversleep the following morning. It was past eleven when, after breakfasting alone, she went along to the morning room to sort through Clara's correspondence as she usually did. The room was chilly on this frosty morning. The fire had only just been lit and she was kneeling on the hearthrug and poking it into a blaze when Clara flung open the door and burst in, still in her dressing-gown, her hair hanging loose around her shoulders, her eyes blazing, one hand clutching the morning copy of the *Daily News*. She brandished it in front of Louise's startled face.

'Have you seen this? Have you? I'll have that wretched editor sacked, I'll have him driven out of the profession. I'll make sure he never works for a reputable paper again!'

Louise put down the poker and stood up. 'I don't know what you're talking about.'

'Don't you? Don't you? I think you do.' She slammed the paper down on the table. 'Read that! Oh, you knew what you were doing all right, didn't you? You made quite sure that wretched Tom Harper knew all about you and your slut of a mother, all about the marriage that never happened, all about my father being laid to rest beside the woman he loved so dearly!' Her voice rose. She seized Louise by the shoulders, shaking her fiercely. 'And where did he obtain that photograph? Where, I say, except from you!'

Shocked and bewildered by the storm of abuse, Louise pulled herself away, picked up the paper and began to read the column on the front page. Tom Harper had done what he had promised. He had devoted two-thirds of it to a glowing description of the distinguished guests, paid tribute to Jean-Louis's achievements, gave a detailed account of Clara's handsome gown of green and gold satin, but then he went on to say what a delightful surprise it had been to meet her half-sister who, like her distinguished linguist of a father, already spoke several languages fluently and had studied the piano under one of the great French masters. The picture that their enterprising photographer had taken that day in the churchyard had been lying in the paper's archives and was now shown to advantage. There she was, just turning from the grave, veil thrown back, sad and beautiful, looking up at Daniel who had his arm protectively around her. It was very effective, very moving, and it maddened Clara.

'But I didn't say all this,' said Louise helplessly. 'It was just dinner-table conversation. The singer, Herr von Standen, spoke scarcely any English so I spoke to him in German. It all started from that. I had no idea who this Mr Harper was.'

'Don't expect me to believe that,' said Clara contemptuously. 'You knew very well and took advantage of it, giving him all your lies.'

'They are *not* lies. I do happen to speak several languages. Papa insisted on it. It was a lifetime passion of his. You ought to know that.'

'How should I know? He never spoke to me of any of these

things,' she said furiously. 'How can I be sure that you are indeed his daughter and not some bastard brat from one of your mother's lovers, foisted upon my foolish, trusting father as his own?'

'How dare you say such wicked things about my mother or about Papa? How *dare* you? They meant everything to one another and to me. It is you who are lying because you're afraid to acknowledge the truth.'

Almost instinctively her hand had gone to the gold locket which she was still wearing that morning, and Clara seized upon it. 'What is that thing you have around your neck? I noticed it last night. What makes it so precious?'

'What has that to do with you?'

'Show it to me.'

'No. Why should I?'

But Clara made a sudden grab at the gold locket, jerking it so roughly that the slender chain broke. She moved quickly away out of Louise's reach. Helplessly the girl watched while Clara opened it. James Ducane's handsome face seemed to turn with infinite love towards the beautiful woman with whom he had lived so happily. For a long moment Clara stared down at it, the hurt and bitterness of years rising within her till it became unbearable. She slammed the locket shut and threw it into the heart of the fire.

'No!' screamed Louise. 'No! How could you?' She pushed past Clara, fell on her knees and thrust her hand into the fire to rescue it. Somehow her fingers caught in the chain and she pulled. By the time she had it in her hands, Clara had gone, slamming the door after her.

The pain of her burned hand was forgotten for a moment as she stared down at the locket, scorched and blackened by the fire and very slightly buckled so that, try as she would, she could no longer open it. She sat there, too shaken and distressed to weep, till the pain of her hand sent her upstairs to plunge it into ice-cold water. She hunted for some soothing ointment and afterwards tied it up with a clean handkerchief while she slowly made up her mind. Somehow she must find a way of having the locket repaired, but how? Where? She knew so little of London and its shops. She could not ask Mrs Bolton or any of the servants. It would be certain to start them gossiping. Then she thought of Christine. She would know.

The quarrel had shaken her more than she realized. She had to get out of the house, walk a little, escape before Clara attacked her again. Outside the day was cold, the garden thick with frost. She shivered but still felt stifled. She pulled on her heavy mantle, put the damaged locket in her small velvet bag, shook her head at Toby, who had jumped up ready to go with her, then crept downstairs, through the hall and out of the front door, thankful that no one had seen her.

Outside the wind was icy but refreshing. She drew a deep breath, glad to be free of the house, and decided to walk instead of looking for a cab. She went down Piccadilly, cut up to Oxford Street and then, worried lest she lost herself, asked a passer-by and was directed through a maze of small, dingy roads that she was assured would take her to Wimpole Street.

She was passing what seemed to be some sort of cheap eating-house when a man lurched out of the doorway and collided with her. He made a grab at one of the hitching-posts along the kerb in order to steady himself and she was suddenly face-to-face with Leo.

It was not possible, it couldn't be Leo, whom she had last seen at the station, Leo who had been condemned to die and then reprieved and exiled to Siberia. And yet it was he, she could not be mistaken even though he was dirty and unshaven, with a long scar down one cheek, shabbily dressed like any young workman, and yet undoubtedly Leo, and she was suddenly frightened. She saw recognition dawn in his eyes, heard him gasp out her name, and then she had broken away from him and was running without looking back, running and running till thankfully she reached the sedate dignity of Wimpole Street, arriving on the doorstep of number 17 breathless and shaken.

Mark, who answered her agitated knock, said apologetically, 'I am afraid Madam is out, miss, and will not be returning till this evening.' But now that she was there, she felt she had to see someone. She asked if Mr Hunter was at home. 'He is but then he isn't, if you know what I mean,' said the butler. 'He most particularly doesn't wish to be disturbed.'

'But it is important, very important,' she urged desperately.

'Well, in that case I could ask him,' he said reluctantly and then was forestalled by Daniel himself opening the door of his study and saying impatiently, 'What the devil is going on? I'm not in to anybody. Didn't I make that clear?' Then his eye fell on Louise. 'Oh Lord, I didn't realize it was you. You'd better come in. It's all right, Mark. I'll look after Miss Louise.'

Once inside the room that had such pleasant memories for her, she felt a huge wave of relief. 'I'm sorry,' Daniel was saying, 'but I do happen to have some very urgent work on hand and the only way to get it done was to shut myself up and refuse to see anybody.'

'I really came to see Christine,' she began tentatively.

'I'm afraid she is spending the day with her mother. Can I help?'

The violent quarrel with Clara, the unexpected shock of seeing Leo, the pain of her scorched hand, all combined to make her feel a little faint. She clutched at the back of a chair to steady herself.

'Are you feeling all right?' he said with concern. 'Can I offer you something – tea, coffee, brandy?'

'I would love a cup of tea.'

'Right. You sit down and I'll give Mark a shout.'

He went out and she sank thankfully into an armchair, closing her eyes for a moment. She was groping in her handbag for a handkerchief when Daniel came back.

'It will be here in a moment. Now tell me what all this is about and what you have done with your hand.'

'Oh, that! It's nothing. I . . . I fell and bruised it, that's all.' Daniel, in his shirtsleeves, with ink-stained fingers, thick brown hair tousled where he had run an impatient hand through it, was so very dear and so wonderfully reassuring that relief and sheer happiness flooded through her. She began to fumble in her small velvet handbag and brought out the gold locket on its broken chain. 'I thought Christine would be able to tell me where I could have this repaired.'

He recognized it at once as he took it from her. 'What happened to it?'

'The chain broke and it fell into the fire.'

'And you burned your hand trying to rescue it? Am I right?'

'Well . . . yes,' she confessed.

'I see.' He thought it sounded a very unlikely story. He too had read Tom Harper's column that morning and it was not difficult to imagine what Clara's reaction might have been, but he said nothing. Mark knocked and came in with a tray of tea and biscuits, putting it down on a small table beside Louise.

'Anything more, sir?'

'No, thank you, Mark.'

The servant went out and Daniel said, 'You pour the tea for both of us while I try to open this.' His fingers were stronger than hers and after a moment he gently forced it open. 'Fortunately it doesn't appear to have affected the portraits at all, see,' and he leaned forward to show it to her. 'I'm quite sure Christine will know of a good jeweller who will straighten it out and remove the scorch marks. Leave it with me and I'll ask her when she comes home this evening.'

'I would be very grateful. I do value it so very much.'

'I know you do. Don't worry. We'll see to it for you and let you know the result.'

He took the cup of tea she had poured for him and smiled at her across it. 'A little different from that delicious brew we drank the afternoon we came from the Gostinny Dvor.'

'I've almost forgotten what it is like to have tea with lemon and no milk.'

'You very nearly converted me. I even persuaded Christine to try it, but we decided you really need one of those delicious Chinese blends to appreciate it.'

She put down her cup with a sigh. 'I mustn't stay too long. I know how busy you are and that I'm wasting your precious time, but something happened on my way here that rather frightened me.'

'Frightened you? In what way?'

'I'm absolutely sure that I saw Leo.'

He frowned. 'Leo? Where was this? Did he see you? Did you speak to him?'

'Not really. He came out of a shop and bumped into me. He looked dirty, dishevelled, not like Leo at all, and yet I knew it was he and I knew that he recognized me and then . . . I don't know why but I was frightened. I couldn't help remembering that last meeting at the station and how he had believed that it was I who had betrayed him to the Okhrana . . . I panicked. I ran all the way here.'

'I see.' He got up and moved away towards the fire, stooping to poke it into a blaze before he turned back to her. 'I hadn't meant to tell you this because I thought you might find it worrying, but now I must. It so happens that a few weeks ago I received a letter from Sir Henry Russell at the embassy. He thought we ought to know that Leo had escaped from the prison camp in Siberia and had probably made his way, God knows how, to Switzerland. It was just possible, he wrote, that his father had taken a hand in it and was now supporting him with money so he could, by now, have reached England. I know through contacts of my own that there are a great many Russian exiles living in London, many of them in dire poverty. It is just possible that Leo is one of them.'

'I feel guilty,' she said. 'He looked so sick, so wretched. I should have stopped, spoken to him, offered him help perhaps.'

'You owe him nothing,' said Daniel vehemently. 'He robbed you of the two people you loved most in the world. Have you forgotten that?'

'No. I could never forget what he did, but, you see, he never intended to hurt *me*. He thought he was running after some impossible ideal.'

'You are a great deal too generous, Louise. If you see him again or feel in any way threatened by him, you must tell me or Lord Warrinder at once. Then if necessary the police can be informed.'

'He must have suffered horribly under the Okhrana. I would not like to see him hunted down here in England,' she said obstinately.

'If he is here, he must have obtained forged papers,' he said thoughtfully. 'If it was known who he was, he would not be welcome here. The Foreign Office might well demand that he be sent back to Russia. We don't know what his purpose is in coming here, so do be on your guard, Louise. If you see him again, tell us at once.'

'I will. I feel better about it now that I've told you. Perhaps I was mistaken. Perhaps it wasn't Leo after all.' She got to her feet. 'Now I must go and leave you to your work. Have you finished your book yet?'

'It's progressing.'

'And then someone like me has to come and waste your time,' she said ruefully.

'Oh, I don't know. A break does you good sometimes. With your nose stuck into it, you can't always see where you are going. Let me have a look at your hand.'

'It's nothing,' she protested.

He gently unwound the handkerchief. 'It's very inflamed. If it blisters badly, you must call a doctor.'

'I will,' she promised.

'Make sure you do.' He put an arm around her shoulders. 'I'll see you out and ask Mark to call a cab for you.'

She leaned against him with a little sigh. 'It's so good to see you again,' she whispered. 'It's been such a long time.'

For the last two months, ever since she had gone to live with Clara, he had done his best to put Louise out of his mind, and had succeeded pretty well. But now quite suddenly the old enchantment was there again. It would be so damnably easy to let it rip for once, and so disastrous. He said almost roughly, 'Come on, let's go,' and at that moment the door was flung open and David burst in.

He took in the picture at once, Louise leaning familiarly against his stepfather's shoulder, read into it more than was there and said coldly, 'I'm sorry. I didn't know you were engaged. I wanted to borrow a couple of books.'

'Go ahead. Take what you like,' said Daniel coolly. 'Louise is just going. She's not feeling all that well. If you're not in too much of a hurry, would you see her back to Arlington Street?'

'Yes, of course.'

He brushed past them towards the bookshelves, selected two volumes and followed them into the hall.

'Mark is calling a cab for you,' said Daniel. 'Goodbye, my dear. Christine will let you know about the locket. Don't fret about it.' He went back into the study and shut the door.

'The cab is waiting, sir,' said Mark, ushering them down the steps.

Silently David handed her into the hansom and then sat beside her, both of them too occupied with their own thoughts to notice the shabbily dressed young man who was leaning against one of the plane trees planted at intervals down the street.

Mark closed the door and presently a serving-girl came up the area steps with a broom and began to sweep dust and leaves across the pavement and into the gutter, very conscious of the man who had by now crossed the road and was leaning against the area railing. She looked up.

'Wot you starin' at?' she said aggressively.

'That girl who went off in the cab – who is she?' He had a funny accent, like some of the pedlars who came down the street from time to time, crying the wares in their big baskets.

' 'Tain't none of your business,' she snapped with a final flourish of her broom.

'She lives here?'

She eyed him doubtfully. 'Don't you go talkin' to strange men now,' Cook had told her over and over, 'you never know what they're after,' and this was a queer sort and no mistake. He wore no hat and his head must have been shaved, because the hair was just beginning to grow all over in a reddish bristle. She was intrigued in spite of herself.

'No, course she don't,' she said scornfully. 'The master brought her back from foreign parts in the summer.'

He felt in the pocket of his shabby jacket, produced some

175

coins and chose one of them as if he were doubtful of its value before he said carefully in his fractured English, 'You know where she lives?'

She tossed her head. 'Course I do. It's in Arlington Street, t'other side of Piccadilly.'

'Arlington Street,' he repeated slowly, as if memorizing it, then he tossed the coin with a lordly gesture at variance with his shabby appearance and walked away.

Cocky devil, she thought, stooping to pick up the shilling that had rolled into the gutter. She pocketed the coin. 'Talk to a foreigner,' Cook was fond of saying, 'and before you can say knife, you'll be whisked off somewhere and never heard of no more!' She decided to keep quiet about it just in case.

Leo walked away, highly pleased with himself. In England for barely a week and by pure chance he had already found out where she lived. Not that he could do anything about it yet, the risks were too great, but he could watch and wait. For the moment that was enough.

In the cab David broke the silence between them. 'What was all that about with Daniel?'

'I actually called to see your mother, but as she was out Daniel asked if there was anything he could do.'

'He told us all this morning that he was far too busy to see anyone – but of course you are not just anyone, are you?'

She turned on him then. 'Why do you dislike your stepfather so much?' she said accusingly.

He was so taken aback he could not think of a ready answer. 'I don't dislike him, we just don't get on,' he said lamely. 'We're too different.'

'I can think of a better reason,' she went on crisply. 'You're jealous because he is kind and generous, and is liked because he thinks of others first and himself last.'

'And you think that is something that I never do?'

'Most of the time you don't. You take everything for granted and don't know how to give. You're so wrapped up in yourself.'

'Well,' he said, baffled and not a little hurt. 'I didn't think you disliked me so much.'

'I don't,' she said exasperated. 'I like you, and Daniel would too if you'd only give him a chance. I just wish you'd take a good look at yourself sometimes.'

Then the cab was pulling up and he was obliged to help her out. By the time he had paid the cabbie, she was already at the top of the steps. 'Louise,' he said following after her, 'please don't run away like that. Won't you stop and talk a little?'

'It's far too cold,' she said, 'and I'm late for luncheon. Clara will be wondering where I am. Thank you for seeing me home,' and she disappeared through the door, shutting it in his face.

God damn it! he said to himself. *How dare she say all that to me! What have I done?* He had half a mind to go up and hammer on the door, except that would probably mean facing up to Clara (which was something he did not relish), and in any case he was due back at chambers. If he were too late, Uncle Harry would want to know the reason why. He shouldn't have let the cab go. Now he would have to walk to Piccadilly and try to pick one up there. *God damn all women!* he said to himself wrathfully as he stormed away up the street.

Chapter 9

A few days before Christmas, Louise was sitting at her bedroom window, looking out on a desolate garden sodden under a thin sleety rain and thinking how different everything had been last year. Then the snow had been thick, a heavy white blanket over the garden and the fields, with the trees shining like silver against a brilliantly blue sky. She had gone skating with Leo on the lake and afterwards they had romped with the dogs in the snow like a couple of children, laughing and chasing one another, carefree and happy without a thought for the future. There had been a party at the villa when they drank champagne to welcome in the new year, filled with hopes and dreams, and now here she was just one year later, wrapped in a thick shawl, alone in a cold and unfriendly house.

Clara had gone to spend the holiday with friends in the south of France, hoping against hope that Jean-Louis would come to her there from his mother's home in Corfu. The house in Arlington Street had been partly shut up, the upper servants given a few days' holiday. Mrs Bolton had gone to spend Christmas with her brother and his wife, and even Ada would be eating goose and plum pudding with her five little brothers and sisters. The only consolation left to Louise was the freedom to come and go as she pleased. She could read, play the piano or take Toby for long lonely walks, with no questions asked. The days since the dinner party had become a fraught battlefield, evenings spent hour after hour in an uneasy silence. At least that was over for the time being.

Christine had written saying that the locket was under repair and would be returned to her soon. Louise knew that if she pleaded loneliness she would be invited to join them, but a stubborn pride kept her silent. She had made a decision to see the year through with her half-sister, and would not run to the Hunters for comfort every time there was a setback.

Later that same day she was in the morning room, trying to coax its particularly sullen fire into a blaze, when she had a visitor. The parlourmaid, whose home was too distant for her to go there and who deeply resented having to stay while others were away on holiday, put her head round the door and said grudgingly, 'A gentleman to see you, miss.' Before she had time to ask who it was, Daniel was there, putting the girl aside, his coat flecked with the sleety snow, his hat in his hand, smiling at her, bringing life and warmth into a day that had seemed comfortless.

'What the devil is going on?' he said cheerfully. 'I thought no one was going to answer the door. The place is like a morgue. What has happened to Cousin Clara?'

Louise had scrambled to her feet, the poker still in her hand, a black smudge on one cheek. 'She's gone to the Riviera with some friends.'

'Has she, by Jove, and given half the staff time off, I presume?'

'Yes, I was just trying to . . .' She moved rather helplessly to put down the poker and he took it out of her hand.

'Oh come on, girl, for heaven's sake, give that thing to me. That's no way to treat a fire.' He threw down his hat, knelt down on the hearthrug and proceeded to show the bad-tempered fire who was master. In a surprisingly short time it began to brighten up. He carefully layered the coal and then stood up. 'There, that's better, isn't it?' he said with satisfaction, wiping his hands on a clean handkerchief, with ruinous results. 'I really called to bring you your locket, all done and as good as new.' He delved into an inner pocket and brought out a small package. 'Christine has already gone off to Bramber with the children to help her mother organize Christmas. It would seem that this year we are to have a family get-together.'

She had already begun to unwrap the packet and exclaimed with pleasure as she lifted out the gold locket. 'It's so good to have it back. I really am tremendously grateful. You must tell me how much it cost.'

'I haven't a notion. You must ask Christine. She dealt with it.' He had already noticed how very pale she looked, the thick shawl wrapped closely around her, the icy touch of the small hands. 'Are you telling me that Clara has gone off, shut up half the house and left you to manage how you can?'

'Oh I don't mind,' she said quickly, 'really I don't. I'd just as soon be on my own. In one way it's a great relief.'

'With those servants who are left having a fine old time in the kitchens and serving you with the leftovers, I'll be bound. It's not good enough,' he said wrathfully. 'Of course you can't stay here like this. You must come to us.'

'No,' she said firmly. 'No, I'm not imposing myself on all of you. It's a family party, you've just said so, and I'm the stranger, the intruder. I am quite sure your wife won't want me there.'

'Don't talk rubbish. Of course she will want you, and I tremble to think what Lord Warrinder would have to say to me if he knew I'd left you here alone to manage on your own.'

'No, Daniel, no. It's kind of you but I must learn to manage my own life. I cannot always be taking and taking. I must look after myself.'

'Plenty of time to do that. Now, don't argue with me, just listen. The family have gone ahead but I am going down on Christmas Eve. I'll call for you and we'll travel down together. God knows Bramber is large enough, and if you feel at any time you can't stand the sight of us any longer, you can go off on your own and read or play the piano if that's what you want.'

'No, Daniel, no, I'm not coming . . .'

'Yes you are,' he went on firmly. 'Be packed and ready by eleven o'clock and bring some pretty clothes with you. This is a time for rejoicing and not for looking back. I'm quite sure your father and mother would agree with me. Now that's settled I really must go. I've all kinds of commissions to do for Christine, bringing you the locket was only one of them. Now remember, eleven o'clock the day after tomorrow, and don't keep me waiting. We mustn't miss the train or we'll be stranded in London.'

'I'll remember,' she said tremulously, 'but I still think . . .'

'No thinking necessary.' He put out a hand, drew her to him and kissed her cheek. 'There, that settles it. Don't come down with me. I'll see myself out.'

In the street the sleet had thickened into snow. He turned up the collar of his heavy coat. Goodness knows what Christine would say to him about it, but the thought of Louise lonely and shivering in that gaunt hostile house was more than he could bear. He strode along towards Piccadilly, mentally going over the list of items he still had to deal with and adding another one – a suitable gift for Louise.

When he had gone she knelt down again on the hearthrug, holding out her hands to the blaze, warmed as much by Daniel's visit as by the heat from the fire. Of course she should have refused his invitation, but the thought of being drawn into that intimate family circle as had happened at Hunter's Lair during the summer had been too irresistible. She was seized with doubts again. Perhaps he had made the suggestion impulsively and was even now regretting it when it was too late. But was it? She could always send a note by one of the servants tomorrow morning saying that after all she had remembered another invitation which she had forgotten, so she obviously couldn't leave London just now – not of course that he would believe it, and in any case she wanted to go. All her good resolutions fled at the thought of seeing Daniel every day, of renewing the shared intimacy that had been theirs. It was all far too tempting.

It was a dismal afternoon, growing dark already. Outside it had stopped snowing and the garden was shrouded in a thin white blanket. She thought she would take Toby for a short walk before the evening meal which, now that Clara was away and the dining-room shut up, was served to her in the morning room.

She went up to her bedroom, dressed herself warmly, put Toby on his lead and let herself out of the front door. Outside the streetlamps had already been lit and stood in pools of yellow gaslight emphasizing the dark shadows between. Almost directly opposite, a man stood on the edge of the amber glow. She had seen him once before, wearing what looked like an old army greatcoat, the collar turned up, his hat pulled down so that it wasn't easy to distinguish his face, yet she was almost certain it was Leo. But if it was he, why did he stand there like that? If he wanted to speak to her he had only to knock and ask for her. If he were in England under an assumed name, he must know that she would never give him away despite what he had done. Perhaps it was not Leo. Perhaps she was only imagining it because of that unexpected meeting on her way to Wimpole Street. Perhaps this was only one of the many vagrants who often wandered through the capital starving and wretched.

She walked briskly down the street, Toby tugging at his strap, and felt the eyes watching her, boring into her back. But when she returned half an hour later, he was gone, the street was quiet and empty and she heaved a sigh of relief. All the same it was that as much as anything which decided her to be packed and ready for Daniel when he came on Christmas Eve. Alone in that great house except for the unfriendly servants, she would have felt horribly vulnerable.

It snowed during that night and all the next day so that it lay heavy on the pavements and she looked out of the train window on to a white world, far too happy to spoil it by any mention of the watcher who might be Leo.

The carriage was at the station to meet them and they arrived at Bramber as the short December day began to draw in. The huge red ball of the sun was sinking behind a frieze of skeletal black trees, and a party consisting of Harry, David,

Isabelle and the two children, with Lord Warrinder giving advice from the shelter of the porch, all in heavy boots and muffled to the eyebrows, was busy putting the finishing touches to a splendid snowman. An ancient top hat was perched at a jaunty angle on its head, two pieces of coal served for eyes, a clay pipe was stuck in the gash of a mouth and a scarlet muffler was wound around its throat. As the carriage came up the drive, they joined hands and began to circle around it, chanting at the tops of their voices, with the dogs joining in and doing their best to trip them up.

'Christmas is coming, the geese are getting fat,
Please to put a penny in the old man's hat.
If you haven't a penny, a ha'penny will do
And if you haven't a ha'penny, God bless you!'

They yelled the last line triumphantly and then stood staring as the carriage slowed up and stopped.

'Good Lord, look who's here!' exclaimed Harry as Daniel jumped down and gave his hand to Louise.

'It's Papa!' screamed Celia, making a rush towards them, 'and Toby too! Goody, goody!' She bestowed a cold wet kiss on Louise and grabbed up the little dog.

Lord Warrinder had come down the steps. 'This is an unexpected pleasure, my dear,' he said kindly, taking both her hands in a warm grasp.

'I've brought Cinderella,' said Daniel, helping Paddy with the luggage. 'She was sitting by the fire with her broom beside her while her sister went to the ball.'

'Then it'll be up to us to provide the fairy godmother, to say nothing of the prince,' said Harry gallantly, coming to kiss Louise's hand.

The only one who made no move towards her was David, not sure whether he was glad or sorry. In this large family party there would be little chance of ever being alone with her. The children were bringing Louise to admire their efforts at snow sculpture. If she noticed him she made no move. He watched for a moment and then walked away.

'Isn't he gorgeous?' said Celia proudly.

'Wonderful. He looks just like Father Frost.'

'Who is Father Frost?' asked Robert, who had a thirst for knowledge.

'Well, I suppose in one way you might call him the Russian Father Christmas. My papa used to tell me that Russian farmers scatter corn over their fields on Christmas Eve saying, "Father Frost, Father Frost, this is for you. Please have a care for our crops." '

'Couldn't we do that?'

'But you haven't any crops.'

'Grandfather's tenants have.'

Christine appeared at the door. 'Who wants tea?' she called. 'Come along in, all of you, it's getting dark.' She took her father's arm. 'You shouldn't be out here in this cold, Papa.' Then her eye fell on Louise, surprise and dismay chasing across her face for a moment before she came down the steps to greet her. 'I had no idea that you would be coming, Louise.'

'Cousin Clara has gone off with friends and left Louise alone, with half the servants given a holiday and the other half on board wages,' said Daniel, a little too quickly. 'I thought she would be happier with us. There's room enough, isn't there?'

'Yes, of course.'

'I – I don't want to upset your arrangements,' began Louise tentatively.

'Don't worry about that. You might have to double up with Isabelle, but you wouldn't mind that, would you?'

'I don't mind anything. It's such a joy to be with you all.'

'Yes, well, come along in then. You must be frozen after that train journey. Bring the bags, Dan. We'll all have some tea and then I'll sort things out,' which she did very satisfactorily, putting Louise in a small room adjacent to Isabelle's up in what had once been the old nursery.

'It's rather a tight fit,' she said apologetically, 'but Isabelle is nearby. Ask her for anything you want.'

'I can't tell you how grateful I am to be here,' stammered Louise.

Christine smiled. 'Then don't try. If we can't share a little pleasure at this time, when can we? We eat very informally this evening so don't worry about changing. Isabelle will call you when it is ready. Now if you'll excuse me I still have a hundred things to see to. Make yourself comfortable.' She hurried away, leaving Louise still faintly worried about her welcome but so grateful to be away from that cheerless great house that she would not let herself fret any more.

'Now Robert is at Rugby, isn't he growing a little too old for this Father Christmas lark?' said Daniel considerably later that night, helping Christine stuff apples, oranges, packets of sweets and other small gifts into two greatly enlarged stockings.

'He'd be very disappointed if Celia had one and he didn't. I think after a term trying to be very grown-up, he's glad to be a little boy again for a few weeks,' said Christine, pushing in a tangerine and beginning to pull the string tight. 'I noticed he had acquired quite a few cuts and bruises but I didn't dare to ask why. He would never have forgiven me.'

'Boys have to grow up and learn to fight their own battles. He'll soon settle down,' said Daniel comfortingly.

'I suppose so.' She sighed. 'I just think it's rather sad.' She tied the string into a bow and eyed the two bulging stockings. 'Thank goodness, they're done. Lord, I'm tired. Mamma was always marvellous at organizing this sort of family gathering, and now she's not up to it, she expects the same perfection from me. It's very exhausting. Hunter's Lair is one thing but here at Bramber you've got to keep up the old traditions in proper style.'

'Poor darling.' Daniel put an arm around her shoulders. 'And now I've made it worse for you by bringing Louise. Are you very angry with me?'

'Knowing you, I'm not really surprised. I should never have asked you to deliver that locket for me.'

'What on earth do you mean by that? Actually I had great difficulty in persuading her to come to us.'

'I'm sure you did, but Louise knows you only too well. You can't resist her lost look, can you?'

185

'Now you're being ridiculous,' began Daniel indignantly, 'it's not like that at all –' but Christine interrupted him.

'Oh forget it. Let's get rid of these stockings or it'll be morning before we've finished.'

They crept along the passage and into the children's rooms, putting the stockings at the foot of each bed and then creeping out again.

'I hope to God they don't wake up at the crack of dawn and start charging around the house,' murmured Christine.

'I'll soon shut them up if they do. Come along, darling, bed for you. God knows why we do it but it's going to be Christmas Day all too soon.'

Despite her very real fatigue Christine lay awake for a while and thought she had been duly punished for being a selfish pig. She had deliberately avoided asking Louise to spend the holiday with them – not that she disliked her, but simply because after the summer she had thought she might well be a disturbing element in their close-knit family group, refusing to admit even to herself that persistent doubt that Daniel liked her far too much. After all, David was already showing signs of being in one of his most aggressive moods, which would be sure to cause trouble. She fell asleep at last with a feeling of gratitude that her brother was here. Harry, with his cheerful temper and good sense, could always be relied upon to act as peacemaker in any family squabble.

For Louise everything about those first few days of the holiday was unalloyed joy: the gracious house; the great hall with its wreaths of holly and ivy; the hissing log fires; the friendly welcome from Lord Warrinder and Lady Clarissa; the way the children accepted her as one of their own, dragging her off almost at once to admire the gigantic fir tree in the drawing-room that they had helped to decorate in scarlet and silver; the bustle of Christmas Eve with a last wrapping of gifts behind closed doors amid laughter and teasing; a lively supper in which even the dogs had their share – it was all so wonderfully different and heart-warming after the dismal chill of Arlington Street and Clara's unconcealed dislike.

When they had all trooped back from church on Christmas morning, it was to find that new guests had joined the party. Christine's sister Margaret, the widowed Lady Ingham, had arrived with her son. John Everard had not particularly wanted to come. It was not that he disliked his grandfather or had anything against Christine and Daniel and his cousins, but they were all so darned intellectual, so often discussed subjects he knew nothing about and played clever-clever games that left him feeling stupid. Like his father, who had died at the Crimea when he was barely three years old, he was far more at home on a horse or walking in the woods with his gun, or chatting with his keepers and tenant farmers, or eating and drinking in the mess with his fellow-officers in the Guards. But he was fond of his mother, who managed his estates admirably when he had to be absent, so he resignedly accompanied her in the carriage that morning while privately making up his mind to disappear after a day or two on the plea of a previous engagement.

He came into the hall a little later than Lady Ingham, having first made quite sure the horses had been properly attended to. He found everyone still standing around, drinking hot mulled wine. It was then he saw Louise for the first time. She was helping Isabelle to refill the silver tankards. She had taken note of what Daniel had suggested, had discarded the dismal black and was wearing a gown of deep red wool trimmed in velvet with a tight-fitting bodice, a full skirt billowing from a tiny waist, cream lace framing her face, her hair shining waves of dark gold in the firelight.

'By Jove, what a stunner!' he muttered to himself. 'Who the devil is she? Where has she sprung from?'

Then she was coming towards him, carrying a brimming tankard of the wine.

'Isabelle says you are her cousin, John Everard,' she said, her faintly foreign accent intriguing him still further. 'I am Louise.'

'Are you living here?' he asked, quite bemused, as he took the cup.

'Oh no, only for Christmas. Do please excuse me but I must continue with my duties.' She gave him a bewitching smile and he watched her move from guest to guest, passing by a scowling David without a glance – by God, he'd have to teach that young whipper-snapper a thing or two! – and then going on to Daniel, with whom she seemed to be on terms of easy familiarity.

Why hasn't anyone told me about her? Where has she come from and what is she doing here? He must ask his mother as soon as he could get hold of her. He took a gulp of the wine, scalded his mouth and discovered that the few days he had been dreading had suddenly become a great deal more inviting.

In the mean time Daniel was introducing Louise to still another guest: a tall rangy man in worn but well-cut tweeds, older than Daniel, she thought, fifty at least, his hair and short beard already grey.

'John Dexter is one of our oldest friends,' Daniel was saying, 'and he can never spare us more than a few days because he is a doctor whose patients always choose the moment he goes on holiday to have a heart attack, or fall into a fit, or get run over, or produce a baby, so that his time off is nearly always cut short.'

'Only too true,' sighed the doctor with a twinkle, 'but this time I may be luckier, since I have a very good stand-in for once.' Shrewd eyes were running over Louise and summing her up medically, a habit of his with nearly everyone he met. *Much too thin, probably doesn't eat enough, lives on her nerves, looks as if a puff of wind would blow her away but tough as old boots, I should say, and I'm very seldom wrong.*

'How's that daughter of mine getting on at your clinic?' asked Daniel.

'Isabelle is a living marvel. Never gets a thing wrong.'

'What does she do there?' asked Louise.

'It's rather what *doesn't* she do! Hands out the drugs, measures doses, rolls the pills for me. I can even leave her to prescribe in simple cases, and she never gets it wrong.'

Daniel smiled. 'It never ceases to rile Christine that years ago she took the same course as her daughter, passed with honours, was awarded the diploma and was never allowed to practise, while Isabelle can now act as your right hand.'

'That's the progress we have made in the last twenty years,' said the doctor drily. 'We have discovered that a woman can have a brain. Isabelle tells me that she would like to become a full-blown doctor now that a medical college for women has been opened up.'

'I know,' said Daniel resignedly, 'she has been badgering me about it for the last six months. First she wanted to go to Cambridge like David, now it's this. What next, I wonder?'

'Are you going to allow it?'

'I don't know, John. It's a long hard course and I'm told the male students make life hell for the girls. It offends their pride, it seems, that young women are allowed to share their examinations and make such a good job of it.'

'She can be very determined,' said Dr Dexter, 'but I shall miss her sorely if she does leave me.'

'Perhaps *I* could come and help you in your clinic,' said Louise suddenly.

'You?' Bushy eyebrows shot up. 'What would a beautiful young lady like you want with work that, I must admit, can be very unpleasant.'

'Isabelle doesn't find it so.'

'Isabelle is different. She grew up with the idea. Christine worked with me for many years, even after the children came. She was out in the Crimea with our medical team and what she learned there was experience to last a lifetime. All that has rubbed off on her daughter.'

'There is one way in which Louise might be able to help,' said Daniel. 'She speaks several languages. Do you still get a number of foreigners at the clinic?'

'Yes, we do, more than ever. Refugees mostly, driven out of their own countries and poor as churchmice. I had a Russian only yesterday, been in some kind of a pub brawl, probably throwing his weight about, and that doesn't go down with the average Cockney. Someone had done their best to carve him up.'

Louise caught her breath suddenly. 'Did he tell you his name?'

'Yes, he did. Igor and something quite unpronounceable. I doubt if it is his real one and I did notice something that struck me as strange. The poor devil had been cruelly flogged within the last few months, I should say, the scars were still obvious and tender on his back. I understand it is actually illegal, though it still occurs in Russian prisons; but not, I would have thought, to the upper classes. This young man had never at any time worked with his hands.'

'Poor fellow,' said Daniel, with a glance at Louise. 'Will he recover?'

'Oh yes, the cuts were unpleasant but superficial, though I did urge him to return from time to time and have them redressed.'

People were beginning to drift away from the hall by now, some of them going to their rooms, others moving to the dining-room, where a light luncheon had been laid out since the Christmas feast would be served at five o'clock to allow the children to take part in it and have their presents distributed afterwards.

'Excuse me, Dr Dexter,' said Louise hurriedly, 'but I did promise Isabelle I would help her make sure everyone has what they want,' and she flitted away.

'It's all a little different from the old days, Daniel,' said the doctor, looking around the great hall fragrant with the scent of the burning logs and the pungent aroma of the mulled wine.

'In actual fact I'd just as soon be spending a few quiet days with Christine and the children, but my father-in-law suggested it and she is very fond of him.'

'Tell me about this girl Louise,' said John Dexter. 'I thought she looked a little disturbed when I mentioned my Russian patient.'

'Yes, well, there is a reason for that. We'll collect something to eat and then I'll tell you all about it. It's just possible we know who this young man is, and if so you may be able to give us some help.'

It seemed to Louise, as she joined Isabelle in the dining-room, that, ever since she had run into Leo and despite the effort she made to put him out of her mind, he kept cropping up, first as the watcher under the trees and now as a patient in the doctor's clinic. She remembered that arrogance so well, and knew that it sprang from his constant need to bolster up his self-esteem. She guessed that the coincidence had struck Daniel too, and felt a wave of relief that she was not alone, that in any desperate need he would be there to give advice and protection.

But this was no time to dwell on gloomy thoughts. Whatever happened during the rest of the holiday, Christmas Day was an unqualified success. Nothing went wrong. No one ate too much, no one got drunk, no one lost their temper, no overtired child burst into passionate tears. Everyone pronounced the dinner to be superb and, after the fruit and the nuts, the pulling of crackers and the donning of funny hats, they all migrated to the drawing-room where the Christmas tree glowed in splendour, the candles lighting the glittering star on the topmost branch where Daniel, at risk of his life, had placed it early that morning.

While the older guests sipped coffee and accepted liqueurs or brandy, the two children were given their orders and began to distribute parcels, with strict instructions not to open or even peep at their own piles till everyone was served.

Since no one had known that she would be there, Louise was overwhelmed by the number of hastily wrapped gifts that began to heap up beside her. Lord Warrinder had come up with the beautifully bound copy of Robert Browning from which he had been reading on the night she first came to Hunter's Lair. Lady Clarissa had glanced through her drawer of treasures and found a pair of delicately scented lilac kid gloves still in their wrapping. There were half a dozen lace-edged handkerchiefs from Isabelle, and the children presented little gaily wrapped packages of sweets and nuts chosen from their own bulging stockings. Christine, hunting rather desperately through her drawers, found an antique cameo brooch;

best of all, Daniel had given her the latest edition of Tennyson's *Idylls of the King* with a note saying that she may have read Pushkin, Ronsard and Schiller but it was now time she was acquainted with the English poets. Then there was a surprise that for sheer unexpectedness nearly moved her to tears.

David had slipped out of the room when the parcel distribution began, and returned with a little bouquet which he dropped lightly in her lap. She picked up the tiny nosegay. He must have gone out into the snow early that morning, hunting through the garden for a few late roses blooming in some sheltered corner. With them he had added a few sprigs of holly and golden ivy, tying it with a ribbon he had begged from Isabelle. She touched the fragile pink petals gently. The last time they had met they had come very near to quarrelling, and yet he had done this. She reached up and impulsively kissed his cheek.

'It's the loveliest thing. I just wish that I could keep it for ever.'

Everyone was now opening parcels and exclaiming with pleasure. The dogs had their share too: Rowley sported a new red collar and Toby was adorned with a huge bow that Celia had tied round his neck. They went scuffling through the piles of coloured paper and gaudy ribbon, hunting for the dropped biscuit or fallen chocolate while Dusty, the labrador, watched with benevolent dignity from his usual place at Lord Warrinder's feet.

Presently, after the servants had come in, clearing the debris and restoring order, the card table was brought out. Lord Warrinder, with his wife, Dr Dexter and Margaret, settled down to a quiet rubber of whist. Robert challenged his father to a game of chess with his splendid new set and gamesboard given him by his grandfather, and with a resigned shrug Daniel gave in. The rest of the party settled for more boisterous games.

John Everard might not shine at charades, or the guessing game where you were called upon to perform some complicated action in the manner of the word, but, ably seconded by

Uncle Harry, he was a wizard at all kinds of amusing card games, and found a special pleasure in instructing Louise, to whom this kind of family fun was totally unfamiliar.

Christine had decided not to take part in anything. The last week had been strenuous and it was heaven to do nothing and watch everyone else busily occupied. There were times when she envied her sister Margaret's peaceful life, where everything seemed to run like clockwork and there were never any sudden shocks or emotional upsets. She had never married again, though Christine knew very well that there were at least two neighbours of hers in Hampshire, worthy well-to-do men, who would have been only too willing to lead her to the altar. 'They're good friends,' she had said comfortably to her sister. 'If I need them I have only to ask and that's enough. No one will ever replace Freddie and I prefer to be responsible for my own affairs. My only real worry is that John Everard has not yet found a suitable wife to provide an heir to Ingham Park.'

Christine sighed. Her own brood were so very different and her life had had its stormy moments. Marrying so far outside her social class had had its share of problems, in spite of Daniel's growing reputation as a writer of distinction. It had been earned in the raffish world of newspapers and literature and was not quite the thing, of course, as envious friends liked to point out. David had been a constant worry, always at odds with his stepfather, and Isabelle, her stay and comfort, was talking of studying for a doctor and had the habit of picking up lame ducks like Alec Rawly. Alec's parents were medical missionaries in Africa and he had no one except an aged grandmother with whom he could spend holidays. He was a nice young man, brilliantly clever, but always in need of comfort and encouragement and lacking in the qualities one would like to see in a prospective husband for one's daughter.

Then there was Louise, in whom Daniel seemed to take so much interest. Christine glanced across at the distant table, where the fun was still fast and furious. John Everard and Louise had their heads very close together while he instructed her how to play. Heaven forbid that *he* should take too much interest. Margaret wouldn't care for that at all. She sighed and stretched herself.

'All the better for your nap?' asked Daniel, smiling at her across the chessboard.

'I wasn't asleep,' she said indignantly, and suddenly knew that she still loved her life. Margaret's quiet, uneventful days would drive her crazy in a week.

Later, when the servants brought in trays of tea and delicious little cakes, Harry said suddenly, 'It seems an age since we were all together like this. When I was a boy, we all sang carols after tea and that German governess used to play the piano – do you remember, Christine? That awful woman who used to rap you over the knuckles for biting your nails, till Papa found out and packed her off.'

'Perhaps I could play for you,' said Louise tentatively. 'I know some of the English ones, Mamma used to sing them.'

'What a marvellous idea. I'll have a look. We've probably still got a book of carols somewhere.'

Harry went to open up the piano and light the candles in the sconces. As he rummaged in the music cabinet, Nanny appeared in the doorway.

'Time you were in bed, Miss Celia. Come along now. It's long past nine.'

'Oh no!' wailed the little girl. 'Oh no, it's Christmas, Mamma. Can't I stay for the carols?'

'It's very late, darling, and you have had a very long day.'

'But this is special. I may stay for the carols, mayn't I, Grandpapa? Tell her. Please!'

'Oh, let the child stay up, Christine,' he said indulgently. 'It's only once a year and she can sleep late tomorrow.'

'Just this once then,' said her mother, nodding to Nanny, who went off frowning at this lapse in discipline.

'Oh, thank you, dear, darling Grandpapa,' crowed Celia, giving him a smacking kiss before dashing off to help her Uncle Harry.

'You spoil her,' said Christine severely. 'You never spoiled us when we were children. Harry and I were terrified of you.'

'Nonsense. I refuse to believe I was such an ogre.'

'You were, you know, but the trouble was that you could be a rather nice ogre,' said Christine affectionately.

'I've found it,' said Harry triumphantly, 'the album and the songbooks. I knew we had them somewhere.' He put the music book on the stand and ushered Louise to the piano stool. 'What shall we start with?'

'What about "I Saw Three Ships Come Sailing in"?' said Daniel. 'We all know that.'

'Right. Ready, everybody? Come on then,' and after a few false starts they were well away.

They followed it with 'Once in David's Royal City', and a great many others. John Everard, who possessed a pleasing light tenor, groped in his memory for the days when he served as a chorister at Eton and sang the first verse of 'O Come all ye Faithful' alone, with the rest joining in the chorus, and they finished with 'The Holly and the Ivy', which was Christine's favourite. When at last they had come to the end and were standing breathless and pleased with themselves, Louise said, 'Do you know the German one – "*Stille Nacht, Heilige Nacht*"? I'm afraid I don't know the English words, but I can play it.'

'I'll sing it with you,' said Harry, whose knowledge of German was far greater than he admitted. 'I got to know it when I was last in Vienna, I think I can just about manage it,' and so they did, very softly and movingly, and the moment proved almost too poignant for Louise, remembering the last time she had sung it with her mother. The tears rolled down her cheeks but she went on playing steadily to the end while the others listened, hushed into silence.

At the end Lord Warrinder said quietly, 'That was quite beautiful, my dear, thank you.'

She sat with head bowed for a moment, unable to speak, and Christine put a hand gently on her shoulder with a sympathetic pressure before the party began to break up.

Robert and Celia were packed off to bed. 'No argument,' said Daniel firmly when they began to protest, 'and no sitting up in bed reading your new books till all hours. Lights out in half an hour. I shall come up and check.'

The servants came in with the drinks table and a tray of tea for the ladies with plates of sandwiches. The gentlemen gathered around while Harry dispensed brandy. Louise refused tea and went from one to the other to say good-night. When she came to Daniel he took her hand, drawing her to him.

'Glad that I persuaded you to come to us?' he said.

'Oh yes, very very glad.' She raised her face to his like a child and he kissed her gently as he might have done Celia. 'Good-night, my dear. Sleep well.'

'She's certainly a beauty,' said Margaret to her sister. 'She'll be breaking a few hearts before she is much older. You're going to lose your David to her if you're not careful.'

'Oh, I hope not. They seem to quarrel whenever they meet. I thought John Everard was making good headway with her.'

'Oh that's Johnnny all over. He likes to charm any personable young woman but he takes it very lightly, and so do they, usually. I only wish he would find the right one and settle down with her. David is different. He's a deep one.'

'I can't see Daniel ever allowing it. For one thing David is only twenty-one and has a very long way to go in the law, and Louise hasn't a penny of her own, poor girl, unless Clara has a change of heart. And I have my doubts about *that* happening. I sometimes wonder what is to become of her.'

The sisters hadn't seen one another for some time and settled down to a cup of tea and a long cosy chat, which there never seemed to have been time for during the day.

In her little room Louise sat on her bed with her gifts strewn about her and looked at the book Daniel had given her. It was a handsome edition, charmingly illustrated. By some accidental quirk of the artist Launcelot – the chief of all Christian knights, the kindest that ever struck with sword, the truest lover and the gentlest – had a distinct look of Daniel, and she was still young and romantic enough to be thrilled by it. She was turning the pages, reading here and there, when someone knocked and Isabelle put her head round the door.

'May I come in?'

Louise shut the book. 'Yes, of course.'

'I just wanted to make sure that you had everything you wanted.' She sat on the bed beside Louise and her eye fell on David's little nosegay, carefully placed in a glass of water on the dressing-table.

'David must think an awful lot of you to have gone to all that trouble,' she said with sisterly frankness. 'It's not like him at all.'

'It surprised me too, because most of the time we seem to be at cross purposes,' said Louise ruefully.

'Oh that's just like David, prickly as a hedgehog but soft as marshmallow inside.'

'I seem to have met only the hedgehog,' said Louise and turned to look at Isabelle. 'Why does he dislike his stepfather so much? You don't, do you?'

'Oh no, we've always been very close, but then I don't remember my real father at all,' went on Isabelle thoughtfully. 'You see, when Daniel first married Mamma he was away for long assignments in foreign countries in connection with his work, and all that time David was very very close to Mamma. I used to feel quite jealous sometimes. Then when Robert was born Daniel decided he wanted to spend more time with us, so although Mamma still loved David very dearly, it was her husband who became the most important person in her life, and I don't think David ever forgave him for that. He was just terribly jealous. Do you understand what I mean?'

'Yes, I think I do. I never thought of it like that,' said Louise slowly.

'It's just one of those family things, I suppose.' Isabelle leaned back on the bed, grinning at her new friend. 'You know, you were a great success with John Everard tonight *and* with Uncle Harry. They went all chivalrous. They never treat *me* like that. Grandmamma says it is because I am far too sensible and men don't like that.'

'But I'm very sensible,' said Louise in protest.

'Yes, but you don't look it. You look beautiful and poetic

and mysterious, as if the wind could whisk you off, like the Lady of Shalott:

> 'Where she weaves by night and day
> A magic web with colours gay
> She has heard a whisper say
> A curse is on her if she stay
> To look down on Camelot!'

Isabelle giggled. 'I had to learn that by heart at school.'

'Oh what utter nonsense,' said Louise indignantly. 'I'm not a bit like that. I'm very down-to-earth. I've had to be.'

'I know you have. I was only teasing. It's lovely having you here. It's like having another sister, someone I can talk to. Celia's a darling but she is still a baby in lots of ways.' She gave a huge yawn. 'I must go. It's terribly late. Aunt Kate is coming soon, she's Daniel's sister. You'll like her. She's an actress and tremendous fun.' She gave Louise a hug and a kiss. 'Goodnight. See you tomorrow.'

In bed, cosily warm and drowsily content, Louise forgot about Leo and the threat that seemed to hang about him. She had a week, seven glorious days, before she had to return to Clara and Arlington Street. The resolve that had taken her there, the intense desire to prove herself as good as Clara, the legitimate daughter acknowledged by the world, had begun to fade. She had grown in confidence, had discovered strengths she did not know she possessed. Here in this house, surrounded by kindness, she was filled with hope, certain that just around the corner there would come a tremendous opportunity, just as it had come to her mother; and she would be strong enough to accept it. At eighteen dreams can be very persuasive and she had not yet learned what her mother had known and what even Clara was being forced to find out: that if you snatch hastily at what you want, then you will certainly have to pay for it in one way or another.

Chapter 10

Kate Hunter arrived on the day that John Everard had at last persuaded Louise to let him teach her how to sit on a horse so that she could join their riding parties.

'You'll never succeed,' said David, finding his cousin's cheerful self-confidence very hard to take. 'I tried last summer and got nowhere.'

'What's the betting, old boy? You probably went the wrong way about it.'

John Everard had a pleasing, outgoing manner that David despised but secretly envied, and maddeningly he was proved right. Horses played a very large part in John Everard's life, and when all the younger members of the house party went walking in the park on Boxing Day, he took Louise round the stables, telling her about his hunting exploits and about the army races he had won. She was a ready listener and he charmed her by the way he spoke to the horses as if they were old friends, persuading her to feed them with carrots from Paddy's store and introducing her to Honey, an elderly mare with liquid brown eyes and a soft nose which nuzzled into her hand.

'I'm not at all afraid of horses,' she told him. 'After all, I used to harness and unharness our pony at the villa, but I never thought of being perched up on his back.'

'Riding Honey will be like sitting in an armchair,' he told her, so confidently that she began to believe him.

The next day the snow had largely cleared and though there had been a frost it was an ideal day to take out the horses.

Early that morning John Everard dug David out of his warm bed and shamed him into accompanying him on a canter through the park. They came back glowing with health and vigour, to an enormous breakfast.

'It's an absolutely ideal day to introduce you to old Honey,' said John Everard, accepting a third cup of coffee from Louise.

'Oh, I don't know.' She hesitated, suddenly faced with an immediate decision. 'I haven't got the right clothes.'

'Isabelle will lend them to you, won't you?' he went on to his cousin.

'Yes, of course I will. Oh go on, Louise,' urged Isabelle, 'don't be a coward. It will be fun, you'll enjoy it.'

'Don't force her into doing something that she really doesn't want to do,' said Daniel, who didn't altogether like the idea and thought John Everard was pushing too hard.

'But she does want to, Papa,' urged Isabelle. 'It's like learning to swim. You shiver on the brink, then when you plunge in, it's marvellous.'

'That's the spirit,' said John Everard. 'Let's say twelve o'clock, and I'll ask Paddy to have the horses saddled and in the paddock.'

Louise looked at the young faces smiling at her and said lamely, 'I shall probably fall off.'

'Well, if you do, we shall be there to pick you up. It's all settled. Twelve o'clock,' said John Everard bracingly. 'I'll be waiting for you.'

'I must be crazy to do this,' said Louise as she went upstairs with Isabelle to try on the riding-habit. 'I shall only make a fool of myself.'

'No you won't. It's not a bit difficult, really it isn't.'

'It's all very well for you to say that, you've ridden since you were a baby.'

'Lots of people take it up when they are grown-up. Daniel never sat on a horse till he was twenty-five, and that was when he was in the Army and he was forced into it with absolutely no experience at all. He told us about it. It was get on with it or be killed.'

'Don't terrify me before I start.' But now the decision was taken, she had to go through with it or look very foolish indeed, and she couldn't endure that. Better to break her neck in the attempt.

The riding-habit was Isabelle's second-best, which she had really grown out of, and it fitted Louise very well, even to the boots.

'You look gorgeous,' said Isabelle generously; 'you've just the figure for it.'

'I won't look so gorgeous when I end up with my face in the mud.'

'You won't fall, Honey won't let you. Come on, John Everard doesn't like to be kept waiting.'

They made their way through the park to the paddock, collecting Daniel, Harry and Lord Warrinder on the way, much to Louise's dismay. She would have greatly preferred to make an idiot of herself in private.

'What on earth is going on in the paddock?' said Kate Hunter some time later, alighting from the station cab and going up the steps to greet Christine while her companion collected their baggage and paid the driver. 'George and I heard screams of laughter as we came up the drive.'

'It's John Everard teaching Louise how to ride,' said Christine. 'Why didn't you let us know when you were coming? We'd have sent the carriage to meet you.'

'George didn't know when he could get away. Who is Louise?'

'It's a long story. I'll tell you later. I was just going down to see how they were getting on.'

'We'll come with you.'

'If you're sure you won't be too cold after your journey?'

'Not in the least. Leave the baggage, George, let's go and join in the fun.'

Down at the paddock things had been going swimmingly. After the first terrifying walk around the field with John Everard leading Honey, when it seemed a frighteningly long way to the ground, Louise found to her surprise that it was far easier than she had imagined. He was very patient with his instructions, not rushing her, explaining everything, as he did with new recruits who sometimes scarcely seemed to know the front of a horse from its backside, and by the time Christine and the newcomers had arrived on the scene Louise was gradually learning how to fall into the rhythm of the horse's step instead of bouncing up and down like a sack of potatoes.

The spectators leaning on the white rail of the paddock, who now included Dr Dexter and David, gave her a round of applause when she pulled up flushed and excited.

'I think that's enough for one morning,' said John Everard, 'mustn't overdo it, you know.' He lifted her to the ground. 'You're a natural, took to it like a duck to water, not like some of the poor wretches I have to deal with.'

'Bravo,' said Christine, 'we'll have you riding to hounds in no time at all. Now come along, my dear, and meet Kate and George.'

Louise hardly knew what she had expected. An actress, Isabelle had said, and she had imagined someone like the players she used to meet at their theatrical parties, someone a little overblown, a little too loud, overdressed, nothing at all like this slim elegant figure in dark-green velvet, the face beneath the fashionable hat not beautiful but striking, a face you would not soon forget. Then there was her companion, introduced as George Westcott, a big man looking even bulkier in his heavy coat with its astrakhan collar, older than Kate, already grey-haired. She wondered exactly who he was.

Then they were walking back to the house, Daniel arm in arm with his sister, followed by Christine, John Everard and the others, all talking horses. David, who had been watching from a distance, fell into step beside Louise. 'How do you feel after all that?'

'Wonderful. A little stiff. Isabelle says that will be worse tomorrow, but I don't mind. It's been a marvellous morning. I thought I'd be terrified and I wasn't. Isn't that strange?'

He thought he'd never seen her looking so happy, so

radiant. 'I would have taught you last summer, don't you remember? But you refused. You wouldn't let me help you.'

'Last summer it was different. Everything here was so new to me, so strange. Now I think I'm beginning to live again, to know where I am going.'

'Oh yes, of course, it's very different now, isn't it? After all, who was I? A nobody, while John Everard is Sir John Ingham of Ingham Park. It makes all the difference in the world, doesn't it?'

She frowned. 'What do you mean by that? I never even thought of such a thing.'

'Didn't you? I thought it was pretty obvious. You've gone a long way in three days, but don't imagine you'll have it all that easy. Aunt Margaret will have a great deal to say when it comes to John Everard choosing a wife.'

'That's the most hateful thing I've ever heard you say to me. I like John Everard very much. Why shouldn't I? He's friendly, he's good fun, I think he likes me and that's the end of it. It's vile of you to suggest anything else. I thought we were good friends, but I'm beginning to know better now,' and she walked quickly away from him.

'Don't go, Louise, please don't go,' said David, hurrying to keep up with her, realizing that in a fit of jealousy he had gone too far and already regretting it. 'I didn't mean –'

'I know exactly what you meant,' said Louise icily, 'and I don't want to hear any more.' She hastened her steps, all the more hurt because, despite his difficult moods, she had always felt drawn to David. If only fleetingly, he had been part of that old world that had gone for ever.

She joined John Everard, and David saw how they laughed and talked together, deliberately shutting him out. He knew he had been unjust but he had hoped for so much from these days together, and instead she was further away from him than ever. To hell with the whole damned lot of them! He turned away into the park, taking a path at random, not caring where he went so long as he could be alone.

During the next couple of days it seemed to Louise as if

everything at Bramber revolved around Kate. It was not that she pushed herself forward in any way, but there was something compelling in her personality and unconsciously it was felt by everyone. She had just returned from a short season in the United States, playing opposite the distinguished American actor Edwin Booth, and they badgered her with questions about it.

'I couldn't believe it when I was approached to play opposite his Hamlet and Macbeth,' she told them. 'English actors have always been hated in New York. Macready was booed out of the theatre and had to run for his life, while they tore poor Edmund Kean to shreds. It was a daunting prospect, but George said it was a challenge and I ought to take it up or I would regret it for the rest of my life. And so, to please him, I said yes.'

'And had them all eating out of your hand in no time,' said Daniel.

'Don't you believe it! Their theatre critics are a good deal tougher than ours,' she went on with a grimace. 'They wrote that I looked too young to be Hamlet's mother and not old enough for Lady Macbeth, but they positively drooled over Portia in *The Merchant of Venice*. I was warned that outside the big cities audiences were quite capable of tearing up the seating and hurling it on to the stage – and someone did throw a knife, but luckily it missed Booth. The worst we had to suffer was being mobbed by dozens of women at the stage door who all adored Edwin, and then being invited to teas and suppers and receptions where we were expected to smile and chat and drink endless gallons of coffee and eat cookies and pumpkin pie, and all after a gruelling performance. I've been on a strict diet ever since I came home, haven't I, George? He has to put up with it, poor darling.'

When she opened her baggage there were gifts for all the family, and she delighted Robert and Celia with two Indian jerkins in soft doeskin fringed and decorated with beads and with feathered headdresses to match. The children were enchanted with them and proceeded to drive everyone mad by leaping out of dark corners with a wild Indian war-whoop until they startled Nanny so much she fell down a flight of stairs, and Daniel put a stop to it. 'In the garden only or I shall take it all away from you,' he threatened, 'and anyone racing around the house or uttering a single war-cry will have his ears boxed. Understand? I mean it.'

'Yes, Papa,' they mumbled, not a little crestfallen.

'Good. Now off with you. I don't want to hear another sound.'

'Not that he would ever touch them,' said Christine under her breath to Kate. 'Daniel has never raised his hand against any of the children, no matter how provoking. He reasons with them instead, and mostly it works.' Her remark was to make what happened a day or so later especially alarming.

Louise was fascinated by Kate and intensely curious to know who George was and what part he played in her life. No one explained, and he himself, though perfectly friendly, really said very little. Curiosity got the better of her and that evening, when Isabelle looked in to say good-night, Louise pulled her into the room and shut the door. 'Don't tell me if you don't want to, but I'd so much like to know more about Kate. I've never met anyone quite like her, and who is George? Is he her husband, her lover or her theatrical manager?'

Isabelle laughed. 'Perhaps a little of all three. George Westcott is actually a solicitor in a very old firm of lawyers. They manage all Grandfather's business affairs and ours too, I suppose.' She dropped down on the hearthrug and spread her hands towards the fire, all ready for a long cosy chat. 'As for what he is to Kate – well, I only know what Mamma has told me. It goes back a very long way, before even she was married.' She looked at Louise thoughtfully. 'In a way perhaps you ought to know about it, because Cousin Clara played an important part in it.'

'Clara!' exclaimed Louise, coming to sit beside Isabelle on the rug. 'I've never heard her mention Kate.'

'No, she wouldn't. She hated her, probably still does.'

'But why? What happened?'

'Well, I suppose it all started when Kate was about your age. She was not famous like she is now, but just a struggling young actress. Cousin Clara had just married Raymond Dorrien, the son of Lord Dorrien and very, very rich. He was also what Uncle Harry would call "no end of a bounder" and he was simply crazy about Kate.'

'Even though he was married?'

'Oh yes, he was the kind who wouldn't let that make any difference; only, you see, Kate detested him. She returned all the gifts and flowers he sent to her and in the end it made him so mad that he decided to break into her lodgings so that he would be there when she returned. Then he could lock the door and do just what he liked with her, if you understand what I mean.'

'What happened?'

'Well, when poor Kate did return that night, she found him lying dead on the floor with blood everywhere.'

Louise shivered. 'How ghastly. What did she do?'

'The police were called of course, and they didn't believe Kate's story. She was accused of his murder and shut up in Newgate for weeks and weeks while Daniel tried desperately hard to find out what had really happened. Grandfather, who was an acting QC then and quite famous, took up her case and defended her.'

'How did he really die?'

'Well, it all came out at the trial of course. It seemed that he had employed two villains to break into the lodgings for him. There was an argument over what he had agreed to pay them. There was a violent quarrel and one of them struck him with a knife. When they realized what they'd done they bolted, but the knife had severed an artery. He was unable to help himself and slowly bled to death. Grandfather won his case of course, and Kate was released.'

They were both of them staring into the fire, a little shaken by the horrific story, then Isabelle went on thoughtfully:

'It must have been dreadful for Clara to be left a widow when she was so young, and after little more than a year of marriage, and in such frightful circumstances. Mamma said she was very bitter. She blamed Kate for everything and never really forgave Grandfather for saving her from the gallows.'

'Where did George come in?'

'At that time he was a junior member of his father's firm and worked along with Grandfather on the case, and in the course of it he fell in love with her.'

'Why didn't he marry her?'

'He would have done, but it was Kate who refused because she wanted to continue with her career as an actress. She found out that George's father was a very strict churchman and would never have forgiven his son for marrying into the theatre, and she knew how George loved and respected him, so there was a kind of compromise.'

'Do they live together?'

'Not exactly. Kate has her own little house in Chelsea and George still lives with his father, who is now nearly ninety, but he does spend a lot of time with Kate.'

'It's like my father and mother,' said Louise slowly. 'You see, Mamma wouldn't marry Father for years and years because of his position at the embassy,' and she wondered if it was that very fact that had seemed to draw her to Kate.

'We all know, of course,' said Isabelle, 'but we don't talk about it. It's just accepted, though lots of people think it shocking. Grandmamma does, as a matter of fact, but she puts up with it as she doesn't want to upset Grandpapa, who has always been very fond of Kate. In the theatrical world liaisons like that are quite common, and nobody thinks any the worse of them for it, but it would be quite different for Cousin Clara. She moves in the very highest society and doesn't approve at all. She doesn't really approve of Daniel either, or of the way we live, not that we care very much. Cousin Clara is a cross that we just have to bear.'

'I rather gathered that,' said Louise ruefully. 'Thank you for telling me all this, it does help me to understand. What a wonderful person Kate must be to go through so much, become a famous actress and yet still remain so warm, so friendly.'

'I know what you mean. When I think of someone like her, it makes me feel very small and useless. I have had all the advantages she never had and I have achieved absolutely nothing.'

'But you have!' exclaimed Louise. 'You should hear what Dr Dexter says about you. It is I who should be envious. Do you really want to be a doctor? The very thought terrifies me.'

'It's odd,' went on Isabelle, 'but everyone thought it would be David who would want to take up our father's profession, but he hated everything to do with sickness while I've always been fascinated, ever since Mamma used to take me with her to the clinic when I was a child. At the moment Daniel won't let me go to medical college. He thinks I will find the courses and the prejudice against women too hard, but I won't, you know, and I shall wear him down in time, you see.' She scrambled to her feet, smiling down at Louise. 'Don't get me started on my favourite hobby-horse or I shall go on till morning. I'm going to be strong and say good-night.' She bent down, dropped a kiss on Louise's cheek and slid quietly from the room.

Left alone, still sitting on the hearthrug and staring thoughtfully into the fire, Louise wondered if the grief and bitterness Clara must have suffered as a young woman helped to explain the violent rage against the father who had neglected her for another love. Did it also explain her obsession with Jean-Louis and her dread of losing him? She got up and sighed. Only a few more days and then back to Arlington Street. Only now she felt different about it somehow, as if, hidden behind Clara's armour, she might perhaps find a glimmer of understanding.

Kate was equally curious about Louise. Christine had told her the bare facts, but said very little about Daniel's involvement except that he had been obliged to spend several weeks in St Petersburg and had accompanied Louise on the long journey to England and then to Hunter's Lair. But Kate, who knew her brother and his wife so well, wondered how much

Christine had deliberately held back. She remembered too how she had felt at eighteen: the insecurity, the fear of what the future might bring, the feeling of being different from others. There had been moments when it seemed that only Daniel had stood between her and utter despair, and she wondered if the same thing had happened to Louise and if it explained the intimacy she had sensed between them, even in the first few days she had been at Bramber. She could not help a certain sympathy for a girl striving to find a place for herself in an unfamiliar world.

She had guessed that David, who had always been a favourite of hers, was going through the pangs of unrequited love and was infuriated by John Everard, who took these things very lightly indeed and was indulging in a flirtation with Louise that both of them seemed to enjoy. It was the kind of thing all young men went through at some time or another and she did not think it would last. What was far more worrying was David's antagonism towards his stepfather. Before she went to America she had thought he had outgrown that adolescent jealousy, but now it was back again, apparent in a number of small ways, perhaps not obvious to those who did not know them well, but she knew that Daniel was keeping his temper with difficulty, chiefly for Christine's sake.

David was particularly objectionable one morning at breakfast. He was sitting at the long table with John Everard while Daniel was at the far end, and Kate did not think anyone had noticed her as she came in and went to the sideboard to pour herself some coffee. The two young men had spread a newspaper between them and were reading aloud extracts from the first of Daniel's articles on the appalling number of prostitutes who thronged the Haymarket and the neighbourhood of Leicester Square night after night, illustrating it with vivid case histories and emphasizing the fact that the authorities did little or nothing to prevent the hideous exploitation of children, boys as well as girls, as young as ten or eleven. It was bold, it was factual and it was written with passion, ripping open what lay beneath the smug hypocrisy of society. On Joe

Sharpe's advice Daniel had not signed it with his own name and it was printed under a pseudonym.

The editor had given it a prominent position in his *Northern Clarion* and a copy had been dispatched to Daniel in London and sent on to him at Bramber, where it had been picked up by John Everard before he could take it away.

'By God,' said the young man admiringly, 'the fellow who wrote all this knows his onions all right. It's a crying scandal, has been for years, and he fair lays about him with a cudgel. Whoever he is, he'll have all the pimps and brothel keepers coming after him with a hatchet if he's not very careful.'

'You know who wrote it, don't you?' murmured David, with a glance at Daniel, who was finishing his breakfast in silence.

'Haven't a notion, but the chap's got guts, I'll say that for him.'

'Oh yes, he's got guts all right,' said David. 'Don't you agree, Daniel? How many nights do you think it took him to find out all those spicy details? I wonder if his wife knew what he was up to.'

'Oddly enough, you don't necessarily have to sleep with a woman to discover the truth about her,' said Daniel, putting down his coffee cup. 'There are other ways. Do you mind?' He took the paper from them, folded it deliberately and went out of the room.

'You don't mean that *he* wrote it?' exclaimed John Everard as the door closed. 'Not Uncle Daniel!' David shrugged his shoulders. 'Well, if that doesn't take the biscuit! Good for him, I say.'

Then Kate brought her coffee to the table. The two young men looked startled, bade her good-morning and then hastily excused themselves as they went off together.

She told Harry about it later that morning when they went for a stroll in the garden. They were old friends. She had known him when she was still only a young girl trying to make a living as a singer in the Supper Rooms on the Mile End Road, where a lively programme of songs, comic sketches, pretty girls and a touch of bawdy drew all the young bloods who were down from university. For a few months she had believed herself in love with him, till their brief romance came to an abrupt end when his father packed him off to Paris to continue his law studies, but their friendship had survived the years.

'If David goes trumpeting it all over town that Daniel is the author of those articles, it could mean trouble for him, couldn't it?'

'Possibly, but Daniel is not unaccustomed to controversy. He'll not let it disturb him particularly. He's weathered storms before now. If he has a cause in hand that he believes in, he'll not give it up quickly.'

'Why does David do these things to him, Harry?'

'Jealousy, my dear, the little green-eyed god. He feels he can't measure up to him, and also he can't endure the plain fact that Louise adores Daniel; she's made it very obvious ever since he brought her back from Russia and makes it quite clear that beside him David doesn't stand a chance.'

'But surely that's all nonsense.'

'Maybe, but I bet I am right.'

'And what does Daniel feel about her?'

'You know Dan, Kate, better than any of us. He has always had great compassion for anyone in trouble, and it must have been hell for that poor girl, more or less abandoned among strangers. Small wonder that she clung to him, and still does, and he wouldn't be human if he didn't feel a little flattered.'

'How do you mean?'

'It's very pleasant when you're just past forty and feel on the downward path, to find that a beautiful young girl believes you to be God's gift.'

'No more than that?'

'Not yet, but it could be, and I think Christine senses it.'

'She couldn't believe that Daniel is in love with Louise!' said Kate incredulously. 'She's even younger than Isabelle.'

'It does happen, you know, and I think it is in Christine's mind. You're very close to him, Kate, talk to him about it.'

'Oh I couldn't. It's too . . . too tenuous. I would be putting into words what perhaps isn't there. But I might be able to talk to Louise. It won't be easy. I can't just go blundering in. I'll have to find an opportunity.' She smiled and took his arm. 'Sometimes I'm grateful that I've outgrown all the agony of falling in love. George is such a safe, solid, reassuring companion.'

'Is that all he is?'

'Isn't it enough?'

'Do you love him, Kate? I've often wondered.'

'It's grown with the years,' she said thoughtfully. 'At first it was mainly gratitude. After the horror of the trial, I was simply grateful for his kindness, his protection. But now it has become far more than that and I couldn't live without him. We are parted for months sometimes when I go away on tour, but when I come back nothing is changed. He is still there and it's infinitely comforting. What about you, Harry? Isn't it about time you found someone for yourself?'

'To comfort me in my declining years, do you mean?' He smiled. 'I've never yet found anyone who measured up to you.'

'What nonsense! There must be dozens of lovely girls who would be only too glad to make you happy if you would let them, and provide you with an heir to Bramber one day.'

'Heaven forbid. I shall be quite happy to see David step into my shoes when the time comes.' They walked on together in a companionable silence.

Then Harry said suddenly, 'You wouldn't consider ditching George and coming to me?'

She stopped dead and stared at him. 'Harry, have you completely lost your wits or is this a joke?'

'It's not senile dementia just yet, but it is not a joke. I knew it was useless. I just thought I'd ask.'

She took his arm again and they walked on. 'Dear Harry, I'm so very fond of you.'

'I know, and it wouldn't work at all, would it? Just as it didn't all those years ago. Oh come on, let's go in. I'm freezing and in dire need of something very hot with a dollop of brandy in it.'

*

They had an impromptu concert that evening, which started because Lady Clarissa wanted to know why her two younger grandchildren couldn't do something to entertain their elders before they were whisked away for nursery supper.

'When I was your age,' she said severely, 'I had to earn my supper.'

'That's a lie if ever there was one,' muttered Harry under his breath.

'And don't you be impertinent,' she snapped at him, as if he were four years old instead of forty.

Celia, who never suffered from shyness and had a very proper opinion of her own ability, came up with a spirited rendering of Blake's poem 'Tyger! Tyger! burning bright/In the forests of the night' which her class had all learned by heart last term. Daniel wondered if she had the slightest idea what it meant, but comforted himself with the thought that lines learned in childhood often came back later in life when they were most needed – just as certain passages in the Bible drummed into him at the Methodist chapel sometimes had an uncomfortable way of reminding him of what he would have preferred to forget. Celia curtsied to a round of applause and ran to him for his approval. He smiled down at her, rumpling her hair.

Robert was more difficult to persuade. He had been learning to play the flute for two years now, but when pressed he turned red as a beetroot and shook his head violently.

'But you played your piece beautifully at the school concert in the summer,' said his mother encouragingly.

'That was different,' he muttered. 'I didn't really know anyone in the front row except Papa, and he sat where I couldn't see him.'

'Suppose we all bury our heads in the sand like ostriches,' said Harry, 'will that do?'

It was Louise who came to his rescue. 'I heard you practising. It's Schubert, isn't it? Suppose I accompany you on the piano. Then there will be two of us being brave together.'

So he was persuaded, did very well and was immensely

gratified when Kate very softly sang the last verse of the old song:

> 'Come then to me and close the door
> And never never leave me more
> Chase every pain from out this breast
> Calming the heart to joyful rest.'

Kate, watching how the children obediently went from one to the other of the guests to say good-night, and how they clung to their father before he passed them over to Nanny, thought fiercely that nothing must be allowed to destroy the happiness of this family, not if she could do anything to prevent it.

If anyone had told John Everard that he would thoroughly enjoy days of such simple family pleasures, he would never have believed them, but to his surprise he did. There was something very delightful about the company of a lovely young woman who listened to his tales, smiled at him bewitchingly and made him feel a hell of a fine fellow, so that when they came back to the drawing-room after dinner he let himself be persuaded to sing a couple of sentimental songs and was then prepared to sit and listen through the rest of the evening, which at other times he would have dreaded.

Louise was of course asked to play, and she chose Mozart and one of Chopin's loveliest ballades. He looked at her, face bent a little over the keys, lit by the candles in their sconces, and wondered what his mother would say if he suggested making her mistress of Ingham Park. Of course there was that business about her father and an opera singer, but Russia was a damned long way away and if anyone did face him with it he could always knock them down, so he sat and thought about it in a hazy sort of way.

On the other side of the room David was in a very different frame of mind. That evening Louise had chosen to put on the white dress she had been wearing the first night they had met, that magical moment in the garden of the villa. He had never forgotten it and nothing had happened since to come anywhere near it. They had seemed so close for those few hours, but then he had gone away, that damned bomb had wrecked her life and it was Daniel, blast him, who had stepped in his way, Daniel who was married to his mother and had absolutely no right to any part of her. Even this evening, when she rose from the piano and he moved over on the sofa, inviting her to join him, she shook her head, smiled and went to a footstool close to the fire, leaning back against Daniel's chair as if some secret intimacy always drew them together. He could have burst with frustration.

Everyone else was enjoying a thoroughly jolly evening. Kate refused all requests to give a Shakespearian recital and instead was persuaded to sing some of the many songs with which she had delighted audiences in the old days, joined at the end by Harry, who gave a spirited rendering of old music-hall ditties, and ending up with a rousing chorus in which they could all join.

Then the servants came in, bringing the drinks table and trays of tea with delicious sandwiches and cakes. When they were all settled with what they wanted, Isabelle asked Lord Warrinder to read to them.

'Something special, Grandpapa, to finish off this lovely evening. You do it so well. I wish I had been old enough to go to the Old Bailey when you were still acting as Queen's Counsel. What was he like, Aunt Kate?'

'Wonderful, my dear. No one came anywhere near him. He could have been a great actor.'

'What utter rubbish,' he protested. 'You make me sound like some posturing mountebank. Ask Harry or your father to read from one of Charles Dickens' novels.'

'The murder of Nancy perhaps,' said Harry. 'I saw the old man performing that shortly before his death. By God, he could make your flesh creep!'

'You don't mean that Dickens fellow wrote about murders, do you?' said John Everard in surprise. 'I tried one of his books once, something about a curiosity shop, dry as dust, only got half-way through.'

'Philistine!' muttered Harry.

'It is New Year's Eve tomorrow,' said Lord Warrinder. 'We ought to be thinking of the future. Isabelle, run and fetch my copy of Tennyson from my study.'

She ran off and was back in no time. 'What are you going to read?'

'I know just the thing: Ulysses returning from Troy, the stress of war over but still not content to dream by the fireside.'

They settled to listen to the rich voice with its fine cadences, not too solemn or too slow, and he held them spellbound to the last few lines:

> 'That which we are, we are,
> The equal temper of heroic hearts
> Made weak by time and fate, but strong in will
> To strive, to seek, to find and not to yield.'

Kate, whose eyes were on her brother, saw the tiny smile that passed between him and Christine and thought it must hold a memory for them, a memory of the days when he was struggling to lift himself from the depths of poverty and ignorance and she was lending him the books he longed for, and she felt reassured. Surely nothing could part these two, and certainly not a golden-haired waif who had come so strangely into their lives, she thought, but she was wrong. The very next day saw the first crack that might if not quickly mended split them apart.

It was foolish enough, an accident that arose out of David's frustration and Louise's over-confidence and should never have happened.

It was such a splendid morning, only a little frosty with brilliant sunshine that edged every twig and leaf with glittering silver, a morning that made one glad to be alive. Harry suggested it at breakfast, an excursion through the lanes and across the Downs to Amberly Castle, where they could halt at the Black Horse for a hot mince pie and a drink.

Christine was strongly in favour. 'What a heavenly idea. You all go, but perhaps I had better stay and keep Mamma company. She is feeling a little frail this morning.'

'Oh no you don't, my dear,' said her father. 'You've spent far too much time this Christmas in worrying over our pleasures. Off you go with the party and enjoy yourself. The children and I will keep Clarissa company.'

'Actually horses terrify me, great brutes,' said Kate cheerfully. 'You go, George, if you feel you can bear it. I'll stay; and if I think I'd like a breath of fresh air, I'll ask Paddy to harness the dog-cart and come out to meet you all.'

And so it was settled. The horses were brought round saddled and ready, all of them, even quiet old Honey, tossing their heads and eager to get going on this keen lively morning. Among these horse-loving people it was simply taken for granted that Louise would go with them, even though since John Everard put her in the saddle she had never done more than a gentle trot round the park. It seemed silly to draw back now, so she hid her anxiety and just prayed that she would not make an utter fool of herself.

'Everyone ready?' asked John Everard, the natural leader of the expedition, with Isabelle, Harry and David circling around him impatient to be off. 'Come on then, let's go.'

Christine was riding beside Daniel, who knew very well how she loved it and how little opportunity she had nowadays to enjoy her favourite sport.

'You go ahead with the others,' he said to her, 'you know what a slowcoach I am on a horse. John Dexter and I will bring up the rear and at the same time look after Louise.'

'Are you sure?' she said, still uncertain.

'Of course I'm sure, my love. You take yourself up there with the best of them. You could show John Everard a thing or two, I'll be bound. That young man is a little too bumptious for his own good.'

She laughed. 'It's so long, I'll probably go flying over my horse's ears at the first fence. Take care, Dan, and don't let Louise do anything foolish,' and she went cantering forward to join the leading party.

Turning out of the park gates, they trotted along a country lane where they could ride three abreast with Louise between them. Then the leaders turned off on to a grassy ride that led through fields left fallow for the winter, but crossed here and there by shallow ditches fringed with reeds and low-growing shrubby plants. The vanguard took them in their stride but Daniel, who was familiar with the terrain, took care to avoid jumping and led his small party through the gateway and across the planks that bridged the ditch. They were jogging along peacefully some long way behind the main party when David came cantering back towards them, swerved and came up beside Louise with a fine display of horsemanship.

'Enjoying it?' he asked, putting a hand on hers.

'Oh yes, very much indeed.'

'We'll be coming out on to the open Downs soon. You don't want to stay behind with the old fogeys, do you? Why not come along with me?'

'Old fogeys be damned!' said Dr Dexter. 'Let me remind you, young man, that I was riding in a point-to-point before you were even thought of!'

'Don't be afraid,' went on David, his hand tightening on Louise's bridle, 'you'll love it and I'll take care of you.'

'Don't press her if she doesn't feel up to it,' said Daniel, a little annoyed at David's persistence.

'Why must you always interfere? Can't you let her decide for herself? You would like to ride with me, wouldn't you, Louise?'

Pulled this way and that and a little afraid she was acting like a silly schoolgirl, Louise said, 'Yes, of course I would, but I might hold you back.'

'No, you won't. I won't let you. Come along then.' He gave Honey a slap on the backside so that she started forward into a sharp trot and then broke into a canter, quite outstripping Daniel and the doctor.

Taken by surprise, Louise was frankly terrified, holding on for dear life with David always ahead and urging her on. She could see one of the ditches coming up before her. The scrub that grew alongside it was not really high, not much more than a couple of feet. David cleared it easily and went galloping on. Poor Honey did her best but, receiving no hint or direction from the frightened girl on her back, she took the ditch awkwardly and landed clumsily. Louise lost a stirrup and was flung off, which wouldn't have mattered so much if she had not hit the stump of a recently felled tree.

David, far ahead, did not at first see what had happened but Daniel, already anticipating trouble, dug in his heels, galloped forward, cleared the ditch, flung himself out of the saddle and fell on his knees beside Louise, closely followed by Dr Dexter, who dismounted a little more gently and came at once to assess the damage.

'Careful, Dan,' he said quickly, 'don't move her. It could be dangerous till I've seen what she has done.'

Louise was deathly white and lying in a queer distorted heap. Frantic with anxiety, Daniel raised her head a little. She opened her eyes, tried to move and cried out in sudden agony.

'Gently, gently,' said the doctor as he knelt on the other side of her.

David had at last come galloping back, looking disturbed. He swung himself out of the saddle.

'What happened?' he said breathlessly. 'Is she hurt?'

Daniel let the doctor take Louise from him and got to his feet, a tearing, burning anger rising up in him.

'Don't you ever think what you're doing, you damned clumsy fool?'

'*Now* what have I done?'

'Don't you realize you could have killed her?'

All the petty jibes of the week, all the half-veiled insults he had ignored, welled up in him into an uncontrollable rage and Daniel let it go. He hit David on the jaw with a force that sent him sprawling on the frosty grass. The boy still held his riding crop in his hand. In a moment he was on his feet and had slashed it wildly across his stepfather's face, leaving a bloody weal across his cheek. For an instant they stood glaring at one another till the doctor's voice cut across them like a knife.

'For God's sake, stop it, the pair of you. Daniel, come and help me.'

The rage vanished, leaving him ice-cold. He got down on his knees again on the frosty ground.

David said in a choked voice, 'Is she badly hurt?'

'I can't tell yet but it's bad enough. Don't just stand there, boy, ride back to Bramber, organize transport. We've got to get her back to the house as soon as possible.'

'Yes, yes, of course.' David flung himself back into the saddle and rode off across the fields like a madman.

Dr Dexter said, 'You've got to help me, Dan. She has dislocated her shoulder. I can put it back but it should be done as soon as possible and it's going to be damned painful for her.'

Daniel nodded, calm now and resolute. As a foreign correspondent he had on various occasions had to deal with injuries to himself and to others, and had a fair knowledge of first aid.

Together, with infinite gentleness, they peeled off Louise's jacket. Then Daniel took her in his arms, holding her firmly, her face pressed against his coat, while Dr Dexter braced himself. He held the dislocated bone in a firm grasp, took a deep breath, and shot the shoulder back into its socket. Louise gave a brief scream, then sat quiet again, dazed. Dr Dexter sat back for a moment, sweat on his face. 'It's a long time since I've had to do that.' He unwound the silk scarf he had tucked into his neck and turned it into a temporary sling to hold the arm in place. 'It's horribly painful, I know,' he said soothingly, 'but I had to do it. It will wear off presently. Now let me take a look at the rest of you.' Apart from a nasty crack on the head and a number of bruises that were going to stiffen up and be painful later on, there didn't appear to be more serious damage. 'We can't do very much till David comes back,' he said. 'I wish it wasn't so damned cold.'

Louise was shivering with pain and shock. Daniel put her into the doctor's arms and felt in his pocket for the silver flask that had travelled all over the world with him.

'Give her a shot of this,' he said. While the doctor poured a little of the brandy into the tiny cup he shrugged off his riding-coat and wrapped it around the shaking girl.

'We could do with a nip of this ourselves,' said the doctor.

'There should be enough. Sorry about that unpleasantness just now,' muttered Daniel, taking the silver cup. 'He got me on the raw.'

'He's been asking for it,' said the doctor drily. 'You'd better let me have a look at that face of yours when we get back, or Christine will be asking awkward questions.'

'I'll think of something.'

He took out a handkerchief to wipe away the blood that was oozing from the cut across his cheek. While they waited there was time for him to cool down, to be angry with himself for losing his temper, to realize that seeing Louise lying there, white and still, had struck him to the heart so that for a moment he was blind to everything else.

It was a longish time before David came back, riding ahead of the dog-cart, driven at a cracking pace by Kate.

'I came as soon as I could,' she said breathlessly as she pulled up. 'How is she? I brought blankets and rugs.'

'Good girl, that's what's needed,' said the doctor. 'Now, Dan, you get in and then I'll wrap Louise up and put her into your arms. With you holding her we can avoid too much jolting on the way back. I don't want that shoulder slipping out again.'

It worked well. Louise lay along the seat, covered with the blankets and rugs and supported by Daniel, while David took hold of Honey's bridle and the doctor took charge of Daniel's horse, which had been peacefully cropping the grass, and they followed the cart in a little procession.

Kate drove as fast as she could but the road was rough going for the dog-cart and she dared not jolt Louise too much. Back at Bramber everyone had been alerted and Daniel carried Louise up to her bedroom with Nanny and the doctor in close attendance, leaving David standing with Kate as Paddy came to take the dog-cart away. He looked so forlorn that she put a hand on his arm. She had noticed the darkening bruise on his jaw and the ugly weal across Daniel's face, but she asked no questions. Time enough for that later.

'Don't worry too much,' she said gently. 'She is in very good hands. Don't you think you had better ride to meet the others? They must be wondering what has happened.'

'Yes, I suppose I should. I didn't want this to happen. I just wanted Louise to enjoy the day with me.'

'Yes, of course you did. She'll understand that. When you come back, perhaps the doctor will let you see her.'

He stood awkwardly for a moment. 'Thanks, Kate. You're a brick.'

'Rather a heavy one nowadays, I fear,' she said wryly. 'Now off you go.'

She watched him climb back into the saddle and wondered what Christine would say when she found out, as she no doubt would, and then went upstairs to give a strictly edited version to Clarissa and Lord Warrinder. She knew that he at least guessed at the truth behind it.

It was a great pity that the Christmas holiday, which had begun so splendidly and gone on with so much simple pleasure and good will, should end in a feeling of disappointment, a certain uneasy tension and a desire to get away as soon as possible and back to ordinary everyday living.

The foolish little accident provoked a number of unexpected reactions, the children being the only two completely unaffected. They appeared in Louise's bedroom for the one minute permitted by Nanny, offering her some rather sticky chocolate, the last remnant of the Christmas stockings, and bringing both little dogs with them to cheer her up.

'I fell off my pony once,' said Robert in a hushed, sickroom kind of voice. 'It hurt terribly.'

'I'd better not leave Toby,' whispered Celia, eyeing the strong bandage that now held the shoulder in place. 'If he jumps on the bed it might be awful. Rob and I will take great care of him.'

Louise gave them a warm smile and they crept out on tiptoe.

John Everard, permitted to put his head round the door, was so struck by her look of frailty, skin pale as a lily, golden hair spread out on the pillow, enormous dark-fringed eyes, that he resolutely approached his mother with the hazy notion that had been floating around in his mind for days, and for the first time in his much-indulged life was met with her firm disapproval.

'My dear boy,' said Margaret, 'you must be out of your mind even to suggest such a thing. Don't misunderstand me: Louise is a beautiful girl and I am very sorry for her, but as your wife, as the mistress of Ingham Park . . . it is totally out of the question. Quite apart from the fact that she is penniless and as far as I can see totally dependent on Cousin Clara – and we all know about *her* – you seem to have forgotten that she is the illegitimate daughter of a French opera singer.'

'You don't need to make it sound as if it were a criminal offence,' muttered John Everard; 'after all her father was an English gentleman and closely connected with Grandfather. It is not her fault surely, and but for that . . . that confounded bomb her parents would have been married.'

'Some twenty years too late,' went on his mother drily. She put her hand on his arm. 'I want you to have the best, dearest, the very best. You know that, don't you?'

He moved away from her. 'Am I to have no say in the matter?'

'But of course you are, it will be your decision and your choice. I am quite sure that when we leave here you'll see it all quite clearly just as I do.'

'Perhaps I will and perhaps I won't,' he said rebelliously and walked away, annoyed with himself and with his mother, anxious now to get back to his own satisfactory life in London among the male society in which he felt most at home.

David was not allowed to see her at all. 'Leave it for a while, my dear boy,' said Dr Dexter, 'and don't worry. She's not seriously hurt, but it has been an unpleasant shock and she needs rest and quiet. I have given her a light sedative.'

David went away, nursing a painful swollen jaw, with a strong feeling that nothing ever came right for him and, for all anyone cared, he might just as well take a running jump into the lake.

Even Harry, who was not given to introspection, suffered a sudden unpleasant certainty, as he watched Kate and George together, that his work at the Bar which he loved, his passion for music which he was rich enough to indulge and his occasional affairs with fashionable young women, who found him an irresistible change from a dull husband, were after all not enough; and his life seemed curiously empty.

However the New Year's Eve ritual must be gone through, and it was a foregone conclusion that they would all be gathered in the drawing-room as the time approached. Louise had been carried downstairs so that she should not be left out. The champagne had been opened and the glasses handed around. The curtains were drawn back and they looked out on a frosted garden, lit by a pale moon into a scene of black spectral trees and ghostly shadows. As the long case clock in the hall boomed out midnight, there came the distant sound of the bells from the village church, and they raised their glasses to welcome in the new year, each one with his own hope for something new and different. Only Louise, clutching the goblet with both hands, felt tears prick at her eyes and had a frightened feeling of going forward into the unknown.

The curtains were drawn again. Kate sat down at the piano and sang the first verse of 'Auld Lang Syne' and they linked hands to join in the chorus. After that they finished off the champagne, ate delicious spicy hot patties brought in by the servants on silver trays, and thought about packing up ready to leave on the following day.

Daniel picked up Louise, under Dr Dexter's stern eye, and carried her off upstairs, with Nanny waiting disapprovingly at the bedroom door. 'About time too,' she said tartly, 'drinking champagne till all hours, and Miss Louise so poorly too! She'll be in a fever by morning, I shouldn't wonder.' She turned back the blankets and then moved to the fire, putting the posset of milk on the trivet to keep warm while Daniel lowered Louise gently on to the bed.

She touched the weal on his face as he bent over her. 'You never told me how you did that.'

'It was my own clumsiness. It's nothing.' He saw the tears still sparkling in her eyes and guessed how she was feeling. 'Don't look back, Louise, never look back. It doesn't help,' and he kissed her gently. But her hand round his neck pulled him closer, responding to him passionately so that it became something else, and deeply disturbing. For a moment he let himself drown in it, then, shaken, he pulled himself abruptly away and stood up.

'Good-night, my dear, sleep well,' he said, and went out quickly as Nanny came bustling up, putting down the cup on the bedside table, plumping up the pillows and tucking her charge warmly into the bed.

Christine was almost the last to go to bed that night. There always seemed to be something that needed to be done. Her mother, who had been a notable hostess in her day, had been more exacting than usual, and Christine was thankful to see her safely in her room with her personal maid in attendance.

'Now don't let your father stay up too long, Christine,' was her mother's parting shot to her daughter; 'he's getting on and he needs his sleep nowadays though he hates to admit it.'

'I won't, Mamma.'

She kissed her mother dutifully and went on down to the hall. It was very quiet. The great logs on the hearth were smouldering into ash. The servants had all gone to bed, except for the butler, who would be finally locking up. There was a streak of light from her father's study. She had guessed that something had happened that day between her husband and her son, partly from their damaged faces, partly from the unnatural politeness between them during the evening, and she suddenly felt terribly tired. It was too much on top of everything else. The strain of caring for the large household over the last ten days had been more than she had bargained for. Thank goodness she would be back among the ordinary everyday problems of Wimpole Street in a day or so. The thought was infinitely restful. She braced herself, crossed the hall and pushed open the study door.

Her father was lounging comfortably in one of the leather armchairs and Daniel was standing on the hearthrug, glass in hand. 'Do you realize, both of you, that it is long past two o'clock?' she said as they turned to look at her.

'Is it? I suppose it must be,' said her father, pulling himself lazily out of the easy chair. 'Daniel and I were enjoying a quiet nightcap together.'

'Brandy, after all that champagne!'

'It's very settling to the stomach. Good-night, Dan, give a thought to what we've been discussing.'

'I will.'

'Good-night, my pet.' He kissed Christine. 'You've looked after us all splendidly but I'm not sorry to return to my usual quiet life.' He went out, closing the door, and she came to perch on the arm of the big chair.

Daniel held up his glass. 'Want some?'

'A sip or two of yours will do.'

He gave her the glass. She took a couple of mouthfuls, choked and grimaced. 'I don't really like brandy. It always reminds me of something horrid, like a violent toothache.'

He laughed, took back the glass, finished off what was left and put it on the table.

'What were you and Papa talking about?' she asked.

'Not a great deal. He thinks that if too many people realize I am behind this press campaign against prostitution and the government's attitude to it, it may prejudice my being accepted as a candidate for the next election.'

'But you've not written the articles under your own name.'

'No, but people may make a guess. David was doing his best to spread it about, and John Everard is not one to hold his tongue. He seemed to think it all a great joke.'

'You wouldn't consider dropping it?'

'Good heavens, no. I happen to believe in what I'm doing

and I don't intend to be frightened off. Maybe it won't change anything but it *could* just make a few responsible people think.'

She sighed. She'd known it was useless before she said it. He would never change his mind on anything which he felt deeply about. But there was something else she had to know.

'Daniel, what happened today? I asked John Dexter, but he put me off with some tale I didn't believe for a moment. That weal across your face wasn't made by a low-hanging bough when you were riding fast under the trees, was it? And David didn't walk into the stable door. It was all a conspiracy to keep me in the dark, wasn't it?'

He looked away from her, stooping to stir up the dying fire, uncertain how much to tell her. Then he straightened up. 'If you must know,' he said reluctantly, 'I knocked the boy down and he retaliated. That's all.'

'With his riding-crop?'

'Yes.'

'Was it because of Louise?'

'It was so damned thoughtless, pulling her away from us, persuading her to ride ahead with him when he knew she was hopelessly inexperienced. He seemed to think the whole thing was a huge joke. He could have killed her. I'm afraid I lost my temper. I'm sorry, Christine. I regret it. He's your son and God knows I've done my best to treat him fairly but this time ... Oh well, it's done now.'

'You're very fond of Louise, aren't you?'

'What's that got to do with it? I would have felt the same if it had been Isabelle or one of the children.' But would he? That uncomfortable Methodist conscience of his reminded him that he might have been angry but would never have gone so far.

'Is everyone in love with Louise?' said Christine in a sudden irritable outburst. 'John Everard and David mooning after her, Harry behaving like some gallant out of a silly novel, even the children are her slaves, and now you. I wish you'd never brought her from Russia. I wish to God you'd left her there to work out her own future instead of burdening us with it!'

He looked at her, appalled. 'You don't really mean that, you couldn't.'

'Yes, I do, I do, every word of it!' she said passionately. 'She has come between you and David and now she has come between you and me, and I can't bear it.' She dropped into the armchair and buried her face in her hands.

'Nothing can do that, nothing at all, surely you must believe that.' He came and knelt beside the chair, putting his arm around her, drawing her against him. 'You're tired. All this has been far too much for you, otherwise you would never say such foolish things.'

'Are they foolish, Dan? Are they?'

'You know they are.' For a moment he held her very close, then he got up and gently pulled her to her feet. 'Come on, my love, bed first and then back home tomorrow. I badly need to get back to work.'

'And I have to check through the children's clothes with Nanny before they go back to school. The little wretches are growing out of everything.'

'That sounds more like my Christine.'

He turned out the lamp and then put his arm around her as they went out into the hall. At the foot of the stairs she stopped, looking up at him.

'And Louise goes back to Arlington Street.'

'Louise goes back to Clara, God help her.'

His arm tightened around her and they went up the stairs, seemingly as close as always, but the uncertainty was still there. The bright new year they had welcomed that evening would find a way of deepening it.

Chapter 11

Louise didn't return to Arlington Street quite as quickly as Christine would have wished, chiefly due to Dr Dexter's strictures. She travelled back with the family from Bramber, but she was still in a good deal of pain, and indeed so poorly when he made a last examination, that he recommended another day or so in bed or at least resting quietly, even though she protested that she was perfectly well.

'I take it that your cousin Lady Dorrien is still away and not expected back for some weeks,' he said quietly to Christine. 'It seems a little unkind to condemn the poor child to the tender mercies of servants.'

'She must stay here. It would be no trouble for us, would it, my dear?' said Daniel quickly before she could answer. 'With Robert due back at Rugby and Celia growing up so fast, there is nothing Nanny likes better than having someone she can fuss over.'

'Good, then that's settled,' said the doctor. 'I only hope she realizes how fortunate she is to have such good friends. I have told her to let me know if there is any more pain. Now I must be off or else my patients will all begin to die on me. The new year is just the time for it.'

'He is nearly as besotted with Louise as the rest of you,' said Christine tartly to her husband after she had kissed her old friend goodbye. 'And you had to back him up, didn't you?'

'What else could I do? We could hardly turn her out when she is still in so much pain.' Daniel frowned. 'Why are you so hard on her? It isn't like you, Christine.'

'No, it isn't, is it? Oh never mind. I had better go and speak to Nanny about it right away.'

Kate had come back to London with them, George having gone to spend a few days with his aged father. She was very fond of her brother, and of Christine too. The time had come, she thought, for having a quiet talk with Louise. Her opportunity came a few days later, when Louise was up, feeling a great deal better and talking about going back to Arlington Street on the following morning.

Louise was in the drawing-room that afternoon, sitting by the fire with Toby on her lap. The soreness in her shoulder was easing now and, for the first time since that stupid accident, she felt herself again, full of new life and new hope. The Christmas holiday had done a great deal for her. She was no longer the shy schoolgirl; she had blossomed in the kindness shown to her. John Everard's marked attentions, David blowing hot and cold as the mood took him, Harry's slightly old-fashioned gallantry, all had given her a new self-confidence.

'May I call on you in London?' John Everard had said to her just before he left, still smarting from his mother's strong disapproval and reacting against it. 'I keep my horses stabled not far from Hyde Park. Would you care to ride with me sometime in the Row?'

Surprised and a little flattered, she said doubtfully, 'If you're quite sure I won't disgrace you.'

'Never! What an idea! The other chaps will all be green with envy. And I have just the horse for you, gentle as a lamb.'

She was not in love with him in the slightest but all the same it was very exciting. It made her feel of value, even though deep in her heart she was only too well aware that none of these young men came anywhere near Daniel. She felt she would be going back to Arlington Street with a new confidence, able to face up to her sister, certain that, whatever the future might bring, she would find a way of dealing with it. The sudden opening of the door roused her from her comforting thoughts.

Toby jumped down, running to greet Kate as she came in, followed by Mark with a tray of tea. 'I thought I might find you here,' she said cheerfully. 'Christine has taken Isabelle and the children to the British Museum with the promise of a special tea afterwards, and Daniel is buried in his work, so it seems we are on our own. I've been wanting to have a little talk with you before you go home.'

The butler put the tea tray on a small table beside her. 'Is there anything more, madam?'

'No, thank you, Mark.'

He went out, closing the door. Toby settled himself on the hearthrug with one eye on the dish of biscuits, and Kate turned to Louise.

'Shall I pour, my dear?'

'Yes please.' Louise admired Kate greatly but was a little afraid of her: she seemed so competent, so self-assured. She took the cup handed to her and said a little shyly, 'What do you want to talk to me about?'

Kate stirred her tea in silence for a moment, then she said unexpectedly, 'You know, you and I have a good deal in common. We're both of us illegitimate for one thing.'

Louise gasped. 'But you are Daniel's sister.'

'Half-sister. I don't think many people know or care very much about it nowadays, but it is true all the same. Same mother, different father. Like you, I am a love child.'

Louise stared at her curiously. 'Does it distress you very much?'

'I didn't find out till I was about your age, and by then I'd already made something of my life and I refused to let it distress me. I was not so lucky as you. I didn't have a sheltered childhood with loving parents. I was six when my mother died and I was put in the orphanage, and twelve when they sent me as housemaid to a wealthy family where the eldest son thought it amusing to chase me up and down passages till I ran away in terror. I was picked up, starving and penniless, by a travelling theatrical company. I owe Roddy Crowne and his wife not only my life but also the gift of being able to trust people again, and it was they who taught me how to act. After that, though God knows I had my ups and downs, I made my own way.'

'You must have had tremendous courage,' breathed Louise.

'Not courage so much as a grim determination never to be defeated, never to let anyone, no matter who they were, trample all over me. And I didn't have so many talents as you have, Louise. What are you going to make of them?'

'I don't know what you mean.'

'I think you do. For one, you have a rare gift for the piano. Isn't it a pity to let it go to waste?'

'It's easy to say that. If Papa had lived, it would have been different. He was talking about my studying in Paris. We were making all sorts of plans, but they cost money and now ... Clara doesn't even approve of my using her piano for practice.'

'What was it that made you decide to accept her invitation to live with her?' asked Kate curiously.

Louise hesitated. The strong desire to prove herself as good as her half-sister seemed now to have become unimportant. She said slowly, 'I think it was because I resented the hateful way she spoke of my mother and the fact that my father loved her so dearly. I wanted her to eat her own words and publicly acknowledge me as James Ducane's daughter.'

'And have you succeeded?'

'No. And I think she hates me more than ever because of it; and yet the queer thing is that now I don't seem to care any longer.'

'That's the spirit,' said Kate. 'Stand on your own feet and cock a snook at the approval of so-called society. I did, and I've never regretted it. Now, to be practical. I think there may be one way in which I can be of a little help. Daniel tells me that you are something of a linguist. Would you like to translate French and German plays for me?'

Louise stared at her in surprise. 'I don't know. I've never tried. I can read French and German with ease, but to turn them into English is something else.'

'Don't think I'm crazy to suggest it,' went on Kate, smiling.

'The fact is there is a shortage of good English plays at the present time, and there is a good deal of interest in foreign drama, but we're not all such expert linguists.'

'I could translate them,' said Louise, her interest suddenly fired, 'but I don't know that I could put them into a dramatic English suitable for the stage.'

'That wouldn't be necessary. What I and my friends want is a good sound translation on which an expert theatrical writer can work. You would be paid, of course. We'll arrange a suitable fee. Would you like to think about it?'

'I don't need to think. I'd love to do it for you if I could. If it turns out not good enough, then I wouldn't accept any fee. I have spoken French all my life and Papa spent years in Vienna from when I was five years old, and he always insisted on my studying the language of the country in which we were living.'

'Good,' said Kate. 'Then that's settled. I will consult my friends and let you have the necessary books. Then it will be up to you.'

'It's very kind of you,' murmured Louise. 'Is that what you wanted to talk to me about?'

'Not entirely. There is something else.' Kate paused for a second, looking at the girl sitting opposite her, the dark-gold hair smoothly drawn back, the large eyes with their long lashes, the flawless creamy skin, the tender vulnerable mouth. It was little wonder if men fell for it. She sighed and plunged in.

'Tell me, are you in love with Daniel?'

Louise stiffened, then drew herself up proudly. 'I don't think you have any right to ask me that.'

'He is my brother, and I think I have every right when during the last few days I have watched how you have been amusing yourself with John Everard, driving David frantic and at the same time have made it very plain where your real preference lies.'

'I have done nothing wrong,' said Louise indignantly.

'No, not yet. Is Daniel in love with you?'

'I'm not going to answer that.'

'*Is* he?' persisted Kate.

'No, of course he isn't.'

'But you very much wish that he was, don't you?'

'No, no, you're quite wrong.' Louise turned away, everything in her rebelling at the way Kate had touched something very important to her, something which had sprung from those painful days in St Petersburg, something which she cherished so dearly.

Then unexpectedly Kate leaned across the table, speaking very gently. 'You're angry with me, and I can understand why, but believe me I'm speaking from my heart. I can guess at what happened. You met at a time of unbearable grief when you were very unhappy, very vulnerable. I know my brother. I know how kind he is, how compassionate. He is a man whom it is very easy to love. But you must understand that he is married and he loves Christine dearly. They had a bitter fight to keep that love and find their happiness together and it has forged a strong bond between them. Don't ever try to kill it. Daniel is loyal. He loves his wife, he loves his children, but he is a man, not a saint, and vulnerable. Something has drawn him very close to you. If anything should happen, if you tempt him beyond endurance, you will destroy him and yourself. If for any reason he were to betray Christine, as some men might do without a second thought, Daniel would never forgive himself. You must understand that.'

'I don't know why you are saying all this to me. I have done nothing wrong,' said Louise defiantly. 'I know I only have a small part of him, but it is mine and I cherish it.'

'Of course you do, and you resent me for dragging it into the open. It is always dangerous to interfere in people's lives, but I do beg you to remember what I have said.'

'I don't think I can ever forget it.' Louise was on her feet and trembling with anger. 'You have made me feel as if I were some . . . some contemptible creature out to win a man simply for her own satisfaction. You needn't worry. I could never be like that, never, and I am leaving here tomorrow in any case, because I would not trouble Christine and Daniel any longer.

But I tell you this: Daniel is my very dear friend and I'm not going to turn my back on him, not for you, not for anyone. Now, if you will excuse me, I have some packing to do.'

She picked Toby up and stormed out of the room, but Kate thought it was a brave show of defiance which would crumble when she cooled down; and she was perfectly right.

Alone in her room Louise stood for a moment, cheeks burning, still shaking with anger at Kate's plain speaking. She felt as if something had been torn away from her, and what had been beautiful and precious had become ugly. She would have liked to walk out of the house there and then, prove to Kate how very wrong she was, but it would be impossible to leave without making lame excuses that would sound ungrateful after all the kindness she had received.

Furiously she began to pull dresses out of the wardrobe and empty the drawers in the chest, stopping for a moment to stare at her face in the mirror. In some way that she didn't understand Kate had robbed her of her innocence. Shielded and protected, up to a year ago her deepest feelings had been reserved for her father and her mother until the tragedy had torn them from her, Daniel had come, a buffer between her and a hostile world, and she had turned to him with a passionate adoration that had as yet no touch of sensuality. She had no real experience to draw on. Her friendship with Leo had been light-hearted, a sisterly affection spiced with a few kisses, holding him always at arm's length. That first meeting with David awoke an interest which might have developed if it had not been swept away by the murderous bomb and forgotten in Daniel's coming. Now she and David seemed to meet only to quarrel, the first instinctive liking lost in exasperation and antagonism.

By the time she had packed almost everything it was seven o'clock, and Isabelle was looking in to say what a marvellous afternoon they had enjoyed. 'Even the children were thrilled, and ate a simply enormous tea. They won't want any supper. I don't know what Nanny will say. Are you coming down? It must be nearly dinner time.'

And Louise knew suddenly that she couldn't face it. To pass the evening quietly with Daniel and Christine had become impossible. They would read in her face that something had disturbed her. She stammered an excuse: she was feeling very tired, had developed a wretched headache and thought she would go to bed early.

'Oh, poor you,' said Isabelle sympathetically. 'I'll tell Mamma.'

Then Christine, a little concerned, came up asking what was wrong and if there was anything she could do, and insisting on a light meal being sent up with a glass of wine. 'You must try and eat a little,' she said, 'or Dr Dexter will be accusing me of neglecting you. Isabelle shall bring you one of my headache powders and you can take it with a cup of tea before you go to bed.'

Louise saw her leave with relief, and when the tray came up she did try to eat a little, though a good deal of it went to Toby. She obediently swallowed the headache powder but it didn't have any immediate effect so she lay awake for a long time. In a way Kate had caused the very thing she was anxious to prevent. For the first time, almost unwillingly, Louise thought of Daniel as a lover, imagined those strong hands of his caressing her, kisses that became more and more passionate. Presently she fell into an uneasy sleep and a wildly erotic dream that made her shiver with a more intense pleasure than she had ever experienced. She awoke sweating, distressed and very unhappy. It drove her out of bed very early, washed, dressed and determined to leave straight away. She asked Mark to call a cab for her as soon after breakfast as possible, even though Daniel protested there was no need for her to hurry away in such a rush.

'If you leave it till this afternoon,' he said, 'I could come with you and see you safely into Arlington Street.'

'No,' she said firmly. 'No, it is time I went. I have troubled you and Christine quite long enough. I know how busy you are, and Christine has the children to worry about. The cab driver will see to what luggage I have. It isn't a great deal.'

Goodbyes were said all round. Celia brought Rowley for a farewell kiss and hugged Toby so tightly that he squeaked in protest.

Daniel watched the cab drive away with mixed feelings, then went back to his desk, covered with galley proofs which as usual his editor wanted corrected and returned as soon as possible. As he settled down to them, he wondered what had happened to drive Louise away in such a tearing hurry.

It was not a great distance. The cab driver good-naturedly carried her luggage up the steps for her as she still dared not put too much strain on her injured shoulder, and he grinned at the large tip she dropped in his hand. 'Any time, lady, any time,' he said, and went back to his cab whistling cheerfully.

Mrs Bolton herself opened the door to her knock.

'Oh, it's you, miss,' she said ungraciously, 'we were not expecting you back so soon.'

'I said I would only be away till the new year,' said Louise crisply, 'and it's already a few days past that.'

'Well, now you're here, you'd better come in,' said the housekeeper, moving back so that Louise saw the man who hovered in the hall just behind her. 'This is my brother, Roger,' went on Mrs Bolton hurriedly, 'he's just going. He dropped in for a few minutes as he was nearby.'

'Good morning, miss,' said the man politely. 'Shall I carry in your luggage for you?'

She didn't know why she took such an instant dislike to him. He was thin and dark, with overlong, greasy black hair brushed straight back, a thin line of moustache and large white teeth revealed in an ingratiating smile. Give him two furry ears and he could have played Red Riding Hood's wolf without any further make-up, she thought, unpleasantly aware that the small piercing eyes were studying her from head to foot before he brushed past her and picked up her valise. Involuntarily she shivered, then told herself she was being ridiculous. He put her luggage beside her and turned to his sister.

'I'll be off now, Agnes,' he was saying, and planted a kiss on Mrs Bolton's cheek before he went down the steps.

The door to the drawing-room was partly open and Louise could see the table with the cups and silver coffeepot. So the housekeeper had been entertaining her brother in style while the mistress was away. Clara wouldn't like that – not that Louise had any intention of telling her. What the servants did was not her concern.

'I'll tell Ada to light a fire and see to your room,' said Mrs Bolton.

'There's no need to hurry. It's not yet midday. Perhaps someone would carry up my luggage. I'll carry Toby.'

'I suppose you know that Lady Dorrien will not be returning for some weeks,' said the housekeeper; 'so naturally we shall not be opening up the whole house.'

'That won't worry me,' said Louise calmly. 'You need not trouble yourself too much on my behalf. I shall be living very quietly till my sister returns.'

She went on up the stairs to her bedroom. The house felt cold and unfriendly after the warmth and welcome at Bramber and Wimpole Street, and she almost wished she had let Daniel come back with her. He would have made her feel safe, and smiled at her instinctive dislike of the stranger in the hall. Then Ada came in, greeting her with pleasure, kneeling down to light the fire and telling her how good the goose had tasted and how exciting the children had found the little gifts she had been able to buy them with Louise's guinea. The luggage was brought up and she began to unpack, carefully shaking out the dresses and exclaiming over the riding-habit which Isabelle had insisted on her taking with her.

'Just fancy,' she said admiringly, 'ridin' on a horse an' all! We'll see you in Rotten Row any time at all now with all the nobs.'

'So you might,' said Louise, wondering if John Everard would keep his promise and rather childishly hoping that he would. A call from Sir John Ingham might make these snobbish servants sit up and take notice.

The fire burned up, spreading warmth and chasing away shadows, and she was just thinking how stupid she was to imagine there was anything sinister about the stranger in the hall when something Ada was saying caught her attention.

'That brother of Mrs Bolton's is a queer one, and no mistake. Did you see him when you come in, miss? That's the second time this week he's called, pokin' his nose in and askin' questions, wantin' to know where you was, cheeky devil, till Cook shut him up, tellin' him it weren't none of his business, and that Mrs Bolton treatin' him as if he were royalty when he's no better than the rest of us.'

'What do you mean, Ada? Have you seen him before?'

'O' course I 'ave. He lives over in Bermondsey. He has a little drapery shop not a stone's throw from where we live, and my Pa says only a few years back he were as poor as poor and his two daughters runnin' the streets barefoot, while now you just ought to see them, dressed up to the nines they are and too grand to speak to such as us, when Ma's known them to come begging for a screw of tea and a cup of sugar. Where's it all come from? That's what my Pa says. Not from the shop, that's for sure. One of them police called there once but nothin' came of it. But they're a funny lot and so's he, you take my word for it.'

Louise was inclined to dismiss it as gossip, and maybe a little envy for someone who had been more successful than they had, but why should he ask questions about *her*? Perhaps the servants talked about the relationship between her and Clara.

Ada went off promising to bring a light luncheon.

'A little bread and butter with some cold meat and a pot of tea is all I want,' Louise said.

During the weeks before Clara came home, Louise felt she had at last broken out of her cocoon of grief and self-pity and emerged into a new life. Perhaps it was putting aside the black of mourning – though she still felt guilty about it. There were still dark moments, she still had dreams of being back at the villa with her father laughing at her for believing that anything could kill him. She would wake in the deep watches of the night and know painfully how utterly alone she was. There was still the frightening certainty that if Clara went back on her half-promises, as she might very well do, nothing stood between Louise and destitution but the few pounds that Daniel had banked for her and which up to now she had scarcely touched. She told herself that she was fortunate. She was housed, fed and clothed – there were thousands of young women far worse off than she was – but it did not help, and in moments of deepest depression she must steel herself against running to Daniel for the sympathy and encouragement which she knew he would willingly give. Kate had closed that escape to her. She had whipped away Louise's self-delusion. Now she must stand alone.

In the daytime it was easier to be brave and look to a future full of interest. For one thing Kate had kept her promise, sending a copy of Friedrich Schiller's *Maria Stuart*, a drama which included an imaginary scene between Elizabeth and Mary, Queen of Scots, a part which Kate hoped to play one day. Louise set to work on it at once, setting up a table in the morning room with pens, ink and an abundance of paper and a new modern dictionary which Kate had thoughtfully included to provide alternative renderings of a difficult word. Written in verse, it was not easy, but it kept her absorbed and that was what she needed.

Just as important was the freedom to play the piano whenever she chose and she took full advantage of it, trying to approach new works as her teacher in Russia had done, and sometimes just playing for her own pleasure.

John Everard too had kept his promise. He called one morning in full regimentals, having just come from the Palace, and looking so handsome that Rennet, the butler, a snob to his backbone, was sufficiently impressed to show him into the drawing-room and himself inform Louise that Sir John Ingham had called and was asking if she would receive him.

Ada, peering round the baize door that shut off the servants' quarters, watched her running joyously down the stairs and into the room with outstretched hands, and reported it gleefully to the kitchen staff, who had always been inclined to look down their noses at Lady Dorrien's poor dependant.

'I've really called to ask if you would accompany me to the Mews so that I can introduce you to Candy,' said John Everard when the first greetings were over. 'She actually belongs to my sister so she is well accustomed to a lady rider.'

'But I couldn't take her from your sister,' protested Louise. 'It wouldn't be right.'

'You needn't worry about that. Clary won't be riding for a while, a year at least probably. You see she is . . . well, she is . . .'

'She is not sick, is she?'

'Oh Lord, no, nothing like that.'

'I know,' said Louise smiling, 'you mean she is expecting a baby. How wonderful for her.'

'That's it,' said John Everard with relief, 'and her husband has forbidden her to ride till it is all over, much to her annoyance. Edward is attached to the Foreign Office and very proper. You and he would get on famously. He speaks several languages too. I tell you what: I'll ask Clary to call upon you.'

'She may not feel well enough,' protested Louise.

'Rubbish, she was as fit as a fiddle when I saw her last. I told her all about you and she said she would love to meet you.'

'If you're sure . . .'

'Of course I'm sure. Clary loves meeting new people. She'll probably ask you to dine with them – *en famille*, of course. And now that's all settled, when will you ride with me? Shall we say next Sunday?'

And that was how it began, and how it went on, and not only on Sundays. Just a few days later Louise, in Isabelle's riding-habit, freshly pressed by Ada and with a dashing new top hat with a long floating veil, rode with John Everard in Hyde Park at the fashionable hour of the morning, and caused quite a buzz of interest among his many acquaintances.

'Who is the pretty baggage I saw you with?' asked one of his comrades in the barracks one morning the following week.

'I'll thank you to speak more respectfully of her,' said John Everard austerely. 'She is a distant cousin of my grandfather and recently come from St Petersburg.'

'You don't say. Anything to do with that poor fellow in the embassy whom those ruffians murdered a few months ago?'

'If you must know, she is his daughter.'

'The devil she is! Where has she been hiding all these months?'

'She has been in mourning,' said John Everard coolly. 'It is only now she feels she can venture into society.'

Louise's sudden appearance created quite a little stir and very soon of course reached David's ears. 'What the devil does John Everard think he's playing at?' he grumbled to Uncle Harry in the robing-room of the Old Bailey after a morning in court. 'He's running around with Louise as if they were already engaged.'

'Stealing a march on you, is he?' said his uncle drily. 'Well, it's up to you, my dear boy. John Everard has a couple of advantages – his title and his love of horses – but if I'm not mistaken, our little Louise is something of an intellectual. What about inviting her to accompany you to one of the picture galleries you're so fond of, ideal places for a lovers' tryst, I've always been told.'

'Oh shut up!'

'Or a concert,' went on Harry imperturbably. 'Clara Schumann will be playing in London soon, I hear. Just the thing to put a girl in the right melting mood. Or a play. As a matter of fact Kate has been lucky enough to secure a box at the Lyceum for *Macbeth* with this chap Henry Irving. The critics say he plays it like some great famished wolf; should be interesting. I thought of asking Louise to accompany us but there is room for four if you care to join the party.'

'No thanks.'

'Please yourself.'

'It's a wonder Daniel hasn't joined the queue of Louise's followers,' muttered David, hanging up his uncle's gown for him and feeling obscurely that he was getting the worst of it.

'He's probably a great deal too busy with clearing his desk before he goes off on his new mission to the Balkans.'

'What mission? He hasn't mentioned it.'

'Very likely not. I gather your mother is very much against it. She thinks it's far too dangerous – in which she is probably right.'

'What the devil is he expecting to do there?'

'Don't you ever read *The Times*? You should, you know. That Crimean peace treaty was a farce. It's a wonder it lasted so long. Now Germany, Austria and Russia are ganging up on Turkey, who for our sins is still our ally. The Prime Minister has been raising hell about it for the past year, even sent the fleet to the Dardanelles just in case, but then the confounded Turks let him down by attacking Bulgaria, going in with fire and slaughter apparently. Dizzy tried to pass it off in the House with one of his witty speeches as being grossly exaggerated but the Opposition have weighed in, talking about the soil reeking with the blood of innocent victims and the air tainted with unimaginable crimes and so on. The *Daily News* and, it seems, the PM himself have decided that Daniel is just the man to discover the real truth. He'll do it too. He won't be put off with any camouflaging lies.'

'I thought he was still occupied with his prostitution crusade.'

'He's gone about as far with that as he can for the time being. A question has already been asked in the House about it. There are some who think he has gone too far in his attack on the government, and the underworld may very well be after his blood if he's not careful. It could be a good thing for him to be out of the country for a while to let it cool down. You know, you're an ungrateful young devil,' went on Uncle Harry caustically: 'you did your level best to spread it abroad that he was the author of those articles. You don't appreciate how damned lucky you are. You could have a stepfather who kept you on a very tight rein and stood no nonsense. Daniel is far too easy towards you. He falls over backwards to give you everything you want.'

David said nothing. His uncle had an uncomfortable way of making him feel very young and foolish, but all the same it did make him think. He accepted the invitation to join the theatre party after all, when he had the pleasure of sitting close beside Louise and watching her enraptured face. It was the first Shakespeare play she had ever seen in English, and it held her spellbound.

Harry, who had seen Macready and Kemble in the part, was inclined to be critical, but Kate argued that this Henry Irving was not just a good actor but a genius, and genius was always controversial. 'In a few years,' she said with conviction, 'he is going to be sensational and I'd give a great deal for the chance to play opposite him.'

After the play Harry took them to supper at Vespers, a highly respectable restaurant often frequented by the legal profession and which he considered suitable for his two young *protégés*, and while he and Kate wrangled amicably about the merits of the production David was making good headway with Louise. He could be extremely charming when he forgot his prejudices and jealousies and set out to please.

He told her about the exciting paintings he had seen in Paris last year, an exhibition of works rejected by the Academicians with contempt and received by the public with derisive laughter.

'They call themselves Impressionists, Louise: Monet, Renoir, Seurat . . . they've cut away from the past. They are the future. I think paintings, like music, are great when they disturb complacency, make people think. They are not designed just to give pleasure. Don't you agree?' he went on earnestly, and asked her if she would go with him to the National Gallery in Trafalgar Square, where he could show her his own favourites and hear what she thought of them.

'If Clara is not home by then, I'd love to come,' she said, and thought that they had recaptured something of the charm of their first meeting at the villa, when they had walked across the fields and talked of music and art and been so happy together.

Afterwards he escorted her home to Arlington Street and, sitting close to her in the cab, he ventured to take her hand in his. As they alighted in front of the house, two men who had been standing under the trees a little distance away moved a step forward into the glow of the gas lamp. Louise started, clutching involuntarily at David's arm.

'What is it?' he asked in surprise, putting a hand on hers and drawing her close to him.

'Nothing,' she said quickly, trying to recover herself. 'I thought I recognized a man I used to know in Russia, but it can't be. It's impossible. I must be mistaken.'

'Who was it?'

'Oh, no one of importance,' she said quickly, and saw that the two men had already melted back into the shadows. By that time the butler had opened the door and she turned to David, giving him her hand and smiling at him. 'It's been a wonderful evening. I've enjoyed it so much. It was so kind of your uncle to include me.'

'And you will come with me to the Gallery on Saturday?'

'I shall look forward to it.'

'Good. I will call for you in the early afternoon.' He hesitated, and then awkwardly kissed her fingers and hurried down the steps to the waiting cab.

Upstairs in her own room Louise stood for a moment, still a little shaken. She could have sworn that the two men standing so close together had been Leo and the sinister Roger Tanner – but what possible connection could there be between them, and why on earth should they be watching her? She must be mistaken. She had never talked to anyone here in England about that very unpleasant business at the villa and that last terrible meeting with Leo at the station. She had never wanted to remember it. It was linked with the pain of that time, it was something she had shared with Daniel and no one else.

Chapter 12

When they came out of the National Gallery into the frosty February afternoon, David said apologetically, 'I'm afraid I have been lecturing you for the last hour. You should have shut me up.'

She smiled at him. 'I liked it. I had an art teacher at one time and he was not nearly so interesting as you,' and indeed on his favourite subject David could be entertaining as well as knowledgeable. He had told her that when he first saw her she reminded him of the angels in early Italian paintings, with a golden beauty that was not of this world. She had laughed at him.

'But I'm not a bit like that. I'm very down to earth. There is a sort of medieval smile, isn't there, and I'm afraid that to me it sometimes looks very like a simper.'

'Philistine!' he exclaimed, and they had gone on wrangling amicably about the merits and demerits of early religious painting as they wandered from one to the other.

Now, standing on the steps and looking across the great square with Landseer's friendly lions, the sun going down in flaming red and gilding Nelson on the top of his column, she felt quite happy and contented.

David took her arm. 'Before I buy you some tea I'd like to show you something else. It's an exhibition of work by a Polish artist who died last year. He was a great friend of Aunt Kate's. I think you would be interested. They are mostly portraits, and some of them you will recognize.'

It was quite a small gallery with about a dozen oil paintings and a great number of charcoal sketches, each one executed with tremendous vigour and power in every bold stroke. She walked from one to the other and was utterly fascinated. Here was a gallery of portraits of London life, a panorama of the teeming streets of the East End – flower girls, crossing-sweepers, a pie seller, a conjuror, a boy with a dancing bear, a hurdy gurdy man, a match seller, a crippled beggar – they seemed to step off the walls and parade in front of her so filled with life that she could almost smell the roasting chestnuts, taste the hot mutton pies. The paintings were unlike anything she had seen that afternoon, great splashes of colour dashed on to the canvas. She recognized a very young Christine, painted with tenderness; a vivid portrait of a young Daniel, facing the world, angry and defiant; until she came to the last and found that she could not take her eyes away. It was some seconds before she realized that it was a very young Clara, not beautiful but intensely alive, with dark haunted eyes that stared out of the canvas as if face-to-face with tragedy and yet defying it.

'When did he paint this one?' she asked David who had come to join her.

'I'm not sure. It must have been at the time of the trial when her husband was murdered.'

'I know something about that. Isabelle told me.'

'It is years ago now, and Clara could not have been more than twenty. He must have made sketches at the trial and painted it afterwards.'

'It's very strange,' she said slowly. 'I never thought I'd feel sorry for her, but now I do. This Karl Landowsky must have been a wonderful artist. They are more than just portraits. They tell you something about the soul of each person. I suppose that sounds silly.'

'No it doesn't. I think I understand what you mean. I do know that Aunt Kate thought he never received the acknowledgement that was due to him, and I'm pretty sure she has been the prime mover behind this little exhibition.'

'It's very remarkable. Thank you for showing it to me.'

Over tea and cakes in the discreet parlour of Fortnum's in Piccadilly, David asked her if she would come out with him again. 'There is a series of concerts to be held at St James's Hall and it is certain that Clara Schumann will be playing at one of them. If you are interested, I could get tickets.'

'I'm not sure,' she said a little doubtfully. 'Mrs Bolton has heard from my sister. She will be returning very soon now, and the whole house needs to be cleaned and opened up again before she arrives.'

'But that doesn't concern you, surely. And in any case, you're not going to allow her to keep you shut up as she did before, are you?'

'I do owe her something, David – but all the same I feel differently about myself now and about her. In fact there is only one thing that troubles me a little.'

'What's that?' he said eagerly. 'Perhaps I can help.'

She had been about to tell him about Leo, about the feeling that he was deliberately haunting her and that one day there would be a confrontation, but then she drew back. David was too young. He would never understand. It would involve telling him about those wretched meetings with Leo in St Petersburg that she had shared with Daniel and that she only wanted to put behind her once and for all.

'It's not much really,' she said a little lamely. 'It's just that I have been wondering what I shall do if Clara marries Jean-Louis, as I think she will. It will change everything for her and for me.'

David had a strong feeling that this was not what she had really intended to say, but he did not press her. There would be time enough when they met again, as he was determined that they should, and very soon. They parted on the friendliest terms, with David promising to obtain tickets and let her know the exact date of the concerts; and when that evening she took Toby for his little walk, the street was largely deserted, no sinister figure lurked under the trees and she was glad that she had said nothing to David. She made up her mind there and then that the next time she saw the man she would stop, ask him what he wanted and threaten him with the police if he didn't leave her alone.

Before anything like that could happen, she was surprised by a visit from Daniel.

The whole house was undergoing a kind of spring clean in readiness for the return of the mistress, and she had taken refuge that day in the morning room. She was working on her translation when a flustered Ada put her head round the door.

'There's a Mr Hunter askin' for you, miss,' she said breathlessly.

Daniel! Her heart gave a huge leap and then slowly quietened. 'Ask him to come up, will you, Ada?'

'Very good, miss.'

That morning she had put on an apron over her neat white blouse and dark blue skirt and, having made up her mind to work all day, she had simply brushed out her hair and tied it back with a ribbon. There was ink on her fingers and a big smudge on her cheek but she didn't care, she was far too happy to see him. She was on her feet to greet him when he came in, still in his heavy coat, his hat in his hand, looking somehow just as she had seen him first on that never-to-be-forgotten day in St Petersburg, and she had to resist the impulse to throw herself into his arms.

'What on earth is going on?' he said. 'I had to pick my way through a barrage of maidservants armed with brooms and buckets and the Lord knows what else.'

'Clara is returning soon and the whole house is being turned upside-down for her benefit.'

'So that's what it is.' He threw down his hat and took both her hands in his. 'I hope that doesn't involve you. This room seems to be heaven in the midst of chaos. What are you so busy with?'

'I'm trying to translate a play.'

'Ah yes, of course. Kate told me something about that. How are you getting on?'

'Sometimes very well, sometimes badly,' she said ruefully. 'I often know exactly what it means but can't always put it into the right dramatic English.'

'Let me see.' Daniel picked up one of the sheets she had laboriously copied out and ran his eye down it. 'It's not bad,' he said judiciously, 'not bad at all, but it's too literary. This is a play, remember, not a novel, and therefore it needs action, drama. May I make a suggestion? Try it over aloud several times before you make your final copy. You'll be surprised how different a sentence sounds when spoken aloud. I sometimes read over my dialogue to Christine. She is a very good critic and often puts me right.'

'I'm afraid I'm no actress, but I think I see what you mean. I'll try it out next time.'

'You do. It will work, believe me,' he said, thinking how very young she looked, striving to hold her own in a difficult world, and how much help he could have given if circumstances had been different and Christine didn't feel as she did. 'Do you still keep up with your music?'

'Oh yes. I have the piano to myself, even if it is freezing sometimes in the drawing-room.'

'Make sure you don't take cold.'

'Oh, I don't mind. All musicians have to suffer for their art sometimes,' she said gaily. 'Now that you are here, can I offer you something? Coffee? A glass of wine?'

'The kitchen will probably go into a convulsion at the very idea,' he said, smiling. 'No, thank you, my dear. Actually this must be a very brief visit. I wanted to see you because I am going away shortly. I shall be out of the country for at least a month, possibly longer, and I wanted to make sure that all is well with you. I would have called before, but there have been so many things I have had to tie up and finish off before I go. I gather that Harry and David and John Everard have all been looking after you.'

'They've been very kind, but I have missed you.'

'I can't believe that. Seriously, now,' he went on, perching on the edge of the table, 'what has occurred to me is that the small sum we brought back from Russia must be all used up by now. To put it bluntly, Louise, I don't like to think that you are utterly dependent on Clara for every trifle. Lord Warrinder agrees with me. I would like to put a small sum of money into your account so that you can draw upon it in case of any emergency.'

'It's very kind of you both, but I really don't need it.'

'You're not just saying that because you don't want to accept money from any of us?'

'No, it is not that,' she said steadily. 'I still have the greater part of what you banked for me. It will cover all the small things I need, and when Kate pays me for the play I shall be rich.'

'You're an independent young woman, aren't you?' he said, smiling again.

'I need to be. So that's settled. Where are you going? David didn't say anything about it when we were together at the Gallery.'

'Didn't he? Well, he's not very interested in my doings. It is actually what you might call a fact-finding mission. It would seem that Turkey, ostensibly our ally, has been behaving very badly, invading Bulgaria, carrying death and destruction into innocent villages, and my paper appears to think I'm the right person to ferret out the truth and find out how many of the atrocities actually happened, or whether they are enemy propaganda put out by Russia and Germany, who have an axe to grind in the matter.'

'But isn't that terribly dangerous for you?'

'Not particularly. I am quite a hand at these things. I can take care of myself.'

'If I were your wife I wouldn't let you go,' she exclaimed passionately.

He grimaced. 'Christine has been doing her best to dissuade me, but work of this kind has been part of my life for years now and I've no intention of running away from it at the first hint of danger. And now I really must be off. I leave very soon and I still have ends to tie up. Don't let Clara smother you when she comes back. You have a wide circle of friends now. Try and remember that.'

And none of them matters a straw without you, she thought with a sudden feeling of despair. He had always been there, and now, if that secret fear of hers were to materialize, if Leo went on haunting her (or worse), Daniel would be out of the country, hundreds of miles away. She should have confided in him before, and now it was far too late.

'Take care of yourself,' she said breathlessly, 'please, please don't let yourself be killed.' She felt for a moment all the agony and terror of last year. She flung herself into his arms as if she couldn't bear to let him go, the light kiss he gave her turning into a passionate embrace in which for a few seconds they were both utterly lost. Then he tore himself free, picked up his hat and fled from the room and down the stairs, falling over a bucket on the way. She heard the front door slam, with a feeling of finality, her hand pressed against the mouth he had kissed, tears running down her cheeks, and yet at the same time wildly, crazily happy.

As for Daniel, he strode down the street furious with himself for giving way to a rush of feeling he thought he had driven out. Ever since New Year he had deliberately immersed himself in his work, spending long hours in his study plotting a new series of articles, this time on the evils of child prostitution as a follow-up to those already published. Joe Sharpe was eager to publish just as soon as the furore that had greeted the first series had died down. He had long sessions with his publisher over the corrected proofs of his new book before it was dispatched to the printer – so long that Christine had complained that she never seemed to see him except at meals, and sometimes not even then.

Harry and Kate had kept him informed about Louise, and David had muttered something about taking her out, and it was not till he knew that he would be out of the country for several weeks, possibly months, that he gave in to the irresistible desire to see her for himself and knew in his heart that the offer of funding her was simply an excuse. He had found it impossible to escape a feeling of responsibility for her, and there was also the worrying question of Leo. He had in fact already asked John Dexter if the mysterious Russian had turned up again, and the doctor told him that as far as he knew he had returned to have his wounds redressed and then simply disappeared, as did many of the patients at the clinic.

The memory of that horrible scene at the railway station was still vivid in his mind, as was the uneasy impression of something very like obsession, even madness, in the eyes of the wretched young man, his head shaven to the skull, his ankles gripped by heavy chains, looking pitifully young and lost in such brutal company. Such a man could harbour a bitter desire for revenge for months, years perhaps, before ultimately giving way to it. But if Leo had turned up again, surely Louise would have confided in Daniel. He thought of telling Christine, but it would involve a lengthy explanation of the days spent at the villa and it seemed better to say nothing when already she seemed so unwilling to discuss Louise. In any case, he was probably making too much of it. He did think of mentioning it to Harry, but in the end he was obliged to leave some days before he had expected and the opportunity was lost.

However, he did say something to Christine on the last evening they spent together. 'I wish you would keep an eye on Louise while I'm away. It seems Clara will be coming home soon now and Lord only knows what kind of mood she will be in.'

'I don't really know why you should be so concerned about Louise. It seems to me she has gathered quite an army of supporters. Harry and Kate have taken her under their wings, even David has got over his sulks and John Everard not only takes her riding in the Row but has persuaded Clary to call and invite her to a family dinner party. Heaven knows what Margaret is thinking about it. Even Mamma invites her to take tea with her now and then, and told me only the other day what a sweet, good-natured and beautifully behaved young woman she is: a hit at me, of course, who was never sweet, good-natured or beautifully behaved. I should say that by this time Louise will be more than a match for Clara.'

There was an edge to Christine's voice and he deliberately made no comment. Something had disturbed the close companionship that had been so much a part of their marriage, and he didn't seem able to mend it, try as he would. Christine had argued bitterly against this new assignment of his.

'I know why you're going. You're deliberately putting yourself into danger simply because you want to get away from me.'

'Oh good God, Christine, you know that's not true. I've been in far more risky situations.'

'That was when you were younger.'

'Well, I'm scarcely in my dotage,' he said, trying to laugh it off.

'You're forty-three. You have far more responsibilities now.'

'I have a reputation to maintain in matters like this, and I've no intention of backing out now.'

She knew that when he spoke like that, any argument was useless, but all the same, when they came to the actual parting, she clung to him, nearly in tears. 'I'm sorry, Dan, I'm sorry,' she whispered. 'It's only because I worry about you so much, God knows why. I should have grown out of it by now but I haven't. Promise me that you won't do anything foolish for the sake of a good story. Don't take any risks.'

'You know me,' he said sturdily. 'I run like a hare at the first whiff of danger! I'll be back before you know where you are, and, if there's a shopkeeper still unlooted in Belgrade, I'll bring you back something that will make it all seem worthwhile.'

It was David who told Louise about Daniel's departure, when he took her to hear Clara Schumann play her husband's beautiful, melancholy music. She thought of Daniel while she let the music flood through her, and wondered if the time would ever come when she would be able to play like that.

About a week later, an official letter arrived from the bank, informing her that £100 had been placed in her account, on which she could draw whenever she pleased, and enclosing a sealed envelope with a note from Daniel: *Don't be angry that I've not taken you at your word. You can always pay me back when the play is a roaring success.*

Despite her brave attempt at self-sufficiency, it did give her a pleasant feeling that in case of necessity she was not utterly penniless.

The next surprise for Louise was not so happy. Clara arrived two days before she was expected and caught everyone at Arlington Street on the hop. Not that the house wasn't ready for her: it had been scoured from attic to cellar. It sparkled and shone. Every carpet and curtain had been cleaned, every item of furniture polished to within an inch of its life, every ornament washed, every mirror gleamed. All had been completed in such good time that there was a day to relax, to draw breath, to enjoy the satisfaction of work well done. Mrs Bolton took a day off and left the house soon after breakfast. Cook, with a larder well-stocked, decided on a simple supper for the staff with something to spare for Miss upstairs, who never raised any objection to what was put before her. Rennet put the last piece of silver back into its chamois wrapping with a sigh of satisfaction, took off his apron and, still in his shirtsleeves, lit his pipe, put his feet up and began a leisurely glance through the morning paper just as the front doorbell rang clamorously. There outside in the road was the station cab, piled high with luggage, and there was Clara on the step, demanding to know why the carriage had not been sent to the station to meet her.

For a few moments all was utter confusion. Servants flew about in all directions. Rennet, struggling into his coat, was heard trying to explain that the telegraph must have gone astray, that they had absolutely no idea she would be arriving that day, but everything was ready for her. All this while the luggage was being carried in and the driver paid.

Upstairs in the morning room, cut off from the rest of the house and quite oblivious of Clara's unexpected arrival, Louise had taken Daniel's advice and was trying out an extremely dramatic speech, giving herself added reality by emphasizing her words with the poker, when the door flew open and Clara stood there, more formidable than ever in her travelling-dress of rich green velvet trimmed with squirrel, and looking blazingly angry.

'May I ask what is going on?' she demanded. 'Rennet in his shirtsleeves, Mrs Bolton gone off no one seems to know where, the servants behaving like frightened rabbits, and now you acting like someone from a Drury Lane melodrama.'

'We – we didn't expect you till the day after tomorrow,' stammered Louise.

'So I gather. And what do you think you are doing with all this?' A sweeping gesture indicated the table, loaded with its pens, ink, books and piled sheets of paper.

'I am translating a play.'

'You're *what*?' exclaimed Clara incredulously.

'It has been arranged for me by . . .' She had been about to say Kate Hunter, remembered in time that Clara was said to loathe her and hastily substituted Daniel. 'And I am to be paid for it.'

'Are you indeed?' said Clara drily, 'and that explains, I suppose, why my sitting-room has been turned into a literary workshop.'

'I had meant to clear it all away and take it to my own room before you came home,' said Louise, hurriedly starting to pile things together and only making the confusion worse.

'Oh, leave it, for heaven's sake! Since my housekeeper appears to have taken the day off, you might perhaps inform Cook that I should be obliged if she would serve a light luncheon in the dining-room in about an hour's time, and condescend to provide dinner at a suitable time this evening,' went on Clara ironically.

'Yes, of course, at once. Mrs Bolton has gone to visit her brother. I understand that his wife has been taken ill. She will be very distressed at not being here, but I'll see to everything.'

'And you'd better tell Ada to come up at once and assist my maid with the unpacking.'

'Very well.'

Everything could not have gone more hopelessly wrong, thought Louise, hurrying down to the kitchen where everyone from Cook to the scullery maid had been galvanized into activity. She had meant it all to be so different. She had intended to be cool, calm and collected, ready to meet her sister on an equal footing with her new feeling of self-confidence, prepared to find a different Clara from the new knowledge she had of her. And now there she was, thrown back to the very first days of humiliation. Only, strangely enough, it was not quite like that, as she gradually began to realize.

There was a difference in Clara. She no longer seemed to feel the need to be so aggressive, so determined always to find fault. That evening when they dined together she actually asked Louise how she had enjoyed her stay at Bramber, and when Louise said it had been like one big family party she didn't make her usual acid comment on the free and easy way Daniel and Christine chose to live their life. She even volunteered a few ironic comments on the notable people she had met during her long stay at Nice, and offered to show Louise the latest fashion magazines she had picked up in Paris on the journey home.

It was all very strange and bewildering. Louise, prepared to do battle if necessary, found little to fight against. It could be very disconcerting, as she discovered a day or so later, when they were in the morning room sorting through Clara's correspondence, which Louise had tried to deal with in her absence. They worked for a while in silence, then Clara said suddenly:

'Are you still busy with this translation of yours?' When Louise said she was working on it in her bedroom during the afternoon, Clara frowned. 'It's ridiculous to shut yourself up there when I rarely use this room after midday. You can work down here, and tell the servants to keep the fire going for you.' She cut short Louise's stammered thanks by saying irritably, 'There's no point in making yourself ill over it. Now, where were we? Is there any other matter I should attend to before I dress? I'm lunching out today.'

Then there was John Everard. Louise had wondered whether to write him a note telling him to forget riding in the Row for the time being, and then in all the agitation forgot it so that, when he came to fetch her as usual on Sunday morning after church, he ran into Clara, dressed in great style for a carriage airing in the park. He shared the family feeling about Cousin Clara as someone to be avoided at all costs, but remembered himself sufficiently to stammer a polite greeting.

She eyed him sternly. 'I gather you are in the habit of riding with Louise in the Row.'

'Yes. She is actually exercising Clary's mare as my sister is not riding just now,' he said hastily.

'I see. And does your mother know about this?'

'Yes, of course,' he said, with the uneasy thought that Clara was just the sort to go blabbing a lot of nonsense to Lady Ingham. 'She met Louise at Bramber over Christmas.'

'Well, take care of her. See she doesn't come to grief,' and she swept by him to where the carriage was waiting for her.

'Phew!' muttered John Everard as Louise came to join him. 'What's happened to the ogre? I expected to have my head bitten off and it didn't happen. Is she turning soft in her old age or what?'

'She is not so old as you might think,' said Louise as they went down the steps to where his groom waited, holding the horses.

'Oh Lord, she must be! She used to frighten the wits out of me when I was a child. Nanny used to say, "You do that again, Master John, and Cousin Clara will get you!" Oh, to hell with her! Come on, let's go.'

He gave her a lift into the saddle and they went trotting down the street side by side. Louise had nearly said, 'She's not too old to be in love,' and then bitten the words back. She had made a shrewd guess at Clara's change of heart but was unwilling to say anything till her guess was confirmed, as it was a week later, when they were in the drawing-room after dinner. She had dealt with the coffee as usual and brought the cup to Clara, putting it on a small table beside her chair. She poured one for herself, came to sit opposite and decided to risk a question.

'Did you see anything of the Comte de Chaminard when you were in France?' she asked innocently.

Clara looked startled for a moment and then she said, 'Yes, I did. He brought his mother to spend New Year with us.'

'His mother? The Greek lady? What was she like?'

'Very small, very slender and utterly formidable.'

'How do you mean?' asked Louise, intrigued.

'It would seem that after her French husband died, and she and Jean-Louis were more or less forced to leave the family château, she went back to her father, the old Greek shipowner, and worked alongside him. After he died suddenly she continued to manage the whole concern herself till Jean-Louis was old enough to take it over, and even now she knows as much about it as he does, and he never clinches an important deal without discussing it with her first.'

She had never discussed anything so personal before, and it was then that Louise knew that her guess must be right. Jean-Louis had waited for his mother's approval, and that strong-minded lady had glimpsed in Clara someone like herself, hard, indomitable, capable of running her home, her children and her husband as well as a shipping empire if it were necessary. Jean-Louis must have asked Clara to marry him, and at long last all her doubts, her torments and anxieties were to be satisfied, so that she could afford to look more kindly at the world around her – even at the interloper, the love child, her half-sister.

Louise had the good sense not to ask any questions. Clara would tell her more in her own good time. All she did was to enquire if Jean-Louis would be coming to England this year.

'Oh yes, at the beginning of May or soon after,' said Clara. 'He is in the United States just now. There is a big deal coming up and he must be there to oversee the details.'

Of course it was not all sweetness and light. It couldn't be, Clara being what she was. She could not yield everything. When she took Louise with her, as she did increasingly, to musical evenings or charity events in which she was involved, she still introduced her as 'poor dear Papa's little ward'. The word 'half-sister' still stuck in her throat, even though she knew that by now almost everyone had guessed the truth.

It was on these occasions that Louise had her first real experience of upper-class English society, and found it very stiff and unfriendly, not at all like it had been at Bramber or Hunter's Lair or in those dear lost days at the villa. The older women glanced at her with active dislike. No penniless foreigner had any right to look like that. Most of the young girls like herself were either painfully shy, or simply stared and giggled when she tried to make intelligent conversation about books, plays and music. On the other hand the men, young and old, found her quite delightful. This did not add to her popularity.

It was at a morning bazaar for homeless children that she made a new acquaintance. The stalls were heaped with all kinds of articles: clothes, scarves, shawls, ornaments of every kind, cheap jewellery, all discarded by the rich because they were tired of it, had worn the dress three times or had no use for Great-Aunt Araminta's birthday presents. Presiding over one of these tables was a tall lady, simply but elegantly dressed, white-haired but looking a good deal younger than her sixty years, who was introduced by Clara as 'my dearest Harriet'. Louise realized that this must be the redoubtable Miss Motford, a distant relative of her own father, who had come to look after the difficult nine-year-old Clara and remained as friend and companion for some thirty years, only retiring shortly before Louise herself came to England.

'Dearest Hattie,' said Clara, kissing her warmly. 'Wherever have you been hiding yourself that you haven't called on me? I want you to meet Louise, Papa's *protégée*, you know, from St Petersburg. She helps me with all my correspondence just as you used to do.'

They chatted for a few minutes and then, Clara being hailed by another group of friends, Louise said shyly, 'May I stay and help you with the stall? Clara has so many friends and I haven't. It makes me feel rather like a dog on a string.'

'Of course you may,' said Miss Motford kindly. 'Actually I shall be glad of more assistance when we really get going.'

She had been out of London for some months on a lengthy

visit to friends in the north, but she knew all about Louise from Clara's first furious letters, and she eyed her now with a good deal of interest.

They talked in a friendly way while the stall did a roaring trade. A great number of young men, dragged there by a mother, wife or sister, found Louise's charming looks very attractive and were easily persuaded into buying a number of completely useless objects.

Lunchtime arrived at last and they closed down, most of the goods now disposed of after a strenuous morning. Clara came back to them saying that she had been invited to lunch with friends but the carriage could take Louise back to Arlington Street.

'Perhaps you would care to come home with me,' said Miss Motford to Louise. 'I live in a tiny cottage in Chelsea, but I can always rustle up something to eat.'

'Thank you. I'd like that very much.'

'Good. I dare say Clara's carriage will take us there.'

It was the narrowest street Louise had ever seen, hardly wide enough even for the horses. There was a row of small cottages, each one painted white, and bright with boxes of spring flowers. They went through a tiny hall into a parlour as charming as the doll's house she had loved as a child. There was another room which Miss Motford called her studio, a tiny kitchen, and a garden not much larger than a pocket handkerchief but absolutely crammed with plants climbing up walls or stacked in tubs, many of them in flower already.

She took Louise upstairs to one of the two small bedrooms to take off her hat and coat. 'This cottage was one of three inherited by your father. He sold two of them but kept the third as a home for any dependent who might be in need of it. Clara's old nanny lived here till she died, and then it was granted to me. It suits me very well. I can look after it myself with the help of a daily woman, and I live very comfortably with all my favourite things around me.'

During the afternoon Louise discovered that Miss Motford was not only very well-read but also did exquisite petit-point needlework, painted charming watercolours of flowers and plants, and seemed to have a wide circle of friends, chiefly from the arts. It was a pleasure to be in the company of such a sensible intelligent person, in whom she felt she could confide and know that her confidences would be treated with respect.

'Tell me,' said Miss Motford, making a cup of fragrant China tea in the tiny kitchen, 'about this adventurer to whom Clara seems to have taken such a great liking. Daniel said he reminded him of a Greek pirate with the manners of a French *chevalier*.'

'Oh, do you know Daniel too?' asked Louise delightedly, having deliberately kept him out of the conversation.

'Certainly I do. I call on him and Mrs Hunter occasionally. I have the greatest admiration for his courage and determination in the causes he takes up.'

'Oh, so do I,' said Louise fervently. 'But for Daniel I don't think I could have gone on living after they murdered Papa and Mamma. As for Jean-Louis, he is all that Daniel says and more,' she went on. 'I suppose you could call him handsome, but in a way he is far more than that. He gives you an impression of immense power and intellect, and I think at times he could be frightening.'

'And Clara loves this paragon?'

'Oh yes, I am very sure of it.'

'I only hope he is worthy of it,' said Miss Motford drily. 'For all the show she puts on and for all her wealth, Clara has never really known happiness.'

They went on to talk of a number of things, of Louise's music and how she longed to study further, of the play she was translating. When they parted, it was with a mutual intention to meet again soon.

Chapter 13

The first draft of the translation was almost finished, as she told Kate proudly when Harry invited her to join his party at the Lyceum, where Henry Irving's controversial Hamlet was stunning theatrical London. 'Simply hideous,' wrote one critic; 'Beyond all praise,' commented another; while to Louise it was a revelation. She was enthralled by a young prince who had discarded the sable plumes and elaborate costume of earlier players and appeared in simple black with only the gold chain round his neck and the glitter of the silver-hilted sword at his side. She shared her enthusiasm with Isabelle, who had taken David's place.

'He is working hard for once, and about time too if he is not to disgrace Uncle Harry,' said his sister heartlessly. 'He is to be called to the Bar later this year.'

'What does that mean?' asked Louise curiously.

'He'll be a real barrister then, and have to work and face life in earnest.' Best of all that evening was to have first-hand news of Daniel. 'He asked me to tell you,' went on Isabelle in a whisper, 'that he hasn't been able to write to anyone very much because he is in some ghastly place where there is little opportunity of getting letters out.'

'Is he in danger?'

'He doesn't say very much, but then he wouldn't, for fear of alarming Mamma. But I have a feeling that he will be very glad indeed to be out of it.'

'If you write, do please send him my love.'

'Of course I will, but goodness knows whether he will ever get the letter.'

The days went by and it was nearly April. Louise's nineteenth birthday came and went unnoticed. It seemed almost impossible that it was only a year since the morning when she had woken very early with a childish feeling of excitement, when there were gifts and congratulations and Leo arriving with a huge bouquet which he had stolen from his father's hothouses. Buried in the midst of the flowers was a tiny Chinese lion-dog, exquisitely carved in green jade.

'It's so beautiful,' she had said, 'but much too expensive.'

'It's not just from me but from Papa and all of us,' said Leo expansively, 'because you admired Mamma's jade collection so much. I thought it looked a bit like your silly little Toby.'

And she had laughed with sheer pleasure on that happy day of sunshine and showers, with no thought of the tragedy that was only a few months away. She had the figure still; it sat on her mantelpiece, ugly and endearing. She looked at it sadly sometimes, remembering the Leo who had brought her the gift, the Leo who no longer existed.

She had not seen him since that evening with David, and had tried to put him out of her mind, though she did wonder sometimes if he was still somewhere close by, watching her when she took Toby walking in the evenings. She told herself that she was being ridiculous.

Then Ada mentioned something about Roger Tanner that, whether she believed it or not, somehow made her feel threatened. It was one afternoon when the girl was attending to the fire in the morning room. 'I've been meanin' to tell you, miss,' she said, piling on extra coal and sitting back to watch it spark into flame. 'It's about that brother of Mrs Bolton. My pa heard something funny about him.'

'What do you mean by funny?' asked Louise.

'Well, peculiar I suppose you could call it, really. It seems that he don't depend on the shop for his livin' at all, and that's true, says Ma, seein' as they hardly sell a thing from one week's end to another.' She paused and then went on dramatically: 'It seems he's got a house up in a smart part of London and he lets it out in rooms.'

'A lodging-house, do you mean?'

'Maybe you could call it that, but it don't have the ordinary sort o' lodgers.' She lowered her voice to a dark whisper: 'They say he lets his rooms to girls ... you know the sort I mean ... girls off the streets who ought to know better ... And they bring in men, more than one a night, they say, and they has to pay part of what they get or else he throws 'em out, bag and baggage ... d'you know what I mean?' She looked doubtfully at Louise, as if she might have gone too far.

Louise frowned. It was something you read about in books but never came up against in real life. 'I suppose you mean it's a kind of brothel,' she whispered, still unwilling to believe the sordid story.

'That's what my pa says, though it don't look like it, see. He keeps books but all they show is the rents he receives, it don't say nothing about what he gets from the girls. To think that all the fine clothes his daughters swank about in come from that – makes you think, don't it?'

'How does your father know all this?'

'There's a man in his factory who used to work for that Mr Tanner. Pa said he told some stories that made your hair stand on end.'

It seemed impossible to believe that Mrs Bolton, a model of rectitude, could possibly be connected with such a person, but then she might not know about the brothel. What distressed Louise more than anything was to think that Leo could be connected with something so detestable. More than ever she wished she could confide in Daniel and be reassured, but he was hundreds of miles away and would not be back for many weeks. She told herself that it was in all probability a tissue of lies told by a man who had been dismissed and bore his employer a grudge for it.

She resolutely put it out of her mind, and it was not too difficult just then since she had a serious problem of her own. The fact was that John Everard was becoming a great deal too persistent in his attentions. One afternoon he turned up in a very dashing carriage and offered to drive her to look at the spring flowers in Kew Gardens. Taken by surprise and tempted by the morning sun, she went with him, and enjoyed herself immensely. Then Clary invited her to a family dinner party with her brother as the only other guest. John Everard had sat gazing at Louise while his brother-in-law prosed on very boringly about a chap called Goethe, and thought to himself how much he would like to take Louise to Ingham Park, ride with her around the grounds, show her his horses, talk to her about what he intended to do when he sold his commission and settled down. The evening ended with him promising to take her to Hampton Court Palace the following week.

'You like history so much, you'll love it,' he urged, and she found it hard to refuse.

'If Clara doesn't want me for anything, I'd like to come.'

'Good. Then that's settled.'

He kept his promise, and she did love it, enjoying as much of the old palace as they were allowed to see, getting hopelessly lost in the maze, with a great deal of laughter, and then walking the length of the palace so wonderfully restored by Christopher Wren for Dutch William, rows of scarlet tulips marching alongside in the flowerbeds, stiff and straight as soldiers.

He had been telling her about the father he scarcely remembered, who had died gallantly in the famous Charge of the Light Brigade at Balaclava. 'Aunt Christine brought one of his horses back from the Crimea, Brownie, who lived till she was twenty-five and is buried in Ingham Park. Aunt Christine's husband was fatally injured when he tried to save Rufus, the whole stone building collapsed on him and the horse during a fearful hurricane. He died a year later.'

They walked on in silence for a little, then he stopped suddenly, oblivious of the other people who were also strolling along the wide path, took her hands in his and said abruptly, 'Louise, will you marry me?'

She stared at him aghast, knowing it was impossible, hating to hurt him, robbed of words for a moment. Then she drew her hands gently away.

'Oh, why did you have to say that? Why? You have spoiled everything.'

She walked on quickly and he kept pace with her. 'Why have I spoiled everything? You must have realized already how very much I think of you.'

'I can't marry you, John. I can't. It is impossible.'

'Why is it impossible?' he said stubbornly.

'There is everything against it, I being what I am and your mother not really liking me – oh, and everything being so very uncertain.'

'But that's one of the reasons why I want to marry you, to give you back what you have lost.'

'To give me an honourable name, that's what you mean, isn't it?' she said bitterly.

'No, it's not that. I love you, Louise.'

'No,' she said in distress. 'No, it's impossible. You must see that.'

He paused for a moment and then said bravely, 'Well, I don't. Is there someone else? Is it David?'

She shook her head. 'No, it's not David, it's not anyone.' She turned to face him. 'I like you, John, I've enjoyed our rides and our walks together so much, but I don't want to marry anyone, not yet, not for a long time. I want to ... to find myself first. Oh God, I can't explain, and I don't want to make you unhappy.'

'I don't understand what all this is about, but I'm not giving up,' he said firmly, taking one of her hands again and holding it in his own warm grasp. 'And don't say I've spoiled everything. We're not giving up our rides together, are we? I can still see you from time to time, can't I?'

'Yes ... Oh, I don't know ... it does make a difference.' She was very nearly in tears.

'It makes no difference at all,' he said sturdily, 'and to prove it I'm going to take you to the hotel at the gate and buy you some tea, and after that we'll drive back and I'll tell you all about Ingham Park. I'm going to ask Mamma to write and invite you there so you can see it for yourself.'

'No, John, no, you mustn't,' she said unhappily.

'You can't stop me.'

John Everard did as he threatened. He ordered a tray of tea in the comfortable lounge of the Gate Hotel, but it was not a success. Louise was blaming herself severely for not realizing what was happening and letting things go as far as they had. Try as she would, it was impossible to recapture the lightness and pleasure of the early afternoon.

He drove her back to London and when he helped her to alight from the carriage captured one of her hands, drawing her close to him. 'It's not the end of everything, is it?' he pleaded. 'I shall see you next Sunday as usual?'

'I don't know . . . perhaps we shouldn't . . .'

'Nonsense, why shouldn't we? I shall call for you at the usual time.'

'No, please.' She drew her hand away. 'I must go now. Thank you for . . . for everything.'

She escaped from him into the house, thinking that next Sunday was five days away and she could make an excuse: a bad headache, the onset of a violent cold, anything.

It so happened that Lady Ingham had come to London that week to spend a few days with her pregnant daughter and was shocked and horrified to find that all the gossip was about the imminent engagement between her son and that pretty little thing from Russia whom Lady Dorrien was befriending. She repudiated the whole thing instantly, saying there was absolutely no truth in the rumour and that her son had been simply taking pity on a friendless young girl whom he had met as a guest of Lord Warrinder at Bramber. She complained bitterly about it to Christine.

'I simply don't know what has got into him,' she lamented. 'I told him down at Bramber that the very idea was quite preposterous, and what happens? I'm told that he is regularly riding with her in the Row and taking her here, there and everywhere as if they were already betrothed. I might have guessed what would happen. She has set herself out to capture him, and it would seem that she has succeeded. She is quite shameless. I wonder Cousin Clara allows it.'

'To be quite honest,' said her sister, driven in all fairness to defend Louise, 'I think it is John Everard who has done the pursuing. Louise has other strings to her bow, you know. Harry has been inviting her to join his theatre parties, David has been escorting her to exhibitions and concerts, even Cousin Clara appears to have had a change of heart.'

'I wish to God Daniel had never brought her from Russia. He must have been out of his mind.'

'I wish that too sometimes,' confessed Christine, 'but he really had no option. He couldn't just abandon her, and Papa supported him very strongly. I am afraid she is here to stay and we must make the best of it.'

'Can you imagine her at Ingham Park? The daughter of a vulgar opera singer, illegitimate and without a penny of her own – what are our neighbours going to think? It makes me shudder at the very idea of it.'

'Her mother may have been an actress but her father *was* James Ducane, you know, a man whom Papa liked and respected, and you must admit that she is not in the very least vulgar. Even Mamma approves of her and you know how very particular *she* is.'

'Anyone would think you doted on the girl!' exclaimed Margaret irritably.

'I don't in the very least, but I do think you're making too much fuss of what may be only a lot of silly rumours. Why don't you ask John Everard outright what his intentions are?'

'What is it about the wretched girl?' went on Margaret with exasperation. 'Even Clary likes her, and Edward Dalroy, who ought to know, told me how delightful it was to talk with a well-educated girl and what wonders she had done persuading John to talk about something other than his horses. Dear God, what kind of a thing am I up against?'

All the same she did take her sister's advice and asked her son a very direct question at the earliest opportunity.

'For once the gossips are quite right,' he said calmly. 'I did ask Louise to marry me a few days ago.'

'You did?' said Margaret faintly.

'And you'll be pleased to know that she rejected me.'

'She rejected you?' repeated his mother, outraged that any young woman had dared to turn down her adored and handsome son.

'Turned me down flat for a number of reasons, one of them because she believes that you do not like her. But don't think I am giving up. I shall ask her again, Mamma, and it's no use your raising any objections because they will do absolutely nothing to change my mind. And there is something more,' he went on with unusual determination: 'I would be glad if you would invite Louise to spend a week with us at Ingham.'

His mother stared at him, utterly aghast. 'You cannot expect me to do that. Everyone will be asking when your engagement is to be announced.'

'So much the better. My fear is that she will refuse, but I tell you now that if you don't ask her, I shall, but it would come better from you.'

And despite all her arguments, all her pleading and much against her will, Lady Ingham did write the letter. Louise received an invitation couched in polite if cool terms – the great lady condescending to a commoner – which nearly made her accept out of sheer devilment, but she did not want to hurt John Everard more than necessary. She knew how much he loved his country home and longed to share it with her. She took refuge in Clara's unpredictable moods and wrote that she believed they were expecting guests and she did not feel she could leave her sister at such a time.

The letter written, she posted it herself and, since it was still early in the morning and she felt most unaccountably lighthearted now that it was done, she went into Fortnum's in Piccadilly and on a whim bought a number of chocolate novelties wrapped in extravagant gold paper tied with coloured ribbons. She took them to Wimpole Street as Easter gifts for Christine and the children.

To her great disappointment Mark said, 'I am sorry, miss, but Madam left with the children a couple of days ago to spend Easter with Lord and Lady Warrinder.'

'I see.' She looked down ruefully at the box on the step. 'I didn't know. I ought to have come before.'

'Perhaps the master could take them down to Bramber for you,' suggested Mark helpfully.

'I thought Mr Hunter was still away.'

'He arrived very late last night and I'm not even sure if he is up yet. If you care to step inside, I will find out for you. Madam left word that she hoped he would follow her to Bramber as soon as possible.'

The servant picked up the box and ushered Louise into the study which she remembered so vividly from her previous visits. 'If you care to wait here, miss, I'll only be a few minutes.'

He disappeared and she wandered around the familiar room, which was unusually neat and tidy. Everything was in its proper place: pens, pencils, ink, stacked paper, no sign of the usual chaos which Daniel forbade anyone to touch since he always knew exactly where everything could be found. She had read one of his reports published in the *Daily News* and been moved by his trenchant account of what had followed Turkey's invasion: villages destroyed, whole families evicted, a cruel toll of homelessness, starvation, sickness and murder.

Mark returned with a tray of coffee and told her that Mr Hunter would be with her in a few minutes.

He was up, washed and already shaving when Mark delivered his message, and his first reaction had been to refuse, to say he was in no fit state to see anyone. He had endured a fiendish journey of a day and a night with little food and no sleep, hidden in a crate in a goods train among every kind of farmyard animal which had all reeked to high heaven. He had seen too much, asked too many probing questions, and been a great deal too outspoken about some of the atrocities he had witnessed. The Turkish police had been on his track for a week and he had escaped from their clutches by a miracle – not that they had any real case against him, but once in their hands it would be only too easy to trump up a charge of spying, and conditions in Turkish prisons were notoriously vile.

He had arrived home, starving, filthy, exhausted beyond

belief, only to be greeted by an empty house and a cool message from Christine that since she had heard nothing at all from him she really couldn't wait any longer, but perhaps he would follow as soon as possible and not disappoint the children. In addition there was a brief note from Ezra Brown, who had been sponsoring his application to stand as Independent candidate at the next election, saying that members of the selection committee were having second thoughts on account of the notoriety he seemed to have acquired for his articles on prostitution, which had even occasioned a question being asked in Parliament. 'Damn, damn and damn again!' he muttered, throwing the letter down. It was altogether too much on top of everything else. He had slept badly, woken unrefreshed, and was in consequence feeling considerably out of sorts and hard-done-by.

'Shall I tell Miss Louise to leave the gifts and you will take them down to Bramber for her?' asked Mark diplomatically, already aware that his master was unusually short-tempered that morning.

'No,' he said with sudden decision. At least someone would be glad to see him. 'Give her some coffee and ask her to wait. I'll be down in a few minutes.' And so he was, in shirt and trousers, his hair still damp where he had washed out the grit of travel, and wearing a flamboyant deep red dressing-gown, a gift from Christine.

'Well,' he said coming through the door, 'what a wonderful surprise. I had begun to think everyone had deserted me.'

Her first thought was how deadly tired he looked, and the second how very much she loved every single thing about him.

'I've thought about you so much while you've been away,' she said, 'and I read what you wrote in the newspaper – but that must only have been part of it. Was it a very dreadful experience?'

'It had its grim moments, but I was lucky,' he said lightly. 'I wasn't murdered and I avoided ending up in a Turkish prison for the next twenty years.'

'Oh Daniel, don't –' and suddenly, almost without any

conscious thought on her part, she was in his arms, then she was kissing him and his arms tightened around her, she felt the hard male strength pressed against her and it seemed like the culmination of weeks of thoughts and dreams. It was marvellous and it was very nearly their undoing. For a few moments his weary frustration, the fatigue and loneliness were all swallowed up in sheer physical pleasure, then with an effort he put her from him and moved towards the table, striving for the commonplace.

'What about pouring some coffee for me and telling me why you are here at this time in the morning. Mark says you brought some Easter gifts for Robert and Celia.'

'Yes, I did. I didn't know they were away.' With an effort, and in a daze of happiness that she did not dare to question, she poured coffee for them both.

He took the cup and moved towards one of the armchairs. 'Come and sit down and tell me what you have been doing.'

'I'd much rather hear about you.'

'It would make very sorry telling, I'm afraid. Tell me, how is Clara behaving these days?'

So she began to tell him about the change in Clara. 'I don't know how to explain, but she is happier somehow and I feel I understand her better.'

'Perhaps the Greek pirate has come up to scratch.'

She smiled. 'I think that might be true. It seems he brought his mother to meet her in Nice.'

'Did he, by Jove? The matriarch inspecting the bride.'

'Perhaps.'

'And what about you, Louise?'

'Oh, I've been working very hard and not getting anywhere very much. I've finished the first draft of the play and . . . and John Everard has asked me to marry him.'

He sat up. 'He's *what*?'

'It sounds impossible, doesn't it, but it's true.'

It gave Daniel a jolt. He got up and moved away to put down his cup. 'It's not impossible at all. Are you going to marry him?'

'No, of course not. I like him very much but I don't love him. I'd stifle at Ingham Park. Besides, his mother doesn't care for me at all.'

'Margaret would not consider a princess good enough for John Everard, but she would come round to it in time. You'd be safe for the rest of your life, Louise.'

'I don't want to be safe, not like that.'

'What do you really want?'

'I'd like to go on with my music,' she said slowly. 'At first nothing seemed to matter to me any more, but now I've begun to realize how important it is to me. I wish I could continue what I had begun in St Petersburg with Monsieur Vincent. I really hunger for that, and it seems that ever since then I have only been marking time.'

'And what else?'

'I wish ... no ... I don't wish that because I know it is absolutely impossible.'

'Come on now, tell me. Nothing is impossible if you really want it.'

'This is ... I wish that you loved me as much as I love you.'

It was so unexpected and was said so simply it took his breath away, so that he couldn't think of an appropriate answer and, in the temporary silence, she went on. 'I told you it was impossible, didn't I?'

He gathered himself together in an effort to make the right reply. 'You must put anything like that out of your mind once and for all. It's not love, Louise, simply an affection born out of the circumstances that drew us together. You must thrust it away from you. Forget it.'

'I can't. I've tried and tried but it is still there.'

'Nonsense,' he said almost roughly. 'There is John Everard, there is David, all the young men you will meet and who will fall in love with you.'

'None of them means anything beside you,' she said with sudden passion. 'If anything had happened to you while you were away, I wouldn't have wanted to go on living.'

He turned to look at her, shaken by a powerful wave of

desire that had nothing whatsoever to do with the steady love he had for Christine and his children. Here in this house, where by chance they were isolated from everyday living, it would be so desperately easy to yield. What matter if afterwards it was hell and damnation?

'Louise,' he said huskily and, at that precise moment when their eyes met, she took a step towards him and he saw a kind of tremor run through her, there was a shrill whistle outside and someone hammered at the front door. They stood breathless, hearing Mark go to open it, a murmur of voices and then a tap at the study door before he came in.

'A telegram for you, sir.'

Daniel took it from him, tore it open and for a moment stood staring down at it. He looked as if he had received a blow in the face.

'What is it?' whispered Louise.

'It's from Lord Warrinder. Robert has had a riding accident, he has struck his head and is still unconscious ... The doctors are afraid that he ... that he ...' He choked momentarily and Mark said:

'The boy is waiting. Is there any answer, sir?'

'Yes. Say I will come as soon as possible. Then put a few necessities in a bag and find out the time of the next train.'

'Very good, sir.' Mark went out and Daniel turned to Louise.

'I must go. Christine will be frantic. If anything should happen to Robert ...'

She understood, had always known what came first with him, and Robert was *his* son, not like David. He was bound to feel it all the more deeply.

'Don't worry about me. I'll go,' she said quickly. 'I don't want to be in the way. I shall pray it's not as serious as it seems.'

'I'll ask Mark to call a cab for you.'

'No, he's busy. I can walk.' She hesitated, then kissed his cheek and hurried from the room.

All the time, as he finished dressing, got himself to the

station and on to the train, his uneasy conscience went on reminding him that he who looks on a woman with desire commits adultery with her in his heart. At the very moment punishment had come like a hammer of fate. He thrust the wretched thought away from him, consumed with an angry impatience because the train was so slow.

Paddy was at the station to meet him with the dog-cart. 'Master Robert were worried about summat, sir,' he said as he drove at breakneck speed along the narrow country lane. 'He were upset, not like himself. I warned him about ridin' Sultan, the nag's too strong for the boy and nasty-tempered too, but he wouldn't take no heed. He come down one mornin' when my back were turned and were off like a shot up on to the Downs. It were an hour or so after when Sultan comes back, lookin' sorry for himself, and then we found him, lyin' like as if he were dead with that ugly black bruise, fair upset me it did ...'

Lord Warrinder was on the steps to meet him. 'Thank God you're here. I took a chance with the telegraph, praying that you'd have returned. Christine is up with the boy. Go to her, Dan, she needs you badly.'

When he came into the bedroom she was standing at the window and turned to look at him.

'You came then.'

'You knew I would as soon as I got your father's wire.'

'I didn't know ... I wasn't sure ... I'd had no word ...'

'I'm sorry. It just wasn't possible to write.'

'Oh Dan ...' She gave an inarticulate little sob and ran to him. He held her close against him.

'How is he?'

'Just the same. He's in a coma ... for two days now ... and the doctor says there is nothing we can do but wait and pray that he will come out of it. It's the bruising, you see, they can't tell how bad it is and they're afraid if they explore they could do more damage ... It could mean ...' Her voice was muffled, her face pressed against his coat. His arms tightened around her.

'Poor darling, it must have been hell for you. But I'm here now and we'll see it through together. He'll be all right, I'm sure he will.'

'I told myself I wouldn't cry, I wouldn't give way,' she said, fiercely sniffing into the handkerchief he gave her. 'Mamma has never stopped weeping and it's so silly, it does no good. Come and see for yourself.'

They went to the bed together, his arm still around her. Robert lay very still, the thick brown hair tumbling over his forehead, so quiet, so unlike himself, so utterly defenceless, he could have been dead already. There was a faint discolouration around one eye that puzzled Daniel till he remembered what Paddy had been muttering on the way from the station. He did not mention it then, for there was too much else to talk about.

Life in the great house had to go on as usual despite anxiety over the sick boy. There was an important case coming up before Lord Warrinder very soon, and when after dinner he was left alone with his son-in-law he asked how his mission had gone in Bulgaria.

'Well enough, I think. I have a quantity of notes I must put into a report as soon as I can.'

'You look exhausted, Daniel. Why don't you and Christine have an early night? Nanny will be on watch and the doctor has sent us a very capable nurse to help us out.'

'Perhaps I will. I wish I had been here when it happened.'

'You couldn't have done more than we did.'

'No, but I could have taken some of the pressure off Christine.'

Later that evening he persuaded her to take a night off from her constant vigil, and he lay on the bed watching her brush out her hair, still dark and lustrous.

'By the way,' he said suddenly, 'when Paddy was driving me from the station, he said something about Robert being not himself. Was that just Paddy nattering on as usual or was the boy really upset about something?'

'Yes, he was,' said Christine thoughtfully. 'I'd almost

forgotten about it in all this trouble, but when he came home from Rugby this time he had the remains of a terrible black eye that worried me. I meant to tell you about it. I think he is being bullied, but you know what Robert is like. I couldn't get a word out of him, only some nonsense about having fallen down on the playing field. That school is too rough for him, Daniel. I wish you hadn't sent him there. Papa brushes it off, he says all boys go through it and it will make a man of him, but I don't agree. Robert is sensitive. He feels things deeply, far more than Celia does.'

Daniel frowned. 'If this is true, I'll have to speak to the headmaster. I'll talk to the boy myself when he comes out of this.'

'*If* he comes out of it,' murmured Christine.

'We mustn't give up hope. I don't think I altogether trust these country doctors. I'll ask John Dexter to come down and take a look at him. We'll hear what he says and then, if necessary, seek further advice, the best there is. Where is David?' he went on a little irritably. 'He should have been here with you.'

'Harry decided to take a weekend break in Paris and took the boy with him. I miss Isabelle,' sighed Christine, 'but she has gone to spend a few weeks with her friend in Edinburgh. I couldn't drag her back. How long can you stay, Dan?'

'I will have to go back immediately after Easter. I must report my findings personally to the PM as soon as possible, but I'll come back as often as I can.'

'What was it like out there? You wrote so little,' she said, realizing guiltily that in her absorption in her son she had scarcely noticed how tired and thin he looked.

'It certainly had its unpleasant moments. There was a serious lack of any decent food, for one thing. I hope I never have to eat bean porridge again as long as I live. I spent most of the return journey shut up in a goods van wedged between a crate of squalling hens and a great many disagreeable and hostile geese.'

She slipped off her dressing-gown and climbed into the bed beside him. 'But why, for heaven's sake?'

'The Turks didn't care for me prying into some of their worst atrocities so they set the police on me. It was touch-and-go for a day or so, but I wasn't going to end up in the hellhole of a Turkish prison if I could help it.' He smiled wryly. 'I'm beginning to think I'm too old for these jaunts.'

'Oh Dan, I'm sorry. I didn't realize how hard it has been for you. You didn't give us any idea.'

'I was never sure of where my letters would end up,' he said.

'It was good of you to bring those Easter gifts for the children.'

'They're not from me, I'm afraid,' he said, yawning. 'It was long past midnight when I got in last night. Louise brought them early this morning and, since you'd gone already, she left them for me to bring.'

'Did you see her?'

'For a few minutes. She looked very well. I gather she has had a proposal from John Everard.'

'Has she, indeed? I know Margaret was terrified that he was going to ask her.'

'Margaret needn't worry. Louise has turned him down.'

'He is very determined, and she could easily have second thoughts about it.'

'I doubt it. Louise has other ideas about her future. It seems the Greek pirate is expected to arrive any time now and marriage is in the air. Clara is apparently softening up. I think there may be some changes at Arlington Street before long.'

'Did she tell you all that? You must have had quite a chat.'

'She hinted at it.' He settled down in the bed and drew her against him. 'I don't know how you're feeling but I'm dead beat. I've been pretty short on sleep this past week.'

Anxiety about their son had drawn them together, but they were still a little on edge with one another. He felt guilty that he had let his thoughts stray away from her, if only momentarily, and Louise still stood between them.

It was a wretched Easter though Cook did her best, providing a bowl of brightly coloured eggs for the breakfast table and an

Easter feast of roast lamb and her own very special meringue trifle. Louise's giant Easter egg wrapped in gold paper and tied with scarlet ribbon stood beside Robert's bed for the happy moment when he would open his eyes and come back to them. Celia, usually so full of life, crept around like a small ghost and could hardly muster more than a wan smile at the big chocolate rabbit with long ears and a pink bow round his neck that Louise had chosen for her.

An urgent telegram brought John Dexter down on the Monday, but there was little he could do except give them hope and encouragement.

'The boy is young and resilient, there is every reason to think he will come out of it. Talk to him from time to time, bring his favourite things to him, let Celia come with the dogs. It is impossible to tell what will trigger off the brain as the bruising slowly heals. If only we could open up the skull and remove the pressure, but it's far too risky. But don't lose your courage, Christine, and call me again if the slightest need should arise.'

Not even to Daniel did he say that in his opinion there was a grave danger of a brain haemorrhage. Nothing could be done to prevent it, and it might *not* happen, so why worry them unnecessarily?

They did as he suggested, but it was nerve-racking and did very little good. In between sessions at his son's bedside, Daniel strove to write a coherent and intelligent report on what he had seen and heard during his weeks in Bulgaria.

It was from Celia that he had a hint at what it was that had been troubling Robert before his accident. In an attempt to cheer her up he took her for her favourite walk through the park to the home farm, but not even a litter of squealing pink piglets, chicks like balls of yellow fluff and a basketful of adventurous tabby kittens took her mind off her brother for more than a few minutes. On the way back she startled him by suddenly saying, 'Papa, what is a whoremonger?'

'Wherever did you hear a word like that?'

'Robert told me that one of the boys at his school said that was what you were. He ran all through the playground shouting that Hunter's father was a dirty whoremonger and it made Rob so mad that he hit him. After that they fought, the other boys joined in and that was how he got that dreadful black eye. Afterwards the headmaster caned him because he would not say how the fight started. He forbade me to tell Mamma about it so I didn't.'

'Does Robert know what it means?'

'He said he looked it up in your big dictionary but he didn't really understand what it meant except that it was something very bad, so he knew it couldn't be you, but he was awfully upset about it. He told me that I wasn't to tell anyone but now . . .' her lips trembled, 'now he's so sick . . . You're not . . . not what those beastly boys called you, are you?'

'No, Celia, I'm not.'

Oh God, thought Daniel. He had embarked on his crusade against the evils of prostitution with the best of motives and under an assumed name, but the truth had leaked out and it had never once occurred to him how it might affect his children. How could he possibly explain it to her? But he had always been honest with them, and Celia was eleven after all. He couldn't just brush it aside with a few glib words. They had been walking through a stretch of woodland; he dropped down on one of the fallen tree trunks and drew her to stand between his knees.

'Listen to me, Celia: a whoremonger is a man who goes among poor women, lives with them and makes them work for him, doing bad things for money.'

'But you don't do that.'

'No, but you know what my work has been, don't you? You know that I sometimes write about bad things to try and put them right. Well, I wanted to do something to help those poor women so I had to go among them, listen to them talking, find out what had driven them to such a life, so that I could write about them, so the ministers who govern the country would then realize what must be done to help them. Do you understand?'

'I think so,' said Celia slowly. 'It's like Mamma, isn't it, when she ran a bazaar to help all those poor women who have babies with no father to care for them?'

'Yes, something like that,' he said in relief, feeling totally inadequate. 'And you won't let it worry you any longer, will you?'

'No, and I shall explain to Rob when he is better.'

'Good.'

They resumed their walk and later that same day Daniel came into Robert's room to see Celia close beside the bed, stroking her brother's hand.

'It's all right, Rob,' she was whispering, 'Papa explained it all to me, so you don't have to fret about it any longer and please, please come back soon. I do miss you so dreadfully.' After a moment she looked up and saw him. He held out his hand and she ran to him. 'Rob isn't going to die, is he? Papa?'

'Of course he isn't. We won't let him, will we?'

He gave her a reassuring hug and saw her run away, a little comforted. Surely, he thought to himself, surely God couldn't be so cruel as to make the boy suffer for what his father had undertaken in good faith and with the best of intentions.

As for Louise, for one marvellous, dizzying, impossible moment she had believed that Daniel loved her as she loved him. Then it had vanished, the telegram destroying her rapture as completely as the bomb had shattered her security and she knew he was lost to her. She went back to Arlington Street that day still a little exalted, a little dazed.

That very afternoon John Everard called and tried his utmost to persuade her to change her mind and accept the invitation to Ingham Park.

'No,' she said. 'No, John, it would not be right, not now. It is kind of your mother to invite me but I know how she really feels.'

'She will love you as much as I do when she learns to know you,' he pleaded. 'I promise I won't hold you to anything against your will, but Ingham Park is at its best in the spring. I want so much to share it with you. Please think again,' and he took her hand in his, drawing her towards him.

He had his own particular charm but she had given way to it far too much already. Gently she disengaged herself and stood out against him valiantly, blaming herself severely for allowing him to believe she cared for him more than she did. It had been so easy to allow a feeling of triumph and a growing self-confidence since Christmas to carry her gaily along, and events had gone much further than she had ever intended.

She saw him leave at last, grieved for his disappointment but thankful it was all over. She still sometimes felt that she was whirling along on the thinnest of ice which at any moment could give way and hurl her into the abyss, a feeling that grew stronger when she was in the drawing-room with Clara after dinner. They were alone that evening and, though they had been on the whole on friendlier terms, Clara could still be bitingly unpleasant at times.

She looked up from her coffee to say abruptly, 'I'm afraid there is something I have to say to you, Louise, something very distasteful. You have been allowing yourself to be talked about among our friends and I don't care for it. I hope you realize that.'

'Talked about?' repeated Louise. 'Whatever for? I'm sure that none of your friends are interested in anything that I do.'

'Oh yes they are, very much so, and it reflects upon me, especially when you play fast and loose with the affections of a popular young man who is related to me.'

'I don't know what you are talking about.'

'Nonsense, of course you do. John Everard has apparently made no secret of the way he has been pursuing you, but I had no idea it had gone so far. Don't you think I should have been informed of what was going on between you?'

'I didn't think you would be interested. Actually his proposal took me by surprise and I have absolutely no intention of accepting it.'

'You are living in my house and under my protection,' said Clara icily. 'I think I deserve some consideration. If you had come to me, I would have advised you strongly to accept him, even though my cousin Margaret would no doubt have raised a number of objections. I would be happy to see you established in a good position for the rest of your life.'

'Perhaps that is not what I'm looking for,' said Louise, flushing. 'I would not wish to cheat John Everard. I like him but I don't love him.'

'Oh, love!' exclaimed Clara with contempt. 'What's that but a young girl's dream?'

'You don't need to be young to dream of love' was on the tip of Louise's tongue but she did not dare to throw it in Clara's face. Instead she said, 'I'm sorry if I have caused you any embarrassment.'

'So you ought to be. I hope that in future, when young men come knocking at my door and asking for you, you will have the courtesy to inform me, as your guardian, and when Jean-Louis arrives you will of course pay him the same courtesy.'

'Jean-Louis?' exclaimed Louise. 'Does that mean . . .?'

'It means that we are shortly to be married. As soon as he comes, the date will be settled.'

'Oh Clara, that's wonderful!' exclaimed Louise. 'I'm so very happy for you,' and impulsively she ran to put her arms around her half-sister and kiss her cheek.

'Yes, well, that's quite enough now,' said Clara awkwardly, disengaging herself from Louise. 'No doubt you had guessed already. There will be a great many changes here of course, but that is something to be discussed when Jean-Louis is here.'

'Will he be staying with us?'

'No, no, of course not. It would not be at all proper. He still has his apartment in Half Moon Street.'

In all the excitement it did not occur to Louise how these changes would affect her and that she might very well be cast adrift once more. For the moment she refused to worry about the future. Kate had been delighted with the translation and had paid her sixty guineas, which seemed an enormous sum, and she did wonder if it had come out of Kate's pocket, or maybe that of George Westcott. Now Kate was asking if

Louise would like to look at *Fedora*, a romantic melodrama by Sardou with a wonderful leading part which she was anxious to find out about before Sarah Bernhardt's eye fell on it.

Life seemed full of promise over that Easter and Louise was totally unprepared for the storm John Everard's proposal provoked in David.

He had returned from a long weekend in Paris with Harry that had included a visit to the opera, together with rather more riotous entertainment celebrating his twenty-second birthday among the artists and writers in the café society of the Left Bank and Montmartre. Before returning home he called into the wine bar near the Old Bailey where fledgling barristers like himself occasionally foregathered to show off amongst their elders and betters. An acquaintance who had once met him with Louise greeted him boisterously, slapping him on the back.

'While you've been gallivanting in Paris, old son, your girl has got herself hitched.'

'What the devil are you talking about? Louise is not engaged to anyone.'

'Not publicly, yet, but it seems that cousin of yours – good-looking chap in the Guards – has popped the question.'

'John Everard has asked her to marry him?' said David disbelievingly.

'That's right. Of course she refused at first, all maidenly blushes, but it's a foregone conclusion, isn't it? She'd be a fool to go on saying no when he has so much to offer and can do just as he pleases – lucky dog – with no disapproving papa to put a spoke in the wheel.'

'I don't believe it,' said David. 'Louise wouldn't do that to me.'

'Oh wouldn't she just? You know girls, Davey, all over you one minute and wouldn't be seen dead with you the next.'

The very next afternoon David braved Clara and stormed into Arlington Street. He pounced as soon as Louise came into the drawing-room where he was waiting for her. 'I'm surprised to find you still in London,' he said sarcastically. 'Why aren't you at Ingham Park with John Everard?'

'I don't know what you are talking about,' she said calmly. 'Why on earth should I be there?'

'You know well enough. You're going to marry him, aren't you? When? This month, next month? How did you persuade Aunt Margaret? That must have taken some doing. Clever puss, aren't you? You had it all planned at Christmas and my damn fool of a cousin fell for it. The poor little orphan doesn't need any of us any longer, does she? She has made quite sure of her future.'

'Have you taken leave of your senses? Where have you heard all this?'

'Oh, don't deny it. John Everard did just as you expected, didn't he, and you said no, with the absolute certainty of saying yes next time he asked. But I won't let you marry him,' went on David violently, forgetting all good sense, grabbing hold of Louise and pulling her hard against him. 'You belong to me, don't you realize that? You've always belonged to me, ever since we first met in the garden at St Petersburg, and I swear to God that no one else, no matter who he is, is going to have you.'

'Let me go,' she said furiously, struggling to free herself from his grip. 'Have you gone raving mad? I'm not going to marry John Everard now or ever, and I don't belong to you or to anyone else. I belong to myself.'

For a moment he still held her, her face only a few inches from his own, then slowly he let her go. 'I don't believe you. I've only just come back from Paris and they told me . . .'

'You shouldn't listen to silly gossip,' she said crisply, rearranging her disordered dress, 'and in any case, instead of coming here and shouting at me, you should be down at Bramber. Don't you know that your brother has met with a serious accident, that he is still very ill, could be dying by now for all you care?'

He stared at her, bewildered. 'Robert is sick? What happened to him? Why didn't they tell me? How do you know?'

'I was with Daniel when the telegram came from your grandfather.'

'Daniel is still abroad,' he said stupidly.

'Don't your family mean anything to you at all?' she said scathingly. 'He has just come back.'

'What were you doing there with him?'

'Oh for God's sake, what do you think? I called in at Wimpole Street with some gifts for the children just before Easter and he had returned that night, driven out of Bulgaria by the Turks and lucky to escape alive. Robert has had a fall from his horse and injured his head. He is still unconscious.'

'Oh my God! I didn't know. Mamma will be nearly out of her mind.'

'That's what Daniel said. He left for Bramber at once. Now you know hadn't you better go too?'

'Yes, yes, of course I must.' He hesitated, distressed at the news and feeling that he had made an utter fool of himself. 'I'm sorry, Louise. I thought . . . I didn't want to believe that you . . .'

'Perhaps next time you won't be so quick to make up my mind for me,' she said. 'And now you'd better go. Your mother and Daniel need you far more than I do.'

'Yes, yes, I know . . . but you're not really angry with me, are you? I can come back, can't I?'

'I don't know . . . Not if all you can do is be insulting.'

'Oh please,' he went on, trying to take her hand, but she quickly drew it away.

'I shall still be here,' she said austerely. 'I'm not going away as far as I know, and I shall be glad to know how Robert goes on.' And with that he had to be content, while Louise saw him leave with a great deal of exasperation and just a little, a very little, reluctant sympathy.

Chapter 14

Jean-Louis arrived from Paris as powerful, enigmatic and fascinating as he had been before, but with the Greek pirate submerged for the time being beneath the charm of his French ancestry, while, sure of him at last, Clara blossomed. There was no other word for it, thought Louise. She was transformed by this late flowering of love so that even Miss Motford, who had entertained the gravest doubts, was quite won over by Jean-Louis when she dined with them one evening, and had to admit to Louise that the unexpected had actually happened: Clara was radiating happiness for the first time in nigh-on forty years.

Louise, paying a flying visit to Wimpole Street to ask after Robert, gave Daniel the glad news and thought he looked incredibly tired. He told her that Robert had opened his eyes, only to stare blankly at them. He still could not speak or move, and intense anxiety continued while patience had begun to wear very thin.

Daniel was shuttling between London and Bramber, trying to complete a detailed report on the Turkish affair and setting out the main points of his article on the evils of child prostitution for which Joe Sharpe was badgering him. At the same time he strove to keep his temper with his stepson, who blamed him for sending Robert to Rugby instead of Harrow, and as a consequence provoked angry words between himself and Christine which he bitterly regretted. Then there was Celia to deal with. Nanny had brought her back to London, since medical opinion pronounced she would be better off at school with her friends than brooding over her brother's condition. He tried as far as he could to spend a little time with her each evening so that she would not feel too abandoned, with her mother at Bramber and Isabelle far away in Scotland.

It had not been easy and he was feeling the strain of it, so it was little wonder that he was glad to relax for an hour in Louise's sympathetic company, listen with amusement to her running on about Clara and her Greek pirate, give her some good advice about the play she was struggling with and forget for a few minutes the gnawing sense of guilt that it was Robert's unhappy doubts of his father that had driven the boy into testing himself to the utmost by riding a horse a great deal too powerful for him.

Louise sat and drank tea with him in his study, and when she got up to leave kissed his cheek. Seeking comfort, he held her very close for a few seconds, then let her go. She ran into David as she was leaving the house.

'What on earth are you doing here?' he asked rather ungraciously.

'I came to ask how Robert was and stayed a little while to talk to Daniel. I think he looks very exhausted.'

'It's not he who's suffering, it's Mamma. She has to bear the brunt of it.'

'You don't seem to be helping very much,' she said tartly.

'I go down there as often as I can,' he said indignantly. 'In any case I would have kept in touch with you – you don't need to come here spending hours alone with Daniel when Mamma is away. What will people think?'

'Who do you mean by "people"?' asked Louise: 'you, or the servants? If you really want to know, I also spent an hour with Nanny and Celia, and I think that is one of the most insulting remarks you have ever made to me.'

'Look here, Louise, I only meant . . . well, you know how it is. It's you I'm thinking of . . .'

'That's quite enough. I don't want to hear any more, and in future when you call, I shall take care not to be in!' With that she stormed down the steps, leaving him regretting his hasty words and unfairly blaming Daniel for his own jealousy and loss of temper.

Isabelle had been right about David, thought Louise, walking much too fast: he was charming and entertaining when he chose, but prickly as a hedgehog. They never seemed to meet without the sparks flying.

She arrived back at Arlington Street just as Jean-Louis stepped out of a cab. He and Clara had a box at the theatre that evening, and Louise thought how handsome he looked in his evening dress, a jewelled cross of some Greek order at his throat and his opera cloak lined with white satin. He greeted her with his own particular courtesy and, while he waited in the hall for Clara to join him, he said suddenly, 'Why don't you join us? I understand the box holds four.'

Much as she would have loved to hear Mozart's *Magic Flute*, she had the good sense to refuse, knowing with absolute certainty that Clara would deeply resent her taking up even so small a part of Jean-Louis's attention.

'Thank you,' she said, 'it's kind of you to suggest it, but I'm afraid I must refuse. I have . . . have made other plans for the evening.'

'I see. Another time, perhaps. Ah, there you are, my dear, radiant as usual,' he went on, turning to Clara as she came down the stairs, while Louise took good care to disappear as unobtrusively as she could.

Now that they were formally engaged, Jean-Louis was at the house far more frequently than he had been before. They entertained a great deal too, and he and Clara were invited everywhere, society hostesses regarding the Comte de Chaminard as a prize well worth inviting to their dinner table. Louise grew to know him far better than she had done before, realizing that he was a man with many interests who could talk entertainingly and knowledgeably on a variety of subjects. He treated her with an easy familiarity, rather as if she were a daughter or a younger sister. She found him full of surprises and very easy to talk to now that she had lost her shyness, but she knew she had to be very careful. When Clara was with them Louise would remain very quiet or disappear altogether, knowing that Clara did not care for anyone, least of all a slip of a girl like her half-sister, to take any part of him from her.

She found out one day by pure chance that he had a deep knowledge and appreciation of music. Believing herself alone, she had settled down for a long afternoon at the piano. Ever since the concert with David when she had heard Clara Wieck play her husband's compositions, she had made a special study of Schumann, practising hard, and she was trying them out for her own pleasure that afternoon. She did not notice him coming in, and it was not till she had come to an end and rested for a moment that she saw him get up out of the deep armchair and stroll across to her.

She stood up in consternation. 'I am sorry. I didn't know you were here. Clara was called out to an old friend who has been taken ill. She asked me to let you know that she would be back by five at the latest.'

'Don't disturb yourself,' he said easily, leaning against the piano. 'I've had a most enjoyable afternoon. Schumann, wasn't it?'

'Yes. I have been practising ever since I heard his wife play some of his music a couple of months ago.'

'You have a quite exceptional talent,' he said thoughtfully. 'Wouldn't you like to pursue it further, studying in Paris perhaps, or even Vienna?'

'Yes, I would, but I am afraid it's not possible for a great many reasons.'

'Perhaps we might think of a way to overcome some of those reasons. In the meantime Clara tells me that she is planning a musical party in a few weeks, probably the last before we go abroad. Will you honour me by playing that evening?'

'Clara wouldn't want that,' she said quickly. 'She will be engaging well-known artistes – professionals. I am only an amateur. I couldn't compete with them.'

'There are quite a number of professionals I've enjoyed far less than listening to you this afternoon,' he said. 'Think about it, Louise, and don't worry about Clara. I can deal with her.'

She had no doubt that he would do as he said, and she wondered what Clara's reaction would be. The musical party was still some weeks off, towards the end of May. In the mean time she practised assiduously whenever she could and waited to see what would happen. She knew now that the couple were planning to marry early in June in the Greek Orthodox church in Paris, and afterwards would probably spend their honeymoon on his yacht, cruising among the Greek islands. So far Clara had said nothing about the future. She wondered what she was going to do if Clara decided to shut up the Arlington Street house and dismiss the servants.

One afternoon, when Louise was taking tea with her in Chelsea, Miss Motford asked her what her plans were when Clara was married.

'I haven't made any,' she confessed, 'except that I must somehow keep myself. Daniel says he can almost certainly get me more translation work, and so does Kate, but I don't know if it will be enough to make a living. It's queer, but at the moment I can't seem to worry.'

'If at any time you are desperate for somewhere to live, you would always be welcome here,' said Miss Motford unexpectedly. 'I have a spare bedroom and I have no doubt that with your many talents you could find some kind of useful work among my many acquaintances.'

'How very kind of you,' exclaimed Louise, touched to the heart by the generous offer.

'I know what it means to be dependent on relatives and how hateful it is having to accept their help, however kind they are,' said Hattie Motford, 'so remember, if such a time comes, you can have a home here.' This was something comforting to hold on to in those dark moments when the future seemed so uncertain.

Whatever battle Jean-Louis had fought with Clara he had obviously won, because she came to Louise one morning when she was working on her French translation and sat down at the table, frowning at her. 'I suppose you know already that Jean-Louis would like you to play the piano at my musical soirée,' she said abruptly.

'He did mention it,' she murmured, 'but of course it all depends on you.'

'Yes . . . well . . . it seems he has a very high opinion of your talent, so you had better make sure that you justify it.'

For a moment Louise was terrified. It was one thing to dream about the possibility but quite another to face up to the reality: a sophisticated audience, at least some of them musically knowledgeable, and all of them deeply critical. Then a wave of pure elation, mixed with sturdy self-confidence flooded through her.

'I can do it,' she said quietly, and knew with certainty that she would not let him down.

'You had better tell me what you will be playing, as I am having a programme printed,' went on Clara, still frowning doubtfully, 'and then we must talk about what you are going to wear.'

But Louise already had her own ideas about that, and that very afternoon she knelt by the huge old trunk in her bedroom and lifted out from its tissue-paper wrappings the gown which had been made for her for her parents' wedding and which she had never worn. She had not looked at it since the day she had packed it in St Petersburg. Wearing it would be like a justification, a celebration of the day that had never been; but now, as she shook out the folds of rich silk, she wondered if she was right. Perhaps after all it would be wiser to forget it, go to Clara's dressmaker and have a new gown made, one in which to start a new life, free of the past. Louise Dufour, she would call herself, daughter of Marianne Dufour, and an artiste in her own right . . . Then she laughed at herself for building a stupid fantasy on the strength of one amateur performance at a concert held in a private house.

She turned back to the dress, holding it up against her. She was slimmer than she had been a year ago. It would probably need to be taken in at the waist a little. For a few moments she was lost in memories. What fun they had had in designing it, her mother overseeing every detail. The lustrous corded silk was the palest, creamiest pink, the skirt flowing from a tiny waist and drawn to the back, falling in flounces trimmed with the finest lace, the tiny tight sleeves also falling away into a cascade of lace. She stripped off her skirt and white blouse and slipped it on, looking at herself critically in the mirror. She liked its simplicity but realized that it needed a touch of colour to give it drama. Geranium-pink velvet, perhaps, in a sash that would fall into a huge bow with trailing ends; and the neck, designed discreetly for a church service, needed to be cut out a little to reveal her white throat and shoulders.

She felt a stir of excitement and a certainty that she could rise to the occasion. It was like creating a new image of herself. She found other things in the trunk that she had forgotten: a pair of satin slippers dyed to match the pink, a gauzy scarf of pink and silver organza to throw around her shoulders. It all needed careful ironing of course, but Ada could be trusted to do that, lovingly taking care of every small detail.

Clara saw it of course, but before it had been transformed, and privately she thought it highly suitable: rather insipid and schoolgirlish, nothing there to overshadow her own appearance on this all-important evening.

The days went by and the programme was arranged. There was to be a well-known string quartet; a lady who played the harp; the Herr von Standen who had sat beside her at that memorable dinner party last December would sing several German *Lieder*; a certain Madame Leoni, who was usually in opera at Covent Garden, would condescend to sing French ballads; a well-known violinist would oblige; and there was Louise, who would at Jean-Louis's request play Schumann in the first part and after the interval for refreshments a selection of the Chopin that she particularly loved.

There was one minor incident during those weeks that showed all too clearly how fragile Clara's happiness still was, how jealousy and insecurity still smouldered beneath the surface. Jean-Louis had tickets for the theatre, but Clara had a raging headache so that at the last moment she felt she could not face it.

'What a pity,' he said, looking down at her stretched on the sofa, very pale and sick. 'I had a devil of a job getting the tickets too. It seems that this young woman, what's her name now?, Ellen something . . .'

'Ellen Terry,' murmured Louise, who was standing by ready with remedies, and sprinkling lavender on a handkerchief in case Clara needed it.

'That's it. Well, she appears to have taken the town by storm. Tickets are at a premium. Are you quite sure you don't feel up to it, my love?'

'When I have a migraine like this, even the slightest sound is agony,' said Clara faintly.

'My poor darling, I understand. When I have any kind of sickness I don't want anyone near me.' He kissed her forehead gently. 'Tomorrow you will be a great deal better and we will do something very special to make up for it.'

'I am so sorry to spoil your evening,' murmured Clara, almost in tears. She would have walked through fire for him, and it maddened her to feel so hopelessly incapacitated by pain and sickness.

'Oh all is not lost,' he said cheerfully. 'It seems a pity to waste these tickets. What about you, Louise? Would you care to accompany me?'

She hesitated. Everyone had been talking about *Olivia*, an adaptation of Oliver Goldsmith's *The Vicar of Wakefield*, and the beauty and charm of the young actress playing the leading part, but all the same Jean-Louis was engaged to her half-sister.

'I think perhaps I had better stay in case Clara should need me for anything.'

'In my experience of migraine, the last thing you want is anyone fussing over you, isn't that so, my darling?' he said with the heartlessness of good health. 'You lie quietly with the curtains drawn and everything peaceful around you, and I'll take this child to the theatre and bring her back safely afterwards.'

'If that is what you want, Jean,' said Clara with a slight edge to her voice.

Louise knew she should have insisted on staying and then thought recklessly, *Why should I?* Clara had every comfort, with Miss Tuft on hand to attend to her slightest need.

'I shall have to change,' she said hesitantly.

'Of course, but don't be too long or we shall be late.'

She fled from the room while Jean-Louis pulled up a chair beside Clara's sofa and took her hand in his, speaking gently and comfortingly.

Louise enjoyed the play enormously, and dining with Jean-Louis afterwards even more though she had protested at first, insisting that she ought to return home in case Clara needed her.

'My dear child, she will be sound asleep by now, and an extra hour won't make any difference. Besides, I need supper and so, I am sure, do you.' So she had given in, and he took her to a discreet restaurant where he was well-known and treated with deference. He proved to be an entertaining companion, discussing the play, listening to her telling him about seeing Henry Irving, capping it with a vivid description of seeing Sarah Bernhardt play Racine's Bérénice in Paris and the shock when he met her afterwards.

'There was this great tragedienne, attired in frills and furbelows, tinsel and jewels, hair standing out like a dark frizzled mop and eyes like holes burned in the white paper of her face, nothing at all like the gentle beauty we have been watching tonight.'

The time seemed to fly by all too quickly till she said guiltily, 'It must be growing very late and we really ought to go. Thank you for a wonderful evening.'

He drank the last of the champagne he had ordered and sat for a moment looking down at the empty glass. 'You know, you remind me of my first wife,' he said. 'Elena played the piano too; not expertly but well enough, and I loved to listen.'

'What happened?' she breathed.

'She was drowned in a boating accident, she and the boy with her. The sea around Corfu can be treacherous, but she had sailed since she was a child and had always loved it. But that day she was caught in a squall and was gone before any of us could reach her.'

Deeply moved at such a confidence from so self-contained a man, Louise could not think of anything adequate to say, but put her hand gently on the strong lean one that lay on the table. After a moment he looked up with a smile. 'It was a very long time ago but sometimes old scars still pain.' Then he stood up. 'You're right, my dear, we must go or I shall be scolded by Clara for keeping you out so late.'

When they reached the house and she thanked him again, he pressed her hand and said, 'I enjoyed the evening. Tell Clara I will call tomorrow to ask how she is,' and he watched her go in before he drove away.

She crept quietly up the stairs but, as she passed Clara's room, Miss Tuft appeared at the door, finger on lips.

'Wherever have you been?' she hissed. 'Madam has been very distressed.'

'I'm sorry. Should I go in to her?'

'She is asleep now but she will want to see you first thing in the morning.'

'Very well,' said Louise, feeling like a schoolgirl being summoned before the headmistress for suitable punishment.

And punished she was, having to endure more than a week of Clara at her most bitingly sarcastic – but never when Jean-Louis was there. He was his usual friendly self but for the sake of peace Louise deliberately kept out of his way, hoping he didn't notice it. However, resentment wore itself out eventually when Clara found she needed Louise's help in sending out invitations, arranging with Mrs Bolton for the hire of more gilt chairs for the drawing-room and supervising the piano tuner, called in to make sure all was right with that splendid instrument.

Daniel received the invitation just as he was leaving for Bramber, and wondered if he could possibly persuade Christine to come up to London and go with him and David. Glancing through the programme that had been enclosed, he guessed that the evening would mean a very great deal to Louise. He had not seen her for some time, deliberately keeping himself away. Surely this must mean that she was on better terms with Clara, and he wondered how much Jean-Louis had had to do with it.

He arrived at Bramber in the early evening and was glad to find Harry already there. His brother-in-law was always good company and, despite his very real anxiety about his nephew's condition, contrived to keep the dinner table amused with a lively account of Jean-Louis, whom he had met on several occasions during the last month.

'What is he really like?' asked Christine. 'Daniel always calls him the Greek pirate.'

'It's a good description. He is that, but a great deal more. Very astute, very knowledgeable, a charmer on the surface, but I'd say in any crisis he could be as tough as old boots. Clara has met her match in him all right. If it should ever come to a clash between them, I'd put my money on Jean-Louis.'

'What do you think he sees in her?' asked his sister curiously.

'Well,' said Harry judiciously, 'the fact is that we are prejudiced, you know, we've all had a very biased opinion of Clara, chiefly because to us she is still the abominable child and the extremely tiresome young woman. But actually she is a very good businesswoman, for one thing. She manages her financial affairs excellently – and they're pretty complicated – and on the whole, when her emotions are not involved, she is a very shrewd judge of people. She would never have survived so long if she wasn't. No one has ever bowled her over till Jean-Louis came into her orbit, and in my opinion it is like calling to like. Don't you agree with me, Papa?' he went on, appealing to Lord Warrinder.

'Yes, I believe I do. I think you've judged her pretty shrewdly. God knows I can't stand her, never could, but I've always been aware that there was more to Clara than appeared on the surface.'

'You seem to know a great deal about her,' remarked Christine.

'Well, I do happen to know her confidential lawyer,' said Harry modestly, 'and her name has cropped up once or twice.'

'In your cups, I presume! I must say I'd like to meet this Jean-Louis,' went on Christine wistfully.

'Come with us to this concert Clara is organizing and you will. I take it we've all been invited.'

'Oh, I don't know,' she said. 'I'll have to think about it,' and they went on to talk of other matters.

Later, when they were alone in the drawing-room, the others having already retired to bed, Daniel brought up the subject again. 'Why don't you do as Harry suggested, darling, and come up to London with me? It would make Louise so happy.'

But Christine shook her head decisively. 'I have thought about it. I know Robert has been in the same condition now for weeks and weeks, but it could change at any moment, for better or for worse, the doctor told me so.'

'But the nurse is here, and your mother and your father too for part of the time. It need only be for one night. It would do you good. You're wearing yourself out with this constant vigil.'

'I know, I know,' she said. 'I do realize how hard it is for you, Dan, but when it is your own child, part of you, it becomes so desperately important.' She leaned her head against him. 'Oh why did this have to happen to us? Why?'

'None of us can answer that.' He sighed. The weeks of nerve-racking anxiety, of never knowing from day to day, were having their effect on both of them.

'You go to this party,' urged Christine. 'Louise thinks so much of you. She will be terribly disappointed if you are not there to hear her play.'

'I don't know,' he said uncertainly. 'Let David go. He can attend it for both of us.'

'Where is Celia this weekend?' asked Christine suddenly. 'She is not sick, is she?'

'Good heavens, no. She has gone to spend a few days with a

schoolfriend. The mother wrote and asked me for permission. It seems they have a whole menagerie of animals, dogs, cats, rabbits, and they live out at Hampstead somewhere. I thought it would do Celia good to be with other people for a few days. Nanny will take her and fetch her home.'

'Poor darling, there is so much you have had to do for me. Are they looking after you properly, feeding you as they should?'

'You can trust Nanny for that,' he said wryly. 'At any moment I expect her to say, "Eat up, Master Daniel, or you'll never grow up into a big strong boy"!' They laughed together and he put his arm around her shoulders as they went up to bed.

It was a warm night for May and the room felt stuffy. When they were undressed and ready for bed, he went to pull aside the curtains and open one of the casements. He stood for a moment, looking out on the sleeping garden, feeling the night air cool on his face, and Christine came up behind him, putting her arms round his waist and leaning her head against his shoulder.

'I'm sorry, Dan,' she whispered. 'I know I'm being unfair to you but I can't seem to help it. Every time I look at Robert lying there, so still, so utterly helpless, I feel I am somehow being punished for what I did to Gareth.'

He turned round quickly so that his arms encircled her, pulling her fiercely against him.

'You must never believe that, never for a single moment. It was he who had cheated *you*, by making you believe that I no longer wanted you. We never intended, never dreamed . . .'

He was suddenly seized by a fierce anger against everything that had seemed to split them apart these last months. They had not made love since Christmas, and he was shaken by a wave of hunger for the intimacy that had always been so much part of their marriage. He cupped her face in his two hands, kissed her hard and then picked her up and dumped her on the bed.

'No, Daniel,' she protested.

'Yes, my love, no argument.'
'Then at least turn out the light.'
'Why? Are you ashamed?'
'Perhaps. I'm no longer as young as I was.'
'You are to me.'

But he turned out the lamp and took her in his arms, as fiercely and as hungrily as he had done all those years ago in the icy cold and grim horror of the Crimea, on the night when they had believed they were saying goodbye for ever, the night when Isabelle was conceived and Gareth lay paralysed and helpless in the ship that would carry him and Christine to England and ultimately to his death.

Chapter 15

Only a few days before the musical evening, Louise saw Leo again. She had not seen him since the night David had brought her back from the theatre and for a terrifying moment she had glimpsed him and that unpleasant brother of Mrs Bolton's watching her from the shadows. She had meant to tell Daniel about it, but then he had gone away and so much had happened since then that it had faded from her mind. Now suddenly, without warning, the threat was there again and a great deal more alarming.

There had been guests that evening and when at last she went up to her bedroom Toby was restless and asking to be taken out. Usually at times like these, when she was occupied, Ada took him to the garden, but in the stress of a busy evening the girl must have forgotten. Louise knew that the kitchen staff would still be busy with the clearing-up. It was a fine evening so she thought she would take him for a brisk walk to the end of the road and back herself.

She threw a light shawl around her shoulders, went quietly down the stairs and out through the hall door, leaving it ajar for a quick return. The street was quiet, the gas lamps hissing gently in their pools of amber light. She walked quickly to the end of the street, Toby tugging at his leash, and on the way back her mind was so occupied with the myriad things she had to do for the concert that she walked into the arms of a man, who had suddenly stepped out of the deep shadows into her path.

He had her in a firm grip before she realized it, and she was staring up into a face only a few inches above her own. The lamplight turned the eyes into dark hollows, emphasized the high cheekbones and showed clearly a thin streak from ear to chin that could have been an old scar. She knew him instantly.

'Leo!' she exclaimed, trying to free herself. 'What are you doing here? What is it you want from me?'

His arm tightened around her. 'You will know soon. It won't be long now.' His voice was low and hoarse and he was speaking in French, the language they had always used between them in the old days.

'What do you mean? What won't be long?' she asked in the same language.

'You'll see. I've waited a long time for it,' and he lowered his head, his mouth clamping down on hers so hard that for a moment she could not breathe. Then furiously she tried to thrust him away from her, and he released her so suddenly that she stumbled and nearly fell. Toby was barking. He tried to snap at Leo's ankles and yelped as he was given an impatient kick. In a sudden panic Louise snatched up the little dog and ran for the house and safety. She paused on the steps to look back. Leo still stood there, half in shadow and somehow horribly menacing. She shivered as she went through the door, slammed it shut behind her and leaned back against it.

Rennet, coming along the hall ready to lock up, stared at her in surprise. 'Is anything wrong, miss?'

'No, no, of course not. I have just been taking Toby for a little walk.'

'I see. Then I had better get on with locking up.'

'Yes, of course. Good-night, Rennet.'

'Good-night, miss.'

Safe in the sanctuary of her own room, she tried to pull herself together. What did he want from her? What did it all mean? Perhaps she should have stayed, tried to talk to him, but there was something crazy about him. There had been a madness in the eyes staring down into hers, and her mind went back to that morning at the villa, to the horrible moment at the railway station when she had felt torn with pity for him. Surely he could not still believe that it was she who had led the police to his hideout at Bluebeard's Castle?

She wondered what she ought to do. She could of course go to the police but she was a stranger, a foreigner who knew nothing about the procedure in England, and it would need so much explanation. How could she possibly make them understand when the situation was so bizarre? This time, she thought, she must tell Daniel. He had been with her from the beginning, he would know what to do. She tried to comfort herself with that and in the mean time did her best to put it out of her mind. So much hung on the next few days. She could not, must not, let herself be distracted.

Time went by all too quickly and the night of the soirée came. Guests would be arriving around eight-thirty for nine o'clock. A light meal was served to Clara and Louise at seven, but she found it very difficult to eat anything and escaped as soon as she could.

Her dress lay ready on the bed. She would have liked this time free to concentrate her thoughts, prepare for the ordeal which had once seemed so thrilling and now was so terrifyingly close, but Clara had demanded that she should help to receive the guests. With the instinct for drama she had inherited from her mother, Louise was aware that the dress was part of her performance, so she would not put it on till the time came. Instead she slipped into the shimmering white gown she had worn on that long-ago evening at the villa, and hurried down to where Clara and Jean-Louis were already greeting the early arrivals. She moved among them quietly and unobtrusively, shepherding the ladies to the room set apart for wraps and shawls and overhearing one or two unflattering comments as they adjusted a flounce or repinned a fallen curl.

'Let's hope that girl has advanced beyond Clementi's first piano exercises,' said one spitefully. 'I cannot imagine what Clara was thinking about.'

'They do say that Monsieur Vincent, who worked with Franz Liszt, was her teacher in Russia,' ventured another timidly.

'Really! Will he be here, I wonder?'

'We are hoping so,' said Louise coolly, handing out the necessary hairpin. 'My old teacher happens to be a personal friend of the count.'

That silenced them, but in actual fact the very thought had frightened her. He had been her most severe critic in the old days. What would he think of her now, having gone blindly along for a year without any expert tuition?

Back in the drawing-room the servants were carrying around trays of champagne, with brandy if any of the gentlemen preferred it. She looked anxiously for the guests who mattered to her more than anyone. She had almost despaired of them when at last Rennet showed them in: Lady Clarissa, exquisite as a figure in porcelain in a gown of filmy black lace, her handsome husband beside her; Harry, who already seemed to know everyone; with David following in his wake and then Daniel, in impeccable evening dress and looking as if he wished he were somewhere else.

They greeted Clara, kissing her cheek as near relatives should, shook hands with Jean-Louis and then came looking for Louise, Lady Clarissa whispering, 'Such a fearful ordeal for you, my dear,' David murmuring, 'It takes me back to the garden at the villa, do you remember?' and lastly Daniel, dear Daniel, taking her hand in both of his and saying, 'How do you feel?'

'Terrified but resolute.'

'That's my brave girl. Christine sends her dearest love and hopes you will forgive her. Remember we're all behind you, cheering,' and he kissed her icy fingers and then her cheek so that for an instant she was warmed and comforted.

As soon as the guests were seated and the quartet had taken up their position at the far end of the drawing-room, the great chandelier blazing above them while the rest of the lights were discreetly lowered, she slipped upstairs to change. Ada was there to help her, and at last, when all was done, she looked down at the flowers on her dressing-table. Jean-Louis had sent white gardenias for her, golden roses for Clara. She hesitated, wondering if it was wise, remembering how her half-sister had frowned when the florist delivered them and she had carried them away to her own room. Yet it seemed churlish to ignore his generous gesture. Recklessly she picked them up and gave them to Ada to fasten in the soft waves of dark-gold hair swept up and away from her face. No bracelets lest they get in the way, no jewellery at all except for the tiny diamonds in her ears and the golden locket that linked her with her mother on this all-important occasion.

'How do I look?' she asked at last, turning round for Ada's inspection.

'Oh, miss, you're that lovely. Suits you a treat that colour does. Not one of those gentlemen will be able to keep his eyes off you.'

She laughed. 'I hope he will be listening to me too.' And then she was hurrying down the stairs to pause at the door, hearing Madame Leoni's voice rising and falling, aware that the moment for which she must brace herself was very near.

When she opened the door and went in, there was an audible gasp. She had always been so self-effacing, no one had expected anything like this.

'My God, what a stunner!' exclaimed Harry. David caught his breath because she had become his magical princess again.

Jean-Louis got to his feet and came to lead her to the piano. She did not know if he had done this to all the performers, but she was very conscious of the gesture Clara made, as if to restrain him. When she was seated, there was an expectant hush. But after the first few minutes she forgot all about them, giving herself up to the music, going from darkness to light, from pain to the heights of romantic love, and sweeping to the dramatic conclusion. The applause almost frightened her, some of the younger gentlemen keeping it up, Harry among them, calling her back and back, demanding an encore. She shook her head, curtsied again deeply and withdrew, but Jean-Louis followed her.

'Give them something more. They won't be satisfied otherwise.'

'Clara won't like it.'

'Never mind Clara.'

So she went back, playing a jaunty little tune that was such a complete contrast it set them all laughing.

It was a wonderful feeling. The first bridge had been crossed. Nothing would ever seem so difficult again. She went away to her own room for a few minutes to draw breath, to dip her hands into cool water, dab a little rice powder on her hot cheeks. Then she went down again and had scarcely entered the room when a small thin man with a shock of white hair came charging up to her, taking her in his arms and kissing her on both cheeks.

'Monsieur Vincent!' she exclaimed breathlessly. 'How very good it is to see you again. How many mistakes did I make?'

'A good many, my child, but none that are not easily remedied, and you have grown up. It is far deeper, far more full of feeling. You have suffered . . . I know what happened, *quelle tragédie* . . . and now maybe you have fallen in love. It shows, you know. Don't blush, you mustn't mind an old man like me saying such things. And now tell me, what are your plans?'

'I haven't any,' she confessed, 'except of course to go on working and, I hope, improving.'

'Nonsense, you must go further, you must study. You must not waste this God-given talent. I will talk to Jean-Louis about you. He and I are friends for a very long time. He will think of something.' He patted her hand. 'It is what your dear Mamma would have wished.'

The interval occupied the best part of an hour, time for the guests to help themselves to the delicious food laid out in the dining-room. There were patties stuffed with salmon and lobster, with chicken and duck and rich creamy cheese. There were the first hothouse strawberries topped with cream, small cakes with almonds and cherries, wines to suit every taste and fragrant hot, black coffee.

There was time for the guests to gather around Clara, offering congratulations while secretly thinking how very unfair it was that someone as rich as she was should marry a man reputed to be worth millions; not an old man either, but someone as glamorous and thrilling as a Greek pirate. There were also one or two who wondered what she was going to do for her father's little byblow, the love child who that evening had undoubtedly contrived to steal a good deal of the limelight.

David, who had made up his mind to capture Louise for himself, was thwarted by Harry, who surrounded her with a number of music buffs like himself and was joined by the German singer, who shook a playful finger in front of her nose.

'When we meet last December,' he said in his fractured English, 'you tell me you play just a little. And it is a lie, a big big lie, because you play Schumann like an angel.'

She laughed and said, 'I don't, you know, not really. It is full of dreadful holes, you ask Monsieur Vincent.'

David felt excluded. Even his grandparents had discovered some old acquaintances and settled down to a cosy chat, while Daniel had been cornered by Jean-Louis, who had read his articles and wanted an insider's view of the Turkish affair. It was all intensely irritating. He helped himself to food and coldly eyed the blushing daughters of his mother's many friends. The girls giggled and stared back, admiring the way his hair fell artistically across his brow and thinking his scowl romantically Byronic.

Replete with fine food and even finer wine, the guests settled down to the second half, roused from a comfortable doze by Herr von Standen's spirited rendering of Schubert's *The Earl King*, drowsing through the harp and violin, waking with a start at Madame Leoni's high notes and prevented from dropping off again by Louise's very skilful selection of Chopin: waltzes that evoked memories of Taglioni's *La Sylphide*, lively mazurkas, dreamy nocturnes, spirited ballades, all ending with a splendid polonaise.

Most of the time Louise was so absorbed in what she was playing that the audience might not have been there. But there was one moment when David, whose eyes never left her, saw her look directly across at Daniel, and it set him furiously wondering what it was that gave the look such significance. Daniel himself, listening dreamily and remembering the distraught, unhappy girl who despite her fragile self-confidence was still facing the world very much alone, knew with an absolute certainty that he had accepted a responsibility from which, even if he had wished to, he could never escape.

Then it was all over and was judged by everyone to have been one of the most successful events of the season. Congratulations poured in on Clara and she tried hard to forget how ravishing Louise had looked, how exquisitely young (what chance did forty-one have against the bloom of nineteen?), and she bit down the rising anger that Jean-Louis had shown her all the attention and courtesy he might have extended to a daughter, a sister or someone even closer.

Louise, escaping from a group of well-wishers, wondered if she could capture Daniel for a few minutes and confide in him about Leo. She found all the Warrinders together and put a hand on his arm.

'Could I speak to you for a moment?'

'Yes of course. What is it? Is something troubling you?'

She drew him a little away from the others. 'Yes. It happened one evening a couple of days ago when I took Toby out –' They were sharply interrupted. Rennet had come in, looking somewhat agitated and carrying what looked like a telegram on the silver salver. He came straight to Daniel.

'For you, sir. It apparently came a little earlier and your manservant brought it round himself as he thought it could be important.'

Daniel hesitated and then took it quickly and tore it open.

'What is it?' said Lord Warrinder. 'Is it Robert?'

'Yes. It is from Christine.'

'He's not . . .'

'No, but there has been a change for the worse and the doctor is worried.' He looked up, his voice unsteady. 'There has always been danger of a brain haemorrhage . . .'

'And this has happened?'

'Not yet, but that is what they are afraid of. I must go. I can't let Christine face it alone. How quickly can I get down to Bramber?'

'You could get the milk train,' said Harry practically. 'It leaves at five o'clock. Time for you to go home, change and still catch it. I would come with you, but unluckily I am in court tomorrow and so is David.'

'I'll come with you,' said his father-in-law. 'I'll take Clarissa home, change and join you at the station. Give our apologies to Clara, will you, Harry? Explain what has happened. We'd better leave at once, Daniel. There is no time to be lost.'

'I'm sorry to spoil your wonderful evening, Louise,' said Daniel. 'You do understand, don't you?'

'Of course. All my prayers go with you. I'll ask Rennet to call Lord Warrinder's carriage and I'll fetch Lady Clarissa's wrap for her.'

'Bless you.'

For a few minutes all was hurry and bustle. She stood at the door to watch the carriages drive away, the opportunity to mention Leo's frightening reappearance lost, something that afterwards Daniel was deeply to regret. So much might have been saved.

Within a few days of that eventful evening Louise was to be plunged from the heights of elation into utter despair. It was all due to a stupid mistake, a foolish misapprehension on Clara's part. Life had more or less returned to normal, with Clara already beginning to make preparations for leaving England and her marriage in Paris. It was Jean-Louis who had insisted on a quiet wedding.

'No celebration, no huge reception with a thousand guests,' he had said firmly. 'We are neither of us children marrying for the first time. Simply a few close friends to wish us well, that is all we want,' and Clara, remembering that long-ago marriage which had ended in so much pain and wretchedness, was happy to agree with him.

Louise was in the drawing-room, still in her plain dress since

Clara and Jean-Louis were due to dine out with friends and she had thought to spend a quiet evening working on her French translation, which had been sadly neglected during the past weeks. She had come down to fetch some books she had left there when unexpectedly Jean-Louis was shown in.

'You're early,' she said in surprise. 'Clara has only just gone up to dress. I will go up and tell her that you are here.'

'No, don't go. It so happens I'd like a quiet word with you. I've been talking to Monsieur Vincent, or rather he has been talking to me, very vehemently. He was greatly impressed with you. Did he tell you?'

She grimaced. 'Not in so many words. He told me that I'd grown up in the past year but he also pointed out my many mistakes.'

He smiled. 'That only proves how interested he was, otherwise he wouldn't have taken the trouble. Come and sit down. I have a proposition I'd like to put to you.' He dropped on to the sofa, and she perched a little apprehensively on one of the small gilt chairs.

'What is it?'

'Clara and I have been discussing your future,' he went on. 'She has decided at last to fulfil the terms set out in the will your father unhappily did not live to ratify. Has she told you?'

'Not yet.'

'I gather that you will have a reasonable income, which will give you some independence, but I don't think it will run to the expense involved in living for a year or more in Paris enjoying the expert tuition and discipline which our Monsieur Vincent tells me you need and could receive at the Conservatoire. That is where I come in.'

'You? I am not sure I understand.'

'Well, it's like this (though I must confess that Clara doesn't entirely agree with me. She is of the opinion that you play the piano very prettily and that's the end of it but I think she is wrong). I believe you need something more, something that would fulfil your promise, and even if it doesn't lead to your becoming a virtuoso pianist playing in concerts all over

Europe, it will give you a satisfaction you have long wanted.' He leaned back on the sofa. 'Now tell me. Am I right?'

'Yes, yes, you are, but . . .'

'No buts. I am prepared to finance you for a year, and more if it should become necessary and if you still wish it.'

'You?' she stared at him. 'But I couldn't possibly accept it from you.'

'Why not? Your sister and I are shortly to be married. I shall become . . . what do you call it over here? A kind of half-brother-in-law. What should be more natural than my doing what I can for my wife's half-sister?'

'Clara wouldn't like it at all,' she said doubtfully.

'She will come round to it,' he said confidently, 'and in any case it doesn't really concern her. One of the pleasures of having money is that you can do precisely what you please with it.'

She stared at him, tempted by his suggestion but still fiercely independent, wondering if it was merely the whim of a very wealthy man, still uncertain what he would expect from her.

'Why?' she said at last. 'Why would you do this for me?'

'Why?' he repeated and for a moment said nothing. Then he got up, moving away from her towards the windows, looking out on the tree-lined street and seeing something quite different, a relentlessly stormy sea and a great emptiness. 'I told you once about Elena,' he said slowly. 'She was Greek and her father was an old patriarch who believed that marriage and babies should be sufficient for any woman. But Elena had always longed to study music, and I promised that when the boy was a little older I would take an apartment in Paris and she could follow her dream. She died before I could fulfil my promise.'

'I'm sorry,' she breathed. She got to her feet and went to him. 'Is that why you wish to give it to me?'

'Let's say it is one of the reasons.'

She felt honoured that this essentially private man should have revealed to her something that must have meant a great deal to him. 'Then I will accept,' she said, 'and will try to do what she would have done. That's a promise,' and impulsively she leaned forward to kiss his cheek. He turned his head, slipping an arm around her waist, drawing her to him. His lips met hers in a light kiss that was a mingling of gratitude and an old, old memory.

It was the greatest ill-fortune that at that very moment Clara came into the room and saw them outlined against the window, his arm around Louise, their heads close together. All the jealousy, all the bitter resentment she had felt for this half-sister, all the doubt and uncertainty and insecurity burst into an uncontrollage rage. She crossed the room, seized Louise by the shoulder and flung her away.

'Go!' she screamed. 'Get out!' and she struck her across the face so violently that one of her rings drew a trail of blood across her cheek.

'Stop that!' Jean-Louis's voice cut like a whiplash. 'Have you gone out of your mind?'

As Louise stumbled to the door she heard the rising hysteria in Clara and the cold icy rage with which her lover answered her wild accusations, then she had shut the door on it and fled up the stairs, stopping on the first landing and leaning against the wall, too deeply distressed to move. After only a few minutes she saw Jean-Louis come out of the drawing-room and, without waiting for Rennet, he flung open the hall door, letting it slam behind him with a resounding crash that shook the whole house.

After a while she pulled herself together and climbed up the next flight of stairs to her own room. She knew Clara well enough to be sure that to try any sort of explanation now would be worse than useless. She must wait till she had cooled down. She wondered how violently they had quarrelled and guessed, from what she knew of Jean-Louis, that he was not a man to take kindly to unjust accusations being flung at him. The offer that had been so kindly meant had hopelessly misfired.

Presently Ada knocked and came in, her face alive with an excitement she knew she ought to suppress.

'There's been a right old turn-up, miss. Did you hear the door? Shook us up proper, that did. Mr Rennet said the count went off like the devil were after him and Madam has shut herself up in her bedroom and don't want no dinner nor nothin'. Miss Tuft says as how she tore that lovely new silk gown she were wearing into shreds, and when she protested, Madam pushed her out of the room and shut the door on her.' She paused to take breath. 'Will you be coming down, miss, or shall I bring you something on a tray?'

'I don't think I want anything. Some tea and bread and butter will be sufficient.'

'It won't do you no good if you don't eat proper,' said Ada, shocked. 'Cook has a lovely chicken roasting in the oven. I'll ask her to carve you a few slices and I'll bring Toby's supper at the same time.' She paused at the door to look back. 'What do you think will happen now, miss? Do you suppose the gentleman will come back?'

'I don't know, Ada, I really don't know.'

How far had it gone? She thought about it all the evening while she picked at the food Ada brought and took Toby for a walk around the garden. It kept her awake for most of the night and by morning she had at last come to a decision. Difficult though it would be, she had to make Clara understand. She could not let her sister ruin her own life when in one way at least it had been Louise's fault. Two proud people would find it almost impossible to break down the wall built by angry words. Somehow or other she must persuade Clara to understand that.

She could not face any breakfast, but she drank the tea that Ada brought to her and then went resolutely down to Clara's room. Just as she reached the landing she saw Miss Tuft come out, looking very unlike her usual composed and dignified self. Now was Louise's opportunity to find Clara alone.

She opened the door without knocking and went in cautiously. Only one curtain had been drawn back. The room was partly in shadow and looked as if a gale had blown through it. Garments were scattered everywhere and shattered glass from some precious perfume bottle crunched under Louise's feet as she went towards the bed. It was a handsome four-poster hung with finely embroidered linen curtains which had been drawn back along one side.

Clara lay against the banked-up pillows, her eyes closed, her dark hair hanging loose around her face, looking so white, so forlorn and sick, that Louise was filled with pity. She was straightening the disordered coverlet when the eyes flickered open and Clara pushed herself up a little.

'*You!*' she whispered. 'You! How dare you come in here? Get out! Get out! I never want to set eyes on you again!'

'I'm not going, Clara,' she said as steadfastly as she could. 'You are making a terrible mistake. You must listen to me.'

'I don't want to hear any of your lying excuses. Go away!'

'No. Not until I have made you understand.'

'What is there to understand? It was there plain for anyone to see.' She pulled herself up higher in the bed. 'I must have been blind not to have seen it before.'

'There was never anything to see.'

But Clara went on unheeding, the bitter words pouring out of her. 'How long has it been going on? How many times has he come here when I was out? Where have you been meeting him? How often did he take you to his bed?'

'Never, never, never!' said Louise forcefully. 'And stop talking like some third-rate novel!' She seized Clara by the shoulders and held her pinned against the pillows. 'You are going to listen to me whether you like it or not. When Jean-Louis was here yesterday afternoon waiting for you, he was not making love to me, he was offering to pay for me to study music for a year at the Conservatoire in Paris.'

'Why should he do that?'

'Because . . .' She had been about to say 'because of his first wife who died so tragically', and then stopped just in time. It belonged to him. If anyone told Clara it must be Jean-Louis himself. 'Because he had been impressed by what Monsieur Vincent had told him about me.'

Clara turned away her face. 'This is all rubbish, all lies. I don't believe you.'

'But you must,' she went on desperately, 'because it is the truth, every single word of it. He told me he had already spoken of it to you.'

'Yes, he did,' she admitted reluctantly. 'I didn't think he meant it. And then, I suppose, you sealed this unbelievable pact of yours with kisses. Is that what you are expecting me to believe?'

'Only because it is the truth. Can't you understand that? It was my fault, mine entirely. In England you are all so cold, so stiff, so unfriendly. At home it was different, we were never like that. I kissed him as I might have kissed my father, to show gratitude and affection.'

Clara stirred restlessly, half wanting to believe, half still fiercely rebelling against it. 'It matters little now in any case. He said terrible things to me, unforgivable things that I can never, never forget.'

'And if he did, what unforgivable things did you say to him to make him so angry?'

'I don't know, I can't remember, I was far too upset. I only know it was the end of everything between us.' She suddenly rolled over away from Louise, beating one fist futilely into the pillow. 'What am I going to do? Dear God, what am I going to do?'

A suspicion suddenly sprang into Louise's mind. Something about Clara's desperation, something about the plain fact that lately she had suffered one or two bouts of sickness – nothing to worry about, soon gone, but perhaps significant. She made a wild guess.

'Clara, are you pregnant?'

'Why should you say that?'

'Are you?' Suddenly she was very insistent.

'I don't know,' she muttered reluctantly. 'I am not sure.'

'But you could be.'

'At my age? Don't be stupid. It's ridiculous, absurd.'

'But still possible. Clara, you must see a doctor. You must tell Jean-Louis.'

'No, never!' she said violently. 'Do you think for one

moment that I'd use that as an excuse to bring him back? I'd die first. If it's true, I'll manage somehow. I'll go abroad. I'll have the child adopted.'

'You would do that to the child of Jean-Louis?'

'If I must. I will not go begging for marriage like some wretched housemaid because her lover has got her with child.' She was staring straight in front of her, nervous fingers plucking at the sheets. 'It can't happen to me, it can't, I won't let it, not now.' She caught her breath in a sob. 'All my life I wanted a child. I was pregnant once before, and Raymond's bloody murder killed it before it was born. I envied Christine because she had everything, a kind father, a husband, a lover, four children, while I had nothing. God forgive me but when the boy was struck down, I thought that now *she* will suffer . . .'

'It was a false alarm,' said Louise gently. 'Robert is not going to die. Daniel sent me the good news.'

'Why does everything go right for Christine and never for me? Why? Why?'

There was no answer to that, and no argument that Louise could make would persuade Clara to approach Jean-Louis, but all the same sharing the painful secret with someone, even the enemy, was a relief. In the end she allowed Louise to pull back the curtains, flood the room with light, bring water to bathe her face, to comb her hair, tidy the bed, ring for a tray of tea and, when it was brought, persuade her to drink a little.

When Miss Tuft came back, looking around her in considerable surprise, Louise said crisply, 'My sister is not feeling at all well. I think she should spend the day in bed and take only a little light food.'

'I did suggest calling the doctor first thing this morning,' said Miss Tuft indignantly.

Louise knew very well how Clara would dread any hint of her condition becoming the talk of the servants. 'I hardly think it is necessary today,' she said tactfully. 'Let us see how she feels tomorrow,' and she went away to wrestle with a new problem.

It had now become absolutely necessary to bring these two

proud, difficult people together; but how could it be done? When Clara made up her mind, as Louise knew only too well, nothing would move her, not even the difficulties of bearing a fatherless child at the advanced age of forty-one, and Louise had an uneasy feeling that Jean-Louis might suddenly take off, return to Paris, take refuge in his yacht out of everyone's reach. Someone must tell him, must make him realize the situation. And it had to be her, there was no one else. She trembled at the thought. It was delving into something deeply private between these two, and she could not gauge his reaction to her interference. If Clara had her pride, then so had he, coupled with an iron will.

She knew there was no escape, she had to face it. She knew where he lived, as during the last few weeks many messages had passed between Arlington Street and Half Moon Street. It required a certain sort of courage to call upon a gentleman in his bachelor apartment, but, having decided, she did not hesitate. In the late afternoon, she dressed herself suitably and thought she would walk the short distance through Piccadilly, glad to be out in the fresh air and away from the stifling, nerve-racking atmosphere of the last twenty-four hours.

His was a tall, well-built house and the small brass plate indicated that he lived on the ground floor. She rang the bell with some trepidation and Gaston, his manservant, opened the door, looking at her in some surprise.

'Monsieur le comte is at home,' he said in answer to her query, 'but he is preparing for the evening. I will ask if he will receive you.'

He showed her into what was obviously a man's room, furnished handsomely in mahogany and brown leather, completely impersonal except for the few books scattered here and there and a faint aroma of expensive cigars. She waited in considerable agitation. Yesterday there had been a warmth between them, a glow of friendship, but now she was venturing into deep waters and was only too well aware of the danger of interfering in the lives of others. It took all her courage, together with the memory of Clara's white, desperate face, to prevent her running out of the room. She was standing by the window and did not hear him come in till he spoke.

'Gaston says you wish to see me.'

He had obviously been in the middle of dressing. He was freshly shaved and wearing a heavy black silk dressing-gown over evening shirt and trousers.

'Yes, I do,' she said, and then suddenly found herself completely bereft of words. You cannot abruptly blurt out to a man that his mistress is bearing his child and ask him what he is going to do about it. She stared at him speechlessly while he shut the door and came further into the room.

'If you are here on behalf of your sister,' he said coldly, 'I am afraid it is useless. She made her opinion of me perfectly clear yesterday.'

'Clara has no idea that I am here,' she managed to say, intimidated by his freezing manner.

'I see.' He did not ask her to sit down but simply crossed the room to take up a position on the hearthrug before he went on. 'In that case why are you here? If you are anxious lest the proposition that I made to you yesterday will now be cancelled, I can assure you that you need not be afraid. I shall fulfil my obligations and will make all the necessary arrangements with Monsieur Vincent on your behalf.'

That stung her at last into speech. She had not once thought of the consequences to herself, and she was hurt and angry that he should assume her only anxiety was for her own future. 'I never even thought about it,' she said indignantly. 'I was only deeply concerned that what was a simple gesture of friendship on my part should be so completely misinterpreted by my sister.'

'Yes, well, maybe it is just as well that I realize her opinion of me as a despicable philanderer before we are married rather than afterwards,' he said ironically.

'But she doesn't believe that, not for a single minute. She loves you. That was why she was so desperately hurt.'

'After the insults she flung at me, I find that very difficult to believe,' he said drily.

He was not the charming, friendly man she had grown to know and like but a stranger: cold, withdrawn, implacable; quite suddenly she lost her temper with him. 'Oh, you don't understand Clara at all, do you?' she exclaimed, exasperated that a clever man should be so stupid.

'And you do, I presume.'

'I've learned to, quite painfully, over this past year,' she said, now plunging in recklessly. Somehow, even if only blunderingly, she must make him understand what she had learned about Clara in the last few months. 'You must realize that Clara has always had everything, except the one thing that really matters. She has never known love from anyone. Her father – my father – abandoned her to servants as a child, her first husband was a rake who amused himself with other women and died horribly. So she armed herself against a hostile world, determined that no one should hurt her again, till you came along and she fell in love. But she has never felt secure, she has always been afraid that like a mirage it could vanish overnight.'

'How do you know all this?' he said, frowning.

'I didn't, not at first, I thought her hard, unfeeling, but now I have talked with those of her family who have known her since she was a child, and I began to understand. When she came back after Christmas, she was different. She was alight with happiness, she glowed with joy. You do understand what I'm saying, don't you?'

'I don't know,' he said slowly. 'Perhaps.'

'You believe you know her, but there are things that Clara would never ever confide to anyone. And now there is something else.' She hesitated but the moment had come and she must risk it. 'Clara is expecting your child.'

'What!' Shock almost robbed him of speech. 'Are you sure of this?' he said at last.

There was silence for a moment. A Frenchman might have brushed it off, but surely not a Greek, a man who had already lost a son. She had taken a chance and only hoped she had been right.

'She has not yet consulted a doctor,' she said, 'but I think it is quite certain, and to bear a first child when one is her age requires a great deal of courage, and love.'

'Is that the real reason why you came here to me today?'

'It is one of them. Someone had to tell you, and I know that Clara would die first.'

He was looking at her curiously. There were some young women who would have exploited the situation to their own advantage, and yet here was this girl pleading for a sister who had never treated her with more than a scant and grudging kindness.

'You are very young,' he said. 'How do you come to understand so much?'

'I don't know that I do. I only grope my way through a jungle, because now there is no one to help me. Maybe it is because I am what I am – illegitimate, a "love child", Mamma used to call me – and even at home people always talked to me more freely than they did to other girls. Already I have learned how very easy it is to make mistakes when you have no guide.' She gathered herself together. 'Now that I have done what I intended to do, I must go. I have been here far too long already.'

'You have set me a problem,' he said, 'do you realize that? You must give me time to think it through.'

'There is something else,' she said earnestly, 'and it is very important. Don't ever tell Clara that it was I who told you the truth. You do understand that, don't you?'

He smiled at her for the first time that afternoon. 'I am not so stupid. We can still remain friends, I hope, whatever Clara decides to do with me.'

'Perhaps. I don't know.'

'I will ask Gaston to call a cab for you.' When it came, he helped her into it and watched it drive away.

She reached her own room utterly exhausted. The errand had taken far more out of her than she had expected. She could only hope that she had succeeded, but if she imagined that Jean-Louis might come galloping along that very evening for a romantic reconciliation she was to be disappointed. They were neither of them twenty-one, able simply to kiss and make up. It was not till the next afternoon, when Clara was up and going about the usual daily tasks with a grim determination to show nothing of her inner turmoil, that there came an unexpected knock at the door.

Rennet went to answer it and a moment later, a little flustered and against his express orders, showed Jean-Louis into the drawing-room.

He did not fall abjectly at Clara's feet, nor did he make any attempt to take her in his arms. Instead he said with a casual cheerfulness, 'It is a lovely afternoon, and I thought we might take a drive out to Kew. Put your bonnet on, Clara, the fresh air will do you good. You weren't looking at all well yesterday afternoon. Louise too, if she cares to accompany us.' But Louise only smiled and quickly excused herself.

If Clara was on the point of refusing, of flying into a rage or of ordering that he should leave immediately, he had spiked her guns by taking up their lives as if nothing whatsoever had happened to disturb them, and amazingly it worked.

With a sigh of pure thankfulness Louise saw the carriage drive away. Whatever was said as they walked under the lilacs, sat in the shade of the giant pagoda or gazed at the water lilies across the lake was no concern of hers.

From that day everything more or less returned to normal, but was possessed with a certain urgency. Not a word was breathed about Clara's condition, but Louise knew a visit had been paid to the family doctor. She did wonder if Miss Tuft had guessed, but she had been Clara's personal maid for more than fifteen years, would go with her into her new life and knew when to keep her mouth tightly shut.

Clara and Jean-Louis were to leave a week earlier than had been planned and would be married almost immediately. The house was to be partly shut up and left with a skeleton staff. Louise had just begun to think that now the time had come to take up Miss Motford's kind offer, and beg a bed till such time as she had gathered her resources together and planned some kind of a future for herself, when she received an urgent summons to the dining-room.

She found Clara already there with her George Westcott who, it appeared, had been James Ducane's English lawyer. With a feeling of unreality she watched her half-sister sign away that part of her inheritance which her father had confidently planned to provide for his mistress and his illegitimate daughter.

Mr Westcott, in his considerate way, explained the details and told her that, since she was still under twenty-one, Lord Warrinder had kindly consented to act as her guardian and would look after her financial affairs. 'He also asked me to tell you,' he went on, 'that you are welcome to stay with him and Lady Clarissa either at Bramber or at Berkeley Square whenever you should wish.' It took her breath away. She found herself stammering thanks while Jean-Louis sat by, leaning back in his chair, saying nothing, except that a hint of a smile hovered about his firm mouth and she did wonder how much he had had to do with it.

Afterwards, when they were alone for a moment, he said, 'How does it feel to be an independent woman of means?'

'I don't know,' she confessed. 'Ever since Papa died I have lived on a knife-edge of insecurity. It seems like faery gold that at a touch could change into trash.'

'No fear of that,' he said. 'Clara is too good a businesswoman. I want you to know that if she and I happen to be abroad still when the time comes, I have given Monsieur Vincent authority to enter your name at the Conservatoire. He tells me that you will have to undergo a preliminary test, but he is quite sure you will come through it with flying colours.'

He had suggested that she should go with them to Paris to attend the wedding, and it was not easy to refuse gracefully, but she was wise enough to realize that although Clara had conceded so much, although there had been a kind of intimacy between them ever since that day at her bedside, her sister still resented the father who had denied her the love she longed for and lavished it on strangers. Louise would not spoil her happiness by her presence at the wedding.

It was in the last week of May that she saw them board the Dover express, Clara giving her an unexpected hug and Jean-Louis kissing her on both cheeks and saying he was already looking forward to attending her first student concert. She watched the train pull slowly out of the station, waved a handkerchief till it disappeared and then returned to the quiet house and began to count her blessings.

There seemed so many that she hardly knew where to begin. Tomorrow she would call on Daniel to give him all the news and ask him whether she should do anything about Leo. Then there was the question of Miss Motford. She had already made up her mind to ask her if she would consider going with her to Paris in the autumn, sharing her apartment and acting for a few months as chaperon, friend and guide.

That evening her mind was so filled with exciting plans that she could not bear to remain in the house. After dinner she put Toby on his leash and went out into the warm night of early summer, walking through streets all seemingly crammed with happy people like herself, gazing into shop windows, watching the carriages roll by, filled with hope for the future, longing to share it with Daniel, who would so readily understand.

She walked further than she intended, and when she returned to Arlington Street it was already dusk, the lamps shining between the pools of dark shadow. At the entrance to the street, beneath the tall plane trees already in full leaf, someone grabbed her from behind and a hand thrust something that smelled sickly sweet against her nose and mouth. She struggled violently to free herself. Toby's leash was torn from her hand and she heard him barking valiantly, then a painful yelp as a kick sent him sprawling into the gutter. She redoubled her efforts but a heavy blanket had been thrown over her head, pinioning her arms to her sides. The drug was having its effect, her senses were swimming dizzily. She was lifted and thrust into what she took to be a cab, since she heard the wheels grind over the cobbles as it jolted forward, throwing her heavily against the seat, trussed up like a bundle. She seemed to be sinking into a dark cloud, her limbs felt as heavy as lead and then she felt nothing more.

PART THREE

Leo

Chapter 16

Daniel was in his study trying to catch up on the great deal of work that had accumulated during the last fortnight. The first few days at Bramber after the musical evening had become a painful blur which he hoped never again to have to live through. Endless vigils beside his son's bedside, waiting, waiting for the inevitable outcome, with the agony of knowing that nothing, absolutely nothing, could be done. 'He is in the hands of God,' the elderly doctor had said sententiously over and over again, till Daniel felt that if he repeated it just once again he would seize the old fool and cram the useless words down his throat.

Only John Dexter had kept him sane. 'Have patience, Dan. Now you know how a doctor feels when he realizes that all his skill is not sufficient, when he can only pray for a miracle.'

'One that never comes.'

'Oddly enough, it does sometimes.'

The strain had caused angry words between him and Christine.

'It's all because of you,' she had said, one day when their nerves were stretched to breaking-point. 'If the boy had not been so distressed by what those bullies at the school told him about you, if you had not been so completely out of touch on that wretched business in Bulgaria just when he needed you most, he would never have acted in such a foolish way. I understand Robert so well. The only way he knew how to fight it was to test himself to the limit.'

'Who has been telling you all this?'

'It seems Celia blurted it out to David, poor child.'

'I thought I had explained it to her.'

'So you did, but how can a child of her age understand such things? You are so busy fighting other people's battles you have no thought for your own children, for me.'

'That's not fair. I wrote those articles under an assumed name. If David had not seen fit to spread it around that I was responsible –'

'Don't be so ready to blame David for everything. It's always been like that, from the very beginning. Gareth once told me that you would always follow what you believed to be right, no matter how it affected those who love you, and he was right.'

There were a good many answers to that but wearily he said none of them. It would only make matters worse.

One comfort had been Isabelle, who had come hurrying from her friends in Edinburgh wanting to know why they had not told her before so that she could have taken her share of the nursing and the anxiety.

But in the end, amazingly, John Dexter had been right. Miracles do happen and it did to them, one night when Daniel was alone with the boy, Christine resting for once, the nurse gone downstairs on some errand.

He had been opening the window, glad to let the cool night air blow away some of the stifling warmth of the sickroom, when he heard a sound from the bed. He turned round, anxiety gripping him by the throat, to see Robert sitting up, uttering inarticulate sounds that tried to turn into 'Father'. Daniel was beside him in a moment, almost weeping in relief, because the miracle had happened, the boy's eyes were clear, they recognized him, though he could not form the words struggling on his tongue.

After that, though improvement was desperately slow, it was there, every day just one more step forward.

'You're fortunate,' said John Dexter. 'The blood clot that was causing so much anxiety must have cleared itself. It will take time. The brain has to learn to work normally again.'

'But he will recover, he will be himself again?'

'I don't see why not, but I would say one thing, Dan. Don't send him back to Rugby. The rough-and-tumble life at a public school is not for him. Keep him under your eye for the next year or two, find a good day school in London by the end of the year, and in the mean time take it easy, don't force him, let him find his own way back.'

The relief was enormous. His bright, intelligent, lovable son would not go through life like a mindless vegetable. At last he could throw off the agonizing burden and return to London and his work, contenting himself with frequent visits. Isabelle had wanted to come with him but he would not permit it.

'Your mother has had a desperately hard time for a great many weeks now. It has worn her out. Now the nurse only comes in at night she will find it a great comfort if you stay with her. There is your grandmother too. It's been a strain on her and she's in delicate health.'

She gave in a little reluctantly and he returned, alone except for Celia, rosy-cheeked and happy now that her beloved brother had come back to her. Nanny scrupulously sent her in to him each evening to say good-night and sit on his knee for half an hour while they discussed weighty matters like what she had been doing at school that day, or whether she should save her weekly pocket money and buy a new book, having lately taken to reading in a very big way.

'Only it is going to take weeks and weeks to save enough to buy *Jane Eyre*,' she said sadly.

That surprised him. He had always encouraged his children to read, but this seemed a little high-powered for Celia's age.

'I don't think that's quite the right book for you, my pet.'

'Lots of girls at school have read it,' she said indignantly.

'Have they indeed? I tell you what. I have that book somewhere and later on you shall borrow it. In the mean time, you save for two weeks, I'll supply the rest and we'll go out one Saturday morning and buy something really thrilling like *The Children of the New Forest*.'

She agreed enthusiastically. Any expedition with Papa was likely to turn out very worthwhile.

*

On this particular morning at the beginning of June he straightened up wearily after some hours at his desk, finished sealing a bulky package for Joe Sharpe at the offices of the *Clarion* and had just decided it was time he had a break with a glass of wine and a biscuit and cheese when Mark knocked and came in, looking a trifle put out.

'There is a young person asking for you, sir. She has brought Miss Louise's little dog, which she says she found wandering the streets. If you remember, some time ago the children had this address engraved on his collar, so she brought him here, but she won't hand him over to anyone but you.'

'Miss Louise's Toby? She must be worried to death at losing him. What does this young woman want to see me for? Give her some money, Mark, and send her packing.'

'I tried that, sir, but she won't go. She keeps on saying that she is sure you will remember her.'

'Oh, very well, I'll come.' He got up and went through to the front door, frowning down at the girl in the pink cotton gown (rather the worse for wear) and the straw hat perched on a cluster of brown curls. 'Well, here I am,' he said rather sharply, 'what is all this nonsense about?'

'Don't you remember me, sir? It's Essie.'

'Essie?' he repeated and then with a jolt he remembered. It must have been a year ago now, before he went to Russia. He had been working on research for his articles when, walking through the filthy streets around Seven Dials late one evening, he'd very nearly fallen over the little bundle crouched against the doorway, huddling herself together against the driving rain. She couldn't have been more than fifteen, a pitiful child who might have been his own daughter.

'You can't stay here,' he had said uncertainly. 'You'll be soaked through.'

'Got nowhere to go,' she muttered, pulling the ragged shawl closer round her thin shoulders.

Pity had overcome him and he had pulled her to her feet. 'Oh come along, child, I can at least buy you something hot to drink.'

There was a food stall close against the railings of St Giles's Church. He bought her a mug of scalding tea and a hot meat pie and saw by the way she tried not to wolf it that she had probably not eaten for days.

'Can't you go home?' he had asked.

'Me stepfather kicked me out when me mum died, said he weren't providin' for some other man's brat. Tried the sewin' for a bit but it don't pay much, and lodgings cost money.'

'How much do you owe?'

'Three weeks – six bob,' she had muttered hopelessly.

He found a half-guinea with a handful of silver and put it in her hands. 'That'll pay the back rent and a week or two in advance. The rest will do for food till you find work.'

She stared speechlessly at the money and then at him. He ordered the stallkeeper to refill the mug of tea and cut short her stammering thanks. 'Get back to your lodging before you're wet through,' he had said abruptly and left her staring after him, thin hands clasped around the refilled mug.

Now that same girl was standing on the steps and had obviously filled out a little.

'How are you getting on, Essie?' he managed to say.

'I'm all right, doin' fine, brought me luck you did, sir, an' no mistake.'

'Where did you find the dog?'

'It were near Leicester Fields. Nosin' round in the gutter, he were, lookin' fair starved so I took him home, gave him a drop o' milk and a bit o' bread. Then I saw the address on his collar so I brought him back.'

'How did you know that *I* lived here?'

She gave him a knowing grin. 'I hear 'em talkin', don't I? Saw your picture in the paper once so when I sees that on the collar, it felt as if it were meant, like.'

'I see. I'm very grateful to you. The young lady who owns Toby will be delighted to have him back.' He felt in his pocket, found a guinea and held it out to her.

'I didn't do it for that,' she said, 'honest I didn't.'

'I know you didn't, but take it all the same. Buy yourself something pretty.'

331

She hesitated and then gave him a beaming smile. 'P'raps I will then.' She gave Toby a pat. 'He were a nice little dog. Wouldn't have minded keepin' 'im but it wouldn't work, see.' She turned to go and then paused. 'There's some of 'em out there as could be having it in for you, mister,' she said in a whisper, 'cos of them articles you've been writing. They don't like the plain speakin', see. You look out for yourself.'

'I will, Essie, never fear.'

'Tata, then.'

He watched her go, stepping out bravely, head up, straw hat at a jaunty angle, and wondered if this time she had found a man who didn't beat her senseless and steal all her money. What future was there for her and others like her? He felt a wave of hopelessness at the impossible task he had set himself. More than eight thousand prostitutes known to the police had been one of the latest statistics, and that took no account of the hundreds of others still *not* known. How could he, one man alone, hope to make any improvement in that figure, or in the conditions in which most of them lived with the men who exploited them? He sighed and turned back into the hall.

'Better ask one of the maids to clean Toby up a little and give him something to eat. The poor little beggar looks half starved. Later on I'll take him back to Miss Louise myself. She must be worried sick about him,' he said to Mark, handing over the small dog.

'I'll take him to the kitchens, sir.'

Daniel turned back to his desk and a couple of hours later, when he had eaten his working lunch and was beginning to feel he had done enough for one day, Mark brought Toby back, looking far more like himself and showing his gratitude by jumping up on Daniel's knee and trying to lick his face.

'The kitchenmaid said he smelled so bad she was obliged to bath him, sir, and then Cook saw that he had a good meal.'

'That's more like it, isn't it, boy?' He got up, putting the little dog on the floor. 'I'll take him round to Arlington Street right away. I have some letters ready for the post.'

He tidied himself up, put on his jacket, took his hat and set off, relaxing a little, free to do as he wished with no questions asked. Lord Warrinder had told him of Clara's amazing change of heart, and he looked forward to a pleasurable hour with Louise discussing her future.

Mrs Bolton opened the door to his knock and stared at him blankly for a moment when he asked for Louise.

'The young lady is not here, sir. Now that Lady Dorrien and the count have gone abroad, Miss Louise comes and goes just as she pleases.'

'But surely she must have told you where she was going. Her little dog was found wandering in the streets. That's why I have brought him back.'

'As to that, I really don't know what to say,' went on the housekeeper unhelpfully. 'She took the dog with her, that I do know, and I'd rather you didn't leave him here with us if you don't mind. Now the house is to be partly shut up with only a reduced staff, it would not be suitable, and in any case Miss Louise was always very particular to look after the dog herself.'

'But surely the fact that she went out without saying where she was going and has not yet returned must have caused you anxiety on her behalf. Have you thought to contact the police?'

'Certainly not. I wouldn't dream of doing any such thing. I'm quite sure neither Lady Dorrien nor Miss Louise would thank me for it. Whatever would the neighbours think? Police coming here and asking questions! She'll come back in her own good time, I dare say. I am sorry, but I am afraid that is all that I can tell you, sir. Good-day,' and she more or less shut the door in his face.

Considerably disturbed by now, he stood for a moment looking at the door, uncertain whether to hammer on it and demand some further information. It seemed to him highly probable that Mrs Bolton was hiding something – but what? That Toby had been found straying, hungry and dirty but with the leather strap still attached to his collar, proved first that he had not just run out of the house, second that he could not have simply lost himself when Louise took him in the park and let him off his lead to run free. This left two more possibilities. She could have met with an accident – though surely by now one or other of them would have been informed – or, worse still, someone had abducted her. It was just possible that, since Toby was found in Leicester Fields, he could have made some attempt to follow her abductor. He simply could not believe that Louise would allow Toby to be snatched from her without some sort of struggle, nor would she just disappear without telling anyone where she was going, particularly just now when everything she most wanted and longed for had fallen into her lap.

He was walking quickly up the road, lost in these worrying thoughts, when someone came running after him and plucked at his sleeve. He turned round to find a maidservant looking up at him anxiously, a shawl clutched around her and partially hiding her face.

'Mr Hunter, sir,' she whispered breathlessly, 'do you remember me? I'm Ada and I always looked after Miss Louise. Can I speak to you for a minute?' She looked around her a little fearfully. 'Some place where we can't be seen.'

He drew her to the shelter of the plane trees at the end of the road and said brusquely, 'Now, tell me, what is this?'

'I don't know quite what Mrs Bolton told you, sir, but that evening, three days ago now, when Miss Louise went out, she didn't take nothing with her. She weren't expecting to go away anywhere. She were just taking Toby for his usual walk. When she didn't come back, I went to her room and she hadn't taken nothin', no handbag nor none of her clothes. I didn't like to say much just then in case there were some reason, but I were puzzled, and in the morning, when I saw that her bed hadn't been slept in, I went and told Mrs Bolton and she said Miss Louise had probably decided to spend the night with you and Mrs Hunter or with that sister of Captain Ingham she's been so friendly with, or even with Miss Motford, but if she had I'm sure she would have said something to me about it, she was always so friendly. Do you think she could have been knocked down in some dreadful accident?'

'I don't know, Ada, but I think if she had one or other of us would have heard of it by now. Lord Warrinder, who is her guardian, is very well-known indeed.'

'There is somefing else,' whispered Ada, with another anxious look around her: 'Mrs Bolton's brother.'

'What about him?'

'I don't know for sure but he's a queer sort, you ask my dad, and he's been hangin' about the house for days, taking tea with his sister and askin' sly questions about Miss Louise.'

'I see. Thank you for telling me all this.'

'You will let me know, won't you, sir, if you find out where she is? I were always so fond of Miss Louise, and of Toby too,' and she bent down to fondle the little dog, who had been frisking around her feet as if glad to see her.

Then she had gone, running along the road and disappearing down the area steps, leaving Daniel more anxious than ever. There was still one possibility worth investigating. Miss Motford. He took a cab to Chelsea, but the little house appeared shut up, and when he knocked at the door a neighbour who was tending her geraniums in her front garden peered over the fence.

'No good your knocking,' she said cheerfully. 'Hattie Motford has gone off to Bournemouth for a few weeks to stay with some old friends. She won't be back for a month or more.' So that door was closed too.

Abductions did happen of course, particularly if there was money involved, but there had been no ransom note, no indication at all, and for the first time Daniel began to think seriously of Leo. He might have considered it sooner if Louise had told him of the two occasions since Christmas when she had seen him, especially the last time.

He returned home and went up to the nursery where Celia was being given her supper by Nanny, and delivered Toby over to their charge.

'Is Louise coming to stay with us, Papa?' asked Celia, her mouth full of her favourite chocolate sponge.

'No, not just now,' he said, 'but she has asked us to look

after Toby for her. He will be staying with you and Rowley for a little while.'

Nanny, who guessed that there was something more behind it, said cheerfully, 'That's all right, Mr Hunter, don't you worry. While we are looking after one we can take care of two, can't we, Miss Celia?'

That settled, Daniel considered his next step. He was alone at Wimpole Street, no one readily available with whom he could talk it over. Harry was concerned with an important case that had taken him out of London temporarily, and David had gone with him. Lord Warrinder was down at Bramber till his next case came up at the Old Bailey. Daniel decided the time had come to go to the police.

Detective Inspector Radford was an old acquaintance with whom from time to time Daniel had enjoyed friendly consultations connected with his work, and he was fortunate enough to find him still in his office this evening.

Inspector Radford was older than Daniel by some ten years, extremely intelligent and very experienced, with a rather cynical view of humanity in general and of the vagaries and waywardness of young women in particular. He had a deep distrust of most foreigners. Since his work had on occasion taken him into the East End, that melting pot of differing and sometimes warring nationalities, this was not surprising. He liked Daniel; he thought his feelings occasionally outran his good sense, but admired his courage and determination; so he was quite prepared to listen quietly and give a considered opinion.

'One thing I'm pretty sure of,' he said at last. 'If this young woman has suffered some kind of an accident that prevented her from identifying herself, we would have known of it by now and would have already begun to make enquiries. An abduction is another matter. As you and I know, it does happen and is usually followed by a demand for money. There have been cases where the unfortunate girl is shipped away abroad and sold off to some foreign hellhole, but scarcely ever from among the class to which your young friend belongs. But

I would point out that in my experience there is a strong romantic element in a very great number of such cases. Tell me more about this young Russian, Leo, who was responsible for the assassination of one of our diplomats and his mistress. What exactly was her connection with him?'

Daniel hesitated, anxious not to say too much and give the wrong impression. 'At the time every effort was made to keep this part of it out of the papers for Louise's sake,' he said, 'but in fact when James Ducane took up his post at the St Petersburg embassy he leased a villa on the estate of Leo's father, Count Davitsky, and installed his mistress and his daughter there. Louise would then have been about eleven; the boy, the younger son of the count, a year or so older. The families were on friendly terms and the boy and girl more or less grew up together.'

'Was she in love with him?'

'No, not at all, I'm quite sure of that – though I rather think his feelings towards her may have been a great deal warmer.'

'You say he threatened her when she found him hiding at her father's villa.'

'Yes. He had evidently persuaded himself that she had deliberately put the police on to him.'

'Did you see him yourself?'

'No, but she was in a very agitated and distressed state.'

'And yet she still prevented you from taking any steps to pursue him.'

'You must understand, inspector, that the whole tragic affair was one of mistaken identity, and though Louise was so deeply upset at what he had done, she was, I think, still sorry for him. She understood very well the fanaticism of these young anarchists from the university. She had more or less grown up with it.'

'And that was what took her to the station when he was banished to Siberia.'

'Yes. I tried to persuade her not to go, but I think she wanted him to know that it was not she who had directed the police to the place where he was captured, the wrecked lodge on the estate where she and Leo had played as children.'

'And he didn't believe her.'

'No, he didn't, and he showed it. He spat abuse at her.'

'What was your opinion of him, since you were seeing him for the first time?'

Daniel thought back for a moment to that unpleasant morning at the station before he said slowly, 'I had the impression of a boy raised in luxury suddenly brought up against an absolutely terrifying experience which he could not come to terms with, and wanting only to blame everyone but himself and punish anyone who had helped to place him there.'

'Has it occurred to you, my friend, that she could have gone with him that night, out of pity, perhaps, or even a misjudged affection, and found herself in some unhappy dilemma because of it?'

'No,' said Daniel. 'I am absolutely certain she would not have gone with him willingly. She was terrified of him. If Leo is responsible, and I am inclined to think it is the only possibility, then he has taken her by force for some purpose of his own. You must know, inspector, that Louise may be only nineteen but she has great depths of courage and strength of will, and through the generosity of Lady Dorrien and her future husband everything she most wanted was opening up for her. Why should she prejudice it?'

Inspector Radford was of the opinion that Daniel was emotionally involved with this young girl for whom he felt such a deep responsibility, and therefore inclined to believe she could do no wrong, but all the same there were aspects of the case that interested him. 'We would dearly like to lay hands on this Russian,' he said. 'We have of course been informed of his escape from his prison guards and that he has possibly entered this country under forged papers, but to find a foreigner masquerading under a false name amongst the myriads in the East End is rather like hunting the proverbial needle in the haystack. One thing interests me,' he went on thoughtfully, 'this fellow Roger Bolton. It so happens we had cause to investigate him some time ago, after an accusation had been brought against him that he was running what we call a "disorderly house" somewhere in the neighbourhood of Soho. Enquiries were made, but absolutely nothing could be proved against him. On the surface he was eminently respectable, and though I still had my doubts the case had to be dropped for lack of evidence.'

'Are you telling me that nothing at all can be done in Louise's case?'

'By no means. I'll get one of my men making enquiries in the neighbourhood of Arlington Street. Someone may have noticed something. Servants are given to peering out of windows instead of getting on with something more useful. I'll also send men to make enquiries in the East End. We have several points of contact, and these foreigners are not always friendly towards one another. One thing I would mention: don't go around asking too many questions yourself. It won't help, you know, only muddy the issue.'

And with that Daniel had to be content. He went home, ate a solitary dinner without much appetite and wrote a letter to Christine. It was his usual habit to tell her about almost everything, but this time he didn't mention what had happened to Louise. His wife had been through so much these last weeks that he saw no point in disturbing her further till he had more concrete information. There was also the plain fact that she had always harboured a faint resentment of his interest in the girl. Later he would realize that it was a mistake to say nothing, but at the time it seemed the wisest thing to do. He added that it might be difficult for him to come down as often as usual, but if she wanted him, of course he would come instantly. Celia sent her love and was well and happy.

The letter signed and sealed ready for the post, there was nothing further to do but wait. He walked up and down his study, consumed with anxiety. It was all very well for the inspector to say, 'Leave everything to the professionals,' but Louise had been his personal responsibility from the very start and he was filled with an enormous impatience. He wanted to go out and scour the London streets for her, which was ridiculous. There was also a faint, frightening possibility that she might already have been whipped out of the country.

He went to bed at last and slept badly, haunted by a frustrating nightmare in which Louise was always tantalizingly just out of his reach. He woke up unrefreshed and with a strong determination to ignore the inspector's advice and pursue a few contacts of his own arising from various enquiries he had followed in the past. But it proved a frustrating day in which he got nowhere, and when he returned in the afternoon Mark handed him a note from the inspector asking if he would call at the station as soon as conveniently possible.

He went at once, with a feeling of dread, and was immediately shown into the inspector's office. 'I gather you wanted to see me,' he said. 'Is there any news?'

'Not exactly.' The policeman got up from behind his desk. 'It so happens that the body of a young woman was found this morning in an alley not far from Leicester Fields. She had been assaulted, badly beaten and finally strangled. There is no indication as to who she was or who did this to her, but she is the right age, she is well dressed, was once very attractive and has fair hair. It won't be very pleasant but I should be glad if you would take a look at her.'

It was quite possible. It took a moment for Daniel to brace himself for what could be a truly dreadful ordeal, then he followed the inspector down to one of the cells.

The body of the girl had been laid on the narrow bed, a brown prison blanket thrown over her.

'Ready?' asked the inspector.

He nodded and the policeman turned back the blanket. It was all there: the golden hair, the dead-white face, the purple bruises on the neck, but it was not Louise. The relief made him feel almost faint. He shook his head.

'It is not Louise.'

'Certain?'

'Absolutely.'

The inspector replaced the blanket with a certain gentleness. 'I had to ask you. We must eliminate all possibilities.'

'Yes, of course.'

Back in the office the inspector said, 'Enquiries have been put in hand and I may very likely have further information for you in a day or two.'

'I shall be very grateful.'

They parted on friendly terms and Daniel walked back to Wimpole Street. The incident had brought him face-to-face with what could and did happen to unhappy young women almost every day. He had never felt so helpless or so alone.

Chapter 17

When she first opened her eyes, Louise could distinguish nothing. She felt strange, light-headed as if she were suffering from a fever, her mouth and throat dry. Then, as the effects of the drug slowly faded, she realized that she was lying on a hard bed with a rough blanket thrown over her. There was a single candle in a heavy iron candlestick on a chest beside the bed, and by its uncertain light the room gradually took ghostly shape. It was utterly bare, with no other furniture of any kind. Directly opposite the bed was a narrow window, partly curtained, through which shone a faint glow as if from a streetlamp outside, and further along a door with heavy bolts top and bottom. In the wall to the right of where she was lying there was a further door, probably leading to the rest of the house, and she realized that she must be in a basement room like hundreds of others in London, let off for a few pence a week to a variety of temporary lodgers.

Her head still felt heavy and muddled but she tried hard to concentrate. It had been evening and she had been walking home with Toby when she was seized from behind. She had a vague impression that there had been two of them, and although no word had been spoken she was certain that one of them had been Leo. But if so, why had he brought her to this place? What did he want from her? And then with a sharp pang she remembered the dog. There had been a scuffle, she had heard him bark and then a yelp of pain. Oh God, what had they done to poor little Toby?

Her mouth tasted vile. There was a small jug and a cup

beside the candlestick. Perhaps it contained water. She tried to pull herself up in the bed and was jerked painfully back. It was only then that she saw with a shock that she was chained to one of the heavy brass bedposts. She stared at the steel bracelet round her wrist and the length of chain padlocked to the post. She tugged at it violently but it would not budge. She fought down a rising panic and found that the chain was just long enough to allow her to sit up a little. Her thirst was becoming intolerable. She stretched out her free hand to the mug and then drew back. Supposing it was drugged or poisoned?

She lay for a few moments, shaken and trembling. To bring her here, to chain her up like a dog, was surely an act of madness. She remembered the night before the concert, Leo staring down at her with that strange wild look. 'I've waited a long time for this,' he had said. For what? Oh dear God, why hadn't she spoken of it to someone? Why hadn't she told Jean-Louis, when Daniel had been forced to leave so unexpectedly? But so much had happened after the concert, both to Clara and to herself, that everything else had been wiped out of her mind. And now the unbelievable had happened and she didn't know what she was going to do. She had no idea of the time, but it must be well after midnight. Why had Leo brought her here and then left her? What would happen if she screamed and screamed for help? Surely someone must hear.

With a mighty effort she raised herself a little and picked up the mug. She took a cautious sip. Except that it was warm and stale, it had no taste at all, and it did just help to moisten her mouth. In a sudden burst of rage at what had been done to her, she took a deep breath and screamed, once, twice and then with a tremendous effort a third time. There was no response of any kind. If anyone passing by heard the cry for help, they took no notice. It was no concern of theirs. The silence flowed back again, heavy and stifling.

She did not know how she endured the endless hours of that night. After her outburst she felt drained, empty of hope, uncertain what to do. She kept telling herself that very soon someone was bound to come. When she did not return to the house that night, surely they must have begun enquiries . . . surely someone would follow it up and find her. She must remember everything that had happened, every detail, in case she had to describe it. It had been late in the evening and there had been two, Leo and another who was exceptionally tall . . . It struck her suddenly that it could have been Mrs Bolton's unpleasant brother – but why? What possible interest could he have in her? Hours went by, desperately slowly, while her mind went over and over it. The streetlamp was turned out, the candle guttered to its end and the darkness closed in on her, silent and threatening. She fell at last into a half-doze filled with nightmares from which she would start up in terror, only to be jerked back by the cruel chain.

At last, after what seemed like an eternity, the darkness faded from the dirty window. Even in smoky, grimy London the dawn had come. Her eyes felt heavy and gritty after the exhausting night, her hair was tangled into a bird's nest. She felt grubby and unwashed and desperately needed to relieve herself. In the growing light she looked round the room in despair and saw now that a bucket had been placed up against the bedpost to which she was chained. There was something horribly humiliating about having to perform so private a function when curious eyes could be watching her, when someone could come in at any moment, but at last sheer necessity overcame her disgust. It was just possible to roll off the bed beside the post that held her prisoner and at last, the pressing need satisfied, she could stand up and look around her for the first time.

It was a depressing sight. Dark-brown wallpaper, the pattern long obscured by dust and soot, hung in long strips from the ceiling, while a ragged curtain was half drawn across the dirty window. She tried to tidy her white silk blouse and navy skirt, which were badly crumpled, and shook out her hair, running her fingers through the lustrous mass, pushing it back and trying to secure it with one of the combs and some hairpins. Then she sat on the side of the bed, feeling better able to face what was coming than if she were lying down. The light gradually strengthened. She was just wishing she could reach the window and perhaps find out where she was when she heard the key in the lock of the inner door. She stiffened and started to her feet as Leo came in carrying a cup and a plate. He kicked the door shut behind him and they stood for a second staring at one another.

The reddish hair that had been shaved close to his skull in the Russian prison had grown untidily long and reached his shoulders. He was dressed like any young working man, in breeches and boots and short jacket, a muffler round his throat, no touch of the aristocrat nor of the shy boy she had once known. His face had a thin, ravaged look. He stood quite still, his eyes raking her from head to foot, and at that moment she realized she was up against something she did not understand, something that terrified her. Then quite unexpectedly he smiled.

'How did the night go, Louise? Did it seem endless?' He walked around the bed and put the cup of tea and the plate with the slice of bread on the chest. 'In the fortress they called it "confined to solitary", only my cell was below the level of the Neva so that the floor was inches deep in black slime and at night the rats came in to keep me company.'

'I don't understand,' said Louise, desperately trying to keep her voice calm. 'Why have you brought me here, Leo? What is it that you want from me?'

He went on as if she had not spoken. 'They did not bring me tea or fine white bread either. It was black bread, and so green with mould that even the rats wouldn't eat it. When the guards fished me out at last I thought I would die, only I didn't. There are worse things than lying in a cell reeking with filth, there is the *knout*. Do you know what a flogging does to you, Louise? The humiliation, the tearing of the flesh, tied to a post like an animal, like one of my father's stinking serfs.'

The savagery in his voice appalled her. 'Why are you telling me all this?' she said, shaken and at the same time deeply distressed.

'Why? *Why?*' he repeated, and suddenly grabbed her by the

shoulders, forcing her back on to the bed, holding her down, his fingers digging into her, his face close to hers. 'Why? Because it was you who sent me there!'

'But I didn't, Leo, I swear I didn't!'

'Don't lie.' He held her pinned to the bed, his breath in her face. 'Who else knew about that lodge hidden among the trees, forgotten for more than a century?'

'There could have been many others, you know there could, some of the peasants, your brother even –'

'Michael despised me, but the family good name is his god. He would never have jeopardized it. And not one of them could have known about my great-grandfather's wine cellar. Don't you remember how we found it one day, you and I, how we laughed when we broke down the door and saw the barrels and even one or two bottles still there thick with dust? We broke one open and it tasted filthy and you said, "We'll call it Bluebeard's Castle and keep it all to ourselves." What a marvellous place to hide. A man could live there for a century and no one would ever know. And you remembered all that, didn't you? That day we met at the villa, you guessed that was where I would go, and you and the Englishman deliberately set the dogs of the Okhrana after me.'

Nothing she could say would convince him that he was wrong, and she slowly began to realize that for nearly a year now he had been obsessed with a dream of revenge. He wanted her to know everything that had happened to him. The weak ineffectual boy, who had never been able to succeed at anything, had in his own mind become a martyr, pursued by the state, rejected by his family, forced into exile; and it was she who was responsible, all that he had been through was due to her, so she must listen and learn and suffer with him and afterwards . . . What did he intend to do with her afterwards? Those feelings he had once had for her, that boyish affection, was it still there? In the hours and days that were to come he varied between brutality and a kind of mawkish tenderness, and she was his victim, his prisoner, he had her at his mercy, he could do what he liked with her; and he never for one moment let her forget it.

The long hours, the endless days, seemed to merge into one another. At first he came and went, talking, talking, till her head ached and all she wanted to do was to bury her face in the pillow and shut her ears against him, only he would not permit it. He would shake her, turn her back to him and go on and on relentlessly.

He made her feel every moment of that nightmare journey across Russia shut up in the cattle-truck with the other prisoners: thieves, rapists, murderers, men who despised him because of what he was, because he could not fight back, men who grabbed the barrels of bread and dried fish pushed into the truck when the train stopped, and knocked the precious tin mug of water out of his hands. He thought he would die, he wanted to die, but he survived because the guard who travelled with them intervened at last, not out of pity or kindness but simply because he had been paid and his instructions were explicit.

He told her about being pushed out when the train reached Irkutsk. It was October and the river had not yet frozen. From there they would take boats into the furthermost regions of Siberia. It was there that he escaped.

Listening to his rambling story about the guard who unshackled him, who turned a blind eye when he joined the other prisoners floundering in the icy slimy mud and, with the help of another prisoner, took his chance and dived into the rush of the river, she wondered how much bribery had been at work. His father was powerful and he had after all only murdered foreigners, not Russians. As for the peasants all those thousands of miles from the capital, they were inclined to look kindly on these political hotheads who struck a blow for liberty. So Leo had made his painful way through forest and river and village, often sick but somehow stumbling forward, on foot, by cart, and at last by train, to Switzerland. His family had rejected him but out of pride had not left him penniless. Money came through a Swiss bank. All this and more he poured into her unwilling ears, day after day. It did explain a great deal, but it did not entirely explain his relentless pursuit of her.

Because she had no choice, she listened to him, sometimes with disgust but at times filled with a terrible pity. At first she tried to reason with him, make him understand that she had powerful friends who would take steps to search for her, that he would suffer for what he had done, but if he were to set her free now she would say nothing and he would escape all blame. No one need ever know. He could leave England, where he was always in danger, where if the police laid hands on him it was more than likely that Russia would demand he be sent back to complete his sentence. She did not think he even listened. He was obsessed with some dream of his own and every hour she grew more afraid.

From time to time he brought her food, cups of weak tea and bread, sometimes with cheese or some kind of meat, but she couldn't bring herself to do more than drink some of the tea and crumble a little of the bread.

Once when he came through the door she heard a scuffle, then a shriek, followed by a burst of raucous laughter before the door slammed on it, and she wondered if the house was one of those Ada had spoken of where the women brought their men, perhaps the very house owned by Roger Tanner. That evening Leo was in a gentler mood. He brought a bowl of water and a towel. He washed her face gently, ran his fingers through her tangled hair, then suddenly bent his head and kissed her clumsily but full on the mouth. She jerked her head back, thrusting him violently away from her, and he slapped her cheek.

'What about those others you have kissed? I've watched them come and go, the soldier who takes you riding, the Englishman who was with you at the station in Petersburg who taught you to despise me. I've not forgotten *him*, and I swear to God that the time will come when I will make him pay.'

It was then that her nerve broke. She felt she was tangled in a web from which she would never break free and which threatened not only her but Daniel too. How could she make him understand, when he was living in a world of his own, a world which had lost touch with reality. She was battering wildly at him with her hands and blood sprang up on the wrist with its steel bracelet.

'Go away!' she screamed at him. 'Go away! Why can't you leave me alone? Can't you see that your very touch turns me sick? For God's sake, go away!'

He captured the hands and held them in a bruising grip. 'Do you really mean that? Do you, do you?'

'Yes,' she said in a burst of wild defiance. 'Yes, yes, yes!'

He released her and stood up, staring down at her, his eyes narrowing, and suddenly she shivered as if an icy wind had blown across her.

'You'll be sorry for that,' he whispered, then turned his back and went out.

The door slammed and she sank back, overcome with utter despair. Almost worse than the nausea from the lack of food, the stifling airlessness of the basement room, the physical discomforts and miseries, was the frightening effect all this was having on her mind. It was as if these last months, when her life had begun to blossom, when at last she could put grief and pain behind her and look ahead with hope, had all been swept away. She was back in the awful despair of those first terrible days: the shock, the bitter pain, the desolate sense of loss, were all there again. And now there was no Daniel to steady her, to give her strength and courage. Now somehow she had to fight her way out alone.

The days dragged by, so long and monotonous with nothing to read, nothing to distract her, that she began to lose all sense of time. Occasionally Leo would come and lie beside her on the bed. He would take her hand and talk dreamily about the past, childish adventures they had shared and which she had long forgotten.

'That's all over and done with. It's in the past,' she would say impatiently. 'We are not children any longer.'

'More's the pity.' And then he would get up and go away, and there were only the long grey days and dark nights to be lived through.

Her certainty that she had only to endure, to stand up against him, that someone would come, slowly drained away from her. She was lost, abandoned among the teeming millions of London's underworld, and there was no one who cared, no one to hold out a helping hand. If only she knew what was in his mind! Now he had her in his power, what was he going to do with her? Keep her here, a plaything, a cowed bitch to serve his pleasure? She felt sanity slipping away from her and held on to it desperately, trying to bring herself back to normality, to the blessed ordinary things of every day. Sometimes when she had suffered sleepless nights she had sought help in her music, reading in her mind the score of a sonata, a concerto, a ballade, as if it were a book, phrase after phrase, her fingers playing a soundless tattoo on the bedcovers. Now, sick and feverish, it was almost impossible to concentrate but after a time the old magic began to work and even soothed her a little so that she slept, if only fitfully.

Then there came a change. For two days she did not see Leo at all. The only break in the deadly monotony was at midday, when the inner door opened to admit a slatternly woman whom she guessed to be some sort of servant from her mob cap and greasy apron. She bombarded her with questions, but the woman stared at her stony-faced, put the usual cup of tea and plate of food on the chest and went out again, slamming and locking the door.

The time stretched interminably till she almost longed for Leo to return. It was late evening on the second day when he came at last, and she sensed at once that there was a difference in him. He was confident, self-assured, as if he had finally made a decision about something. He was wearing a long coat which he took off, shaking it out. He was carrying a riding-whip which he tossed on to the bed, and she wondered if he had taken a journey out of London.

He lit the candle and then stood looking down at her with a smile that for some reason made her blood run cold. 'It's taken most of the day but it's all arranged,' he said.

'What is?'

'We're going away, out of this place, just you and I.'

'Going where?'

'Can't you guess?' he smiled tantalizingly. 'But there is something else first. Turn over.'

'How?' she said drily, lifting her chained wrist.

He laughed as if she had said something amusing, as if the chaining-up of a young woman were no more than a child's game. He took a small key from an inner pocket and unlocked the steel bracelet on her wrist.

She was off the bed in a flash, had run to the outer door, was already struggling with the bolts almost before he realized it. Of course it was ridiculous. She didn't stand a chance. He was beside her in an instant, had taken firm hold of her. She struggled gamely, but close confinement and little food had left her without any strength. He picked her up, carried her to the bed and dumped her on it, face downwards.

'Lie still, damn you!'

'No,' she said breathlessly. 'No, let me go.' She was still making a brave effort to fight him, but now one hand pressed her down into the pillow while the other relentlessly tore at her clothes and, while she lay quivering, he took up the whip and brought it down on her bare flesh. It was so agonizingly painful that she was forced to bite hard at her clenched fist to stop herself crying aloud. All the time his words punctuated the strokes.

'You belong to me, Louise, not to the soldier, not to the Englishman, not to any of those other nobodies who run after you, but to me, to me, and don't you ever forget it!'

Then with a gesture of disgust he flung the whip across the room and, as if the thrashing had somehow purged all the resentment out of him, he began to caress her bruised flesh, murmuring endearments, calling her his darling, his love, his little one. He turned her back to him gently and stroked her face, one hand fumbling at the buttons of her blouse so that he could press his lips against the curve of her breast above the lace-trimmed chemise.

She guessed then with a dreadful certainty at what was to

come and did not know how she was to find the strength to fight against it. The pain in her back was exquisite, turning her sick, robbing her of what little strength she had, so that it took every atom of her will-power to make one more desperate attempt to escape from him. But he held her pinned down with a surprising force. She tried to draw her body into herself, and away from him, but it was impossible. He was lying on top of her now and was thrusting into her. The pain was intense. She bit her lips to stop herself crying out as everything in her tried to reject him. She was being violated in her most secret being, she was being split apart. She flung out a hand as she tried helplessly to pull herself away from him and her groping fingers touched the iron candlestick and closed around it. Filled with a blind rage at what was being done to her, she lifted it with a sudden access of strength and brought it crashing down on his head. It struck him on the temple. He gave a sort of stifled groan and very slowly rolled off her. The candlestick fell from her hand and the candle went out in a splutter of hot grease and a smell of burning.

For a moment she was too shocked, too horrified at what she had done, to move. Then she pulled herself away and sat up. She touched his head gingerly and her fingers came away sticky with what must be blood. Had she killed him? Was it possible? She was trembling so much that she couldn't think, only that she must escape now quickly, in case he was not dead but only stunned, in case someone else should come in and stop her.

She clambered off the bed, still shaking so much that she could scarcely button up her blouse and adjust her disordered clothes. The shawl still hung on the bedpost where it had been thrown on that first evening which seemed a year ago. She put it over her head and wrapped herself closely. If she looked like a scarecrow it could not be helped. All she could think of was to get out of the house as quickly as possible.

He still did not stir and she crept to the door and drew back the bolts. They moved easily, someone must have oiled them. She turned the heavy key and, on an impulse she didn't understand, locked the door behind her and took it with her, clutched in her hand. She climbed the area steps and then stopped for a moment to get her breath and look around her, trying to find out where she was. Across the road was a patch of grass with some tall trees. For the moment the square was empty and she scurried across the carriageway and into the shelter of the trees before stopping to look back at the house that had been her prison. It was one of a row of tall well-built lodging-houses and she saw the number – 7 – clearly lit by the streetlamp.

She leaned against the trunk of one of the trees, feeling faint and sick. Where could she go now? If what she suspected about Roger Tanner was true, she dared not go back to Arlington Street. *Daniel*, she thought, Daniel, her refuge, her hope. Somehow she must find her way to Wimpole Street. He would know what to do. She clung to the thought like an anchor in a stormy sea.

It was a nightmare of a journey, although it was not all that far. When she made her way to the end of the square where it opened into a wider thoroughfare she realized that she was in Oxford Street, and somewhere at the far end of it she could find her way through to Wimpole Street. It should have been a warm summer night, but the rain had begun again, not heavy but quite sufficient to soak the thin shawl and penetrate through to her skin. She was splashing through filthy puddles in her light sandals, and a chill little wind blew round corners and made her shiver. Her back felt as if it were on fire, a pain so sickening that every now and then she had to stop, lean up against the wall and fight a deadly faintness that threatened to overwhelm her. Every time it happened, it required just that much longer, just that much more will-power, to pull herself together and go on.

It was past midnight but there were still people on the streets: solitary walkers, couples, bands of noisy hooligans who amused themselves by pushing the wretched huddled creature out of their way so that she stumbled into the gutter, just one more of the countless homeless creatures who haunted the streets by night.

Once, taking temporary refuge in a pillared doorway, she saw a policeman walking his beat with his usual measured tread, and drew closer undercover in case he should round her up as a vagrant and lock her in a cell for the night.

At last, through a tangle of alleys where cats screeched at one another over stinking food and she fell over a dead dog, bruising her knees painfully, she reached the familiar street, grimly hanging on to the last remnant of her strength until unbelievably the house was there in front of her. A lamp shone a faint glow at the top of the steps. There was a gleam of light from one of the ground-floor windows, but she was too spent to notice any of these things. She dragged herself up the steps, managed to reach the handsome brass knocker, then slithered down the door into a crumpled heap at the bottom.

Daniel, who was still up, having found sleep difficult these last few nights, was the first to hear the knocking. Frowning, he went to the door, drew back the bolts and opened it. The bedraggled figure leaning up against it fell forward at his feet.

'What the devil?' he exclaimed, then went down on his knees as the light fell upon her face. 'My God! Louise! What has happened to you?'

She was by now beyond words and simply clung to him convulsively as he lifted her in his arms, just as Mark came hurrying down the stairs pulling his dressing-gown around him.

'What is it, sir?' he said. 'What has happened?'

'It's Miss Louise.'

Daniel carried her into his study and put her down on the sofa. The light from the lamp fell on the white face, the dark-gold hair, the soaked, bedraggled figure splashed to the waist by the mud and filth from the streets. She clutched at his hand, still fearful, still shaking, as if Leo might pounce on her out of the shadows.

'It's all right,' Daniel was saying gently. 'It's all right. You're safe now. You're here with me.'

He pulled out a handkerchief and began to wipe some of the rain and mud from her face as Mark, having shut and rebolted the door, came in looking shocked.

'Whatever can have happened to Miss Louise, sir?' he whispered.

'I don't know yet but we can't leave her like this. Go and wake Nanny – quietly, mind, we don't want to rouse the whole household – and ask her to come down here. The poor child is soaked through. We must get her to bed with blankets and hot-water bottles. Nanny will know what's best.'

Mark hurried away and Daniel turned back to Louise. He picked up a glass of brandy he had poured for himself earlier in the evening and then forgotten to drink. He put his arm around her and raised her a little. 'Take some of it. It will warm you.'

She swallowed a couple of gulps, choked and then pushed his hand away. Now she was safe, the horror of what she had done was beginning to overwhelm her. She was staring at him, the eyes wide and terrified in the white face. The words came out jerkily.

'He chained me up like a dog, he beat me and . . . and I killed him, Daniel. He was trying to . . . he had forced me to . . . I felt as if . . . as if . . .' but she could not put into words the horror of what he had been doing to her. 'Then I hit him with the iron candlestick. There was blood and he did not move so I thought he was dead and then I escaped . . . I ran away.'

It sounded fantastic but there was no mistaking what she had said, and he had to know more, for her sake.

'Who did you believe you had killed, Louise?'

'It was Leo . . . it was always Leo, every day, every hour. I had to stop him, don't you see, I had to . . .' The tension broke into choking sobs.

'Where, Louise, where did all this happen to you?'

'Where?' She looked bewildered for a moment.

'Can you remember?' he urged. 'Try, it is very important.'

'Soho . . .' she gasped at last. 'I think that is what it is called. It was a square with grass and trees and a streetlamp. It was number. I saw it clearly. Oh God, I killed him and then I let myself out.'

She put out a hand, still clutching the key, and stared down at it. He took it from her and put it on the table.

'It's all over, Louise,' he said gently. 'You're here now and you're safe with me and I don't believe that you killed him. You're not strong enough. I've no doubt he is only stunned. Don't think of it any longer. Try and put it out of your mind.'

By that time Nanny had come in, greatly distressed at the state Louise was in but immediately reassuring and very capable.

'You carry her upstairs, Mr Hunter, and we'll have those wet clothes stripped off in a jiffy. We'll have her wrapped in warm blankets and I'll prepare a good hot drink for her. Mark, you go down to the kitchen, stir up the stove and put the kettle on. There are two stone bottles to be filled. The poor lamb, what have those savages done to her?'

Daniel picked her up and went up the stairs, preceded by Nanny, who had already whipped the coverlet off the bed. 'Shall I call Hannah to give me a hand? She is a good sensible girl.'

'No, I'll help you. I don't want the servants gossiping about this. We'll have to find a suitable story for them in the morning. You understand, Nanny?'

This was no time for niceties, it was imperative to bring warmth back to the chilled and shivering Louise as soon as possible. If her slim, beautiful body moved him, it was only to a deep pity, as Nanny pulled off the lace-trimmed chemise and he saw the vicious strokes of the whip still oozing blood. He drew a sharp breath as his eyes met Nanny's horrified look.

'Who can have done this wicked thing to her?' she whispered.

'I don't know yet. I can only guess.'

'I have a good salve which will help to soothe and heal,' she said. 'Cover her, Mr Hunter, while I fetch it.'

By the time she returned with the ointment and one of Christine's lawn nightdresses, Mark had come in with the two filled bottles and a blanket which he had thought to warm before the kitchen stove. They wrapped it around her and finished their work as quickly and as gently as they could.

The stress of the last week, the lack of food, the close confinement, the exhaustion, had all taken their toll on Louise. Now she lay in a kind of haze of warmth, the pain soothed a little, only half aware of what was happening to her. Daniel smoothed back the damp hair that Nanny had combed and then on an impulse bent and kissed her forehead.

'Dear, dear Daniel.' She touched his face with the comforting feeling that she had come home and nothing now could harm her any further.

He straightened up. 'Take care of her, Nanny,' he said, and went out quickly.

Mark was waiting for him on the landing. 'This looks like being a bad business, sir,' he whispered.

'Indeed it does, and this is not the end of it, I'm afraid. I can only guess at what has been done to her but I want you to send someone for Dr Dexter as early as reasonably possible. I want to catch him before he leaves for his clinic. Stand by to help Nanny if she needs you, and if anyone asks questions say that Miss Louise has been taken very sick and that we are taking care of her. I have to go out for a while but I'll be back as soon as I can. Understand?'

Mark nodded. He had served Christine's family ever since the day he had gone to start work at Bramber at the age of twelve, and was devoted to her and all those dear to her. 'I'll see to it, sir. I'll speak to Cook and Hannah as soon as they are up and Cook will have a word with the rest of the kitchen staff.'

'Good.'

Daniel went down to his study and considered his next step. Obviously Inspector Radford would have to be informed as soon as possible, but not before Daniel knew more about what had happened himself. Somehow Louise must be protected. If she had really killed Leo, whether deliberately or in self-defence, it would be a field day for certain portions of the press. He could see only too clearly how the whole story could be exploited: the young Russian who had once been her lover, who had thrown the bomb that killed her parents, who had followed her to England, risking everything for her. Had she gone with him willingly or hadn't she? What had driven her to murder? Such a tale would be enough to blight her whole life, make her an outcast in decent society, destroy all her hopes for a musical future.

He looked at the key on the table and made up his mind. He was not sure what he could do but he would see the house himself, find out all he could before he went to the police.

It was almost four o'clock, nearly dawn. He put on a long dark coat, jammed on an inconspicuous hat pulled down to his brows, picked up the key and went out. A cruising cab took him near to Soho Square. He gave the driver a handful of silver and told him to wait. The gas lamps had been turned out but there was already a faint lightening of the sky. He walked into the shadow of the trees and looked across at the row of tall houses, picking out number 7. There were very few people about at this early hour as he crossed the road and went down the area steps.

All was quiet. He could see very little through the dirty window so, with a quick look around him, he put the key in the lock. He opened the door cautiously and stepped inside. There was just enough light to see that there was no bleeding corpse, no handcuff and chain, no iron candlestick, in fact no sign of habitation at all. The room had a deserted look, the bed with its threadbare counterpane neatly tucked in, a chest beside it, an inner door firmly closed. An anonymous room waiting for its next lodger. Louise was either suffering from delusions or someone in that house had made absolutely sure that no clue as to her abduction, no hint of what had taken place in this room in the last few days remained.

He was baffled but not altogether surprised. It was fairly obvious that Leo had not been working alone. He stood quite still for a moment, remembering what Ada had said about Roger Tanner asking questions and his sister refusing to report

Louise's disappearance. If Daniel had not called with Toby, he might never have known till it was too late. The sooner Inspector Radford got to work on his theory the better.

He went out, shut the door quietly, relocked it and took the key. The police might find it a useful clue. As he went up the area steps and glanced back at the house, he was just too late to see that a curtain at one of the upper windows twitched for a moment and then fell back into place.

Chapter 18

Dr Dexter arrived soon after seven o'clock and was met by Daniel as soon as Mark opened the door to him.

'What the deuce is going on?' he said a little testily. 'Your messenger scarcely allowed me time to finish a cup of coffee. Who wants me so urgently? Not you, Dan, obviously. One of the servants?'

'No, it's Louise.'

'Louise? What has she been up to? Not fallen off her horse again, I hope.'

'No, it's worse than that.' Daniel drew the doctor into his study and very briefly outlined what had happened during the last week. 'I don't know yet for certain what was done to her but she arrived on my doorstep in a very distressed condition in the middle of the night. Nanny did what she could but now it's up to you.'

'Is this Leo, this Russian you speak of, the same man you told me about last Christmas?'

'Yes. All I could gather was that he abducted her, chained her up like a dog and assaulted her. She cracked him over the head with the nearest heavy object and made her escape.'

'Good for her. Have you informed the police?'

'I did immediately I knew she had gone out one evening and vanished but that was already three days after it had happened. They put out feelers but with no results. I'd like your opinion of her condition before I go to the inspector this morning. No doubt he will want to question her himself.'

'I see. Well, we'd better get on with it, hadn't we? Lead the way.'

Daniel left him at the door of the bedroom and then went back to his study. The doctor had a few quiet words with Nanny, who was an old friend, and then looked down at Louise with his friendly smile. She was still deadly pale with a bruised look about her eyes, the dark-gold hair spread out on the pillow, and he thought irrelevantly that no young woman had the right to go through such an ordeal and still look so incredibly beautiful.

'Well, young lady,' he said cheerfully. 'It seems that you are in the wars again. Shall we take a look at the damage?'

She shrank away from him, trembling. The very fact that she knew him, a fellow-guest with whom she had talked and laughed at Bramber, somehow made it worse. It might have been easier to talk to a stranger. But John Dexter had a way of becoming impartial when he was making an intimate examination and his touch was sure and deft. He discussed the condition of her back with Nanny and suggested treatment as if dealing with a young woman who had been cruelly beaten was the most ordinary thing in the world. He turned back the blankets, his probing fingers gentle, and asked a number of shrewd questions in such a way that she found herself telling him jerkily what he wanted to know without realizing it. Then it was all over. He tucked the bedclothes around her.

'There, that wasn't too bad, was it? Now, I want you to take it very quietly for the next few days. Do whatever Nanny tells you and try to eat some of the food she brings you. Just a little at a time, don't force it. I will come again tomorrow.'

He gave Nanny some instructions while he washed his hands and dried them on the towel she gave him, and then went down the stairs to where Daniel was waiting for him.

'Well, what's the verdict?'

'Not too good, I'm afraid. Her back is nasty and very painful of course, but treatment will help that and young flesh usually heals quickly. She needs feeding up too. At the moment Nanny says she won't touch anything, but that's not the worst. I'm afraid there is no doubt at all that he raped her. I imagine the beating aroused him to some sort of a frenzy and then . . .'

'Oh my God!' muttered Daniel. 'I'd like to wring his blasted neck!'

'Quite so,' said the doctor. 'I couldn't agree more. Let's hope the police lay their hands on him. She must have suffered a great deal of pain, and there was bleeding too. Nanny told me that. It is a horrible shock for a young and innocent girl who has probably never even realized what sex actually means, and instead of being led into it by a loving husband, she is torn apart by a brute. She'll recover physically of course, but the worst effect will be mental. It could have an extremely traumatic effect that hasn't even surfaced yet. You'll need to be very patient with her. Is Christine coming back from Bramber?'

'Very soon, I hope. She can leave Robert now from time to time in Isabelle's capable hands. I don't think she altogether trusts me. She thinks I live in a pigsty when she's not here.'

'Have you told her about Louise?'

'Not yet. I didn't want to worry her unnecessarily till I knew more about it. I shall write now, naturally.'

'And in the mean time do you intend to keep Louise here with you?'

'Of course. Where else can she go? Now Clara and Jean-Louis have gone off to Paris she is totally alone, and I'm not going to permit her to go back to the tender mercies of that harpy at Arlington Street when I have a strong suspicion that she had a hand in the abduction. If you consider we need a nurse to help out with Nanny, perhaps you can recommend someone suitable.'

'It's not that, Dan. She doesn't really require that kind of nursing. It's just that – well, so young a girl here alone with you and your wife away ...'

'Oh, for God's sake! I'm scarcely alone, with Nanny and Celia, two dogs and a house full of servants, to say nothing of David, who should be coming home pretty soon now. What are you accusing me of?'

'Nothing – but others might. You should realize that. You're too well-known, Dan, and you've never quite fitted into polite society in spite of Christine, have you? You're too outspoken, too unorthodox, you follow what you believe to be right and ride roughshod over others, you've made enemies. Think about it and persuade your wife to come back as soon as possible, that's my advice, and don't let that policeman badger Louise with questions till I have seen her again. Doctor's orders, tell him that. Now I must go. They'll be queuing up at the clinic. I'll be back tomorrow. I'd like to keep an eye on her for the next few days.'

Daniel looked after his old friend, disturbed and not a little angry. It had never occurred to him for a single instant that there could be any impropriety in caring for Louise here in his own home. He had acted at once, both from compassion and from the very deep sense of responsibility he had always had for her. What the devil did John Dexter think he should do now? Pack her off to a hospital, where she would probably die in a week from some filthy infection? Medical care had improved since he was a boy, but no one with any means at all would dream of going to hospital if they could avoid it, and he certainly was not going to let her go anywhere near Mrs Bolton at Arlington Street. The very idea of sending her away from the house in her present condition was unthinkable and he dismissed it from his mind, quite certain that when Christine came back she would agree with him. Now there were other matters that needed attention. He must look in on Louise and then take himself to Scotland Yard. He started up the stairs and collided with Celia, coming down at her usual breakneck speed. He just managed to catch her in his arms.

'Nanny says Hannah must take me to school today because Louise has been taken sick and she is looking after her,' she said breathlessly.

He put her down firmly on her feet. 'That's right, pet.'

'Wouldn't she like to know all about Toby? Shall I take him in to her?'

'Not just now, Celia. Perhaps this evening when you come home from school. Off you go now or you'll be late. Look after her, Hannah.'

'I will, sir,' said the maid, coming down more sedately and taking the child's hand. 'Come along, Miss Celia, walk nicely now. There's no need to run.'

Daniel went on up the stairs, knocked at the bedroom door and spoke to Nanny. 'How is she?'

'Resting nicely now. I gave her just a little of Madam's drops.' Christine had a large bottle of laudanum for emergencies but kept a strict watch over its use.

'Go easy with that, Nanny.'

'Don't you be afraid, Mr Hunter. I wouldn't give it without asking the doctor first, but it will help soothe the pain in her back.'

Daniel went along to his own room, washed, shaved, changed his clothes and made his way to Scotland Yard, fortunate enough to find the inspector still in his office dealing with what had come in the early hours.

He sat back in his chair and listened quietly to Daniel's account of the eventful night.

'Hit him on the head and then escaped, did she? A young woman of spirit, obviously,' he said drily. 'Do you believe that she killed him?'

'I doubt if she did more than knock him out temporarily, but if she did do him any real harm someone in little more than two hours took very good care to whisk him away and leave absolutely no sign of her ever being anywhere near the place.'

'Did they indeed?' said the inspector, looking at him sharply. 'And how do you happen to be so sure of that?'

Daniel cursed himself for giving away what he would have preferred to keep to himself. 'After I'd made sure she was in good hands, I took myself to Soho Square. The room was almost completely bare and quite uninhabited.'

'The girl couldn't have made a mistake, described the wrong house?'

'No, she'd suffered too much there. It was indelibly printed on her memory. In any case she brought the key away with her, clutched in her hand. There it is,' and he put it on the desk.

'Hm, interesting,' said the inspector, frowning, 'but all the same you should not have gone there. I warned you not to interfere. You should have contacted us at once. We might have been able to catch them red-handed.'

'You wouldn't have thanked me for calling you up in the middle of the night and sending you out on a wild-goose chase,' said Daniel. 'I was there almost within two hours of her escape.'

The policeman leaned across his desk and said very deliberately, 'I am going to ask you a straight question and I want a straight answer. Is it possible that the girl has had an unpleasant experience, possibly through her own fault, and has invented the whole fantastic story to explain it? Such things do happen, you know.'

'If you knew Louise as well as I do, and if you had seen the pitiable state she was in (and still is), you would not have doubted her for a single moment.'

'If you'll pardon me saying so, you haven't had as much experience of such cases as I have. She is probably already regretting the dramatic tale she poured out to you in the middle of the night.'

'Not at all,' said Daniel, nettled by the policeman's tendency to believe the worst of Louise. 'Last night she was in such a state of mental and physical exhaustion, she could not have invented anything. The horror was too real, too vivid. But when she recovers physically, she will keep her troubles to herself. She always has done. She meets them head-on and does not ask for sympathy.'

'Well, that's as may be,' said the inspector. 'When can I see her?'

'Not till tomorrow. The doctor was very insistent about that.'

'I am good at dealing with hysterical young women.'

'Louise is not in the least hysterical, she is more likely to be silent, withdrawn. I doubt if you will get much out of her.'

'That remains to be seen. In the mean time I'll put one of my men on to hunting up this Roger Tanner. I am almost sure he owned a house somewhere in Soho, and with any luck this could be the one. He'll not escape me this time. As for the Russian, if he's not dead he will more than likely have taken refuge among his own kind, and we have contacts there. It may take a little time but we'll winkle him out, you can be sure of that.'

'There is one other thing,' said Daniel. 'I would be grateful if the story and Louise's part in it could be kept out of the newspapers.'

'Not as easy as you may think,' said the inspector, 'especially if any of those bloodhounds get a whiff that the man responsible was the anarchist who threw that bomb. It makes such a damned good story.'

'I am sure the whole family would be grateful, especially Lord Warrinder, who is after all her guardian and closely related,' went on Daniel, sure that his father-in-law would back him to the hilt.

'We'll do our best, can't say more than that,' said Radford. Keep me informed, and I'll be along to see the young lady as soon as possible tomorrow morning.'

In the event nothing worked out quite as planned. Daniel wrote to Christine that same day with an account of Louise's abduction, but found it difficult to go into the long story of her relationship with Leo. He regretted now that he had not told her about it when he came back from Russia, but what had happened at the villa and at the railway station in St Petersburg belonged to the past which Louise was valiantly trying to put behind her, and he had seen no point in dragging it all out into the open. The result was that Christine did not realize fully the seriousness of the situation and its effect on Louise. Then, just when Robert was on the way to full recovery, Lady Clarissa suffered a heart attack.

'Of all the maddening things to happen,' wrote Christine:

> 'It isn't as if it's a very serious attack either, no more than a 'warning twinge', the doctor says, but you know Mamma. She is convinced that she is dying, and nothing

will pacify her but that her daughter should be by her side. It's upset Papa, too, when he is really more frail than she is nowadays. I can't see myself getting away for at least another two or three weeks, and I can't tell you how I am longing to get back to our ordinary everyday life in our own home. Poor darling, it must be very hard for you. Do look after yourself. Do eat properly and don't work too hard. I know what happens when I'm not there with you. Why don't you ask Kate to come and stay for a few weeks? She and Louise always got on well together. Failing her, what about that nice Miss Motford? I am sure she would come if you asked her. She has a great admiration for you.'

Daniel read the letter with a good deal of exasperation. Surely his mother-in-law, surrounded with servants and nurses, did not need his wife dancing attendance on her? But he knew only too well that Christine, who had never really got on with her mother, would for that very reason feel guilty if she deserted her now. Kate had gone to Edinburgh to star in a short Shakespearian season, and Miss Motford was apparently still in Bournemouth. There was nothing to be done but carry on caring for Louise as best he could and let a spiteful society think what it damned well liked.

He sighed and turned to the rest of the letter:

'The one really wonderful thing is that Robert is getting on so well he wants to go back to school – which the doctors won't allow – and, since he is also forbidden to ride or indeed indulge in any strenuous exercise, he has mapped out a course of study for himself and spends hours in Papa's library. You know what a boy he is for books. He knows I am writing this and sends his love. He misses you very much.'

Just as much as he missed the boy's lively company, he thought, and Isabelle too. He folded the letter, put it away and considered his next step. He must send for Louise's trunk at Arlington Street; he had his usual monthly column to write for the *Forum*, a magazine of some literary fame whose editor was clamouring for the copy; he had commitments to the *Clarion* and the *Daily News*, all to be completed within the next couple of days. Thank goodness for Nanny, who was stalwartly standing by and could be relied upon to care for Louise's needs.

Detective Inspector Radford was also suffering from frustration. He had been more impressed with Louise than he cared to admit. Unlike most victims of such attacks, who pour out their sufferings, real or imaginary, in excessive detail, she was quite calm, almost withdrawn, keeping to dry facts, all emotion under strict control. Only once did she betray any feeling at all, and that was when she asked him what would happen to Leo if they found him.

'He will be charged under English law with abduction and assault, but at the same time, seeing who he is, it is more than likely that Russia will be informed and may demand his extradition. Any further punishment will therefore be their decision.'

'Oh no, no!' she said, turning away her face. 'Dear God, must he go through all that again?' Was it compassion, he wondered, or some lingering childish affection?

In other areas he found himself up against a stone wall of lies and evasions. Roger Tanner had quite simply vanished. His wife swore that he had gone away about a fortnight previously, on business, and she had no idea when he would be returning. He certainly owned the house in Soho Square, but for the past six months it had been let to a certain Mrs Lupton, a stout, formidable woman who looked the inspector in the face and lied with a brazen confidence which proved impossible to break down. She ran it as a lodging-house for young women of good character, she insisted, no gentlemen being admitted; as for foreigners, she had no truck with them as being far too unreliable. The basement room had been empty for weeks, for the simple reason that it needed doing up and she hadn't the money to waste on it. When a timid neighbour ventured to suggest she had seen someone come and go up and down the area steps, she fixed the shrinking woman with a stony eye and said she obliged a friend now and again and could provide names and addresses if the police wanted them. There was absolutely no proof that it had served as a prison where Louise had been chained, tormented and raped, though the inspector knew that her description of the room was correct in every detail.

'I damned well know that I have a case against Roger Tanner,' he said to Daniel, 'but I can't *prove* any of it. A clever lawyer could tear it to pieces in five minutes.'

'You think he was manipulating Leo for his own purposes?'

'Exactly. The young man had money, you tell me, and knew very little of England and of London. He was easy prey for a man like Roger Tanner putting on an act of loyal friend, quick to understand, sympathize and give assistance. He no doubt played him along, intended to let the boy have his will of the girl and then step in. He would know all about the substantial inheritance that had come to her from her sister and her wealthy bridegroom. He knew she was comparatively friendless, an illegitimate orphan who was no one's particular responsibility, and he was determined to get a good deal of that inheritance for himself. He would as it were "rescue" the girl from her abductor and demand a hefty ransom.'

'And Leo? What did he intend to do with Leo?'

'That's anybody's guess. But Tanner had the whip hand. He knew who he really was. A word to the authorities and it would have been all up with the poor devil. Roger Tanner must be chewing the carpet with rage at this moment because she has got away and robbed him of all his hopes. She has not only escaped his clutches but left him needing to cover his tracks, and he'll be itching for revenge on someone. I've not given up, I'll get him one of these days. But I'd advise you to watch your step very carefully in the next few weeks.'

Daniel did not take the threat very seriously. He'd been in

tight spots before and always survived. It was Louise's safety rather than his own that concerned him. With Roger Tanner and Leo still at liberty she could be in constant danger. He sent Mark to Arlington Street to collect her trunk and all her other possessions. Mrs Bolton had been grilled unmercifully by one of the inspector's best men and was not in the mood to be helpful. She had vehemently denied that her brother had taken any but a passing interest in Louise. Why should he, when he had a business to run? As for his visits, they were merely out of kindness to his sister whom he knew to be lonely. The other servants had always been resentful and jealous because of the trust and confidence that Lady Dorrien had placed in her.

'If it had not been for the girl, Ada, who was maid to Miss Louise, I doubt if I would have come away with anything at all,' Mark reported back to Daniel. 'She packed everything, including Toby's basket and rug. I was able to reassure her that Miss Louise was being well cared for. The poor girl is to be dismissed very soon and did ask if she might call, but I advised her to leave it for a few weeks. I hope I did right.'

'Perfectly right. You did very well. Have everything taken up to Miss Louise's room. Later on I'll go up and tell her about it.'

It was four days now since the night she had escaped, and Louise, on doctor's orders, was still keeping to her bed, more exhausted mentally and physically than she had ever thought possible.

Celia had brought Toby back to her, looking fat and sleek, and he went into such an ecstasy of delight at seeing his beloved mistress again that the little girl spread one of Rowley's rugs on the bed and lifted him on to it.

'Nanny doesn't allow me to have Rowley on my bed, but I don't suppose she'll mind this time as you have been so ill.'

The child had accepted without question the simple fact that Louise had been taken sick and found it perfectly natural that her father and Nanny should take care of her.

When Daniel came up this evening to see Louise, he was

given a noisy reception from the little dog. 'You know it is the luckiest thing,' he said, tickling behind Toby's ears so that he squirmed with pleasure, 'that our address was still on his collar, otherwise I might not have known what had happened to you for several more days.'

'I know. I never thought to change it,' she said. She had in fact deliberately left it, because it somehow made her feel that she belonged somewhere and wasn't just a bird of passage with no real home anywhere.

'I have had your trunk and books and so on brought round from Arlington Street,' he went on, pulling up a chair and sitting beside the bed. 'I thought you would feel happier with all your own possessions around you.'

She pushed herself up against her pillows. 'Does that mean that I don't have to go back to Arlington Street?'

'Not unless you wish to, and I strongly advise against it. I am sure you will be a great deal safer here with us.'

She was staring at him, hands clasped, her eyes huge in her pale face, her mind racing back to all Kate had said to her here in this very house after the Christmas holiday. 'But I can't stay here . . . I mustn't impose on you like this. It isn't right. Christine wouldn't like it.'

He smiled. 'What nonsense. Christine knows all about it and sends you the kindest of messages. She would have been back from Bramber by now if Lady Clarissa had not been taken ill.'

'But I'm causing you all so much trouble,' she said distractedly. 'It's so much extra work for Nanny when she has Celia to care for, and then there is you. I know how hard you work. There must be somewhere I could go. Perhaps I could stay with Miss Motford for a while . . . tomorrow I must get up. I must look out for myself.'

'You'll do no such thing, my girl. You'll obey doctor's orders and, as for causing trouble, Nanny is in her element. I've told you before: now that the children have largely outgrown her, she looks forward to having someone she can care for and fuss over. As for me, I have been obliged to work against time in some very strange places. Sometimes I think it gives an added stimulus. As soon as you feel more like yourself, why not try to finish the translation of *Fedora* you were working on? I am afraid our piano is not so grand as the one in Clara's drawing-room but it is adequate, I believe, and you are free to practise on it whenever you like.'

All those things she had enjoyed so much seemed remote from her, as if they had happened to someone else in some other world. Had she really played in that concert to such a large audience? She tried desperately to remember the opening bars of the Schumann and her mind went completely blank. 'It's all gone out of my mind,' she whispered. It's all vanished as if it never happened.' She shivered and pulled the dressing-jacket closer around her. It was a very pretty one which Christine often wore. It filled him with an impatient longing for his wife to be back here with him, and at the same time with a tenderness towards the girl with her frail beauty. He wanted to take her in his arms, bring her comfort and strength, as he had done once before. Instead he stood up and put a hand on hers for a moment.

'Don't fret. It will all come back. I have times when my mind is like a blank sheet of paper, but if you don't try too hard it passes and thoughts flow again.'

Someone knocked and one of the maids put a head around the door. 'Cook says when would you like dinner served this evening, sir?'

'Oh, in about half an hour, tell her, and in my study not in the dining-room.'

'Very good, sir.'

'I'm eating there now since I'm on my own,' he went on to Louise. 'Perhaps in a few days you will join me there. You must not shut yourself up here away from us all. It won't do you any good. Now I must go. Nanny will be bringing up your supper very soon now so I shall say good-night.'

'Good-night.' She reached for his hand and held on to it. 'I don't know how to thank you.'

'There is no need. I'm only glad I was here. Good-night, my dear, try to sleep.'

'I will.'

But that was when the nightmares began. For the first few days the relief of knowing herself safe had been so great that she had lived in a kind of daze, still in a good deal of pain, not only from her back but her whole body felt battered, almost as if it no longer belonged to her. But now very slowly, as the physical tension eased so the mental torment took its place, and the nights were the worst of all now that Nanny, following doctor's orders, had cut down on the laudanum.

'It's no use drugging her,' he had said. 'She must fight her own way out of the trauma.'

Louise would fall asleep but soon seem to be reliving every horrific moment. Sometimes she was suffering with Leo on those nightmare journeys which he had described so vividly; sometimes she was suffocating in his arms, trying to fight him off like some terrifying monster; and she would wake trembling, pouring with sweat and her whole body shaking with horror that she could not control.

She became obsessed with the idea that she had somehow brought it on herself. She should have found a way of dealing with him at the very beginning. Then she blamed herself for all that had happened to him, driving him into a kind of madness, and she would pray that the police would not find him. Perhaps she really had killed him. Was it possible? Night after night she went through the whole horrible incident, felt the bite of the whip, his hands on her breast, the taste of his mouth, the heavy body crushing her, invading her, felt the weight of the heavy candlestick in her hand, the sticky blood on her fingers, till she thought despairingly she would remember it for ever.

But despite the tormented nights, her physical strength continued to return. Dr Dexter encouraged her to get up, and it was a relief to unpack with Nanny's help, to dress in her own clothes, to begin to return to ordinary life. At the end of the following week she came slowly down the stairs one evening to have dinner with Daniel in the study.

It had taken a great deal of persuasion on his part. It was the first time she had ventured downstairs, as Celia or one of the servants took Toby for his daily walks. She knew it was foolish. She knew she should not give way to the fear, but it was as if her bedroom was a sanctuary, the only place where she felt really safe.

Daniel got up from his chair when she came in. The book-lined room which belonged to him so particularly, bathed in the golden sunshine of the June evening, seemed to take her into its heart. He persuaded her to sip a little sherry and, although when the food came she ate scarcely anything, the inner tension slowly began to relax. He talked about the work he was engaged on, asked her if she had ever read any George Eliot and recommended her latest book *Middlemarch* as a splendid picture of an English country town. He told her that Kate was having great success in Edinburgh and wanted to know how the translation of *Fedora* was progressing. 'I've been thinking,' he went on: 'would you like to work in here? You could have a table in the window, spread your books there and then come and go just as you wish.'

'But this is *your* room, where *you* work,' she objected, 'and I know how you hate to be disturbed.'

'I'm not always here. I do have the use of a desk at the newspaper offices and quite often work there, especially when time is short. You think about it and let me know how you feel. It would seem a pity not to finish the play after you have done so much good work on it already.'

'I'll try.' Perhaps when she unpacked her books it would help to cure the deadly apathy that had seized her.

'Good. Then I'll set it up for you.'

When they had eaten and the table was cleared, she got up to go, but he persuaded her to stay a while longer. 'Coffee will be coming in soon and I have something to show you. The first copies of my new book arrived this morning.'

She took the book in her hands, her face alight with interest. 'Oh, how splendid it looks.'

'You're the first. Even Christine has not seen it yet.'

'May I read it?'

'If you wish. Now when I glance through it, I am only too well aware of its faults, when it is too late to remedy them.'

'I suppose all authors feel like that, but I am sure you have no need.'

She was on a footstool beside his chair, turning the pages rapturously when the door burst open and David came in with a rush. He stopped abruptly, taking in the picture.

'I'm sorry,' he said. 'I thought you'd be alone. Good evening, Louise. Am I disturbing something?'

'Not in the least,' said Daniel easily. 'But I was not expecting you for another few days.'

'The case finished yesterday with a spectacular triumph for Uncle Harry. We came back from Oxford this morning.'

Louise had scrambled to her feet. 'If you will excuse me, Daniel, I think I'll go up to bed,' she said. 'You and David will have so much to talk about.'

'If you wish, my dear. Good-night.'

'Good-night, David.'

She brushed past him and went out quickly while he looked after her, frowning. 'I didn't expect to see Louise here.'

'I don't suppose you did. She is staying with us for a while.'

'Is Mamma here?'

'No. She would have been by now, but your grandmother had a heart attack and she felt she had to stay with her. She is still down at Bramber.'

'Poor old Granny. Is it serious?'

'Your mother says it was only a slight attack, but you know how nervous your grandmother is of any illness. Have you eaten? I dare say the kitchen could rustle up a meal if you haven't.'

'I dined with Uncle Harry and afterwards had a brandy with him at his club. There was a very queer story going around about Louise having been abducted. It sounded crazy to me. Is it true?'

'Perfectly true. It is why she is staying here.'

'What the devil happened to her?'

'She was grabbed one evening when she was walking the

dog. It was very unpleasant and has had an appalling effect on her. She shies away from shadows.' Daniel paused for a moment, uncertain how much to tell David and deciding to keep to the bare facts. So far few details had escaped, and he did not altogether trust David to keep his mouth shut. So he said nothing about Leo or the way she had been beaten and assaulted, only that she had been abducted, obviously with the purpose of demanding a heavy ransom for her release, and that she had contrived to overcome her captor and make her escape.

'She found her way here one night drenched to the skin, very shocked and disturbed as you can imagine.'

'What a frightful thing to happen. Do the police know?'

'Of course. I went to the Yard immediately. Inspector Radford has the case in hand but so far with little success. The housekeeper at Arlington Street deliberately hid the fact that she had disappeared for several days and we suspect she may have had something to do with it. Anyway it was obvious that I couldn't let Louise go back there, alone and distressed.'

'No, of course not. Does Mamma know about it?'

'Naturally. I wrote at once and she agrees with me. Now, tell me how things have been with you.'

'Pretty well on the whole, though I was only dogsbodying of course. Uncle Harry was pleased with me. He actually said I'd come up with one or two ideas that hadn't occurred to him.'

'Good for you. I thought you looked uncommonly pleased with yourself,' said his stepfather a little drily. 'You seem to be finding your feet in the legal world at last. Are you intending to stay in the apartment you were sharing with that colleague of yours?'

'Well, as a matter of fact that's why I am here. He has a friend come over from Paris for a few weeks so I thought I'd come back here if it's all right with you and Mamma.'

'Of course. This is your home. Make what arrangements you like. With any luck your mother will be with us in a week or so and we shall be back to normal. In the mean time I dare say we shall carry on well enough.'

*

But Daniel was wrong. It didn't work out well at all, and the disturbing element was David. He had come back very full of himself. Very soon now he would be called to the Bar, and in the autumn he would be working full-time in his uncle's chambers, in a very junior position, of course, but it was the first rung on the ladder. He knew how lucky he was, but he had grown in self-confidence during the last few months and with it had come the firm intention to win Louise for himself. Even though they quarrelled whenever they met, he still wanted her. No other girl had meant anything to him since that first meeting, well over a year ago now, and to find her living in the same house was an unexpected bonus.

He set himself out to please and was hurt and then angry when he found that she was doing everything she could to avoid him. She did not join them when he dined at home, but remained shut away in her own room, and yet if he came back unexpectedly in the day he would find her in the study with Daniel, sharing a working luncheon with him and seemingly on the easiest of terms. He did not realize that in actual fact she avoided almost everyone and shrank away from any physical contact, that only with Daniel did she feel at ease. Gradually David's hurt turned to that childish jealousy of the stepfather who had always seemed to stand in his way.

As for Louise, she was still fighting an inner turmoil that constantly threatened to overcome her surface calm. Her feelings for David had always been mixed. He had sometimes been so delightful that she would warm to him, and then for no real reason the sparks would fly and they were fighting one another. Now in her disturbed state she could not cope with his attempts at friendly intimacy. Once, when he came into the study where she was bent over her books, the heavy gold hair pushed to one side exposing the tender neck, he impulsively stooped to kiss it lightly, and was astonished at her violent reaction as she sprang to her feet, slapping his cheek hard.

'Don't touch me!' she exclaimed fiercely, then caught her breath in a stifled sob and ran from the room.

He did not realize, how could he, that she was beset by

inner fears for herself and her future, fears which grew worse instead of better that week, when the doctor came to give her a routine examination.

'Physically you are making a good recovery,' he said cheerfully, sitting on the side of the bed and taking her hand in his. 'Now tell me all about yourself. How are you coping? No bad dreams, no nightmares?'

'None at all,' she lied bravely, knowing that she must fight them herself, as she had to fight the fear that shook her whenever she ventured out of the house. Only the day before, she had put Toby on his leash and walked resolutely up the street, finding it delightful to be out of the house with normal everyday life going on around her, then on turning a corner she had walked into Leo, the hat pulled down, frowning heavily. For a moment she could not move, only stand there shaking, then the stranger muttered an apology, raised his hat and stood aside to let her pass, and it was not Leo at all; but she was so frightened that she picked up Toby and ran all the way back to the house, shutting herself up in her bedroom, burying her face in the pillows and wondering desperately if it would always be like that.

'If you are unhappy about anything at all,' went on the doctor, getting up, 'then tell Daniel to send for me. Otherwise I'll be back in a week, and do try to eat a little more. You are too thin, my dear.' He smiled, patted her cheek and went downstairs.

She dressed very slowly and presently, thinking he would be gone by now, went down to the study; but the door was ajar and he was talking to Daniel. She stood still for a moment, paralysed by what she heard.

'Is it still possible?' Daniel was saying.

'It's too early to be sure. It's not very common in these cases, but you can't rule it out,' said the doctor. 'I am afraid she could be pregnant.'

'If she is, could you do something about it?'

'You know I can't, though God knows there have been times when I have wished I could. Apart from the moral scruple, it is against the law.'

'Then it's time the law was changed, at least for some cases.'

But she did not hear any more. She felt as if someone had kicked her savagely in the stomach. It had never once occurred to her that she could be pregnant, and now it hit her so hard that all joy, all her precarious hold on sanity and good sense, seemed to drain away from her. She went back upstairs to her own room and tried to face up to it.

It could not happen, it must not. How could she endure those long months of waiting for a child, an illegitimate child born not from love as Louise had been but sprung out of terror, out of loathing? Her future dissolved into horror. Where could she go, where hide herself, with no friendly hand held out to help and comfort, only contempt, only those who would say she must have brought it on herself and so now must suffer the consequences?

She shut herself away for the rest of the day and when, feeling concerned, Daniel knocked and asked if there was anything he could do, she told Nanny to say she had a raging headache and wanted only to lie quietly in a darkened room. But daily life goes obstinately on, even if you feel you are slowly dying inside. She existed through the next few days, going about white and silent while Daniel guessed that something was wrong but didn't ask questions, only wondered if he should call John Dexter. The time for her usual monthly period came and went without anything to show for it and when the doctor came the following week she nerved herself to speak of it.

'Don't let it worry you, my dear,' he said gently. 'Many things can cause this: shock, stress, anxiety, especially in a young girl like yourself. Your courses will resume in their own good time.'

'It doesn't mean that I'm pregnant?' she whispered through stiff lips.

'Good heavens, no. Is that what is upsetting you? Forget it. Put it right out of your mind and think towards the future. You've much to look forward to. We are all expecting great things from you, you know. Tell me, have you tried out

Daniel's piano yet? I don't think he will raise any objection to your daily practising.' He spoke with a cheerful confidence but she didn't believe him. He was only saying these things to give her heart till the blow fell, till she must face the grim truth. Through the hours of torment a way of escape had slowly crept into her mind.

She said tentatively, 'I've been finding it difficult to sleep and Nanny says you won't allow her to give me any more of the laudanum that helped so much with the pain in my back.'

'I'm not very much in favour of drugs,' he said slowly; 'in my opinion they often give superficial comfort and only serve to conceal what is actually causing the trouble. Still, taken in moderation I don't suppose it will do you any harm. I'll tell Nanny, but you must use it sparingly. It can kill, you know, as well as give comfort.'

So the big bottle came back from Christine's medicine chest and day after day she stared at it there on her washstand, and the resolution grew and hardened in her mind. She felt as if everything in her had dried up, she was useless. She couldn't work, couldn't think clearly any longer. She spent a whole day staring down at her translation of *Fedora* and nothing happened. Everything she had done seemed wooden and lifeless and she hated it.

One night that week Daniel, lying wakeful as he did sometimes, got up and went down to his study to fetch a book he had left there. He noticed the flickering light as he crossed the hall and saw that Louise was there in her dressing-gown, candle in hand, staring down at her work table with its pile of neatly written manuscript. She started when he spoke to her and nearly dropped the candle.

'Here, give that to me,' he said as he took it from her. 'What on earth are you doing down here at this time of night?'

'I was thinking about all this,' she said, picking up the thick manuscript in both hands and shaking it. 'It's no good, it's useless, it doesn't mean anything, does it, it's all rubbish. I can't think properly any more, that's why. I thought ... I thought I'd come down and tear it up, destroy it, put it on the fire where it belongs.'

'You'll do no such thing, unless you want to burn the house down,' he said. 'You mustn't let yourself think like that. We all get depressed about the work we are doing, it happens to me, and it always hits you in the middle of the night, but if we were to give in to it, then nothing would ever be done. Now be a good girl and put all those sheets back into their folder. I'm going to take you up to bed before you catch your death of cold. When you look at it again, you'll feel quite differently about it.'

'Will I?'

'Of course you will.'

She let him take her arm and lead her up the stairs. He went into the bedroom with her, placing the candlestick safely on the table by the bed.

'Now, would you like me to go down to the kitchen and rustle up a cup of hot milk to help you to sleep?'

'No. No, thank you. I'm all right now.'

'Sure?'

'Yes.'

'Good-night then, and promise me you'll put all such foolish notions right out of your mind.'

'I'll try,' she whispered.

But, try as she would, she was still gripped by black moods, until something happened that brought her despair to a crisis.

One afternoon, alone in the house except for the servants, she went down to the drawing-room and for the first time opened up the piano. She sat down, letting her hands rest on the keyboard and then very slowly began to play a Chopin nocturne. Suddenly her mind went blank, she couldn't remember a note, her fingers had lost their skill, she was touching the keys clumsily, fumbling helplessly like a child at her first piano lesson. She could remember nothing. It was all gone, all vanished, as if something inside her had broken. She wanted to weep but even the tears had dried up. She slammed down the piano lid and went out, colliding with David who had just come in with Daniel.

He put a hand on her arm. 'Just the very person I wanted to

see. I have something to tell you.' She stared at him blankly, then wrenched herself away and ran up the stairs. 'Now what have I done?' he exclaimed helplessly. 'Do you know? What the devil has happened to Louise these days?'

'The doctor did say she might be subject to difficult moods,' said Daniel.

'Moods? Is that what you call them? I might not exist so far as Louise is concerned, yet I've noticed she is always happy enough with you.'

'Isn't that rather childish?' said Daniel sharply and went away to his own room, leaving David staring after him, frustrated and angry.

He had bought expensive tickets for a concert and had looked forward to inviting Louise to go with him. It was maddening to have all his hopes dashed. He ate a silent dinner with his stepfather and went alone, brooding all through the Mozart concerto without hearing a note, and telling himself that if one thing was certain it was that something was going on between Daniel and Louise. A jealous anger rose in his throat, bitter as gall.

He came back late, having met up with a couple of friends, but despite the fact that he had drunk rather more than usual he still could not sleep. The night was warm and the room felt stifling. He got up and pushed the window wide, glad of the cool night air on his face. It was then that he heard the music, very quiet and very hesitant. What was Louise doing playing the piano at this time of night? He stood there a while, listening to the faint disjointed notes, then there was a slight crash with the murmur of voices. She was obviously not alone and anger stirred up in him again.

He opened the door and went quietly down the stairs. The door to the drawing-room was partly open, the room lit only by a single candle on the piano. He could see Louise in her flimsy white nightgown, her hair hanging loose around her shoulders, kneeling on the floor with Daniel beside her holding her in his arms, her face pressed against his shoulder, so very close, so intimate. Did they make love everywhere, he thought with a burning anger: in the study, in her bedroom, in his mother's drawing-room? This was not the first time either, that was obvious. He was tempted to crash in on them and then drew back with disgust. So it was true, as he had always known. All this time, from their very first meeting in St Petersburg!

The anger grew, almost choking him, not against Louise but against the man he hated, who had ruined and defiled her innocence. What a wonderful opportunity this had been, when circumstances had placed her in this house under his care, with Christine away at Bramber, knowing nothing, utterly and cruelly deceived.

He had not noticed the broken glass nor the dark-brown stain on the carpet. If he had listened more intently he would have heard not a lover's endearments but Daniel's stern reproach as he strove to bring Louise back to her senses, to make her realize the enormity of the act of which she was guilty. He too had heard the faint sounds of the piano and his mind, flying back to that night at the villa, knew that in some way a crisis had been reached. He had gone down to the drawing-room and stood for a moment at the door, the old memory gripping him. But Louise's stumbling, pitiful efforts at the piano were quite unlike what he had heard that night, and no storm raged in thunder and lightning outside the windows. Then as he waited there, unwilling to interrupt too suddenly and alarm her, a gentle draught blew the candle flame and he saw the glass half full of some dark-brown liquid, saw her pick it up, and acted. He was beside her in a second, had grabbed it with difficulty out of her clutching fingers so that it fell, spreading a dark stain on the cream carpet, and she sank to her knees, sobbing helplessly. Her words, tangled and distraught, told him all he wanted to know. The moment had come to be firm and uncompromising if he were to save her from herself.

'I'm ashamed of you,' he said. 'I thought you had more courage. How dare you try to destroy yourself for something that may never happen, is very unlikely to happen. I've always believed you to be so brave, and now you've let me down, let all of us down.'

'I've lost everything,' she sobbed. 'I can't play any more, I can't think any longer, I can't work, nothing has any meaning for me ... I hate – I *loathe* myself.'

'Nonsense. When I was in Bulgaria I saw wretched women treated far worse than you were, women who had lost husband, home and children and yet had the courage to pull themselves up and try to help others. Would you be less than those poor peasants? Shame on you!'

Her face was buried against him but he went on talking, talking, hoping that something was getting through to her. 'This is only a temporary setback, something we must all of us go through at some time in our lives. To give in to it is to lose all self-respect, and that is what is important. You can't live without it. You know what I should do? By rights I should make you go down on your knees and scrub away the stain on Christine's beautiful carpet. And it would not have been a way of escape, you know, all it would have done is make you very, very ill.' He tilted up her chin so that she was facing him, looking directly into his eyes. 'Promise me here and now that you will never, ever try anything like this again.'

The crisis was passing. She felt sick and faint and unutterably weary. She leaned against him, infinitely glad of his strength, thankful in her secret heart that he had come at the crucial moment and saved her from a folly that could have had even worse consequences.

'Listen,' he said resolutely, bringing her down from high drama to plain common sense. 'I'm going to take you to bed and then I'm going down to the kitchen to brew a strong cup of tea for us both so that you can pull yourself together.'

And so David, still painfully watching from his bedroom, saw them come up the stairs, Daniel's arm around Louise until she stumbled, when he picked her up and carried her the last few yards into her bedroom. He stayed there for a while because she would not let him go, holding on to his hand as if it were a kind of lifeline to sanity. David, sick with a mingling of anger, jealousy and a very real wretchedness, threw himself on his bed. He did not see Daniel come out and go downstairs, return with a tray and two homely cups of tea, stay with her till she drowsed at last and then, tired to the very bone, return to his own room, never dreaming that David had seen and misinterpreted and was meditating a vicious and destructive revenge.

Chapter 19

Christine came back from Bramber two days later. She sent a telegram announcing her arrival and Daniel went to meet her at the railway station, taking Celia with him. The child saw her mother first and charged along the platform, flinging her arms around her with shrieks of joy while her father followed a little more sedately.

'Glad to see me?' whispered Christine as his arm went around her and he kissed her.

'By God I am,' he murmured fervently; 'it's been far too long.' He summoned a porter to deal with the luggage and find them a cab. 'I rather hoped you'd bring Robert with you,' he said as they walked together down the platform with Celia dancing along, still clinging to her mother's hand.

'I did think of it, but it's so stifling in London during the summer and the doctor thought he would be better off in country air. Isabelle is staying down there with him.'

'How is your mother?'

'Oh heavens, you know Mamma. Still fretting, but there's really nothing to worry about and I felt I just couldn't go on playing sick-nurse any longer. I want to know everything that has been going on while I've been away. I've felt so cut off down there. How is Louise? You really didn't write very much in your letters.'

'All in good time, my love,' he said, settling her in the cab, sitting beside her and taking Celia on his knee.

'Is she still with you?'

'Yes, she is. It's a long story.'

'And you've had to cope with it all on your own, poor darling. It will be different now I'm here,' and she slipped an arm through his. 'Oh, it feels so good to be back with you again.'

'I've had to learn a new poem for the school concert,' announced Celia importantly. 'It's called "The Brook" and it's ever so long.'

'Is it, darling? You must recite it for us one evening.'

Christine was like a fresh breeze blowing through the house, thought Daniel with infinite relief. It was not that the servants had neglected their duties: they were all far too conscious of their good fortune to be so foolish. Cook had always ruled the kitchen staff with a stern hand, while Nanny looked after the upper servants. Daniel had never been exacting, but having the mistress in charge was vastly different from dealing with an easygoing man. The house sprang to life and for a few days everything went along swimmingly.

There was a great deal to be discussed. News had come from Paris, where Clara had married her Greek pirate and they had gone to spend a few weeks with his mother in Corfu before joining the yacht cruising among the Greek islands.

'So Clara has brought it off at last,' said Christine, a little unkindly. 'I never thought she would. I wonder if it will last.'

'I don't see why not,' remarked Daniel. 'He didn't strike me as a man who ever acted impulsively.'

'I think perhaps he hopes for a son,' ventured Louise.

'At her age? Surely that's very unlikely.'

'Actually Clara is a year younger than I am,' said Christine, 'and these things do happen, and work out very well. Look at Robert Browning and his Elizabeth. She bore him a healthy son when she was in her forties and had been an invalid for years.'

'I think Clara longed for a child more than anything,' went on Louise, thinking of those hours she had spent wrestling with Clara's obstinate determination to wreck her life.

'Did she tell you that?'

'No, not exactly . . .'

'Well, if anyone would know, then I suppose you would.'

Daniel had still not told Christine the full story of Louise's tortured relationship with Leo. She thought the girl looked very thin and pale and, though nothing could take away her essential beauty, she had lost the golden glow of health that had been so much part of her. She felt sorry for her, was kind and thoughtful and did not comment when she kept mostly to her own room, taking care to disappear as soon as meals were over and she was no longer working on her translation in Daniel's study. He knew very well that she was fighting her battle in her own way, and he gave her what silent encouragement he could. Christine was far too busy in those first few days rectifying what had gone wrong in her absence to worry more about her than making sure she had what she wanted, with Nanny to keep an eye on her. Harry came to dine with them one evening, and kept them enthralled with an account of the trial in which he had played a spectacular and successful part.

The only thing that troubled Christine was that David, although he had done well according to his uncle, was in one of his blackest and most difficult moods and she could not understand why.

She had been back for over a week when Margaret, who was spending a month with her daughter in London, called on her one morning and annoyed her intensely by attacking Louise. Usually the two sisters were on the best of terms, but that day Margaret was on the warpath.

'I could scarcely believe my ears when I heard that the girl was still staying here, alone in the house with only Daniel, and you down at Bramber. It seems that, not content with ruining John Everard's life, the wretched young woman is now trying to come between you and Daniel.'

'Oh really, Margaret, what is all this nonsense? You were horrified when John Everard proposed to her, weren't you? So you should be delighted that she refused his offer so very firmly.'

'That's all very well, but do you know what her refusal has

driven the poor boy to do?' wailed Margaret. 'He has volunteered to join a special force that is being sent out very soon to deal with rebellious tribesmen in Afghanistan, of all dreadful places!'

'I simply can't believe that his decision is Louise's doing,' said Christine impatiently. 'He's never been the romantic type who rushes off to some distant place to bury his grief. It is far more likely that he is bored to death with his ceremonial duties here in London and has decided he'd like to see some real action before he gives up his commission and settles down to life in the country.'

'And at the same time dies of some horrible fever or gets himself murdered by those savages, I suppose?'

'Why should he? John Everard is a good soldier and knows how to look after himself. He is far more likely to come home in a year or two, loaded with honours and ready to settle down at Ingham Park with some nice girl.'

'And I suppose you think that Daniel can look after himself too,' went on Margaret with an unusual touch of spite. 'He must be out of his mind, keeping her here for all these weeks alone with him, instead of sending her back to Clara's house where she belongs. It's being talked about, you know. I hear it everywhere. All that ridiculous business of her being abducted. What are the police doing about it? Nothing, as far as I can see. I think it far more likely that she ran off with some man, found it didn't work out as she had hoped, ran back to Daniel and concocted the whole dramatic story. He's always had far too much sympathy for her and she knows that.'

'You've been reading too many trashy novels,' said Christine with considerable annoyance. 'I know exactly what happened. I know what Daniel is doing and I'm in complete agreement with him. As for the police, they have the matter very much in hand, even if they haven't found the wretch who abducted her yet.'

'You're far too trusting, Christine.'

'Oh, for heaven's sake, Margaret! I know Daniel and I know Louise. And if a lot of silly women choose to gossip about us, then let them. I have lived with Daniel for some twenty years, and if I'd taken any notice of the rubbish that has been said about him and about how we live and bring up our children and about our friends, then I would have left him years ago. It's not like you to repeat such things.' She leaned forward and took Margaret's hand in hers. 'It's not that I don't sympathize with you over John Everard, but if he wants to break away from home and live his own life for a time, then you must let him go. I know that ever since dear Freddie died at Balaclava you have had to be father as well as mother to John and Clary, but the time comes when you have to let them go. All these young men are the same. I feel exactly the same about David but it doesn't stop me worrying about him. It seems that is what mothers are for.' She smiled and patted her sister's hand. 'Now, drink up your coffee while it is still hot and tell me about the baby. It is due very soon now, isn't it – the first grandchild! What a mercy it is that Clary has such a nice, sensible, quiet husband. You've no worries there.'

Of course it was all rubbish. There was nothing between Daniel and Louise except his ready compassion and his desire to help. Margaret had a grudge against the girl, that was all, and was far too ready to think badly of her.

And yet, hadn't there always been something between them from the very start? What had happened in St Petersburg to draw them so close together? The girl was so young, so friendless, was it any wonder that she had fallen under his spell? Christine kept trying to push the thought away from her and it kept coming back. There had been so many tiny instances, and one day she caught herself watching them when they were together and was disgusted with herself. In all their married life Daniel had never shown the slightest interest in any other woman; and yet in some curious way Louise was different. She had broken into their close-knit family life and, perhaps without meaning to – Christine granted her that – had wrought havoc.

Ever since his mother had come back to them, David had been quietly simmering in his own particular hell. He was so eaten up with jealousy, he wanted to shout his stepfather's perfidy into his mother's face. Time and again the angry words trembled on his lips and then for some reason he bit them back. In the end it was something quite trivial that set it off, and after that nothing could stop him.

They were in the drawing-room after dinner. Louise had excused herself and gone to her own room. Daniel was tired after spending the day wrestling with an article attacking industry for its callous refusal to allow any compensation for injured workpeople and their families, a burning cause championed by the *Clarion*. With the piece safely dispatched to the post, he was leaning back wearily, an unopened book on his knee, a glass of brandy beside him on the small table.

Celia had come down in her dressing-gown to say goodnight and stunned them all with a recitation of 'The Brook', delivered at such breakneck speed that Daniel thought it sounded more like a raging torrent than Tennyson's babbling stream. 'Bravo, my poppet,' he said when she looked to him for approval. Celia, glowing with pride, was kissed and packed off to bed.

Just then Christine, gathering the coffee cups together, noticed for the first time a rather strange patch on the cream carpet near the piano. Hetty, the housemaid, had scrubbed it clean but it still had a peculiar ruffed-up appearance. When Mark came in to fetch the trolley she asked him about it.

He gave a quick glance at Daniel and said smoothly, 'A cup of coffee was spilled, madam. The housemaid worked all the morning on it but I'm afraid, despite her efforts, it's not quite as it was before.'

'I see. Well, it can't be helped, I suppose.'

Mark went out, closing the door, and Daniel said, 'I'm sorry, my dear. I dropped that cup and I do apologize. It was very careless of me. Stand a table over it, then no one will notice.'

'How typical of a man to say that!' said Christine. 'You can't just put a table in the middle of a room for no purpose.'

And that was the spark that set David alight. He turned on

Daniel savagely. 'Why don't you tell Mamma the truth for once? Why go on lying to her? I know what really happened that night, and on other nights. Isn't it time she knew what has been going on in this house while she has been away?'

Christine looked from one to the other with an uneasy feeling that this was the final confrontation between Daniel and Gareth's son that she had always dreaded.

'What is all this, David? What are you talking about?'

And then it all poured out in one long bitter stream. 'I had come in late that night so I wasn't asleep. I thought I heard the piano and it seemed so strange that I went down to the drawing-room. There was only one candle burning but I saw them, both of them, lying together on the floor.' His voice choked. 'Can you imagine how I felt? I was sick with disgust, with rage. I wanted to hit him, kill him, for what he was doing to her.'

'I don't believe you,' said Christine faintly; 'you must have been mistaken. It's impossible. Daniel, tell me it isn't true.'

Daniel had sat up but he made no denial. 'Let him go on,' he said calmly. 'Let him pour out the rest of his fairy tale.'

David, who had expected an angry denial, hesitated and then went on. 'I was so sick and ashamed that such a vile thing could be going on in this house that I went back to my room, and later I saw them come up the stairs together. He carried Louise into her bedroom and he stayed there with her. Deny that if you can.'

'I've no intention of denying anything,' said Daniel quietly. 'Now your mother has heard your little flight of fancy, she can hear the true story of that night and judge between us. I'd hoped to spare Louise, to say nothing about this wretched episode for her sake, but the truth is that she tried to kill herself by swallowing three-quarters of the bottle of laudanum prescribed for her by the doctor.'

'Kill herself!' exclaimed Christine, shocked. 'Surely not. Why should she do such a terrible thing?'

'Because she believed after days and days of torturing anxiety that she might bear a child.'

'*Your* child?' said David furiously.

'No, not mine,' went on Daniel steadily. 'Neither of you know all that happened to her. For her sake we have tried to play it down, but she was brutally beaten and savagely raped by the man who abducted her. She has suffered a great deal in consequence, not only in body but also in mind. She felt she had lost everything that was most dear to her, even her music. She could no longer play the simplest melody and she was filled with despair. I knew that something was wrong, I had known it for days. I too heard the piano that night, heard her pitiful attempt at the music she loved so much, so I went down. I stopped her only just in time. In the struggle the glass was dropped. That's the true story of the stain on your carpet, Christine. I did my utmost to give her hope, to make her realize the futility, the enormity of what she was doing.'

'And I suppose you spent the rest of the night still persuading her to go on living,' said David with a bitter irony.

'Most of it,' went on Daniel calmly. 'I suppose in a way I was a lifeline to sanity. If you had continued your spying a little longer, you would have seen me go down to the kitchen and bring up two cups of tea, hardly nectar for enraptured lovers.'

Christine's eyes were fixed on his face. 'Is this true, Daniel?'

He frowned. 'Of course it is true. You don't doubt me, do you?'

'Don't listen to him, Mamma,' said David fiercely. 'Oh, he is so clever, so plausible, so glib, he can make you believe anything, but you have not been here these last few weeks as I have. I tell you, I have watched them together day after day. Do you know that he has even made room for her in his study, that sacred room that as children we were never allowed to enter except by invitation, and they have been spending all day together there. I have seen them, laughing, talking, sharing meals, close as lovers. You must believe me, Mamma, I swear it is true. He has spoiled and violated an innocent and lovely girl whom I have dreamed of making my wife. I love her, I have loved her from the first moment I saw her in the garden at St Petersburg, and he has always come between us, he has taught her to despise me.'

'Oh, for God's sake, don't be such a fool, boy,' said Daniel impatiently. 'Is it my fault that you have put Louise against you? Has it never occurred to you that the fault could be in yourself, and not in others around you?'

'Oh, it's so easy for you to say that. You've hated me from the very beginning, haven't you, just as you hated my father because he loved my mother so much. And when he was hopelessly crippled in that hospital ship at Balaclava, you took her away from him, didn't you, for your own satisfaction? It's true, isn't it? Isabelle is your daughter, isn't she? And when she was born my father realized the painful truth and he killed himself, and you had what you had always wanted, my mother, and all she could give you in money and position and a place in the world.'

There was a shocked silence. It was out in the open at last, part truth, part lies.

Christine said through stiff lips, 'Who told you that, David?'

'Cousin Clara, last year at the Bramber garden party. I wouldn't believe her at first; I couldn't, Mamma, I loved you too much; but I've grown to realize that it has never been you, but him. It is true, isn't it?'

'Yes, it is true that Isabelle is my daughter,' said Daniel calmly.

'But it was not like you said, David. You think you understand everything, but you don't. How could you? You're too young,' said his mother in a shaking voice.

'Oh, I understand very well. I'm not a little boy now, you know. You couldn't resist him, could you, you believed everything he told you, just as you do now. Do you know who it was who found Louise's Toby wandering in the streets and brought him back? It was one of the prostitutes he is so fond of writing about. She came here, bold as brass, demanding to see him personally. Mark told me. He seemed to think it funny but I was disgusted.'

'Is that true, Dan?'

'Yes,' he said wearily. 'If you must know, about a year ago I fell over her in a dark alley, a mere child, soaked to the skin. I bought her food and gave her a few shillings to pay the rent she owed. It had helped her back on her feet. When she brought Toby back, she wanted to say thank you, that's all.'

For a moment there was silence. Outside the windows was the calm of a summer evening, a light breeze stirring the leaves of the lime tree, the sleepy murmur of birds.

Then Daniel said coolly, 'If you've quite finished dredging up all you can find against me, distressing your mother and shaming the girl you profess to love so dearly, what do you intend to do?'

David, who had plunged in without thinking of the consequences, expecting a battle royal, with himself ready to console his weeping and betrayed mother, suddenly discovered that his bomb had fizzled out and left nothing but smoke and ashes. 'I can't stay here, Mamma. You must see that, not so long as he is here. Uncle Harry has a spare room, he'll put me up.'

'You'd better be careful how much you tell Harry,' said Daniel. 'He is very fond of his sister.'

'You think you know everything, don't you?' said David with a last flash of defiance, 'but you won't get away with it this time. I'll make very sure of that,' and he went out, slamming the door so hard that the whole house shook and leaving behind him a strained and uneasy silence.

'I could kill Clara for saying that to the boy,' said Christine wretchedly. 'It's just the sort of spiteful thing she would do.'

'She did it for the plain reason that she envies you, my dear.' He sighed. 'It's all so long ago. We never meant it to hurt. You were going to devote your life to him, I was taking myself away from you for ever, and whether Gareth killed himself because of his unbearable pain or because he knew Isabelle wasn't his child scarcely matters now. He was a doctor, he knew he was dying and he took a way out.'

'It still haunts me sometimes.' Christine was staring down at her clasped hands. 'I didn't realize that David felt so very strongly about Louise.'

'He has a queer way of showing it,' said Daniel with some exasperation. 'He quarrels with her at the slightest provocation. He doesn't seem to realize that just now she shrinks from contact with practically everyone.'

'Except you. You are her lifeline and all-important. I've always known of course that she was in love with you, Dan. Are you in love with her?'

'Oh for God's sake, of course I'm not in love with her. You don't believe what that crazy boy has been pouring out to you, do you?'

'There must be something in it.'

'He's so eaten up with jealousy, he saw what he wanted to see. All I have done, and God knows it's not been easy, is to try and buoy her up, bring her back to life, help her to forget what must have been an agonizing experience.'

'You've always been so concerned for her, right from the very beginning. What happened in Russia to draw you so close together? You've never really told me.'

'There was nothing to tell. I was there, I stood between her and utter loneliness and desolation, not like those stuffed prigs at the embassy who weren't willing to lift a finger to help or even try to understand. I did what I could, I was a shoulder to cry on, that's all, and she was grateful,' he said, deeply hurt and a little angry that she seemed to doubt him when he had done nothing. If now and then he had been shaken by that purely physical attraction, he had thrust it sternly away from him.

He did not realize how desperately hard the months had been for Christine since Robert's accident. Although he had taken his share of the burden as far as he could, he had been able to escape from time to time. He had not been forced to endure day after day the torturing anxiety of a mother watching her dearly loved son move closer and closer to death. The strain had at times brought them close to quarrelling, and then thrown them passionately together again.

She had come back to him joyously, with a wonderful feeling of renewal, as if they had gone through a trial of fire and their love for one another had emerged stronger than ever. She had been shocked and distressed by David's brutal attack. It couldn't be true, it was not possible, and yet . . . if not at this time then what about all those other occasions when they had been together? After all, what did she really know? All these wretched thoughts jumbled together in her mind while the room slowly darkened and Mark came in to draw the curtains and light the lamps. He asked if they required anything further.

'No, thank you,' said Christine. 'Nothing more tonight.'

'Very good. Good-night, madam. Good-night, sir.'

He went out and Daniel sat down, picked up the book and drew one of the lamps closer to his chair, trying to bring the situation back to normality. 'I have been thinking, my dear, that we really ought to do something about having gaslight installed,' he said, as if this was just any ordinary evening. Several houses in this street have had it done and it would save the servants a good deal of hard work.'

'I believe that Papa has been enquiring into it for Berkeley Square,' said Christine absently, 'but I like lamplight. It's softer, gentler, with no glare.'

Then abruptly she sat up, the resolution hardening in her mind. She was after all Daniel's wife and this was her home. She had a right to decide with whom she shared it.

'Daniel,' she began firmly, 'I think the time has come to send Louise away. You have surely done enough for her and she is very well provided for now. Papa told me all about Clara and the generosity of Jean-Louis.'

'Send her away? What are you talking about? You can't mean it. She is not a servant, to be dismissed, and besides where is she to go? She has no home, no place she can call her own.'

'She can go back to Arlington Street, can't she, till she makes up her mind what she is going to do?'

'Never! I'm not letting her go back there. The house is partly shut up and that housekeeper is still on the inspector's list of suspects. Heaven knows what could happen to her in that place.'

'Well, she can take lodgings, or an apartment somewhere. After all, arrangements are being made for her to go to the Conservatoire in Paris in the autumn. Isn't that right?'

'If you insist on her being pushed into the street, she'll never get to Paris. You don't seem to understand. She still needs the comfort and support of a place she knows and people she can trust. Ask John Dexter if you don't believe me. Take them away and I don't like to think of the consequences.'

'Aren't you exaggerating? Does she matter to you so much?'

'It's not just Louise,' he said impatiently. 'I'd feel the same for anyone who has gone through what she has. Don't you realize that in less than a year, ever since that damned bomb destroyed everything for her, she has gone through a great deal more than any young girl should be expected to endure: thrown among strangers, fighting a lonely battle. It has taken its toll and this last savage attack has brought her to breaking point. Here she stays till she recovers and is able to look forward calmly to the future on which she has set her heart.'

'If you are so determined about this, then I am not staying here. I'm not sharing my home with Louise.'

'You are my wife. This is your home.'

'Not any longer, it seems.'

'You're surely not letting yourself be influenced by all that crazy nonsense David saw fit to throw at me?'

'I don't know, Dan, I don't know. I need to get away. I must have time to think.'

'I don't believe this. It is ridiculous. Are you walking out on me?'

'Yes . . . no . . . Oh dear God, I don't know what to do,' she said distractedly. 'Oh, why did all this have to happen to us? I was so happy.'

'You still could be, if that wretched boy hadn't poisoned your mind.'

'He is crazily in love with Louise.'

'Don't make excuses for him. He doesn't know what love means,' said Daniel contemptuously.

She turned on him pleadingly. 'Daniel, please send her

away, with a nurse if you think it necessary, or to a hospital if she is sick. Make sure she is cared for, but not in this house.'

'No,' he said obstinately. 'No, I'm not going to do it. It would be cruel and unnecessary. Here she stays till she has recovered sufficiently to work out her own life.'

'Very well, if you have made up your mind . . .'

'Christine,' he said with an appeal she found difficult to resist, 'why are you doing this to us? You have always been so kind, so compassionate.'

'I think you have been more than sufficiently kind and compassionate for both of us,' she said, getting to her feet, needing to escape from him before she weakened. 'It must be very late. I think I'll go up to bed.'

Rebuffed, he said coldly, 'Very well, if that's what you want.'

'Will you come up later?'

'Perhaps. I have one or two things I should look over before the morning. Good-night, my dear.'

He got to his feet, kissed her cheek and let her go. Then he turned out the lamps and went to his study, looking through something he had written earlier and not taking in a word of it. Later he stretched out on the sofa where he occasionally slept when he was working through the night, too deeply disturbed and unhappy at the division between them to sleep, and trying to tell himself that she would think better of it in the morning. But this time he was wrong.

Christine was up very early and was already half dressed when the maid brought her morning tea. She had slept badly, lying awake hour after hour, hoping he would come and knowing he wouldn't. He had his pride and would not plead.

'Is my husband up?' she asked.

'Yes, madam. He asked for coffee to be taken into his study.'

'Tell Cook I don't require anything for breakfast, just tea and toast.'

'Very good, madam.'

The girl went back wide-eyed to the kitchen, reporting that

something was up. The master had spent the night in his study and Madam was already starting to pack.

When she was dressed, Christine went up to the nursery floor, where Nanny was combing the tangles out of Celia's hair. 'If you'd only stand still for a minute, I could do it in half the time,' she was saying as Christine came in.

'You go and start your breakfast,' Christine said to the little girl. 'I want to talk to Nanny. No argument now, off you go. Now,' she went on as soon as the door was closed, 'I'd like you to pack everything Miss Celia needs for the summer, Nanny. I'm taking her to Bramber this morning and then we shall be going on to Hunter's Lair. Put your own things together too. I'd like you to come with me.'

'I'll see to Miss Celia's things of course, and Rowley's rugs and towels straight away,' said Nanny steadily, 'but I shall not be coming with you, madam.'

'But Nanny, why? I'm going to need you.'

'Miss Celia can look after herself very well now, or you could take Hannah. She's a good girl and has been taking the child to school every day. I have never disobeyed you in my life, Miss Christine,' she went on with the directness of an old and valued servant, 'but I don't think it's right to leave that poor young thing, Miss Louise, here alone. If you'd seen her that night, more dead than alive she was, but we nursed her through it and I've become very fond of her since she has been in my care. And in any case, who is going to make sure that Mr Hunter takes proper care of himself and eats as he should with only the house servants? I am sorry if it inconveniences you but I must do what I consider to be my duty.'

Christine stared at her completely, taken aback. She had always thought of Nanny as being utterly devoted to her, and to know that she also felt a similar loyalty towards Daniel had surprised her.

'Very well, if that's how you feel,' she said at last. 'I'll have a word with Hannah.'

'Miss Celia will be very upset at missing these last weeks at school,' said Nanny.

'I can't help that. Just get her ready to leave by mid-morning,' she said sharply, cutting short any further argument. She went out quickly and down the stairs.

The study door was closed. She hesitated and then went in. A glance around showed her the table set in the window, Louise's books neatly stacked, the pens, ink, piles of paper. So David had been right about that. Daniel got up from behind his desk.

'Did you want me?'

'Only to tell you that I'm going to Bramber and then will pick up Robert and Isabelle and go on to Hunter's Lair tomorrow.'

'Won't it be difficult opening up? It's the first time this year.'

'I'm taking Hannah with me. Betsy is already down there and I can always borrow a couple of servants from Bramber. I'm taking Celia with me.'

'Do you have to take the child?'

'She will be better with me.'

'Christine,' he said with sudden desperate appeal. 'Why are you doing this to us?'

'It's your decision.'

For a moment they stood staring at one another, two proud people refusing to give an inch. Then he turned back to his desk. 'I believe there is a train at noon. I'll tell Mark to have everything ready and see you on to it myself.'

'There is no need. I can take care of it.'

'I dare say you can, but I'll be there all the same.'

And he was. He bought their tickets, found a reliable porter, saw the three of them into the first-class carriage, with Hannah a trifle overcome at travelling with the mistress, and did his best to console Celia, who was protesting loudly at missing the end-of-term events including the all-important concert.

'Never mind, darling,' he said; 'you can recite "The Brook" to Grandfather. He will be very interested.'

'You will be coming soon, won't you, Papa?' she whispered, giving him a final hug.

'Yes, pet, very soon. Now be a good girl, look after Rowley and don't worry your Mamma.'

He kissed Christine's cheek, got out, shut the door and walked quickly down the platform.

'Papa is not waving to us,' said Celia, half out of the window, 'and he always does.'

'Your father has other things to worry him,' said Christine, all the more sharply because she could feel the prick of tears, 'and for goodness' sake come away from that window. When the train starts you'll be getting smuts in your eyes.'

Chapter 20

David found all too soon that his savage outburst, which had driven a wedge between his mother and his stepfather, gave him no satisfaction at all. His mother had gone back to the country, but David didn't know what had happened between them. If he had hoped to bring his stepfather to his knees, he had not succeeded. No retribution had fallen on Daniel's head. Louise was still at Wimpole Street, where she was now even more distant to him. He had achieved nothing but a bitter aftertaste of shame, a kind of disgust at himself which he sought to drown by going off on foolish escapades with the wilder elements among the young men in the law and drinking too much, which had the effect of making him so bad-tempered and difficult that even his good-natured uncle became exasperated with him.

'What the devil is wrong with you?' he said irritably one morning when David had been more than usually stupid over some tedious but necessary research, which the juniors in chambers were expected to undertake with proper expertise for their elders and betters. 'I've no particular objection to you dumping yourself in my spare room without so much as a by-your-leave,' went on Harry, 'but I do expect a little co-operation in return. Have you quarrelled with your stepfather again?'

David mumbled something and then suddenly swung around, flushed and indignant. 'And if I have, isn't there a very good reason? Haven't you noticed? He's –' he bit back the vulgar word and substituted something else. 'He's carrying on an affair with Louise.'

'He's *what?*' exclaimed Harry.

'It's true, I tell you. I've seen them all the weeks I have been staying there, ever since we came back from Oxford.'

'Poppycock! You're off your head, boy. Haven't you realized by now that Daniel, unlike the rest of us sinful mortals, has high ideals? He still believes in things like fidelity, loyalty and honour. He doesn't parade it – rather the opposite – but it's there underneath, my boy, rock-solid, and if you've gone to your mother bleating some tale of Daniel so much as laying a finger on that young woman under his protection, then I'll have your blood for it. So shut up and get down to some real work for a change. I used to admire your father; he was a good, hard-working doctor, and you may not believe this but he and Daniel found a kind of respect for one another out in that hellhole of the Crimea. God knows what he would be thinking now of his idiot son.'

Harry on the warpath could be formidable, especially where work was concerned, as David knew to his cost. He buckled to and did not argue, but he was still sore and frustrated and very unhappy, convinced that all he had done was to make an almighty fool of himself and achieve nothing.

As for Louise, when she had come down that day and learned that Christine had gone back to the country, she was overcome with guilt. 'I couldn't believe it when Nanny told me,' she said unhappily to Daniel that evening. 'She did not even come to say goodbye. Was it because of me?'

'Good Lord, no. Actually she left in rather a hurry. She is taking the children to Hunter's Lair because the doctor has recommended sea bathing for Robert,' he went on, keeping his voice absolutely neutral, 'and I agreed to her opening up the house for the summer. The boy loves it there.'

Outwardly he was just as usual, but inwardly he was deeply hurt and not a little angry that Christine should condemn him for something about which he felt so strongly. Why couldn't she understand that he felt as great a responsibility for Louise as for his own children?

So the house settled back into its daily routine, except that

Daniel did not spend long days in his study while Louise was finishing her work of translation. There had been repercussions from his articles about the Turkish oppression in Bulgaria, and he was called to the Foreign Office to answer questions.

One evening, as they ate together, Louise said rather shyly, 'I have finished my work on *Fedora* at last. Would it be too much to ask you if you would read it?'

'It will be a pleasure,' he said, and noticed how much better she looked. There was a little colour in her face and she had lost the strained, haunted look. It was as if she had come back to life, he thought, as he read the manuscript through with her, making shrewd comments here and there and suggesting changes which made her sigh with envy.

'I just plod along doing a pedestrian translation, and with a few words you have turned it into a thing of drama and movement and colour.'

'I couldn't do it without your firm foundation,' he said and thought that, even if his sister never used any of the play, she had done a great deal towards helping Louise when she needed it most. The dread of the future was still there but she was winning her battle against it, he thought.

Louise woke one morning to a feeling of malaise and the pain that, had always accompanied her period; but this time, maybe because of the rape, it was far worse than anything she had ever experienced. The maid, coming in with her breakfast tray, saw her sitting up in the bed, hugging her knees, bent over and looking so ill that she ran for Nanny, who knew at once what was wrong and provided simple homely remedies and a couple of hot-water bottles. When Louise did not appear at dinner that evening and Daniel asked if she was sick, she told him in very delicate language exactly what had happened. He knew very well what it meant to Louise, and made no comment except to ask if he should send for the doctor.

'No, no, Mr Hunter, no need to trouble him. She will do very well.'

When the worst was over it was as if a black cloud had

rolled away. Unbelievably the danger was past. It was as if the flow of blood had purged away the horror, the hideous violation that had so haunted her. It was like being freed from a prison, and in the joy of release she found to her inexpressible relief that the inhibition that had kept her in its iron grip had vanished with it, and she could play the piano again. Half afraid, she started very tentatively with a childish exercise, and then played with more and more confidence. Daniel, coming in late one afternoon, heard the music rippling through the house and thanked God for it. He had spent an irritating afternoon with his editor over an article he had written.

'It's too strong, Dan. Tone it down a little.'

'But we want people to sit up and take notice. We want to wake them out of their apathy.'

'Yes, we do, but not too much, it only makes them resentful.' Against his will Daniel had compromised and now despised himself for it.

He stood for a moment listening in the hall, and then went up to the drawing-room and opened the door quietly. Louise was sitting at the piano, leaning forward, utterly absorbed in what she was playing, the loosely tied golden hair falling across her forehead.

For a moment he was carried back to that night at the villa, the darkened room and a raging storm of pain and grief. He shivered. Did Christine realize what she was doing to him? He was being blamed for something he had not done and at that moment, deeply stirred, a gesture, a moment of weakness could turn it into reality and unimaginable disaster. For a moment he let his mind dwell on it, then he gently closed the door and went away.

Roger Tanner, who for some weeks had kept himself discreetly out of sight, now felt it safe to reappear. To his fury he was immediately pounced upon by Inspector Radford who regrettably could not pin any charge on him, but could call him in for questioning. This he did, for a day and a night, but was then forced to release him with a heavy threat that he could be recalled on the slightest suspicion.

Tanner denied all knowledge of Leo, through he knew very well where the Russian was holed up. The half-mad foreigner was still in possession of a regular supply of money and could easily be parted from it with a few flimsy promises. The only reminder of those few hectic days that could have wrecked them both (but for Roger's quickness of wit in clearing the room) was an ugly scar running from Leo's forehead to his ear, and a hatred for Daniel which had taken a forcible hold on the boy's disordered mind. Roger, more calmly, came to the same conclusion. The sooner that interfering toff was taught a lesson, and a very painful one too, the better.

He discussed it one night with some of his cronies, whispering together in a dirty underground drinking-den called Nick's Bar, unaware that Essie, the little prostitute who had rescued Toby, was huddled in a corner, sipping gin until her latest protector ran out of money and it was time to stagger home.

Essie pricked up her ears and wondered how she could warn Mr Hunter. She dared not go to the house, since if she were seen and suspected she'd be skinned alive for it. She had never been able to write more than her own name, so a letter was out of the question. She was still pondering it when one evening, in the Strand not far from the Temple, she spotted David. She had no idea who he was but she had seen him go in and out of the house in Wimpole Street, so he must be connected. Perhaps he could convey a warning.

He was with a group of other young men but she sidled up to him and pulled at his sleeve. Impatiently he shook her off, thinking her one of the dozens of women soliciting for custom at that time in the evening, but she persisted.

'Do listen please,' she whispered. 'It's about Mr Hunter.'

That brought him up short. 'What about him?'

'Tell him as they're after him, and they mean it this time. He'll know who they are. I heard 'em talking. You tell him not to go walking the streets alone at night.'

'What is all this? You're not making sense.'

'He'll know. Tell him, mister, tell him, please, please!' Then she was gone, disappearing into the usual crowd thronging the Strand on a Saturday evening.

He walked on, disturbed and uncertain what to make of it, and was met by the chaffing of his friends.

'Who's the dollymop, David?'

'Fancies you, does she? A bit early, isn't it?'

'Oh shut up, all of you. It was nothing like that.'

'What was it then?'

'Oh nothing, just some nonsense or other. Come on, you lot, where are we going this evening?'

He dismissed it from his mind for that night, but it came back the next day and he wondered whether to do something about it. He knew his stepfather had enemies, but this was altogether too ridiculous, too melodramatic. He had not seen Daniel since the night he had walked out of the house. It would be too absurd to go back now. He could almost hear the incredulous laughter at his naïvety in taking Essie seriously. Besides, Daniel had been in a good many tight situations and had always been able to take care of himself. Let him take his chance this time. David decided to do nothing.

A week or so after Essie had delivered her warning, Daniel was dining with Joe Sharpe at the Garrick. He was not a club man, preferring as a rule to entertain his friends in his own home, but he liked the Garrick, whose members were largely drawn from actors, writers, poets and men of letters generally. Thackeray and Trollope were members, and once, many years ago, he had brushed shoulders with Dickens. It was an ideal place to entertain Joe, who loved good food and enjoyed cocking an amused and appreciative eye at the literary giants of the day.

After they had eaten they migrated to the smoking-room where, comfortably ensconced in deep armchairs with coffee and brandy between them, Joe got down to what for him was the crux of the whole evening. 'Next spring,' he began, leaning forward, 'I'm thinking of launching a London-based edition of the *Clarion*.'

'Good God! Is that wise? You'll be up against some very stiff opposition.'

'I've calculated for that, which is why I've taken some time to make the decision. The truth is, Dan,' he went on earnestly, 'the *Clarion* has grown too big for its boots. The time has come to expand. The London edition will follow the northern one basically, but with special features applicable to the capital. Now, I've been keeping my eye on you. You have your finger on the pulse of events down here and yet at the same time have never forgotten your roots in the industrial north. With that in mind, I'd like you to take it on as editor. What do you say?'

Daniel, taken by surprise, stared at him for a second. 'It's tempting, Joe, very tempting.'

'You and I have known one another for more than twenty years. We've fought over issues now and again, God knows, but you know my mind on most things as well as I know yours, and within that framework, you'd have a fairly free hand.' To be in editorial control of an outspoken, forward-looking newspaper like the *Clarion* was something he had dreamed about but never hoped to achieve.

'I'd like to think about it,' he said at last. 'It could change a number of things, and I do have my wife to consider, my children, my home life.'

'Think it over by all means. Talk about it with Christine. Only don't leave it too long before you decide. I'd like to have it settled in my mind before I embark on the next move.'

They went on talking until nearly midnight, and parted outside the Garrick on the best of terms, Joe to his modest hotel in the Strand and Daniel to Wimpole Street. It was a fine summer night, the sky full of stars, and he felt too elated by the proposition put to him to call a cab. He decided to walk home, both to clear his head of the brandy fumes and to think about the new opportunity that had suddenly opened up before him, his only sharp regret that he couldn't go home, wake Christine from her first sleep and discuss the whole exciting project with her.

His enemies had been waiting for just such an opportunity for some considerable time. They had watched him go into the Garrick and left a spy to report on his coming out, one of Roger Tanner's shambling hangers-on who would willingly have sold wife and children for ninepence. He saw Daniel part from his friend, wave his stick dismissively at a cruising cab and start to walk up New King Street.

The spy judged accurately that his victim was proposing to walk home, and hurried on ahead to warn the ambush.

Daniel went on his way up Oxford Street, swinging the silver-topped cane Christine had given him, which he used occasionally when the leg so badly damaged in the Crimea decided to act up. He was still considering the changes he might have to make in his life if he decided to accept Joe's offer as he came into Wimpole Street and into the inky darkness beneath the grove of tall trees. It was there that they fell upon him, all three of them.

The first blow, on the back of his head, sent him sprawling forward and he only saved himself from falling by coming up against the trunk of one of the trees. He swung round to face his attackers and just had time to notice that two of them were masked when a vicious blow almost dislocated his jaw. Then he was grappling with someone tall and dark and immensely powerful, but still managed to get in some shrewd blows of his own. But he was fighting against two of them and the other, thin and wiry, was attacking with all the ferocity of a wild animal. The spy was enjoying himself tremendously: armed with a large iron bar and keeping just out of reach, he dodged in and out, hitting out bruisingly at arms and legs wherever he could.

Daniel, strong and furiously angry, was fighting back with all his strength. He had sent the tall man crashing to the pavement and had turned on his second enemy when the spy swung his iron bar with a crippling ferocity against his leg. The pain was so exquisite that he crumpled to his knees, a vicious kick in the stomach knocked him backwards and then his enemy was on top of him, clinging like a savage cat, one hand on his throat, pressing down, strangling. Somehow he managed to drag the hand away as he gasped for breath. The struggle had carried the two out of the inky shadows and a faint light shone on the reddish hair; the mask had slipped, he saw the scarred face and knew instantly who it was. The glitter of a long thin knife had suddenly appeared in Leo's hand. Daniel gripped the wrist with all his strength, striving to hold it away from him, but he was already weakening. Suddenly there was the distant sound of running feet, a shrill whistle and someone shouted.

'The peelers!' gasped the spy, throwing down his iron bar and beginning to run.

The tall man had seized Daniel's tormentor. 'Leave him, you fool!'

'Never, never, till I kill him!' he whispered, bending Daniel's hand back till the bone almost broke and the knife pierced through shirt, skin and flesh; and Daniel felt nothing, only a strange numbness until it was withdrawn with a great rush of blood and agonizing pain.

'Come away, for Christ's sake!' The pressure was lifted. Daniel gasped for breath as his enemy was dragged off him.

By the time the policeman had come panting up from the other end of the road, they had all melted away into the darkness and the young constable hesitated, uncertain whether to pursue them or try to help their bleeding victim. His colleague, summoned by the whistle from a neighbouring road, came running up and then stopped dead. 'Oh my Gawd! Have they killed him?'

'Not yet, but he's in a pretty bad way, bleedin' like a stuck pig. The sooner we get him to the infirmary the better. We'll have to call for the ambulance.'

'Wait a bit.' The second policeman, an older man, dropped on his knees and was peering down at Daniel. 'I know this gent. It's Mr Hunter, lives close by. He's a friend of the inspector, he won't want to go to no infirmary.'

'D'you know where he lives?'

'Can't say for certain.'

Daniel, coming up through a dizzy haze of pain and weakness, muttered, 'Number 17 – key in my pocket.'

'Right. We'll get you there, sir, don't you worry.'

With some difficulty they hoisted Daniel to his feet. Supported by the two brawny policemen, his head swimming, his shirt clotted with blood, his whole body one intolerable agony, he reached the house; while one of them supported him as he leaned against the portico, the other raised the heavy knocker.

Daniel was hanging on to his senses by the merest thread when the door was opened by Mark in his dressing-gown. He drew a sharp breath at the sight of his master.

'Sorry, Mark, afraid I'm pretty well washed up ...' mumbled Daniel and despite all his efforts slid out of the policemen's hands and collapsed across the threshold.

'My God, what has happened to him?' breathed Mark, going down on his knees.

'He were attacked, three of 'em there were, and they fair had it in for him.'

'Could you two officers give me a hand with him?' said Mark. 'We're mostly women here.'

'Just you tell us where,' said the older of the two. 'The inspector would want him treated proper.'

'It's only the one flight,' said Mark.

Louise, who slept lightly these days, had come to the top of the stairs, her dressing-gown huddled around her, and stood there appalled at what she saw.

'I'll show you,' she said quickly and went before them into the big bedroom, whipping off the coverlet and spreading clean towels as the two policemen put him gently on the bed.

'Looks pretty bad to me,' said one of them. 'Needs a doctor. I could rouse up the police surgeon.'

'Thank you, officer,' said Mark austerely, 'but we'll be sending the stable boy for Mr Hunter's own physician.'

'I'll go,' said Louise quickly. 'I know where Dick sleeps. I'll tell him,' and she hurried from the room.

'Suit yourself,' went on the policeman, 'but the inspector

will be wanting to talk to him tomorrow.' He leaned across the bed. 'Can you hear me, sir? Did you know any of the wretches who were attacking you?'

And Daniel, only just about hanging on to his senses, muttered, 'I could put a name to one of them.'

'Good. That's what the inspector will be wanting to know.'

'Yes, well, there'll be a proper time for that,' said Mark. 'We'll have to see what the doctor has to say.' He began to urge the two policemen away, thanking them for their assistance, seeing them to the door and coming back to find Louise had already brought a bowl of water and a towel and was gently wiping some of the mud, blood and sweat from Daniel's face.

'The boy has gone but it's going to be a little time before the doctor gets here,' she said anxiously. 'Isn't there something we can do?'

'Yes, there is. We must get these clothes off him to start with, but not you, Miss Louise, it wouldn't be decent,' said Mark. 'You go and rouse Nanny – quietly now, we don't want the servants too disturbed – and then you can go back to bed.'

'I shall do no such thing,' she said indignantly. 'He helped me when I was hurt and sick and now I shall do what I can for him.' Even when Nanny came down, greatly disturbed but with all her nursing skills immediately brought into operation, Louise still refused obstinately to leave everything to them.

'If it is only to fetch and carry, I'm staying here to do what I can,' she said firmly.

It was after two o'clock when Dr Dexter arrived, his hair tousled, his nightshirt tucked into his trousers. By that time they had stripped off Daniel's bloody shirt and stained trousers, put a large pad on the welling blood from the knife-thrust and tried to deal with his other wounds as best they could. His jaw had stiffened so that he could scarcely speak, and the least touch on his injured leg caused so much pain that they could only put a pillow under it to try and ease it and then throw a light blanket over him. His whole body was so intensely painful that he just wished they would all go away and leave him to grit his teeth and fight his own battle with it. The doctor's coming started it all up again.

'A fine state you've got yourself into,' he said, looking down at Daniel dispassionately and then setting to work with his usual calm efficiency. He bathed and bandaged the blow on the back of his head which was only superficial but had clotted his hair with blood. He discovered a couple of cracked ribs from a brutal kick and was worried by the blow to the stomach, which was extremely tender when he prodded it, and he shook his head over the leg, where the bruising blow had almost shattered the careful reassembly of cracked and splintered bones that he himself had done more than twenty years before in the makeshift hospital at the Crimea. But what really worried him was the knife wound in Daniel's chest. He sighed for some means by which he could see through flesh and into the depths of the body. It was so perilously near to vital organs. Daniel wasn't spitting blood, thank God, and his heartbeat was steady, but there was still the danger of infection. Where had that knife been before it was plunged into the living tissue? They could only wait and pray.

He was strict in his instructions. 'Don't let him get up, or even sit up. I know Daniel: at the earliest possible moment he will want to leap from his bed, but not this time. You can raise his head a little and if he is thirsty, which he will be, give him something to drink, but only very little at a time. Some brandy and water would not go amiss. I don't care for the look of him. I'll be back again by midday.'

Inspector Radford arrived at eight o'clock sharp and battled his way through, despite the combined efforts of Mark and Nanny. 'I promise I won't stay longer than a couple of minutes with him,' said the policeman, 'but there's nothing like striking while the iron is hot.'

'I doubt if he will even hear you,' said Mark drily.

Daniel could barely speak above a whisper with his cracked jaw and horribly bruised throat.

'My constable says you recognized one of your attackers,' said the inspector. 'Who was it?'

'The Russian,' muttered the hoarse voice.

'Are you certain?'

'Absolutely. He was kneeling on me, a knife in his hand, saying the same word over and over in Russian.'

'You know the language?'

'Enough to understand the word "kill" ... "kill" ... till someone dragged him off me.'

'Right. Perhaps this time we'll nab him. Don't you fret about it, sir. We'll get to work while you concentrate on making a good recovery.'

The inspector left, and Louise came from the window where she had been standing, bringing a cool damp towel to wipe the sweat from Daniel's face, raising his head a little to trickle the brandy and water through cracked lips, and wondering how she was ever to repay him for all he had suffered on her account.

For several days he hovered between bouts of intense pain and a semi-drugged consciousness of what was going on around him. Only once did he rouse himself when, on the first day, through an aching haze he heard John Dexter say quietly to Nanny, 'Better telegraph his wife. She should be here.'

'No,' he gasped, 'no, not Christine.' He tried to sit up and the doctor gently pushed him back.

'Why not, Dan? Christine would want to be here with you.'

'No,' he went on, furious because he could only manage a cracked whisper. 'No, I'm not at death's door yet.' She would come, of course she would, out of a sense of duty – and he didn't want that, no matter how sick he felt.

'Gently now, take it easy, we'll see how you go on,' said the doctor, wondering what had happened between these two very dear friends of his. 'Now don't do anything foolish like trying to get out of bed. That chest wound of yours could still be very serious.'

'I doubt if I could lift a finger,' muttered Daniel, subsiding back against his pillows.

'Good, then don't attempt it till I come again tomorrow. And take heart. 'You and I have known worse. Give it a few days more and with any luck I'll have you on your feet again,' he went on cheerfully and left, taking Nanny with him for his further instructions.

David heard nothing about it till several days later, when an acquaintance at the wine bar said casually, 'How's that stepfather of yours? I hear he copped a right nasty one, attacked by a bunch of thugs on his way home one night and left half dead.'

'When was that?'

'Some days ago. Didn't you know?'

'I'm not living at Wimpole Street at the moment.'

It had been a shock, and he felt overcome with guilt. That little tart had tried to tell him and he had pushed her away, refused to listen, done nothing about it. It might not have prevented the attack, but at least Daniel would have been forewarned.

His feelings towards his stepfather had always been so mixed: envy, resentment, a bitter, consuming jealousy and, very deep down and only rarely acknowledged, a half-reluctant admiration for what he had achieved. He tried to ignore the news and couldn't. He had to see for himself how badly he was hurt.

Early the next morning, before he went to the Temple, he took himself to Wimpole Street. He still had his key and let himself in. The house was quiet, the servants busy with their usual tasks, Nanny and Louise breakfasting together in the morning room. He went quietly up the stairs and into what he always thought of as his mother's bedroom.

He paused in the doorway. A window had been partly opened and a gentle breeze stirred the curtains and freshened the room. He crossed to the bed. Daniel had been propped up by pillows, his eyes were closed and his right hand, lying outside the coverlet, had the wrist tightly bandaged. David was so accustomed to his stepfather's excellent health that it was a shock to see how very pale he was, with dark shadows under his eyes, bruises showing up lividly, the thick brown hair escaping from a bandage damp with sweat. He felt overcome with guilt and wished he hadn't come. He was about to tiptoe out again when Daniel's eyes flickered open. He frowned, taking in David before he said huskily, 'What the devil are you doing here?'

'I heard what happened,' he said awkwardly. 'I came to see how you were.'

'Very good of you. Apart from a cracked jaw, a hellish pain in my chest and the doctor's warning that I shall probably be on crutches for the rest of my life, I am fine,' he said in a hoarse croak, his throat still painful.

David stirred uncomfortably. 'Is Mamma here?'

'No,' said Daniel, frowning, 'and I don't want her told about it either. She has had enough to put up with. Give me a few more days and I shall be up and about again.'

Perhaps it was then that David began to grow up. It was going to take a very long time of course, but he did suddenly become uncomfortably aware of how petty some of those long-time prejudices had been, and for the first time felt a touch of shame. He said suddenly, 'I knew, and I should have warned you, but I didn't.'

'Knew what?'

'A little tart begged me one night to tell you that this might happen, that you had enemies plotting against you. She begged me to warn you and I thought . . . Oh, I don't know what I thought, that she was making a fuss about nothing just because she liked you. I thought if I came here after all that had happened, you would simply laugh at me.'

'Perhaps I might have done. If I hadn't been so damned pleased with myself that night, I might have taken some precautions,' said Daniel tiredly. 'It's not all your fault. I've known for some time that there were one or two gunning for me.'

'Do the police know?'

'Yes. I happened to recognize one of the assailants.'

'Who was it?'

'It was the man who abducted Louise.'

David stared at him. 'But you had never actually seen him, had you?'

'Yes, I did once, a long time ago in St Petersburg.'

'But how, why? Who is he? You never told us.'

'No.' In a moment of weakness he had let slip what he still would have preferred to keep to himself, for Louise's sake. Now it was going to be difficult to withdraw. He leaned back against his pillows wearily. 'It's a long story.'

'Why did you never tell us?'

'There were some very good reasons.' He felt suddenly as if all strength had drained away from him. Pain, always lying in wait, suddenly grabbed at him like a tiger. He closed his eyes in an effort to fight it and at that moment Louise came hurrying in, carrying a tray. She took in the situation at a glance and crossed quickly to the bed.

'Why didn't you tell us you were coming?' she said reproachfully to David. 'Daniel is really not well enough to see anyone, and now you have been exhausting him.'

'I'm all right, don't fuss,' muttered Daniel.

'I'm just going,' said David, 'but I'll be back very soon.' For a moment he stared across at Louise. She looked as fresh and lovely as on the summer morning at the villa, with her gold hair neatly braided, in a gown of flowered cotton with a crisp white apron. What man wouldn't willingly be ill to have such a nurse? He felt choked with a mixture of conflicting emotions. 'Look after him,' he stammered at last and went quickly from the room.

After those first pain-filled days Daniel began to recover far sooner than anyone had expected. One day Dr Dexter, making his usual morning visit, found him out of bed, in nightshirt and dressing-gown and still very shaky.

'I thought I told you not to get up till I gave the word,' he said sternly.

'Can't stand lying in bed being mollycoddled,' growled Daniel, 'never could.'

'Well, you can get right back on that bed this minute and let me look you over.'

'Must I? It took me long enough to get myself off it.'

'Go on, man, don't argue.'

He made a long and careful examination, prodding away at several tender places and refusing to be hurried. At last he straightened up.

'You are a damned lucky chap,' he said, giving Daniel a hand to sit up. 'If that wound in your chest had been infected, it could have finished you off. As it is it's healing clean as a whistle. How's the leg behaving?' he went on, helping Daniel into his dressing-gown.

'Giving me hell,' he said feelingly.

'I rather thought it might. You'll be limping again for a good few months, I'm afraid. Where's that handsome stick Christine gave you?'

'I had it with me that night as a matter of fact. I thought I'd said goodbye to it, and so I would have done but for Louise's Toby. She took him walking one afternoon and he was so busy rummaging in the undergrowth under the trees that she went to investigate and there was my stick, a trifle battered, but she has cleaned it up.'

'Good, because I'm afraid you're going to need it. I'll tell you one thing, Dan,' went on the doctor, bringing up another chair and sitting down, 'this trouble of yours has done wonders for Louise. I've never seen such a change. She has been so concerned for you that she has forgotten about herself almost completely. There couldn't have been a better therapy.'

'I'm glad it's done somebody some good,' muttered Daniel ruefully.

The doctor looked at him for a moment, then leaned forward and said bluntly, 'What's gone wrong between you and Christine?'

'Nothing's gone wrong, so far as I know.'

'Oh come on, Dan. I've known you both for a very long time and you can't tell me nothing's wrong when you refuse absolutely to tell her anything about this near-fatal accident of yours, and she likewise forbids me even to mention her name to you.'

'What do you mean by that?' said Daniel, looking up quickly. 'Did she call you in? Is she sick?'

'She's not sick, very far from it. She's pregnant.'

Daniel sat up abruptly. 'Pregnant!' he said incredulously. 'But she can't be.'

'Why can't she? She's not much more than forty. Women have borne healthy children at fifty before now, and she has an advantage. She has had four already.'

'But it's ridiculous. Celia is eleven.'

'What does that matter? Celia will probably be delighted at the thought of a small brother or sister. Christine was a little dismayed at first, but she's fine now.'

'Why did she ask you to go down to Bramber? Is something wrong?'

'Nothing at all. But I think she had suspected for some time and couldn't believe it, and she does not altogether trust your father-in-law's doctor.'

'How long?'

'Near three months, I should say.'

Oh God, what had he done to her? For many reasons they had not slept together very often since Christmas, but there was that one night when tension and anxiety over Robert had thrown them together in a blind passion, and out of it, unbelievably, there had come a child. She must have guessed already when she came home and David had come between them with his crazy accusations, splitting them apart.

'Well,' said the doctor, getting to his feet. 'I'm afraid I have broken my promise to her but I thought you ought to know. Now it's up to you.' He looked down at his friend for a moment. 'I rather gather that Louise has been the stumbling-block.'

'Did Christine tell you that?'

'No, but I'm right, aren't I? I did warn you, if you remember.'

'I did what I believed to be right,' said Daniel stubbornly. 'It's not my fault if Christine chooses to misinterpret it.'

'Yes, well, think about it. I must go. I do have other patients, you know. Now don't try to do too much. I'd hate you to undo all my beautiful work on you.'

He put a hand bracingly on Daniel's shoulder and went, leaving his friend stunned at a development that he had never dreamed of and found difficult to face. His first thought was to go to her, and then he drew back. Why should he be the one to make the first move, when he was in the right? And in any case, trussed up as he was he couldn't think of making any kind of journey for another week at least. He burned with frustration, so much so that it put him back for a day or two and he became in consequence exceedingly difficult with his willing nurses.

'Easy to see who's getting better,' said Nanny wisely, having nursed David and Robert through all kinds of childish crises. 'Men are little boys at heart, you know,' she said comfortingly to Louise. 'Don't take any notice if he snaps at you, simply carry on with what you are doing for him.'

Daniel's work might be controversial, and his style of living disapproved of in conventional circles, but he was also well liked. Joe Sharpe left an encouraging note before he went north again, reminding Daniel to try not to get himself killed before they had launched the London *Clarion*. Several other colleagues expressed sympathy and good wishes, and a few days after it happened the *Daily News* came out with an account of the brutal attack on one of their most distinguished and popular writers.

The *Daily News* was not normally delivered to Hunter's Lair, but sometimes came in via the servants. Robert, coming into the scullery one morning with a pair of filthily muddied boots, saw that the tiles had been recently scrubbed and, obeying rules strictly enforced at Hunter's Lair, looked for something to stand them on while waiting to be cleaned. He pulled a newspaper from the pile kept handy by Cook for just such emergencies, spread it under his boots and suddenly caught sight of his father's name in a headline. He carefully tore off the relevant sheet and took it to the window to read. The next minute he was charging through the house shouting for his mother.

He found her in the garden, cutting back shrubs that tended to become unruly during the winter months, with only one aged retainer coming in to tidy up. 'Don't shout like that, dear,' she said reprovingly. 'Anyone would think the house was burning down.'

'It's worse than that,' said Robert dramatically. 'Some beastly murderers have nearly killed Papa!'

'What! Oh, nonsense! If anything had happened to him, someone would have let us know.'

'But it has, Mamma, look!' and he held out the half-sheet of newspaper. 'I saw it when I was looking for something to put under my dirty boots.'

She dropped on to one of the chairs on the terrace and began to read the article with growing anxiety. Why had they not let her know, if it was as serious as it seemed? She was his wife, wasn't she? What were Mark and Nanny doing hiding it from her? When did it happen? She looked at the piece torn from the paper but there was no date.

'Rob,' she said, 'run and find out the date of the paper, see when it was published.'

He was off like a shot and back within seconds. 'It was well over a week ago, Mamma. He could be dead by now.'

'Of course he's not dead!' But all the same alarm sprang up in her. It was not long since John Dexter had been here with her. Why hadn't he said anything about it? she thought angrily, forgetting that in her turn she had forbidden him to mention her pregnancy to Daniel.

Rob was looking at her anxiously. 'Shouldn't we go to him, Mamma?'

'I don't know. I'm not sure. I have to think. And Robert, don't tell Isabelle and Celia about this, not yet, not till we know more about it. And don't look so worried. He will be all right, I'm sure of it. Your father has faced up to far worse things than a beating and has always come through.'

Left alone at last, her first reaction was that she must go to him and then, like Daniel, she drew back. That girl was still there with him, caring for him, doing all the things she should be doing, and she was suddenly shaken by a fierce jealousy. He had not sent for her, he did not even want her in his hour of need, she thought, and found it all the more painful when she was bearing this unexpected child. She pressed her hand against her stomach with a strong inclination to burst into tears, but then she braced herself. If he had his pride, then so had she; but there was one thing she could do to satisfy her strong need to know exactly how he was.

She could send a telegram to Nanny, with a prepaid reply, which she did that very afternoon, driving their little dog-cart into Rye with Robert beside her. The reply came in the early evening in Nanny's stilted phrases:

Mr Hunter going on nicely now but still unable to walk far. Miss Louise has been a capable little nurse. We all hope, dear madam, that you are keeping well and will soon come back to us. Janet Renfrew.

At least it was something to know that he was recovering and not still at death's door as the newspaper had hinted, but otherwise it gave her very little comfort.

Chapter 21

Ever since David had left Daniel that morning, he had been in a very confused state of mind. On the night when he had let jealousy, anger and a lifelong resentment carry him into those wild accusations, he had believed every word of them. Hadn't he seen them together with his own eyes, time and again? Daniel had countered the attack very plausibly, but David would not let himself be convinced. But now he had begun to have second thoughts. The vicious attack which had nearly killed his stepfather should have given him pleasure, but only succeeded in making him feel horribly guilty, and had made it exceedingly difficult to accept Daniel's half-amused tolerance when he made that reluctant call at Wimpole Street. But the most maddening, the most frustrating thing was what Daniel had let slip about the Russian. Who was he? What part had he played in Louise's life, and why had he never been mentioned before? Why did Daniel know so much and no one else? He went back the very next day, determined to worm the truth out of him, sick or not, and was thwarted by Nanny who said, 'The doctor is with him, Master David, and after all that pulling about he likes to be left alone for a while. Why don't you come round one afternoon for a nice cup of tea with us?' and she patted his arm as if he were two years old instead of twenty-two.

He asked Uncle Harry if he knew what it was all about and unexpectedly he said, 'Actually I do know something. Dan did consult me because there could be a legal aspect. If you want to know the ins and outs why don't you have a word with the inspector? He knows all about it.' David did so, and found Inspector Radford entirely uninformative.

'David Fraser?' he said questioningly, looking up at him when he penetrated to his inner office. 'You must be Mr Hunter's stepson. What can I do for you?'

'I'd like more information about this Russian who is alleged to have been responsible for Louise Dufour's abduction,' he said crisply, 'and also for the attack on my stepfather. Why has none of this appeared in the press? Why has it all been kept so secret?'

'Orders from on high,' said the policeman shortly, 'to play it down for the sake of the young lady's reputation. If we lay hands on him this time, it may be very different. Why don't you ask Mr Hunter? He will no doubt tell you what he considers you should know. I am afraid I can say nothing. More than my job's worth.'

So, frustrated and more than a little angry, he went back to Wimpole Street, where the sight of Louise and Daniel together threw him into hopeless confusion again. They looked so close, so familiar with one another. Daniel was up, partly clothed but still in a dressing-gown, his injured leg stretched out before him on a footstool. Louise was in a low chair close beside him, pad and pencil in hand. He was dictating something to her.

David stood in the doorway listening for a few minutes till Daniel came to an end, stretched himself painfully and said, 'I think that's enough for this afternoon.'

'Right,' said Louise. 'I will write it out properly and bring it to you for corrections.'

'So far there have not been any.' He patted the top of the golden head. 'You're a clever little puss, aren't you?'

'If I am, I have learned it from you.'

He laughed as she got up, pushed aside her chair and saw David.

'Goodness, look who's here. Why are you standing there, David? Why don't you come in?'

'Didn't want to interrupt the fine flow of eloquence.'

'We're honoured,' said Daniel drily. 'I rather thought that, so far as you were concerned, I was out in the wilderness.'

'I'll carry on with this,' said Louise hurriedly; 'it won't take me long,' and she went out quickly.

'Well, now you're here, what do you want?' said Daniel.

'I did come several days ago but you were undergoing treatment.'

'Oh Lord, yes, a horrible experience, I'm afraid. John Dexter is very thorough and it hurts like hell for an hour or so afterwards. What is it that brings you here this afternoon?'

'I want to know about this Russian who tried to kill you and seems to have been pursuing Louise. Isn't it about time you told me the truth?'

'A foolish slip of the tongue on my part,' said Daniel ruefully. 'I wasn't myself that day. I shouldn't have mentioned it. It really doesn't concern you at all. It belongs to Louise.'

'Louise is very important to me. You must know that by now. I have made it plain enough, and if it is important to her then I think I ought to know.'

'In that case why don't you ask her?' said Daniel. 'It's her story. It will come a great deal better from her than from me.'

'But will she tell me?' said David, a little taken aback.

'That's up to you, isn't it? If you mean anything at all to her, I think she will, but I tell you one thing, David, and I mean this,' he went on, his voice hardening. 'We've gone to a great deal of trouble to play this down for the sake of Louise and all it might mean for her future, so don't go blabbing it out to your colleagues in chambers or to your drinking pals in the bars and clubs. Understand? If you do, I swear to God I'll make you sorry for it.'

'What do you take me for?' exclaimed David indignantly.

'I don't always know,' said Daniel slowly. 'Sometimes I have wondered. I liked your father in spite of everything and I've often wished I could like you more for your mother's sake. Make quite sure that you don't let either of them down.' David made an impatient movement towards the door and Daniel stopped him. 'Just one more word of warning before you go. Louise knows nothing of your hysterical outburst of jealousy a few weeks ago. The poor girl had enough troubles of her own.

I saw no reason to burden her with it, and neither did your mother.'

'But Mamma believed me, didn't she?' said David defiantly. 'She left the house the next day.'

'Your mother and I parted temporarily for quite another reason.'

'Which you don't propose to tell me.'

'Exactly. It is no concern of yours. What I do say is, be careful what you say to Louise. She may react quite fiercely.'

'I know what I'm doing.'

'Do you? You're fortunate. There have been quite a number of occasions when I would have been glad to have been able to say the same,' said Daniel ironically.

David stared at him for a moment and then plunged out of the room and down the stairs. He found Louise in Daniel's study, golden head bent, carefully writing up the rough notes she had made. She looked up as he came bursting in.

'What is it? Does Daniel want me for something?'

Daniel, always Daniel! 'No, he doesn't,' he said curtly. 'Actually he has sent me to you. I asked him a question and he said you were the right one to answer it.'

'Is it important? Can I finish this first?'

'What's that you are doing for him?'

'It's a column he writes for one of the monthlies, a sort of comment on current affairs, and it's overdue. The editor is growing very impatient.'

'Won't tomorrow do?'

'I suppose so,' she said doubtfully. 'If I finish it off tonight, we can always send it by hand tomorrow instead of trusting it to the post.' She put down her pen, closed her notebook and turned to face him. 'What do you want to ask me?'

She looked so fresh, so eminently desirable in her white blouse and dark-blue skirt, curling strands of golden hair falling about her forehead. There were quite a number of girls he could have had for the asking; so why did it have to be this one who enchanted him and was at the same time so elusive, so indifferent towards him, so far out of his reach, and who so obviously admired and loved his stepfather? He was swept by an angry tide of impatient jealousy.

'This Russian who must have followed you from St Petersburg, who apparently tried to abduct you, and has now tried to kill Daniel – who is he, Louise? What does he want from you? Why have we been told so little about him? Was he your lover?'

'My lover!' She stared at him for a moment, eyes widening, and then unexpectedly she began to laugh. 'It sounds like one of those sensational novels from Mudie's library. Of course he wasn't my lover. The very opposite in fact. Is that really what you have been thinking?'

'I and possibly a great many other people.'

'I know,' she went on more seriously. 'That's why Daniel, your grandfather too and the police have tried to play it down, because the real truth is so much more complicated, so unbelievable, so bizarre, so horrible, that I sometimes shudder when I remember that he is still out there, somewhere, watching and waiting.'

'Daniel knows, doesn't he?'

'Oh yes, Daniel knows. He was there at the beginning. I don't know what I would have done without him.'

'Who is this man, Louise?'

She looked at him for a long moment before she said slowly, 'Do you remember when you and your uncle came to visit us at the villa that we spoke of someone called Leo?'

'Was that the boy I saw in the garden with you, the one who brought you peaches and called himself a revolutionary? I remember wondering whether you were in love with him.'

'Oh no, never. I'd known him since I was twelve and I suppose, being an only child for so long, I thought of him as a brother, a boy with whom I could enjoy all the adventures which girls aren't supposed to enjoy. We had the run of his father's vast estate and discovered all kinds of secret hiding-places where we could picnic and take the dogs.' She paused for a moment before she went on thoughtfully. 'I suppose in a way Leo was always a misfit. He could never match up to his brilliant family and at the university he joined a group who called themselves anarchists, perhaps to make himself feel important. You see, it was he who threw the bomb that killed my parents.'

'Oh my God! It doesn't seem possible. How could he do such a thing?'

'Oh, not deliberately. It was all a terrible mistake. The bomb was intended for the Commissioner of Police, a man very much hated, who was in the habit of driving through the city incognito. In the terrible confusion Leo escaped and for several days no one knew who had committed the outrage.'

'And then what happened?'

'Must I go on? It was such a dreadful time I don't want to have to remember any of it.'

'Please, Louise, it is important and you mean so very much to me. I want to know everything about you.' He came to her then, wanting to take her hand, but she avoided him before she went on quickly:

'At the end of that week I went down to the villa and found him hiding there. He didn't even know what he had done, and the realization came upon us both like a bolt of lightning. Daniel had followed after me, and Leo was convinced we had set the secret police on to him because barely a week later he was arrested in the wine cellar of an old ruined house on his father's estate, a place where we had met and played games as children. He believed I had directed the police there but I hadn't. I had never told anyone, not even Daniel, not till afterwards when it was all over.'

'But why didn't you? Surely you must have wanted him punished for what he had done?'

'Part of me did, but I couldn't help remembering the gentle boy I had known who was often so unhappy, and all the joyous times we had shared.'

'What happened then?'

'He was condemned to be hanged, but owing to his father's close friendship with the Tsar the sentence was changed to fifteen years' hard labour in Siberia. Here in England you have no idea how terrible that is, and to a boy like Leo it must have been like being condemned to a living hell. I begged Daniel to take me to the station on the day the convicts boarded the train. All his family had rejected him, he was so alone, and I wanted him to know that it was not I who had sent him there. But he didn't believe me. It was horrible. They were shackled together like cattle, and Leo spat his fury and rage at me before he was dragged away. Afterwards when Daniel brought me to England I tried to put it out of my mind. It was all part of those terrible months that I had to come to terms with if I was to go on living. I can't tell you how wonderful it was when he brought me to Hunter's Lair. I had never known a proper family and suddenly I had become part of one. I felt safe and secure for the first time since it had happened and I had lost everything.'

'But that wasn't the end of it, was it, Louise?'

'No, it wasn't. But haven't you heard enough? It's over and done with. I want to forget it.'

'But you can't, don't you see that? Not while he is still out there somewhere. What does he want from you, Louise?'

'I don't know. Revenge, perhaps. I think he wants to punish me. One day just before Christmas, I was on my way to Wimpole Street and I ran into him – but so changed, so wild, so different from the boy I had known that I was terrified. Then Daniel told me that he had received information from St Petersburg that Leo had escaped and was believed to have made his way to Switzerland. There was nothing to prevent him coming to England under an assumed name. I saw him twice more after that. He would stand under the trees in Arlington Street, watching and waiting.'

'Why didn't you go to the police?'

'I was afraid they would laugh at me, a foreigner, a young girl, imagining things that weren't there.'

'Did you tell Daniel?'

'I meant to but didn't want to trouble him when he was so busy, and then he went to Bulgaria, and there was Clara and Jean-Louis and their marriage to occupy me. I tried to put it out of my mind. Was it really Leo, I asked myself, or was I only imagining it? I was so happy when I took Toby walking that evening. Everything had gone so well. Clara had been kind and Jean-Louis unbelievably generous. I had the promise of studying music in Paris, everything that I had most longed for was coming true, then suddenly it was all snatched away.'

'What did he do to you, Louise?'

'It's over and it's finished with. It has taken me a long time to put it out of my mind. Don't make me bring it all back, please.'

'How did you escape?'

'There was a heavy iron candlestick,' she said reluctantly. 'I hit him with it and then I ran away.'

'To Daniel.'

'It was the middle of the night. There was nowhere else to go.'

She was standing outlined against the window, hands tightly clasped to stop them trembling. Daniel's warning flew out of David's head. He plunged in recklessly. 'How soon after that did you and he become lovers?'

'Lovers?' She stared at him as if he were crazy. 'Daniel and I, lovers? Surely you can't believe that.'

'Oh I don't blame you, not for a single moment, it must have been so easy for him, alone with you here, my mother away at Bramber.'

She was still staring at him. 'Daniel and I have never been lovers.'

'There is no need to lie to me. I understand, Louise. I know how attractive Daniel can be. He charmed my mother into loving him just as he has charmed you.'

She stared at him for a moment longer, then all the emotion that she had been trying to repress exploded into a fierce anger and the words poured out.

'How dare you speak to me like that, so – so condescending, as if I were some ignorant serving-girl running away from a silly adventure! Have you any idea at all of what Leo did to me? Can you imagine how it feels to be chained to a bedpost like a dog, unable to move more than a few feet day after day? For a week I lived in a kind of hell while Leo forced me to listen to everything that had happened to him on that appalling journey to Siberia, over and over again, every sordid detail till I thought I would go crazy. He wanted me to know what it is like to be shackled so that every movement causes pain, to live on water and dry bread, hour after hour after hour he went on, a kind of insane mental torture till I didn't know whether to loathe him or to feel pity for a madman.'

She paused to take a sobbing breath and David said quickly, 'I didn't realize – don't go on if it distresses you,' but now it was as if she couldn't stop herself. Let him know the worst and then think what he liked.

'Day went into night and then into day again and I lost all count of time. Then one evening he came in and was different. I was frightened at what he might do. For the first time he unlocked the padlock on the chain and I made a desperate attempt to escape. He threw me back on the bed and lashed me with a horse whip and then . . . and then . . .' She choked for a moment at the hideous memory and then suddenly swung round and almost hurled the words into his face. 'And then he tore off my clothes and he raped me.'

'Oh my God, no! Not that! Not that!'

The look of shock on David's face halted her for a moment and then she went on more quietly. 'I suppose it was that which drove me over the edge; I can't remember, only that I felt for the candlestick and swung it against his head. It was horrible. There was blood on my fingers, I thought I had killed him. I was shaking so much I couldn't move but I knew this was my only chance. I had to escape before he recovered consciousness or someone else came in. I don't know how I did it, only that somehow I got out of the room into the night and into the rain, a few clothes huddled round me, and all I could think of was reaching safety. I still don't remember how I found my way here, all I know is that I would have died if it had not been for Daniel that night. I have lived through that hideous experience over and over again for weeks and weeks. I lived with the terrible fear that I might bear a child, Leo's child, a madman's child. Can you imagine that? No, of course you can't, how could you? You don't know how patient Daniel was with me, how he talked to me and, when in despair I could no longer play the piano, my fingers as paralysed as my mind, he stopped me trying to kill myself. All this he did for me, and all you can think of is that we were lovers! What he did for me was far more than any lover would do. He brought me back to life, made me feel whole and sane again. Is it any wonder that when those murderers attacked him I would have done anything for him, anything in the whole world?'

Stunned by her courage, shocked at her appalling frankness, all David could say was, 'I'm sorry. I did not realize ... I saw you together, I felt so sure ...'

'You saw what you wanted to see and did not look any further,' she said scornfully. Then quite suddenly realization flooded through her. She swung round on him. 'You told your mother,' she said incredulously. 'You made her believe ...'

'I don't know what she believed,' muttered David wretchedly, 'except that she went away the very next day.'

'I remember now. I couldn't understand why she had left so suddenly.' She turned on him then with a blazing anger. 'How could you do such a wicked thing? How *could* you? I don't think I can ever forgive you for that. It was hateful, mean and cruel. It has spoiled something deep and wonderful between Daniel and me and driven apart two people I have learned to love very dearly.'

'I'm sorry, Louise, I'm so desperately sorry. It was you I was thinking of all the time. I couldn't bear to think of someone I'd admired so much, set on such a high pedestal, someone I love so ... so greatly ...'

'Love!' she repeated. 'Love! What do you know of love?'

'I realize now that I was wrong, but I was driven out of my mind because I thought I'd lost you. Can't we start again?' he pleaded. 'Can't we forget this and let it be as it was when we parted that day in St Petersburg, both of us hoping that we would meet again?'

There was something so naïve about his appeal that it touched her against her will. 'Perhaps,' she said, 'I don't know. All that was in another world.'

He reached out, taking her hand to draw her towards him, but she pulled herself free.

'Don't touch me.'

'Have I become so hateful that you can't even take my hand?'

But she only shook her head, unable to explain that ever since the rape any kind of physical contact with a man had become shudderingly repulsive.

They were silent for a moment, both of them far too shaken to speak, and it was at that fraught moment that Daniel appeared in the doorway, leaning heavily on his stick and supporting himself with one hand against the doorpost.

Louise moved at once to his side. 'You shouldn't have attempted to come down the stairs. You know what the doctor said.'

'I can't remain marooned on the upper floor for ever. I admit that for a few moments I thought I was going to fall from top to bottom, but I didn't.' He had taken in David's distracted look and Louise's unusually flushed face, but he made no comment. He moved slowly to one of the chairs. 'Do you think we could have some tea? I have become horribly addicted to it during the last few weeks.'

'Yes, of course, I'll see to it,' said Louise. 'David is just going, aren't you, David?'

'Yes, yes,' he said, feeling far too shaken to stay and make polite conversation over tea. 'I'm due back at chambers and it's already late.'

Somehow he got himself out of the room and out of the house, still reeling from what he had heard and very aware that he still had a long way to go before he could hope to win Louise's love, or even her liking. The innocent young girl whom he had dreamed about had become a woman who had suffered horribly. But strangely, after the first shattering realization, it had not diminished his passionate determination to win her for himself, it had in fact given it an added strength, and with it came a burning desire to strangle the man who had violated her.

Daniel asked no questions and Louise said nothing about David's hurried departure. She poured tea for them both, talking of trivial matters until she excused herself and took refuge in her own room, still disturbed and very angry. How could David have done such a thing? Out of spite and jealousy he had tried to wreck his mother's marriage and destroy the trust and friendship between her and Daniel. Surely Christine could not seriously believe that she and Daniel were lovers? And yet she *had* left the house so suddenly. Struggling with her own malaise and wretchedness, Louise had accepted Daniel's explanation unquestioningly and it was only now, looking back, that small things assumed significance. The very fact that he rarely mentioned Christine, his refusal to allow her to be told about the attack that could have killed him, all spoke of a deep hurt and a pride that refused to give way. Now it was she who must try to repair the damage. The first thing to be done was to leave Wimpole Street, but quietly, sensibly, not running away in a guilty panic. Daniel had helped her back to health and sanity. Now it was up to her to show him she could stand on her own feet.

It was many weeks since that evening when Leo had done his best to destroy her life, and it seemed as if she had been living in a different world since then; but the plans that had been in her mind at that time still made good sense. She set about putting them into action.

One morning she nerved herself to call on George Westcott in his city office in Moorgate. He greeted her with surprise and pleasure, assuring her that there would be no difficulty at all in arranging for money to be transmitted to her through the bank's offices in Paris. Then she called upon Miss Motford, asking her if she could take up her invitation and stay with her for a few days while they discussed the suggestion that she should accompany her to Paris for the first few months as friend, companion and chaperon. Hattie Motford might be sixty but she still had a great zest for life. She had heard something of what had happened to Louise and was delighted at the prospect of moving out of her quiet uneventful existence into a far more exciting life on the Continent.

Down at Hunter's Lair, Christine was faced with an ultimatum from her thirteen-year-old son.

'If you don't go back to Papa and find out exactly how he is, then I shall go on my own,' he announced one morning with determination. 'I've got lots of pocket money saved up. I can buy my own ticket. It's not right, Mamma. He could still be in the most awful pain. One of us ought to be with him.'

'Louise is there,' said Christine obstinately.

'Louise is nice, and I like her, but she's not family. I'm not joking, Mamma, I mean it.'

Christine looked at the young frowning face and began to weaken. 'Wait for another day or two,' she said, 'and maybe I'll come with you.'

'Just you and me!' said Robert joyfully. 'Oh great! Couldn't we go tomorrow?'

'We'll see. There are certain arrangements that have to be made here first.'

It was not a question of giving in, she told herself. Life doesn't stand still just because you and your husband happen to be at loggerheads. There were a number of family matters that needed to be discussed and settled. There was for instance the question of a new school for Robert, since he would not be returning to Rugby. There was Isabelle, who was still determined to enrol at the medical college for women that had only opened four years ago, whether her father gave his consent or not. There was her close friendship with Alec Rawly, who had come to spend a few weeks' vacation at Hunter's Lair. To her dismay they seemed to have grown a great deal closer since the weeks she had spent in Edinburgh. Of course she knew he was brilliantly clever and would no doubt go far in his profession, but he was still so shy, so awkward, his parents were still missionaries in Africa and as far as she knew he was utterly dependent on what he earned, with a few extra pounds from his grandmother. A most unsuitable match for her lovely, gifted daughter. All these anxieties she badly needed to discuss with Daniel. Whatever he might have done he was still the children's father. If Louise was still there, then Christine would only stay long enough to settle the problems in a businesslike way and then return to Hunter's Lair.

On the day that Christine and Robert boarded the London train, Daniel was reading a long letter from Louise. A few days before, when they were dining together in his study, which they had been doing ever since he was up and about again, she told him of the plans she had made and that she was going to leave Wimpole Street the next day to stay with Miss Motford in Chelsea.

'All this without telling me one word about it,' he said, a little hurt. 'I could probably have given some help.'

'I knew if I told you that you would have tried to persuade me to stay here longer, and I mustn't. It's so very tempting, but don't you see, I must leave to go ahead on my own. I mustn't depend on your kindness and hospitality any longer. Miss Motford is wonderfully sensible. She will make sure I don't do anything foolish.'

'Louise, you're not running away from here because of something David has said to you?'

'No, of course not. David talks a lot of nonsense. I have never taken him seriously. I'm going to miss you terribly, but I have got to be brave and take the first steps alone. Hattie Motford and I thought we might go off to Paris for a few days and look for a suitable apartment for September, and then I must start to practise and practise if the Conservatoire is to accept me.'

'You could always practise here.'

'I know I could, but you have your own life and your work and I've trespassed on it for too long already. Besides, Monsieur Vincent lives in Paris and I think I could persuade him to give me some extra tuition. I need it badly after these months when I have done so little.'

And so she had gone, and written him a long letter pouring out all she had not been able to say to him, thanking him for all he had done and meant to her, a slightly incoherent letter with a tearstain here and there (she was after all not yet twenty and had gone through a considerable emotional storm during the last few months). He missed her already. Ever since he had opened the door on that night in June and seen the huddled form lying across his doorstep, deeply distressed and desperately needing his help, he had been concerned for her, even to the extent of quarrelling with his wife. Their marriage, their mutual love and understanding were surely too solid and enduring to be wrecked by a jealous boy's spite. Ever since he'd heard Christine was pregnant he had known the division between them had to end. If it had not been for his blasted leg, he would have found his way to Hunter's Lair by now.

A disturbance outside roused him from his thoughts. He heard Mark open the door, the sound of voices, a boyish treble demanding, 'Where is Papa?' and the study door was flung open. He dropped the letter on his desk as Robert charged across the room and flung his arms around him.

'Careful,' he said as he returned the hug. 'I'm still fragile.'

Robert was looking up at him anxiously. 'We read the most dreadful things about you. Are you sure you are really better?'

'Almost as good as new.' He put his hands on the boy's shoulders, looking down into his face. 'What's more important, how are you?'

'Fighting fit,' said Robert, a new expression of which he was rather proud. 'Do you know, Papa, that I can swim the whole width of the cove and back again without stopping to rest.'

'Splendid. I see I shall have to look to my laurels.'

'Now that I know you are really all right, may I go and see Nanny? It seems such ages since I was here.'

'Off you go then.'

'And ask her to arrange for some tea,' said Christine, who had appeared in the doorway. 'I'm parched after that train.'

'Right. I wonder if this is Cook's baking day,' said the boy with a grin as he dashed off, leaving his parents facing one another across the untidy room.

'Robert is looking wonderfully well,' said Daniel.

'Yes, he is. The difficulty now is making sure that he doesn't do too much. How about you?'

'Oh, I'm well enough except for this leg of mine. "Pamper it for a few months," John Dexter says, "and it will be as good as new," but it certainly doesn't feel like it.'

'Why didn't you let me know what those wretches had done to you?'

'I didn't want to worry you unnecessarily. After all, it's you who are the important one now. When is the stranger due?'

'So John told you, did he, the traitor? He promised me.'

'He thought I should know, seeing that I'm the father. I suppose I am the father? I can't think of another likely candidate at Bramber except perhaps Paddy on a good day.'

'Oh Daniel, don't be such a fool!'

And then, as if with a single thought, they had moved together. He had taken her hands and was drawing her close to him and she was half laughing, half crying. 'I couldn't believe it at first. It seemed so silly. A baby, at my age! It's so ridiculous. Everyone will be laughing at me.'

'They're more likely to be green with envy. I think it's wonderful news, makes me feel young again. Have you told the children yet?'

'Isabelle knows but not Robert or Celia.'

'I tell you who will be overjoyed, and that's Nanny. You and she will have to start refurbishing the nursery.'

'We shall, shan't we? Celia will have to move out. By the way,' she said, trying to sound casual, 'is Louise still here?'

'No, she is staying with Hattie Motford. I gather they are planning a quick trip to Paris to arrange for an apartment when Louise starts her course at the Conservatoire.'

'Is she quite well now?'

'She says so. You will see her when she comes back to pick up her trunk and her books.' He dropped down in the big chair by the desk and she perched beside him, his arm around her waist. As if absent-mindedly the fingers of his other hand crumpled Louise's letter into a ball and rolled it into the waste-paper basket.

'You're going to stay, I hope,' he said, his arm tightening around her.

'Until you're fit enough to come back with me to Hunter's Lair.' She reached across and touched his face. 'You don't look at all well to me.'

Then Robert was back, carrying a dish of scones warm from the oven, a large smear of strawberry jam across one cheek, followed by Mark with the tea tray. Family life was already beginning to return to normal.

Later that evening, when Christine had gone up to bed and Daniel was preparing to follow, he picked Louise's letter out of the waste-paper basket and, without re-reading it, struck a match and burned it to ashes. There was nothing incriminating in it, only a youthful outpouring of love and gratitude, but it might be better if Christine never saw it. It was the end of the affair – if it could be called an affair, he thought a little regretfully. But he was wrong.

In the next few days Daniel and Christine did not go over and over what had driven them apart. Louise had gone; Christine was back, mistress in her own home; and if now and again there still remained a lingering doubt, she had never really believed in her son's wild accusations.

In fact the only point on which they failed to agree did concern David. He called to see his mother as soon as he learned that she had returned to Wimpole Street, and Daniel deliberately took himself out that day, leaving mother and son to settle things between them. Later on he had to be present to discuss David's being called to the Bar. It was an ancient ceremony full of tradition and Harry, who had come in to see his sister, explained what happened.

'I shall arrange a place for you, Christine, and for Father. After all Pa is pretty eminent these days and it will do the boy no harm to have a High Court judge beaming down with pride on his grandson. And of course there will be a place for you, Daniel.'

'You can count me out, Harry.'

'But Dan, you must be there,' exclaimed Christine. 'You must be in the place of his father.'

'David has never thought of me in that way. His grandfather can easily occupy that place. I'm the outsider. In any case I don't really feel I can cope with all the necessary standing.'

'I could arrange a chair for you,' said Harry helpfully.

'Thank you, but I'm not in my dotage yet.'

Nothing that Christine said could persuade him to change his mind, not even when she reminded him that even if he did not attend the ceremony he could join them all later. 'Papa is taking us to a celebration dinner at Vespers.'

'I'd rather not be the spectre at the feast,' he said lightly.

'Oh, Daniel, how can you say that? Why are you being so difficult? You've not forgiven David, have you? He is truly sorry for what he said that night.'

'It's not a question of forgiveness. I think he behaved abominably, but I have seen him twice since then. I did my best to be tolerant, I even gave him some good advice, but that is as far as I'm prepared to go.'

So it all went through without him and when Christine returned very late that night she found her husband in the drawing-room reading, his leg stretched out on a footstool. He closed the book and looked up at her, thinking how very young and pretty she still looked, her pregnancy not yet apparent, and wearing a new gown in pale blue corded silk, deeply flounced and trimmed with darker blue velvet.

'How did it all go?' he asked.

'It was marvellous. It seems that David has done very well. I was so proud of him and he looked so handsome in his wig and gown. Ever so many people came to congratulate me on being the mother of a future QC. I know I oughtn't to boast about my own son, but it was very gratifying.'

'Good. Perhaps it means he has grown up at last and will

behave in future like a responsible adult and not an exceedingly tiresome adolescent.'

She dropped down next to his chair and put her hand on his. 'Oh Daniel, do try to be friends with him, for my sake.'

'Haven't I always? It's rather like trying to be friends with a bad-tempered, spoiled puppy that bares its teeth at every friendly overture.' He hauled himself to his feet. 'Don't let's talk about him any more. It's a very unprofitable subject. Come to bed with me instead.'

'That's a very improper suggestion.' But she let him take her hands and pull her almost roughly into his arms.

'Am I permitted to make love to you? Or is it taboo just now?'

'No, of course it isn't. It's months and months away.'

'Splendid, then what are we waiting for? Come upstairs with me, take off all that finery and let's get on with it!'

A few days later a fire broke out in a filthy congested street near Seven Dials, almost completely destroying a dilapidated lodging-house. The police were called in, because arson was suspected and because of the identification of one of the victims. The house had been occupied almost entirely by foreigners, most of whom escaped serious injury. One, severely burned, had been taken to the city infirmary; the other, of particular interest to Inspector Radford, was already dead by the time he was brought out.

'He must have tripped as he tried to escape, and fallen facedownwards into the fire, poor devil,' said the police constable, 'and then of course he suffocated.'

The inspector looked down at the horribly ravaged face and then at the charred identity papers in his hand.

'It certainly looks as if he could be the man we've been after, but I must try to get further identification. Have him brought to one of the police cells rather than the mortuary, and I will contact those who met him face to face.'

And that was why a policeman called at Wimpole Street the very next morning and asked for Mr Hunter. He was one of the two men who had come to Daniel's rescue that night, and he gave him a broad grin. 'Glad to see you looking more like yourself, sir. Inspector Radford's compliments and he would be obliged if you could call at the station at your earliest convenience.'

'What's it about?'

'Well, sir, it looks as if we've nabbed one of those wretches who attacked you. The inspector would like you to take a look at him.'

'Very well. Tell him I'll be along in about an hour.'

Christine appeared in the hall as he came in and shut the door. 'What was all that about?'

'I'm not sure. It seems the police have at last succeeded in tracking down one of the men who tried to murder me.'

'Good,' she said; 'it's about time they did something about it. I hope they make him suffer for it.'

At the Yard Daniel was shown immediately into the inspector's office and given a brief account of the fire. 'From the papers we found on him, he would seem to be the Russian we have been looking for, but I still need further identification. Unfortunately the poor devil's face has been burned so it may be difficult. I have sent one of my men to fetch Miss Dufour. She should be here in a moment.'

'Couldn't you have spared her that? It's bound to be a very painful experience for her.'

'I'm afraid not, because this is a case where we need to be as certain as it is possible to be, since we shall be obliged to send a report of his death to the Russian authorities.'

'I see. I hadn't thought of that.'

They waited in silence and it was not long before Louise was ushered in and the inspector rose to greet her. She looked very pale and was obviously relieved to see Daniel. He gave her a reassuring smile.

'Is it . . . is it Leo?' she asked breathlessly.

'We believe it is. I am sorry to have to subject you to what will no doubt be a painful ordeal,' said the inspector gently, 'but I'm afraid I have no choice. I had him brought here to make it easier for you. Are you ready? Will you be good enough to come with me?'

He led the way out of the room and, as they prepared to follow, Daniel took Louise's cold hand in his for a moment and pressed it warmly. Then they had descended the stairs and the policeman on duty in the cell at the bottom opened the door and let them in. There was an acrid smell of burning that still clung to the body, stretched on the narrow bed and covered with a prison blanket.

'Ready?' asked the inspector. Daniel nodded and he turned back the covering blanket.

It was not pleasant. More than half the face had been ravaged by the fire, the reddish hair burned close to the scalp on one side, the eye puckered and seamed, the mouth hideously distorted.

For a shuddering moment Louise stared with a horrible fascination. 'I don't know,' she whispered at last. 'It is very like and yet . . . I couldn't be sure.' She gave a little choking sob and Daniel drew her against him with an arm around her shoulders.

'And you, sir?' asked the inspector.

'I feel much the same. It's like, very like, and yet, with those injuries, how could we swear to it?'

'I thought you might say that,' said the policeman, replacing the blanket. 'We do have other means of identification which I should like to show you.'

They went back to his room and he produced the charred papers. One of them was the identity card which all Russian prisoners were forced to carry. There was the convict's number in heavy black type, and beneath it the name of Count Leonid Ivanovich Davitsky.

'These other papers,' went on the inspector, 'are either forged or perhaps belonged to a fellow-prisoner who escaped with him and died on the way to liberty. It is apparently the name by which he was known in England and which has made him so difficult to trace. There is one other thing I would like you to see, Miss Dufour. He was wearing a ring which perhaps you will recognize.' He put a man's gold signet ring into her hands. On it was engraved a small bear cub and the single letter D.

'Oh yes, this belonged to Leo,' she whispered. 'Though his father had rejected him he was still proud to be a Davitsky. It is the crest of the house. He was wearing it when . . . when I was his prisoner.'

'Thank you, my dear, and thank you, sir. You have been very helpful. We cannot, I'm afraid, actually swear to his identity but we can come as close as anyone can hope to be. Would you like to keep the ring?'

She shook her head. 'Let it be buried with him. He was so proud of it. He will be buried, won't he? Not thrown into some lime pit.'

The inspector smiled faintly. 'That is not our custom. In any case it depends on the Russian authorities and the wishes of his family.'

'There must be some place for foreigners who have died in this country. If it costs money, I will pay.'

'Don't distress yourself. We will let you know as soon as the authorities have been informed.'

He saw them to the door and outside Daniel said a little brusquely, 'I am surprised that Miss Motford didn't come with you.'

'She didn't know. She is away for a couple of days visiting a sick relative. She is coming back this afternoon.'

'Well, you're not going home to an empty house and brooding over it. You are coming back with me.'

'No, Daniel, I don't want to trouble Christine. I'm all right. It's just that it has been rather a horrible shock.'

But Daniel had already waved his stick to a passing cab. 'Don't argue,' he said as he helped her into it.

It's not really fair, thought Christine, as Daniel brought her in to the drawing-room, *that she should still look so beautiful*, in lilac muslin with a tiny jacket of a darker velvet and a leghorn straw hat with a pale mauve rose weighing down the brim on the golden hair. *It makes me feel old and plain and commonplace.* Then she saw the pallor, the sparkle of tears, the trembling mouth, and hated herself for even thinking it. She took both Louise's hands, drawing her close and kissing her cheek.

'My dear child, you look so distressed. What happened?'

'It was ghastly,' said Daniel. We both need coffee, hot and strong with a nip of brandy to take the unpleasant taste away.'

'Nothing simpler. Call Mark, will you, and then come back and tell me all about it.' He relayed the whole wretched incident while she still held Louise's hand in hers and felt the girl tremble.

'Perhaps in one way it's a good thing it has happened,' she said gently. 'It's the end of a very dark chapter, isn't it?'

'Yes, I suppose it is. I felt it was like closing the door on part of my childhood. Why did all those happy hours have to end so badly?'

'We could go on asking ourselves a question like that for ever,' said Daniel, 'and still there is no answer. Now you can go forward with no more worries, everything will be plain sailing, no more memories of Bluebeard's Castle.'

'No more Bluebeard's Castle,' said Louise a little sadly.

'What was that?' asked Christine, intrigued.

'It was an old hunting-lodge where Louise and Leo used to picnic and play games once upon a time, and it was where he took refuge before they arrested him.'

'I really must go,' said Louise, putting down her cup and getting to her feet.

'There's no hurry, surely. Why not stay and lunch with us?' urged Christine.

'No, it's kind of you but I really have a great deal to do. In two days we're off to Paris for a week.'

'I'll ask Mark to call a cab for you,' said Daniel, 'and don't worry about the police. I'll deal with any repercussions and let you know about it when you return.'

Outside, while they waited he said, 'You do know, don't you, that whatever happens we are still here whenever you need us?'

'Dear Daniel,' she murmured and touched his face lovingly.

Then the cab was there and he kissed her cheek, handed her in and watched it drive away before he returned to Christine.

'What a lovely creature she is, even after all she has been through these last few months,' she said. 'It really wouldn't have been the least surprising if you had fallen in love with her.'

'Except that I didn't.'

'Not even a little bit?' she teased.

'Not even a little bit.'

She didn't quite believe him, but now it was no longer important. In a way, knowing her Daniel, it even made him more securely hers. 'I wonder how she will get on in Paris. There's one good thing: Hattie Motford is wonderfully reliable. After all she had years of experience with Clara.'

Daniel said nothing. For some reason the savage wound in his chest, though long-healed, sometimes gave him a twinge. He wished he could feel absolutely certain that the dead man he had seen that morning was indeed Leonid Davitsky and not some poor unfortunate who had died in his place.

PART FOUR

Bluebeard's Castle

Chapter 22

It was one of those overcast summer days towards the end of August, and Louise was busy with last-minute packing since she and Miss Motford would be setting out very early the next morning for Paris. On their earlier visit they had found a pleasant, airy apartment on the first floor of a large house overlooking the Parc Monceau. From the windows of their sitting-room they could look towards the grass and trees, where people walked their dogs and children ran and played while the nursemaids chatted with their admirers. Since money was no object Miss Motford had decided it was better than a poky dark flat among the students on the Left Bank which they had explored at first. The great disadvantage was that the only piano available was a very battered instrument indeed, but Louise had high hopes of being able to hire a better one and, if that failed, felt sure Monsieur Vincent would be able to give assistance in finding somewhere she could practise. She had already written to him and received an effusive reply, saying he would be delighted to see her and give her a few weeks of intensive tuition.

She stopped delving into the chest of drawers for a moment and stared at herself in the mirror, feeling how very exciting it was that at last she was to embark on something which she had wanted for such a very long time. She thought how pleased her mother would have been, and her father too – in his quiet way he had been proud of her skill. It was not that she entertained any wild hopes of ever becoming a concert pianist, which would be ridiculous at her age, but she would be working at something she loved, and she hoped to acquire a skill and an expertise that could lead in all kinds of interesting directions. She sighed and pushed away the heavy hair which she had tied loosely back with a ribbon. It was thrilling but it was also frightening. She was very conscious of how much she owed to Jean-Louis. Whatever happened, she must justify his faith in her.

She turned back to emptying the top drawer of handkerchiefs and gloves and felt something hard and cold that had rolled to the back. When she brought it out, she saw it was the little Chinese dog in green jade that Leo had given her on her birthday last year, and that she thought he had probably stolen from his mother's large collection. She stared down at its endearingly ugly face. It had been a happy day. She had laughed and kissed him, never dreaming that the light-hearted friendship could end in a tragic and horrible death in a burned-out slum in Seven Dials. It was a constant reminder of what she had tried so hard to forget, and yet she could not bring herself to throw it out, or sell it or give it to someone else. At last she wrapped it in one of her handkerchiefs and stowed it away in a corner of her valise.

She looked round the room. All was packed now except for a few last items which would go in tomorrow morning. The heavy luggage, the two trunks with her music and books, had all gone ahead. Miss Motford's daily woman, a widow with one young son who lived near by and was glad of the extra money, would come in two or three times and look after the house. Louise was just thinking she could do with a quiet sit-down and a cup of tea when she was surprised by a loud knocking at the front door. Perhaps Hattie had forgotten her key. She ran down the stairs to open the door; it was not Miss Motford who stood on the step but David. She had not seen him since she had left Wimpole Street, and was acutely conscious that she was wearing her oldest blouse and skirt, that her hair was all over the place, her hands were grubby and she didn't want to see him at all.

He was looking very elegant, very much the young man

about town, and for a moment they stared at one another until he said, 'May I come in?'

She moved aside for him to enter the tiny hall and opened the door of the parlour so that he could follow her into the cosy little room.

'What brings you here?' she said, a little impatiently.

'Do you have to be so unfriendly?'

'I'm not unfriendly. It's just that I had not expected anyone and I'm very busy. Hattie and I are to catch the early boat-train tomorrow morning and everything has to be packed and ready by then.'

'I know. That's why I'm here. I wanted to come and say goodbye.'

'I see. I thought you'd be down at Hunter's Lair.'

'No. I've actually been in Scotland. I have a great-uncle who has a castle at Glenmuir on the west coast, and I've been enjoying long country walks and a bit of rough shooting with my cousins. I've only just come back, which is why I have only now heard about Leo. If I'd known before, I would have come with you. Was it a very distressing time for you?'

'It wasn't pleasant but Daniel was with me.'

'So now it is all over, all finished with; you are free of him for ever. It must be a tremendous relief.'

'Yes, in a way I suppose it is. Look, David, I don't really want to talk about it if that's all right with you. I believe I have to congratulate you on being called to the Bar. You are a fully fledged barrister now.'

'For what it's worth. The real work starts in earnest in the autumn. But what I really came to tell you . . .'

But then he was interrupted. Miss Motford let herself in, shutting the front door and saying cheerfully, 'Would you believe it, it has started to rain and of course I had no umbrella . . .' She came into the sitting-room and stopped abruptly. 'I see you have a visitor. It's David, isn't it? Have you called to see Louise? Look, I'm dying for a cup of tea. I'll go and make one and perhaps you will join us?'

'Thank you but I only came for a few minutes,' said David

453

and Miss Motford, with a quick glance from one to the other, said cheerfully, 'Right, you go ahead. I'll pop out to the kitchen, take off my wet coat and put the kettle on,' and she went off, leaving them alone together.

'What I really came to tell you,' said David hurriedly, 'is that I expect to be in Paris myself for several months this winter. Uncle Harry has decided I should take a course on international law at the Sorbonne starting in November, and I thought you and I could see something of one another.'

'I shall be working very hard by then,' she said doubtfully, 'and Clara writes that she and Jean-Louis will be back from Greece at the beginning of October and intend to spend the winter in Paris, so I doubt if I shall have very much time.'

'Why are you deliberately making excuses to avoid me?'

'I'm not. I'm simply stating facts. Of course I shall be pleased to see you sometimes.'

'May I have your address?'

'If you wish.' She spelled it out to him and he wrote it carefully into the diary he took from an inner pocket. He put it away and gave her a wintry smile. 'Now I suppose you're waiting for me to go and leave you in peace?'

'Not at all,' she said politely. 'Stay and take tea with us if you wish.'

'Thank you, no. I know when I'm not wanted. But I still love you, Louise. You do know that, don't you?'

'Oh, not now, David, please.' But his eyes were on her and for some reason she trembled. Then unexpectedly he took a step towards her, gathered her in his arms and kissed her fiercely, taking her breath away so that when he released her suddenly, she staggered and clutched the back of a chair to steady herself.

'Don't forget, I'll see you in Paris in November, if not before,' he said, then took up his hat and gloves and went quickly out of the room. She heard the front door slam while she stood breathless and shaken by the overwhelming realization that, for the first time since the rape, she had not felt disgust or revulsion but something else, a warmth, an inner stirring, a response, a feeling almost of pleasure. She found it utterly disconcerting.

Hattie came in with a tray and glanced around her. 'Has he gone?'

'Yes.' She pulled herself together with an effort. 'He really came to tell us that he will be coming to Paris in November and wanted to know if he could call upon us.'

'That will be nice company for you, my dear,' said Hattie placidly. 'Now, come and sit down and have some tea. You look tired. While we drink it, we'll go over everything and make sure we've done all we should before we go off in the morning.'

Paris was still very quiet, its inhabitants just beginning to trickle back from the summer holidays. The Opéra and the Comédie Française were shut; the season not yet begun. After they had settled into their apartment, Louise was eager to see as much of the city as she could before she settled down to some strenuous practice. She had been so young when her father had moved from Paris to Vienna that she remembered little of it, just one or two moments that had remained part of her childish memory. She had never forgotten the day her father had taken her to Notre Dame, to what must have been a benediction service, the priest raising high the host in its great gold monstrance, the clouds of incense, the voices of the choir rising exultantly in a soaring hymn of praise; the enormous elephant at the Zoological Gardens, nosing gently with his trunk at the bun in her small hand; her father pointing out the dark door through which Danton had gone to his death on the guillotine, a revolutionary but a brave man who had refused to make his escape, saying, 'Can a man take his country with him on the soles of his feet?' She had not understood it then but for some reason the words had stayed with her.

Hattie Motford knew the city well already, but was quite willing to go with her, and proved a valuable guide, as ready to explore the bookstalls along the Seine, its alleys and byways, as to gaze into the shops in the fashionable streets, shaking her head at Louise, who wanted to show her appreciation by buying her all kinds of costly trifles.

The apartment began to assume a home-like atmosphere. The maid they had engaged, who was middle-aged with a badly crippled husband, proved after a doubtful start to be something of a treasure. Inclined to look at two English ladies with the gravest suspicion, she started off by laying down her own rules of service, but was taken aback, first by Louise's excellent colloquial French and second by Miss Motford who, far from being one of those fussy elderly ladies who could easily be brushed aside, had a calm, no-nonsense manner and kindly but firmly put Colette in her place. In no time at all she was boasting to her sister – and anyone else who would listen – that, though firm, they were not always prying into the larder and making notes as to the levels in the butter, eggs and coffee supplies, but were very appreciative indeed of her excellent culinary abilities and enjoyed the good meals she supplied each evening. In fact everything was going along swimmingly, till the day Louise went to her first music lesson with Monsieur Vincent.

He tore her to shreds, wanting to know what she had been doing all summer to play so deplorably. He reduced her to the level of a schoolgirl stumbling through her first exercises and she sat, head bowed, miserably remembering those weeks when her fingers had been as numbed and useless as her mind, and knew she could never explain that terrible time to him. He very nearly brought her to helpless tears, except she knew how much he despised such weakness. She sat stubbornly silent till he came to the end of his tirade.

'Practise, practise, practise, six hours a day for at least a week,' he admonished her, 'before you come back to me, and then we shall have to see how you have improved.' It was only then that she humbly confessed her dilemma in finding a suitable piano and that she had intended to ask for his help. 'Piano? Piano?' he repeated. 'What are you talking about? You have the opportunity to use one of the finest instruments in Paris, as I know from experience.'

'I have?' She stared at him bewildered. 'I don't understand.'

'Didn't Jean-Louis tell you?' And when she still stared blankly at him, he went on impatiently, 'Maybe in the stress of arranging his marriage, he asked your half-sister to give you the information.'

'What information?'

'As you know, Jean-Louis has a house in Paris, out on one of the avenues near the Bois de Boulogne. It is of course partly shut up till they return, but there is a skeleton staff and the housekeeper has been instructed to allow you in to use the piano in the music room whenever you please. It is a pity that you had not been informed. No doubt it slipped your sister's memory at such a happy time.' Slipped her memory, or perhaps been forgotten on purpose? There was still that touch of jealousy. 'Go there tomorrow and start work immediately, and don't let me see you again until you can make a better showing than today.'

But when she was getting her music together to go, he softened a little, putting a hand on her shoulder. 'If I've sounded harsh, it is for your own good. Standards are high and I've already been speaking of your talent to the director. I know you can do it, so don't let me down.'

'I won't,' she said fervently, 'I swear I won't.'

She went back to their apartment, cheered by those last few comforting words, and poured it all into Hattie's sympathetic ears.

'I knew their address,' she said, 'but I've never been to the house. The only thing that troubles me is that for the next couple of weeks I shall be leaving you alone for most of the day.'

'Don't worry about me, my dear. I have always loved Paris and it is years since I've been here. There are one or two old friends I shall call on. I might even take the river boat down to Passy. I will come with you one day and listen, if you will allow me. I should enjoy that.'

So it was settled, and the next morning Louise found her way to the Avenue du Bois de Boulogne and stared at the splendid house, half hidden by a thick hedge of laurel, and hoped that Monsieur Vincent was not mistaken, as she had received no other information. Then she braced herself, went up the steps and raised the heavy knocker. The door was opened by an austere lady in black silk, a lace cap on her hair, who gave her a very intimidating stare that made Louise's heart sink. Then unexpectedly she smiled.

'You must be Mademoiselle Dufour,' she said.

'Yes, yes I am,' said Louise timidly.

'I had expected someone older, nearer to Madame's own age,' said the housekeeper. 'But never mind, come in. I've been expecting you for some days. Monsieur de Chaminard told me you would be coming.'

She led the way through an impressive hall, up a splendid stairway and along a gallery, and ushered her into a room where the curtains were drawn and the furniture shrouded in dust sheets. She moved around the room, drawing back the velvet curtains and whipping off the dustcovers, and there in the place of honour stood a magnificent piano. Louise gazed at it, thrilled beyond words. The housekeeper opened it up.

'Would you like the candles lit?' she asked.

'Oh, no. I can see perfectly,' said Louise.

'When you are ready to leave,' went on the housekeeper, 'just touch the bell and I will come and show you out.'

'Thank you. You're very kind.'

The housekeeper went out and Louise seated herself at the piano, hardly daring to touch the notes. Then she let her hands stray into a few bars and realized her good luck. It had a splendidly rich tone and was perfectly tuned. After the first tentative start she was well away. They had already decided what she would play for her test and the board of the Conservatoire had also set one piece, a particularly difficult Liszt sonata. Gradually she began to lose herself in the music, and it must have been well after one o'clock when she stopped for a while, flexing her fingers and easing her back. She crossed to the window, looking across the peaceful street. A black and white cat was stretched lazily in the sun. She was about to return to the piano when there was a loud knock on the door and a trim maid came in, carrying a tray which she placed on a small table.

'Madame Réger thought you might care for some refreshment,' she said.

'How very kind of her.'

The maid curtsied and went out. There was a silver coffeepot, a plate of fresh croissants with some delicious-looking cream cheese and a small bunch of black grapes. Louise, who in her anxiety had eaten very little breakfast, was suddenly ravenously hungry. The coffee was hot and strong, the croissants still warm from the oven, and the cheese delicious. She ate it all and then went back to the piano, refreshed and grateful for the kind thought and ready for another two hours of hard work. At last the dreadful numbness of the summer had gone for ever.

At the end of a week's hard work she went back to Monsieur Vincent and, although his praise was grudging, she knew he was pleased. She worked hard for another two weeks and each day the housekeeper sent up a tray of different refreshment, for which she was very grateful.

A few days before the test, she had an unexpected visitor. Absorbed in her work, she did not hear anyone come in. She had just decided it was time to finish for the day when someone clapping loud and long startled her. She swung round on the stool and a young man got up from one of the deep armchairs and strolled across to her. He was very good-looking, sleek, with dark hair and a small moustache and the air of a soldier about him. She stared at him as he strolled across to her.

'You must be my uncle's new wife's little sister,' he said. 'I'm delighted to meet you at last. My name is Victor. You really play extremely well, you know. I've been greatly impressed.'

'But what are you doing here?' she stammered, still surprised by the unexpected visitor.

'My uncle permits me to stay here when the regiment is in Paris. We are due to leave for Algeria in a few weeks' time.'

He had bold eyes that examined her from head to foot, and he was already pleased with what he saw. She started to put her music together.

'Don't go,' he said, 'not till we've become better acquainted. Tell me about yourself. Why all this intense practice?'

'I'm hoping to be accepted to study at the Conservatoire,' she said. 'The examination is the day after tomorrow.'

'Judging from what I have been hearing, you'll get through with flying colours.'

She put her music into the portfolio and got up. 'I really must go. I'm later than usual and my friend will be anxious.'

'You are not staying here, then?'

'No. We have an apartment near the Parc Monceau.'

'I'll see you out,' he said, going ahead to open the door for her.

'You need not trouble. I know my way by now.'

'No trouble.' They went down the stairs and he opened the door for her. 'Shall I call you a cab?'

'I prefer to walk. It does me good after sitting for so long,' she said. She walked away briskly and he looked after her.

Her hair was tied back like a schoolgirl's, she was simply dressed in blouse and skirt: a mouse of a girl but with a rare beauty and a certain elegance. It might be fun in the last three weeks of his leave to introduce her to the delights of Paris, which he guessed she had not yet enjoyed. Céline, who danced at the Opéra Comique, was proving far too expensive a luxury these days. It was high time to choose another companion, one a good deal more intriguing. He must find out more about her from Madame Réger, who was always a mine of information.

The day of the test came. Louise felt she had not done as well as she should have done, but now it was over and she must wait for the result. She went along the next morning at midday, when the list of successful candidates would be put up on the noticeboard. A little group of hopefuls were gathered around it. She waited till they had moved away before she dared to approach. She stared at it for a moment, unable to believe her eyes. There was her own name, heading the list. Sheer elation rose up inside her. She must share it with Hattie at once. She turned to run and almost at once collided with Victor, leaning against one of the lamp standards, handsome and elegant.

'Told you so,' he said. 'I knew you'd succeed, so I'm here to take you to a celebration luncheon.'

'Oh no, I couldn't,' she exclaimed. 'I couldn't do that. I must tell my friend. She'll be so anxious.'

'Then we'll find a cab and I'll take you both to lunch,' he said, and waved his stick. The cabbie drew up and before she realized what was happening to her Louise was inside giving the address, and they were on their way to Parc Monceau.

When they reached the house Louise ran up the stairs, followed more leisurely by Victor. She flung her arms round Hattie.

'They've accepted me. Isn't it wonderful?'

'I knew they would. You've worked so hard.' Then she drew away. 'But who is this gentleman you have brought with you?'

'Oh dear, I was so excited I forgot. He is Captain Victor de Charmandon. He is a nephew of Jean-Louis and is living at his house as he's on leave. He has heard me practising and wants to take us both to lunch. This is my dear friend Hattie Motford.'

'Delighted to meet you,' said Victor, gallantly kissing the hand Hattie extended to him. 'Now, if you two ladies are ready, we'll go. I told the cab driver to wait.'

'But we couldn't possibly go out to lunch looking like this,' said Hattie in dismay.

'Why not? You both look charming to me, and I know the very place, nice and quiet, where the food is wonderful. I'll give you five minutes to titivate, then we'll go.'

'Well, just this once,' said Hattie. 'It is a special day. Come on, Louise.'

In five minutes, wearing their newest and smartest hats, they picked up gloves and handbags and were off.

It was a small restaurant but with a distinguished clientèle.

Victor was known and they were given a secluded table where they could talk in peace. The food was delicious and Hattie, who had a discerning taste, said the cool white wine they were drinking was far better than vulgar champagne. While they ate and talked, Victor studied Louise. She was not at all the little mouse of a girl he had at first supposed. She was lively and interesting on a great many subjects and, though a little shy, had more sense in her little finger than Céline had in her whole body. He was going to enjoy the last three weeks of his leave, introducing her to the café life of Paris.

During the day Louise worked hard, getting settled in at the Conservatoire, but three or four times a week Victor would turn up with a new suggestion. Once or twice he even included Hattie, who approved of him as a nephew of Jean-Louis. He took Louise to the cafés where the artists, poets, actors, singers and dancers met, and she was thrilled when he pointed them out to her. He took her to the opera and, it must be confessed, yawned himself through most of *La Traviata*, while Louise wept. He took her later to the Opéra Comique and to the circus, where she adored the fabulous horses and was spellbound by the trapeze artists. On Sundays he took her driving in the Bois de Boulogne and once to the races at Longchamps, where she was enchanted to win a small bet.

The three weeks passed all too quickly. Not since the time with John Everard had she been escorted everywhere by a reasonable young man. Victor, who was no fool and nearer thirty then twenty, and who knew how quickly he could damn himself in Louise's critical eyes, behaved impeccably.

So they came to their last evening together. The next day the regiment would be embarking for Algeria and Louise asked if he would take her to the Red Kite. It was a nightclub everyone had been talking about, much frequented by the young set, who liked their entertainment to be spicy. The Red Kite had the reputation of always going just beyond the limit. Louise was curious.

'You won't like it,' said Victor.

'Why won't I? I'm not a prude.'

'Very well,' he said. 'If you really want to we'll go, but don't say I didn't warn you.'

So they went, and she had to admit even the wall decorations gave her a slight shock, but she wouldn't back out now. They found a quiet table, not too near the rowdy youths, and as it was their last evening Victor ordered champagne.

After a particularly outrageous sketch, which made even Victor frown, she was just about to say, 'I don't really like it here. Do you think we might leave?' when a young man came crashing up to their table.

'What the devil are you doing here, Louise? This is no place for you.'

'David!' she exclaimed in dismay.

He glared at Victor. 'I suppose it was you who brought her here,' he hissed.

'It was actually. Any objection?'

'Yes, and I have a very good mind to punch you on the nose.'

'Just you try it,' said Victor dangerously.

'Stop it, you two. Stop at once!' exclaimed Louise. 'Go back to your friends, David, and leave us alone.'

He looked from one to the other. People around were staring, so he went back to his own table, still muttering furiously.

'And who is that objectionable young man?' said Victor. 'I thought for a moment he meant what he said.'

'He did. I knew him in England,' said Louise. 'He is studying law at the Sorbonne. Victor, you were right and I was wrong. I don't like it here at all. Do you think we could leave?'

'Of course, my dear, at once.' He stood up, threw down some money and put her shawl around her shoulders. Outside he waved down a cab.

'I'll see you home.' At the apartment house, he got out with her. 'This is our last evening together. I'd appreciate a cup of coffee. Do you think I might come up for a few minutes to say goodbye?'

She hesitated. She knew Hattie was out that evening.

'I'd really rather you didn't.'

'Why? Don't you trust me?'

'It isn't that.' She found it totally impossible to explain that ever since the hateful events of last year, she could not endure to be alone with a man she did not know and trust completely.

'You just don't like me, is that it?'

'No, no. It isn't that. It isn't really. I feel so ungrateful, when these three weeks have been so wonderful and I have been so happy.' She suddenly put her arms around his neck and kissed him hard on the lips. 'There, that is just to say thank you,' and she would have run up the stairs, if he had not caught her hand and turned her back to him. He kissed her very gently.

'And that is my thanks to you. You won't forget me entirely, will you? Think of me sometimes, roasting under the African sun.'

'I will, indeed I will, and all the lovely evenings you have given me.'

Then she was really running away from him. He watched her disappear and thought, *Somewhere, at some time, some wretched man must have terrified her,* and it was going to be a long time before she gave her trust to anyone else.

'Turned you down, did she?' said the cabbie, still waiting for his fare.

'Shut up,' said Victor sharply. 'Avenue du Bois de Boulogne and make it snappy.' He got in and they drove quickly away.

The next morning the florist delivered a box. When Louise opened it she saw a dozen white roses, each one quite perfect, as if the dew of the morning were still on them. With them came a card: *Only these seemed worthy of my lovely puritan maiden. With my love, Victor.* She was deeply moved by his understanding and generosity.

Hattie came in from the hall. 'A visitor for you, Louise. What heavenly roses. Who sent them?'

'Victor. It was our last night together. His regiment leaves today.'

'You're going to miss him. That means you'll be in to supper tonight. I must have a word with Colette.'

She went on into the kitchen and, looking decidedly shame-faced, David edged into the room.

'I really came to apologize,' he said, rather humbly for him.

'So you ought. You behaved disgracefully last night. Were you drunk?'

'No, I wasn't. It just made me mad to see you in such a place.'

'You needn't have insulted my friend. It was my choice, not his, and I didn't like it anyway. We left soon afterwards.'

'Who is he, Louise?'

'He's the nephew of Jean-Louis. I met him at their house and he took me out once or twice during his leave. How long have you been in Paris?'

'Only two days.'

She went on snipping the ends of the roses, before arranging them in a vase. Then she gave him a sudden smile. 'Same old prickly David. But I'm very glad to see you. I am longing to hear news of Daniel and Christine and everyone. Why not come to supper, and we can have a good long talk?'

'May I?'

'Of course you may. What about Sunday? Jean-Louis and Clara will be here next week and I shall be busy.'

'You wouldn't come out with me now?'

'No, David. I've lots of work to do for my lectures at the college tomorrow.'

'Sunday then?'

'Sunday it is,' and David went off, looking a great deal happier than when he came in.

Louise took the card and one of the roses into her bedroom, putting the flower in a glass of water. Then she fetched some crusty rolls, a piece of cheese, a jug of coffee and an apple, and settled down happily to an afternoon of really hard work.

Chapter 23

When Jean-Louis and Clara returned, the house was opened up for them and Louise saw it for the first time in all its splendour: the drawing-room with walls panelled in pale-green and gold; the dining-room with walls of red damask and velvet curtains to match; the master bedrooms; and on the second floor the night and day nurseries, set up while they were away with every modern convenience in pale blue and white, and now only waiting for the new heir to the shipping wealth.

They did not entertain a great deal at first, but Jean-Louis was an important figure in the world of finance and it was necessary from time to time for him to invite business acquaintances and their wives to dinner parties. Unfortunately Clara sometimes had trouble with her pregnancy and there were evenings when she found it impossible to act as hostess to her husband's guests, so that it became his habit quite often to ask Louise to take her place, acting like a daughter of the house. She was frequently able to talk to the guests in their own language, which gratified them immensely. She felt she owed Jean-Louis so much that she was glad to do it, and indeed quite often found it very enjoyable. The only problem was that Clara felt this slip of a girl was ousting her from her rightful position as mistress of this great house. Louise tried to make Clara understand that it was not so, and that she often spoke of her half-sister, but all the same it did lead to quarrels and little moments of jealousy.

Sometimes Jean-Louis would take her out for the evening too. They went to concerts, and he took her to see Sarah

Bernhardt give a startling performance in one of Sardou's more lurid dramas. She was also entranced by Eleanora Duse in *Medea*, the story of a woman most cruelly betrayed by a faithless husband.

Altogether these winter months were proving very interesting, she told David when they met for an hour or two. They were both working hard but found time to be together, and for once they were not quarrelling as they had done so often before, but instead finding out new things about each other.

Christmas came but because of Clara's condition they did not entertain, except for a few close friends who called in. Then early in January Louise came in from the college one afternoon to see Hattie gazing in rapt admiration at a beautiful small piano installed in their sitting-room. It was in a dark rich wood and the silver candle sconces were very handsome indeed.

'Where did it come from?' she gasped.

'Can't you guess? It is Jean-Louis's Christmas gift, but was not ready in time. The men put it in this morning and the piano tuner will come tomorrow to make sure all is right. He said it was to thank you for all you've done for him and Clara these last few months.'

'But I haven't done anything. I've enjoyed it. Oh, how did he ever guess that all my life I longed to own my own piano?'

'Jean-Louis is good at guessing things.'

Louise approached it almost with reverence, opened it up and played a few notes. 'It has a lovely rich sound already, not tinny like other small pianos. I must go and thank him at once.'

'The best way you can thank him is by going on doing whatever you can for him and Clara.'

'But I do that gladly. Oh, Hattie, how very, very fortunate I am to have so good and kind a friend.'

When she went to thank him that evening he said, 'I thought it might help you to try out knotty problems at home rather than having to go to the practice rooms at the Conservatoire. Monsieur Vincent advised me, so it should be a good one.'

'I'm sure it is, and it's such a handsome one too. Why are you so very good to me?'

'Because it pleases me,' he said, smiling and pinching her cheek. 'And if you want to please me still more, you'll go and sit with Clara for a while. She is very low today and I'm worried about her.'

'Of course I will. I'll go now. I'll ask her if she would like me to read to her. She enjoys that sometimes. And thank you again, a thousand times.'

She spent the whole evening with her sister, sympathizing and reminding her of how happy she would feel when she held her baby in her arms for the first time.

Within a few days the whole de Chaminard household was in a state of tension. Everyone knew that the famous doctor engaged by Jean-Louis had been called. By morning a colleague had joined him. It seemed now that the baby would be born a month prematurely. There was a day of great anxiety when Jean-Louis scarcely left his wife's bedside and Louise did not go home but remained to help in any emergency. But the baby was not the great-grandson of a Greek pirate for nothing. He struggled into life weighing less than five pounds but still very much alive, as his screams testified.

There were still two or three very anxious days, when everyone seemed to go about on tiptoe – would he live or die? Then the tide turned. Clara began to recover. The baby, already named Alexander by his anxious father, took a stronger grip on life. But one great danger remained: his mother was unable to breastfeed him, and he took against the wet-nurse brought by the doctors. In the end it was Hattie who solved the problem, purely by accident. She happened to notice that her dairyman was accompanied on his rounds by a rosy-faced, plump country girl with a swelling bosom and asked him who she was.

'My daughter, Marie,' he said. 'She lost her first not much more than a week ago, died within two hours of birth. She was so upset, she asked if she could come out with me to try and take her mind off it.'

'What was the trouble?'

'The midwife couldn't understand it. My daughter has milk enough to feed twins, and yet the little one could not survive. Only God knows why such things happen.'

'Would she be willing to act as nurse to another baby?'

'Willing? Why, madam, she'd go down on her knees to thank you just to hold another baby in her arms, even if it belonged to another woman.'

'It might be worth a try. Tell her to come tomorrow, neatly dressed, and I'll see what I can do.'

So Marie turned up the next morning in a clean cotton blouse and skirt, her hair newly washed, her best shawl around her shoulders, and nervously got into the cab with Hattie and Louise. When they reached the big house, they went straight up to the nursery. Alexander lay in his magnificent cot, grizzling and miserable. Marie took one look at him and exclaimed, 'Why, the poor little mite is starving!' Without waiting for anyone to stop her, she lifted him out of his cot and held him. He stared at her with enormous dark-blue eyes and it was love at first sight. Then she unbuttoned her blouse and held him against her bosom. After a few moments he had found what he wanted and he began to suck: the battle was won.

After that nothing was too good for Marie. She was installed in the nursery, given an undermaid to serve her needs and even the English nanny imported by Jean-Louis forgot her stiffness towards the intruder when she saw how her charge improved.

Louise could go back to the apartment, to the joys of her new piano and to take up her neglected work at the Conservatoire, only too grateful that now at last everything was going smoothly. She could get on with her own life once again.

The weeks seemed to fly by. Already it was the middle of

February, and baby Alexander was making great strides, putting on weight every day. Louise thought that for the first time since she had known her, Clara, with her little son and her kind and thoughtful husband, was completely happy.

Jean-Louis had been talking about organizing a small recital for Louise later in the spring, to introduce her to the general public. It was an exciting, if frightening, prospect, but Louise's teachers at the Conservatoire were discussing a suggested programme and beginning to work towards it. Now and again, as her eyes fell on the little Chinese dog sitting smugly on her mantelpiece, she thought of Leo, but she must put him out of her mind. Leo was dead. She had seen him with her own eyes. He had gone out of her life for ever and she must not let herself think of him any longer.

She was alone in the apartment that week. Hattie had some old friends who lived in Lyons, and this was a good time to visit them for a few days. Louise did not mind being alone. She had plenty to work at, and David was always at hand to take her out to supper or walk with her on Sundays in the Bois de Boulogne, where the first signs of spring were already showing. Life was good and she enjoyed it. She had a letter from Daniel, saying he expected to be in Paris soon on an assignment and looked forward to seeing her and perhaps hearing her play.

And then something happened, so appalling, so utterly unbelievable that it could not be true; it could only be a dream, a nightmare from which she would wake, and laugh at herself for believing in it.

She awoke very early one morning. Though the curtains had been drawn back it was scarcely light, but there, standing not a couple of feet from the bed, was Leo, staring down at her, the same Leo and yet different. His hair was a reddish colour; she remembered so well. But he was dead, lying in his grave! She was so paralysed with fear that she could not stir or speak. Then he moved. He came down to the bed, put out a hand and touched her face with icy fingers.

'I'm real, you know. I'm not a ghost. Get up, Louise, get dressed. We're going away, you and I – together at last. This time you will not escape. We're going back to Russia together, we're going back to Bluebeard's Castle, just as I intended last year, only I was a fool. I trusted an Englishman and he let me down. He was only concerned for himself.'

It was then that she came to the dreadful realization that it was not a dream. It was real and it was happening. But how had he got in? Had he stolen the key from Colette, or had he bribed the concierge? She said stupidly:

'But I saw you, the fire had killed you, the police showed you to me.'

'That was my good luck. I'd changed identity with Igor the day before the fire broke out.'

'Do you mean you killed him?' she said in horror.

'The fool tripped and fell, but I left him and got away. You all thought it was me, didn't you? Even the stupid English police. Only Papa never really believed it. The money still came through the bank, and I followed you here. It has taken a long time but now it is all done. Hurry, Louise, get dressed. The express for Berlin leaves at eight and it is all settled – our tickets, our seats on the train.'

Slowly the truth dawned. He was here in her room. She was alone in the apartment and in his power. Perhaps it would be best to play along with him, to pretend to agree. Once out in the street she could escape from him. There would be people, the police. Shut up in this room she was at his mercy.

She scrambled out of bed, while he stood sentinel at the door. She dressed quickly. It was cold, so she put on her thickest skirt and warmest blouse, her boots and heavy winter coat. She had a small carrier bag and began to stuff things into it, all the money she had. She wished it had been more, but it was their custom to draw a cheque from the bank at the start of the month and already half had been spent.

'What are you doing there?' he said suspiciously.

'Only putting a few necessities together. I must leave a note for my maid. She will be here soon.'

'No,' he said. 'Leave nothing and hurry.'

Somehow she must leave a message. But how? On her

dressing-table there was the pencil she used occasionally to darken her eyebrows for the stage. On a scrap of paper she scrawled hurriedly, *Leo – Bluebeard's Castle.*

He had seized her arm and was shaking her. Somehow she contrived to push the slip of paper out of sight under the hand-mirror. Then he had grabbed hold of her and was pushing her out of the door. Should she try to hammer on the door of the ground-floor flat? But they were an elderly couple and would be sound asleep at this hour.

Although it was early there were people in the street, hurrying to work, but he kept a bruising hold on her arm, waved down a passing cab and pushed her into it. Perhaps at the station, she thought, there would be passengers and railway staff and it would be easier to get away; but she was wrong. While Leo felt in an inner pocket for their tickets, she made a wild dash for the porter standing near by.

'Help me,' she said frantically. 'This man is abducting me, taking me away from Paris, from my friends. Tell me where I can run, where I can find a cab?'

The man stared at her as if she were crazy. Then Leo was beside her, saying smoothly, 'Take no notice, this is my sister. She ran away with a lover and my father has sent me to bring her home.'

The man looked relieved. Young girls running away sounded more plausible than wild talk about abductions.

'This way, monsieur,' he said, 'your carriage is here. Hurry, the train will be leaving in a few minutes.' He ushered them into the compartment and slammed the door. The huge train snorted, letting out steam. As she fell into the seat, it jolted forward and then seemed to settle itself for its long journey, moving slowly and majestically out of the station. She knew there were no more than three short stops before Berlin. Hope died and she huddled into a corner of the carriage.

The days of travelling became a nightmare, day merging endlessly into night as they moved further and further east. She knew the few French francs in her bag would not be enough to carry her back even if she were able to escape from Leo's clutches.

So far as everyday things were concerned, he seemed normal enough. He bought her food at the few stops, urging her to eat and drink, but he never left her side. Even when she was forced to find her way to the unpleasant smelly lavatories, he stood guard outside the door.

Once at Warsaw she made a wild dash to the telegraph office. If she could only send a telegraph to Jean-Louis, he would know what to do. He would notify the police, set wheels in motion. But she had scarcely begun to write the form when Leo was there, had snatched it away and torn it up, forcing her back to the carriage. She knew now he was crazy, obsessed with a dream of going back to the years of growing up, the fun and games they had enjoyed as they played together in that old hunting-lodge, which must have crumbled into ruin by now. He talked of it incessantly, till in despair she wrapped her thick shawl around her head so that she could no longer hear and huddled in a corner of the carriage, hopeless and crushed. What he would do if they ever got there, she dared not think. Build one of those enormous bonfires he had loved to make, and burn down the house and them with it?

When Colette arrived at the apartment at seven-thirty, she made a tray of tea as usual and took it up to Louise's room. When there was no answer to her knock, she opened the door and went in. The room looked as if a gale had swept through it: bed untidy, clothes scattered everywhere, and no Mademoiselle Louise. Toby was asking to be let out. There was no note, no message to say where she had gone. But as she put down the tray she saw the corner of a scribbled note.

Leo – Bluebeard's Castle. She stared at it for a moment before she could take it in. Perhaps someone had abducted Mademoiselle Louise, but why? And who was Leo? What should she do? Call the police? No, she must go to David first. She knew where he lived and she must get a cab now, at once. She put on hat and coat and hurried out, hailing the first cab she saw and urging the driver to make haste. When she reached his lodging, David was drinking coffee with Daniel, who had arrived late the night before to spend a few days in Paris.

'Mademoiselle Louise has gone, vanished!' she exclaimed, barely inside the door. 'It's terrible. Some wicked wretch has stolen her away.'

'Gone!' exclaimed David. 'Where has she gone?'

'This was all she left,' and Colette pushed the slip of torn paper into his hands. He stared at it.

'I don't understand – what does it mean?'

'Let me see,' said Daniel. He took it out of David's hand.

'Leo is dead,' went on David. 'You told me so yourself, dead in that fire.'

'We believed it was Leo,' said Daniel slowly. 'I thought so, as did Louise and the police, but I always had an uneasy feeling that we could be wrong. Suppose another man, who had his papers, died in his place?'

'Oh my God, and now he's kidnapped her!' exclaimed David. 'We must get the police to go after them. What does she mean by Bluebeard's Castle?'

'It's where they used to run and play games when they were growing up. She told me he was obsessed with it, when he took her last year. It's a partly ruined lodge on Count Davitsky's estate. No, not the police, David. It's Jean-Louis we want. He has a finger in everything. He will get the police in motion here and all over Europe. We must go to him now, at once, and then you and I will go after them. Go back to the apartment, Colette. Do everything necessary and don't tell anyone. When is Miss Motford coming back?'

'At the end of next week.'

'Good, then go every day as usual and take care of Toby. We will find Mademoiselle Louise. You can be sure of that.'

They quickly packed a few necessities, then took a cab to the Bois de Boulogne, dropping Colette off on the way. They found Jean-Louis leisurely breakfasting and glancing through *The Times*. He was astonished to see them so early and listened to the story they poured out to him. Daniel gave a brief account of what had happened to Louise the previous year and he frowned.

'Why wasn't I told of this? Louise is as dear to me as a daughter. You must know that.'

'She was very unwilling to talk about what had been a terrible experience, and you and Clara were away on your honeymoon. She did not want to upset you or her sister.'

Jean-Louis was immediately practical. 'I will alert the police here in Paris, and I have certain links with other countries. I can inform all those stations where the trains stop. Somehow we must stop this wretched man before he can do more harm. You say you and David are going to follow them?'

'Yes,' said Daniel, 'because I am certain I know where Leo's obsession is going to take him. God knows what he intends, but I am very afraid for Louise's safety.'

'You're going to need money,' said Jean-Louis, 'and that fortunately I can provide, even some foreign currency.' He went to his desk, unlocked a drawer and brought it to them. 'Try and let me know if you have any sightings of them, and I promise, as far as I am able, I'll have the whole of Europe between here and Russia on the look-out for them. I shall say nothing to Clara as yet, so as not to worry her. She is very occupied with our son.'

'How is he? I know you had anxieties when he was born.'

'Progressing by leaps and bounds every day. I hope you'll all be back safely before his christening.'

'Please God, we will,' said Daniel fervently.

Immensely relieved that they could leave so much in the extremely capable hands of Jean-Louis, they caught the midday express for Berlin, hoping and praying they might catch up with Leo and his unhappy captive.

The first news that Daniel and David had of them was at Warsaw, when they went to the telegraph office to send a wire to Jean-Louis.

'Funny thing,' said the man chattily as they filled in the form, 'there was a young woman here earlier on, writing a message she was and a young man comes up, snatches it away from her and tears it up. Then he marches her off, as if she were a prisoner – queer that.' It must have been Louise. It came as a great relief to know they were on the right track.

The train went on, hour after torturing hour, never fast

enough for them, the snow growing ever thicker as they travelled east.

When they reached St Petersburg, Leo took a cab to the Europa, booked a room and locked her in. He was taking no chances on her making a desperate dash to the British Embassy. Then he went down and spoke to the hotel manager.

'Have a tray of tea prepared. I'll take it up myself.'

'Certainly, sir.'

'Tell me, is it possible to get a carriage through to Pavlosk?'

'More than possible,' said the hotel manager. 'The snow is not lying as thick as last year.' He was none too sure of this odd pair. 'But if you are thinking of the Davitsky estates, the count is not there.'

'I know that,' said Leo. He was well aware his father always took his mother to their house at Livadia on the Black Sea at this time, to avoid the bitter cold.

'Have a carriage harnessed and ready to leave by nine o'clock in the morning.'

'Will you be requiring breakfast?'

'Tea, coffee and hot rolls at eight o'clock.'

When the tray of tea was brought, he took it to their room. Louise was kneeling by the wood-burning stove, trying to get warm. He put the tray between them and poured the tea. 'Come along, Louise,' he said cheerfully. 'Drink up. It will warm you.'

She took the cup in her numbed and trembling hands, too sick and weary to do more than sip it and eat a little of the food. Now, she thought desperately, the moment had come. Shut up alone with her, he would ravage her body as he had done last year in that basement room, and this time there would be no Daniel to whom she could run for help. But strangely none of this happened. Leo urged her to eat and drink. He seemed wrapped in an obsessive fantasy that had grown throughout the months and occupied all his thoughts. He had no fear of not being able to carry out what he had planned. His father might be away, but the servants were all still at the great house. He was still Count Leonid Ivanovich Davitsky – the young master, and the steward of the household would always obey the young master.

Louise wrapped herself in a rug and lay on the edge of the big bed, wishing she were dead. But one does not give up so easily at nineteen when there is still hope. Leo stretched out beside her.

'You think I'm mad, don't you? But I'm not. I know exactly what I am doing. We are going back to the days when we were happy, when we had so many dreams of the future, you and I and the dogs at Bluebeard's Castle.' She turned her face away from him, but he went on dreamily talking of what had never really existed. 'Try to sleep,' he said at last. 'We've a long day tomorrow.' He rolled over and touched her cheek for a moment. 'You and I together at last.' She shuddered as the cold fingers stroked her face.

Then he yawned, stretched and fell asleep.

They arrived at the great white house by midday, the horses floundering in the snow and the carriage close to overturning. The steward, an elderly man who had been with the family since boyhood, stared at Leo as if he were a ghost.

'But master,' he stammered at last. 'We thought – we understood . . .'

'That I was dead,' said Leo crisply. 'Well, I'm not. I'm very much alive, and master here in my father's absence.'

'But the house is partly shut up.'

'Surely there is one room heated?'

'There is your mother's sitting-room.'

'Very well, take the lady there and see she is served with a tray of tea and some food. We have had a gruelling journey.'

The steward nodded to one of the staring servant girls and Louise, too numbed by the cold and too despairing to protest, followed the girl up the stairs to the pretty, spacious room with its fine furniture which she had known so well in those far-off days of her childhood.

'Now,' went on Leo, 'don't stand there gaping at me, Stefan. There are things I must know. Is the sleigh still in use?'

'Of course, it is always ready,' said Stefan, recovering from his first amazement but still very doubtful of this young master who seemed to have come back to them from the dead.

'Good. Then first thing tomorrow have it taken out and harnessed ready with two of the horses. I want a basket packed with food and wine, and put in some fire-lighting material and plenty of logs.'

'But where are you intending to go at this season of the year?'

'We are going to the old hunting-lodge.'

'But you can't go there,' said Stefan, more and more convinced that he was dealing with a madman. 'It is already a ruin. The peasants have been stealing wood all winter to burn in their stoves.'

'Don't argue with me. I know what I am doing. Let me know when it is ready. I will drive myself.'

Stefan watched him bound up the stairs with the gravest doubt of this crazy young master, but he was accustomed to obedience and set about following his orders.

In the comfortable room Louise was kneeling on the rug as close as she could get to the iron stove pouring out welcome heat, the tray of tea beside her.

'What do you intend to do?' she said hopelessly as Leo came in.

'What I have dreamed of for the last six months, what has become reality at last,' he said exultantly. He poured tea for himself in the tall glass and smiled down at her. 'At last we are going back to Bluebeard's Castle.'

'But you can't,' she said aghast. 'It may not even still be there.'

'It's there all right. I am certain of it. And I know exactly what I intend to do, you and I together at last.'

They set out in the morning soon after nine. The sleigh had been made ready with a basket packed with food, piled high with logs and kindling for building a fire, and fur rugs to wrap around them. It was a brilliantly sunny morning, the snow sparkling and the horses keen in the sharp air, eager to be out of their stables after the long winter months.

Stefan watched Leo drive away, then dispatched a servant to the city with instructions to telegraph at once to the count, telling him of the reappearance of his son and asking for instructions. If Count Davitsky returned, as he well might, it would be two days at least before he would reach St Petersburg, and in that time anything might happen.

It was near noon before they reached the old house. Although its outbuildings had been largely stripped, the main structure was still intact. The huge room, where so many parties had once gathered, was there still with its huge stone hearth, though the floor was filthy with bird droppings. Mouldering tapestries still clung to some of the walls, and the heavy oak door with its iron bolts still swung on creaking hinges.

'Help me, Louise. Don't stand there shivering.'

She began to carry some of the logs up the stairs. 'What are you going to do?' she asked helplessly.

'Light a fire, of course, just like the old days. Don't you remember?'

'But you can't. The chimney must be choked by now. You'll burn the place down.'

He gave her a quick look but only said, 'Nonsense. It was always wide enough to take an ox.'

He piled the kindling and set it alight. Then he shut the great oak door, shooting the iron bolts and killing any hope she had of escape. Though where she could have run in this wilderness she hardly knew. The fire had already begun to roar up the great chimney and spread on the wide stone hearth.

'It will be warmer soon,' he said. 'Open the basket. Look and see what they have given us. I'm starving.'

She cleared the floor and laid out the food on the clean white wrapping. A small roast chicken, a pie of some spicy meat, cheese and fresh bread, bottles of wine and even two glasses, as if it were all no more than one of their summer picnics. The absurdity of the situation would have made her laugh, if it had not been so frightening.

'Eat,' he said, tearing the chicken apart and offering her half. 'You'll feel better if you do. Remember how the dogs used to watch every mouthful?' He smashed the neck of one of the wine bottles and splashed it into the glasses. 'It's good. Some of Papa's best.' He pushed a glass towards her. 'Go on. Drink.'

When she began to eat, she found she was starving, and every mouthful seemed to give her fresh strength. Was she just going to sit there and let him burn the house down and them with it? She began to look around as she drank the wine. There must be some way of escape. There had to be.

Leo was lying back against the piled fur rugs, putting more logs on the fire and watching them crackle and burn as he recklessly poured more wine. She watched him for a moment, then got up and began to prowl around the room. The windows were useless: small casements so rusted into place that she could never hope to shift them, the panes of glass heavily barred. There was another room, which she remembered as opening on to a staircase that went up to the roof but when she opened the door, very quietly, she saw nothing but a black void, the staircase long since stolen.

'What are you doing?' he said.

'Nothing. Just looking around.'

'Come and sit by me.' He looked up as she passed and pulled her down beside him. 'Remember how we used to sit and gaze into the fire and tell each other stories about it?'

'We were children then.'

'Not *so* young, and we were happy. Where did all that happiness go?'

'We grew up, that's all.' The fire blazed and crackled and to her horror she saw a flame leap out and lick up the corner of one of the mouldering tapestries. 'Take care, Leo. You'll set the whole place alight.'

'Does it matter?'

'It does to me!' She had so much to live for now: her music, her concert, the whole future. She had to escape from him, but how? In desperation she tried to pull him to his feet but he wouldn't move, only putting his arms around her and holding her close against him. She fought to free herself.

'Don't be a fool, Leo. Let me go.'

'Never,' he laughed. 'I promised myself this for months and now it has happened.'

She pulled herself away and ran to the great oak door, but the bolts were far out of her reach. He followed her, swinging her back into the room as the fire began to grow. The tapestry was smouldering now. In a few moments it would burst into flame.

Although it was only three o'clock the short winter's day was over and the room was darkening. She struggled to free herself and suddenly, away in the distance, she heard the sound of bells – troika bells. She remembered the one from the great house which his brother Michael used to drive so brilliantly, at great speed with its three horses galloping abreast. Did it mean that someone was coming? It had to. It must. The bone-dry wood was already bursting into flame. Terror seized her and she fought wildly to free herself from him. Outside there was help. She tore herself away and ran to the window, banging on it, screaming, though she guessed she could not be heard. Leo came after her, dragging her back.

'You are not escaping me now. We're here together and we're going together.'

A great cloud of smoke gushed down the wide chimney, bringing the body of some dead bird with it. It scattered the burning logs, the fire creeping out towards every corner of the room. She fought to free herself but he held her with a madman's strength.

Outside a few peasants had drifted up from the village, staring in wonder at the burning house they had known for so long, when the troika sped up, driven by one of the stablemen from the big house. Three of the peasants ran to the terrified, snorting horses and David and Daniel leaped out of the carriage.

'There's a woman in there,' shouted David, hoping they would understand French, gesticulating. 'We've got to get her out.'

One of the more responsible peasants, the headman of the village, came forward. 'A woman? Who?'

'The madman who is burning the house down has her with him. We've got to break down the door before it's too late.'

They acted then with surprising speed. One of the peasants had brought a hatchet and two others a long heavy pole. They went up the steps and hacked at the great oak door till the ancient hinges gave way at last and it fell in. Gusts of smoke and fire blew into their faces but Daniel plunged in. His fist smashed into Leo's face and he dragged Louise away, pushing her into David's arms.

'Get her outside as fast as you can. I'll try to bring this crazy fool.'

'Leave him,' shouted David, but Daniel had seized Leo by the arm and was pulling him to the door.

A few women had come to join their men. They took Louise gently from David, one of them putting a ragged shawl around her. Choked by smoke and half fainting, she said wildly, 'Where is Daniel?'

'My God, he's still in there. Help me,' David shouted, and together with the village elder he plunged back into what was now a flaming hell.

Leo had torn himself away and a smouldering rafter had fallen, knocking Daniel to the ground. They heaved it away and dragged him out between them, falling outside into the snow, scorched by the flames and choked by the smoke.

For a moment they lay there, unable to move. Then Louise screamed and pointed. Somehow Leo must have found a way to the roof. He was standing on some crazy pinnacle, shouting exultantly, words they couldn't distinguish. Then, suddenly, it seemed to give way beneath him and he fell screaming into the furnace. Louise buried her face in her hands; and for a moment, scorched and burned, shocked and horrified, they sat in a huddled group, clinging together, too shaken to move or speak.

The village elder was the first to pull himself together. 'You cannot stay here,' he said to them in his fractured French. 'It is too cold and your burns must be attended to. I will drive you back to the big house. The sleigh is still here.'

And indeed it was. Leo had driven it into a ramshackle building some way from the house and the horses, still harnessed, were snorting and tossing their heads as they smelled the fire. The peasant backed it out and helped the three of them into it. There was still one of the fur rugs left in it, and he wrapped it around them. Although it was not late it was very dark, except where the night sky was lit by lurid flames and showers of sparks from Bluebeard's Castle. Some of the peasants still stared at it, a place they had known all their lives, now a blazing ruin soon to be gone for ever.

The troika followed them, the sound of its bells adding a macabre touch to that terrible scene. When they reached the great white house, Stefan came hurrying to meet them with some of the servants, only too thankful to see their return. They were helped from the sleigh and taken up to the room where Louise had spent the previous night. Warm, with the lamps lit, it seemed a haven of peace and quiet after the horror they had just come through.

'Where is the young master?' whispered Stefan to their escort.

'So that's who it was,' said the peasant. 'I wondered but I wasn't sure, I thought he was dead. The crazy fool had set the place ablaze and before we could drag him out, had climbed on to the roof. He stood there shouting something. Then it must have given way and he fell into the burning house.'

'God rest his tormented soul,' said Stefan, crossing himself devoutly. 'His unhappy father will have to be told when he returns.'

The peasant nodded and trudged away into the night, while Stefan went to find out what he could do for his three exhausted guests.

'You need a doctor,' he said, 'but there is no one within a dozen miles. The count's own physician comes down from the city.'

But the servants were already applying their own peasant remedies, crude but helpful. Louise had escaped the fire but David's arm had been cruelly scorched, and the hands which had lifted the rafter from Daniel were badly burned. The servants covered them with the goose grease and bound them with soft white linen. Daniel had the worst injury. The rafter had bitten deep, burning away his coat and shirt, and leaving a savage wound on his shoulder and upper arm. They covered it with thick grease and wrapped the linen over it.

Stefan wanted to prepare bedrooms for them but they shook their heads. It was as if the terrible experience they had been through had bound them together and they did not want to be parted. So he brought blankets and rugs and wrapped them up warmly. The servants carried in trays of tea and they drank it thankfully, easing their parched, smoke-dried throats. Presently they brought bowls of soup and would have brought food, but the three could eat very little. All they wanted was the peace and quiet of the room after the turmoil of that terrible day. There was little Stefan could garner from the medicine chest but he did bring a bottle of laudanum, which the countess sometimes took when she could not sleep, and suggested it might ease the pain and help them to rest. Then he built up the wood in the iron stove so that it would burn all night, turned down the lamps and left them. Louise was stretched on the day bed, the two men sunk in the huge armchairs. They did not talk much: only a few words about Leo's sudden appearance like a ghost from the past, and how Colette had come to tell them and how they had enlisted the help of Jean-Louis and then followed them on that interminable journey.

Tomorrow there would be St Petersburg and doctors, with telegrams to go to Jean-Louis, to Christine and to Lord Warrinder, but for now there was only peace, and thankfulness that it was all over. Leo had gone out of their lives for ever, but it would be a long time before they could put out of their minds the hideous moment when he had plunged into that burning hell.

Epilogue

At the beginning of April, spring had come to Hunter's Lair, daffodils were blooming in the garden, primroses starred the woods. The trees everywhere had burst into green leaf and sunlight rippled across the sea.

Louise, Daniel and David had come home by easy stages to face a barrage of questions from the police, first in Paris and then in London, and a great deal of harassment from eager journalists, who saw an opportunity to write up a dramatic story, far more thrilling than any novel.

In the midst of all this turmoil, Daniel's second son decided to be born. He slipped into the world with as little trouble to himself and to his mother as Dr Dexter had prophesied. Indeed, Christine made such a rapid recovery that within a few days they were able to turn their backs on London and travel down to the peaceful haven in Sussex with Nanny, Cook, Betsy and Hannah in close attendance.

On one of these sunny mornings Daniel was lying back in his chair, watching his wife with his baby son. She was breast-feeding him herself for the first two or three months, on the advice of John Dexter. Presently Nanny came in and took the baby away for his morning sleep in the cot in the next room.

'Have you thought any more about a name for him, Christine?' said Daniel lazily.

'I've had one or two ideas. Papa would like Laurence, because it was his father's name and it has a fine manly sound, but I'm not too sure,' said Christine, giving Daniel a quick look before she rebuttoned her dressing-gown. 'Would you mind if we called him Gareth?'

'Mind? Because Gareth was once your husband? Of course I wouldn't mind. If Gareth had lived and things had been different for us, he and I would probably have become great friends. I always admired him as a doctor.'

'Could we decide on that then? Gareth Laurence. It has quite a good sound, doesn't it?'

'A very good sound. I can see it written up in large letters somewhere,' he said smiling, and got to his feet, a little stiffly. His shoulder still pained him from time to time. He moved to the window and opened it.

'What are you looking at?' she asked.

'Come and see for yourself.' She crossed to him and he put his arm round her waist, drawing her close to him. 'Look at those two, down there.'

Louise and David were walking along the edge of the sea, Toby and Rowley gambolling ahead and giving little barks as the waves rolled in over their paws.

'They look happy together, don't they?' said Christine. 'Do you think she will marry him? I know David wants it.'

'One day, perhaps. Just now they are far too young. I know Louise is determined to go back to Paris soon. Jean-Louis is going to organize a small recital for her in the winter. David must learn to share Louise with her music. It means a great deal to her.'

She looked up at him questioningly. 'How are things between you and David?'

He smiled. 'He and I have learned a good deal about each other in these last few weeks. I don't think we are likely to forget it in the future. Now I must go and do some work. I have another son to provide for. Joe Sharpe wants to open the London edition of the *Clarion* in the autumn and there is still a lot to be done if I'm to edit it.'

'You're going to like that, aren't you?'

'Yes, I am. It's what I've always wanted. Now, my love, I really must go.'

'And I must get dressed and interview Cook. It will be Easter soon and the children will be home for the holidays. Goodbye to our peace and quiet.'

'I tell you one thing for sure,' said Daniel, smiling. 'Celia is going to be thrilled with her new baby brother. Now I'm off. What's for lunch today?' he added, as he went out through the door.

'Grilled Dover sole, caught this morning. My nice fisherman friend brought them to me.'

'Good for him.'

Christine opened the window a little and waved.

'Coffee time,' she called.

Louise waved back. 'We're just coming in.'

Then Christine saw Louise stop and take something from her handbag. She threw it as far as she could into the sea. The little Chinese dog fell in with a splash and sank.

'What was that?' asked David.

'I've thrown away the very last remnant of the past. Now we can start again.'

'Can we?' he asked.

'Of course we can.' She smiled at him and slipped an arm through his. 'Shall we go in?' They moved towards the house.

Christine pulled the window shut, leaned her forehead against the glass and said a little prayer of gratitude that Daniel and David had come back to her, when for a few hours it had seemed that they might not. Then she went to get dressed ready for her busy day.